THE BLOOMSBURY GROUP

EX LIBRIS

THE BLOOMSBURY GROUP

Henrietta's War by Joyce Dennys
Henrietta Sees It Through by Joyce Dennys
The Brontës Went to Woolworths by Rachel Ferguson
Miss Hargreaves by Frank Baker
Love's Shadow by Ada Leverson
A Kid for Two Farthings by Wolf Mankowitz
Mrs Tim of the Regiment by D. E. Stevenson
Let's Kill Uncle by Rohan O'Grady
Mrs Harris Goes to Paris and Mrs Harris Goes to New York by Paul Gallico

A NOTE ON THE AUTHOR

The son of E.W. Benson, an archbishop of Canterbury (1883-96), E.F. BENSON was educated at Marlborough School and at King's College, Cambridge. After graduation he worked from 1892 to 1895 in Athens for the British School of Archaeology and later in Egypt for the Society for the Promotion of Hellenic Studies. In 1893 he published *Dodo*, a novel that attracted wide attention. It was followed by a number of other successful novels including his hugely popular *Mapp and Lucia* series. In 1938 he was made an honorary fellow of Magdalene College, Cambridge. He died in February, 1940.

Mrs Ames first published in Great Britain 1912
This paperback edition published 2010 by Bloomsbury Publishing Plc

Bloomsbury Publishing Plc, 36 Soho Square, London W1D 3QY

A CIP catalogue record for this book is available from the British Library

ISBN 978 1 4088 0858 0

10 9 8 7 6 5 4 3 2 1

Typeset by
MPS Limited, A MacMillan Company
Printed in Great Britain by Clays Ltd, St Ives plc

www.bloomsbury.com/thebloomsburygroup

Mrs Ames

E. F. Benson

BLOOMSBURY
LONDON · BERLIN · NEW YORK

CERTAINLY the breakfast tongue, which was cut for the first time that morning, was not of the pleasant reddish hue which Mrs Altham was justified in expecting, considering that the delicacy in question was not an ordinary tinned tongue (you had to take things as you found them, if your false sense of economy led you to order tinned goods) but one that came out of a fine glass receptacle with an eminent label on it. It was more of the colour of cold mutton, unattractive if not absolutely unpleasant to the eye, while to the palate it proved to be singularly lacking in flavour. Altogether it was a great disappointment, and for this reason, when Mr Altham set out at a quarter past twelve to stroll along to the local club in Queensgate Street with the ostensible purpose of seeing if there was any fresh telegram about the disturbances in Morocco, his wife accompanied him to the door of that desirable mansion, round which was grouped a variety of chained-up dogs in various states of boredom and irritation, and went on into the High Street in order to make in person a justifiable complaint at her grocer's. She would be sorry to have to take her custom elsewhere, but if Mr Pritchard did not see his way to sending her another tongue (of course without further charge) she would be obliged . . .

So this morning there was a special and imperative reason why Mrs Altham should walk out before lunch to the High Street, and why her husband should make a morning visit to the club. But to avoid misconception it may be stated at once that there was, on every day of the week except Sunday, some equally compelling cause to account for these expeditions. If it was very wet, perhaps, Mrs Altham might not go to the High Street, but wet or fine her husband went to his club. And exactly the same thing happened in the case of most of their friends and acquaintances, so that Mr Altham was certain of meeting General Fortescue, Mr Brodie, Major Ames, and others in the smoking room, while Mrs Altham encountered their wives and sisters on errands like her own in the High Street. She often professed superior distaste for gossip, but when she met her friends coming in and out of shops, it was but civil and reasonable that she should have a few moments' chat with them. Thus, if any striking events had taken place since the previous afternoon, they all learned about them. Simultaneously there was a similar interchange of thought and tidings going on in the smoking room at the club, so that when Mr Altham had drunk his glass of sherry and returned home to lunch at one-thirty, there was probably little of importance and interest which had not reached the ears of himself or his wife. It could then be discussed at that meal.

Queensgate Street ran at right angles to the High Street, debouching into that thoroughfare at the bottom of its steep slope, while the grocer's shop lay at the top of it. The morning was a hot day of early June, but to a woman of Mrs Altham's spare frame and active limbs, the ascent was no more than a pleasurable exercise, and the vivid colour of her face (so unlike the discouraging hues of the breakfast tongue) was not the result of her exertions. It was habitually there, and though that and the restlessness of her dark and rather beady eyes might have made a doctor, on a cursory glance (especially if influenza was about), think that she suffered from some slight rise of temperature, he would have been in error. Her symptoms betokened not an unnatural warmth of the blood, but were the visible sign of her eager and slightly impatient mind. Like the inhabitants of ancient Athens, she was always on the alert to hear some new thing (though she disliked gossip), but her mind appreciated the infinitesimal more than the important. The smaller a piece of news was, the more vivid was her perception of it, and the firmer her grip of it: large questions produced but a vague impression on her.

Her husband, a retired solicitor, was singularly well adapted to be the partner of her life, for his mind was very much akin to hers, and his appetite for news no less rapacious. Indeed, the chief difference between them in this respect was that she snapped at her food like a wolf in winter, whereas he took it quietly, in the manner of a leisurely boa constrictor. But his capacity was in no way inferior to hers. Similarly, they practised the same harmless hypocrisies on each other, and politely forbore to question each other's sincerity. An instance has already been recorded where such lack of trust might have been manifested, but it never entered Mrs Altham's head to tell her husband just now that he cared nothing whatever about the disturbances in Morocco, while she would have thought it very odd conduct on his part to suggest that a sharply worded note to Mr Pritchard would save her the walk uphill on this hot morning. But it was only sensible to go on their quests; had they not ascertained if there was any news, they would have had nothing to talk about at lunch. As it was, conversation never failed them, for this little town of Riseborough was crammed with interest and incident, for all who felt a proper concern in the affairs of other people.

The High Street this morning was very full, for it was market day, and Mrs Altham's progress was less swift than usual. Barrows of itinerant vendors were crowded into the road from the edge of the pavements, leaving a straitened channel for a traffic swelled by farmers' carts and occasional droves of dusty and perplexed looking cattle, being driven in from the country round. More than once Mrs Altham had to step into the doorway of some shop to avoid the random erring of a company of pigs or sheep which made irruption on to the pavement. But it was interesting to observe, in one such enforced pause, the impeded passage of Sir James Westbourne's motor, with the owner, broad-faced and good-humoured, driving himself, and to conjecture as to what business brought him into the town. Then she saw that there was his servant sitting in the body of the car, while there were two portmanteaus on the luggage rail behind. There was no need for further conjecture: clearly he was coming from the South-Eastern station at the top of the hill, and was driving out to his place four miles distant along the Maidstone road. Then he caught sight of somebody on the pavement whom he knew, and, stopping the car, entered into conversation.

For the moment Mrs Altham could not see who it was; then, as the car moved on again, there appeared from behind it the tall figure of Dr Evans. Mrs Altham was not so foolish as to suppose that their conversation had necessarily anything to do with medical matters; she did not fly to the conclusion that Lady Westbourne or any of the children must certainly be ill. To a person of her mental grasp it was sufficient to remember that Mrs Evans was Sir James' first cousin. She heard also the baronet's cheerful voice as the two parted, saying, 'Saturday the twenty-eighth, then. I'll tell my wife.' That, of course, settled it; it required only a moment's employment of her power of inference to make her feel convinced that Saturday the twenty-eighth would be the date for Mrs Evans' garden party. There were a good many garden parties in Riseborough about then, for strawberries might be expected to be reasonably cheap. Probably the date had been settled only this morning; she might look forward to receiving the 'At Home' card (four to seven) by the afternoon post.

The residential quarters of Riseborough lay both at the top of the hill, on which the town stood, clustering round the fine old Norman church, and at the bottom, along Queensgate Street, which passed into the greater spaciousness of St Barnabas Road. On the whole, that might be taken to be the Park Lane of the place, and commanded the highest rents; every house there, in addition to being completely detached, had a small front garden with a carriage drive long enough to hold three carriages simultaneously, if each horse did not mind putting its nose within rubbing distance of the carriage in front of it, while the foremost projected a little into the road again. But there were good houses also at the top of the hill, where Dr Evans lived, and those who lived below naturally considered themselves advantageously placed in being sheltered from the bleak easterly winds which often prevailed in spring, while those at the top wondered among themselves in sultry summer days how it was possible to exist in the airless atmosphere below. The middle section of the town was mercantile, and it was here that the ladies of the place, both from above and below, met each other with such invariable fortuitousness in the hours before lunch. Today, however, though the street was so full, it was for purposes of news-gathering curiously deserted, and apart from the circumstance of inferentially learning the date of Mrs Evans' garden party, Mrs Altham found nothing to detain her until she had got to the very door of Mr Pritchard's grocery. But there her prolonged fast was broken; Mrs Taverner was ready to give and receive, and after the business of the colourless tongue was concluded in a manner that was perfectly creditable to Mr Pritchard, the two ladies retraced their steps (for Mrs Taverner was of St Barnabas Road) down the hill again.

Mrs Taverner quite agreed about the strong probability of Mrs Evans' garden party being on the twenty-eighth, and proceeded to unload herself of far more sensational information. She talked rather slowly, but without ever stopping of her own accord, so that she got as much into a given space of time as most people. Even if she was temporarily stopped by an interruption, she kept her mouth open, so as to be able to proceed at the earliest possible moment.

'Yes, three weeks, as you say, is a long notice, is it not?' she said, 'but I'm sure people are wise to give long notice, otherwise they will find all their guests are already engaged, such a quantity of parties as there will be this summer. Mrs Ames has sent out dinner cards for exactly the same date, I am told. I daresay they agreed together to have a day full of gaiety. Perhaps you are asked to dine there on the twenty-eighth, Mrs Altham?'

'No, not at present.'

'Well, then, it will be news to you,' said Mrs Taverner, 'if what I have heard is true, and it was Mrs Fortescue's governess who told me, whom I met taking one of the children to the dentist.'

CHAPTER ONE

'That would be Edward,' said Mrs Altham unerringly. 'I have often noticed his teeth are most irregular: one here, another there.'

She spoke as if it was more usual for children to have all their teeth on the same spot, but Mrs Taverner understood.

'Very likely; indeed, I think I have noticed it myself. Well, what I have to tell you seems very irregular, too; Edward's teeth are nothing to it. It was talked about, so Miss - I can never recollect her name, and, from what I hear, I do not think Mrs Fortescue finds her very satisfactory - it was talked about, so Mrs Fortescue's governess told me, at breakfast time, and it was agreed that General Fortescue should accept, for if you are asked three weeks ahead it is no use saying you are engaged. No doubt Mrs Ames gave that long notice for that very reason.'

'But what is it that is so irregular?' asked Mrs Altham, nearly dancing with impatience at these circumlocutions.

'Did I not tell you? Ah, there is Mrs Evans; I was told she was asked too, without her husband. How slowly she walks; I should not be surprised if her husband had told her never to hurry. She did not see us; otherwise we might have found out more.'

'About what?' asked the martyred Mrs Altham.

'Why, what I am saying. Mrs Ames has asked General Fortescue to dine that night, without asking Mrs Fortescue, and has asked Mrs Evans to dine without asking Dr Evans. I don't know who the rest of the party are. I must try to find time this afternoon to call on Mrs Ames, and see if she lets anything drop about it. It seems very odd to ask a husband without his wife, and a wife without her husband. And we do not know yet whether Dr Evans will allow his wife to go there without him.'

Mrs Altham was suitably astounded.

'But I never heard of such a thing,' she said, 'and I expect my memory is as' (she nearly said 'long', but stopped in time) 'clear and retentive as that of most people. It seems very strange: it will look as if General Fortescue and his wife are not on good terms, and, as far as I know, there is no reason to suppose that. However, it is none of my business, and I am thankful to say that I do not concern myself with things that do not concern me. Had Mrs Ames wanted my advice as to the desirability of asking a husband without a wife, or a wife without a husband, I should have been very glad to give it her. But as she has not asked it, I must suppose that she does not want it, and I am sure I am very thankful to keep my opinion to myself. But if she asked me what I thought about it, I should be compelled to tell her the truth. I am very glad to be spared any such unpleasantness. Dear me, here I am at home again. I had no idea we had come all this way.'

Mrs Taverner seemed inclined to linger, but the other had caught sight of her husband's face looking out of the window known as his study, where he was accustomed to read the paper in the morning, and go to sleep in the evening. This again was very irregular, for the watch on her wrist told her that it was not yet a quarter past one, the hour at which he invariably ordered a glass of sherry at the club, to fortify him for his walk home. Possibly he had heard something about this revolutionary social scheme in the club, and had hastened his return in order to be able to talk it over with her without delay. For a moment it occurred to her to ask Mrs Taverner to join them at lunch, but, after all, she had heard what that lady had to tell, and one of the smaller bundles of asparagus could not be considered ample for more than two. So she checked the hospitable impulse, and hurried into his study, alert with suppressed information, though she did not propose to let it explode at once, for the method of them both was to let news slip out as if accidentally. And, even as she crossed the hall, an idea for testing the truth of what she had heard, which was both simple and ingenious, came into her head. She despised poor Mrs Taverner's scheme of calling on Mrs Ames, in the hope of her letting something drop, for Mrs Ames never let things drop in that way, though she was an adept at picking them up. Her own plan was far more effective. Also it harmonized well with the system of mutual insincerities.

'I have been thinking, my dear,' she said briskly, as she entered his study, 'that it is time for us to be asking Major and Mrs Ames to dinner again. Yes: Pritchard was reasonable, and will send me another tongue, and take back the old one, which I am sure I am quite glad that he should do, though it would have come in for savouries very handily. Still, he is quite within his rights, since he does not charge for it, and I should not think of quarrelling with him because he exercises them.'

Mr Altham was as keen a housekeeper as his wife.

'Its colour would not have signified in a savoury,' he said.

'No, but as Pritchard supplies a new tongue without charge, we cannot complain. About Mrs Ames, now. We dined with them quite a month ago: I do not want her to think we are lacking in the exchange of hospitalities, which I am sure are so pleasant on both sides.'

Mr Altham considered this question, caressing the side of his face. There was no doubt that he had a short pointed beard on his chin, but about halfway up the jawbone the hair got shorter and shorter, and he was quite clean-shaven before it got up to his ear. It was always a question, in fact, among the junior and less respectful members of the club, whether old Altham had whiskers or not. The general opinion was that he had whiskers, but was unaware of that possession.

'It is odd that the idea of asking Mrs Ames to dinner occurred to you today,' he said, 'for I was wondering also whether we did not owe her some hospitality. And Major Ames, of course,' he added.

Mrs Altham smiled a bright detective smile.

'Next week is impossible, I know,' she said, 'and so is the week after, as there is a perfect rush of engagements then. But after that, we might find an evening free. How would it suit you, if I asked Mrs Ames and a few friends to dine on the Saturday of that week? Let me count - seven, fourteen, twenty-one, yes; on the twenty-eighth. I think that probably Mrs Evans will have her garden party on that day. It would make a pleasant ending to such an afternoon. And it would be less of an interruption to both of us, if we give up that day. It would be better than disarranging the week by sacrificing another evening.'

Mr Altham rang the bell before replying.

'It is hardly likely that Major and Mrs Ames would have an engagement so long ahead,' he said. 'I think we shall be sure to secure them.'

The bell was answered.

'A glass of sherry,' he said. 'I forgot, my dear, to take my glass of sherry at the club. Young Morton was talking to me, though I don't know why I call him young, and I forgot about my sherry. Yes, I should think the twenty-eighth would be very suitable.'

Mrs Altham waited until the parlourmaid had deposited the glass of sherry, and had completely left the room with a shut door behind her.

CHAPTER ONE

'I heard a very extraordinary story today,' she said, 'though I don't for a moment believe it is true. If it is, we shall find that Mrs Ames cannot dine with us on the twenty-eighth, but we shall have asked her with plenty of notice, so that it will count. But one never knows how little truth there may be in what Mrs Taverner says, for it was Mrs Taverner who told me. She said that Mrs Ames has asked General Fortescue to dine with her that night, without asking Mrs Fortescue, and has invited Mrs Evans also without her husband. One doesn't for a moment believe it, but if we asked Mrs Ames for the same night we should very likely hear about it. Was anything said at the club about it?'

Mr Altham affected a carelessness which he was very far from feeling.

'Young Morton did say something of the sort,' he said. 'I was not listening particularly, since, as you know, I went there to see if there was anything to be learned about Morocco, and I get tired of his tittle-tattle. But he did mention something of the kind. There is the luncheon bell, my dear. You might write your note immediately and send it by hand, for James will be back from his dinner by now, and tell him to wait for an answer.'

Mrs Altham adopted this suggestion at once. She knew, of course, perfectly well that the thrilling quality of the news had brought her husband home without waiting to take his glass of sherry at the club, a thing which had not happened since that morning a year ago, when he had learned that Mrs Fortescue had dismissed her cook without a character, but she did not think of accusing him of duplicity. After all, it was the amiable desire to talk these matters over with her without the loss of a moment which was the motive at the base of his action, and so laudable a motive covered all else. So she had her note written with amazing speed and cordiality, and the boot-and-knife boy, who also exercised the function of the gardener, was instructed to wash his hands and go upon his errand.

Criticism of Mrs Ames' action, based on the hypothesis that the news was true, was sufficient to afford brisk conversation until the return of the messenger, and Mrs Altham put back on her plate her first stick of asparagus and tore the note open. A glance was sufficient.

'It is all quite true,' she said. 'Mrs Ames writes, "We are so sorry to be obliged to refuse your kind invitation, but General Fortescue and Millicent Evans, with a few other friends, are dining with us this evening." Well, I am sure! So, after all, Mrs Taverner was right. I feel I owe her an apology for doubting the truth of it, and I shall slip round after lunch to tell her that she need not call on Mrs Ames, which she was thinking of doing. I can save her that trouble.'

Mr Altham considered and condemned the wisdom of this slipping round.

'That might land you in an unpleasantness, my dear,' he said. 'Mrs Taverner might ask you how you were certain of it. You would not like to say that you asked the Ames' to dinner on the same night in order to find out.'

'No, that is true. You see things very quickly, Henry. But, on the other hand, if Mrs Taverner does go to call, Mrs Ames might let drop the fact that she had received this invitation from us. I would sooner let Mrs Taverner know it myself than let it get to her in roundabout ways. I will think over it; I have no doubt I shall be able to devise something. Now about Mrs Ames' new departure. I must say that it seems to me a very queer piece of work. If she is to ask you without me, and me without you, is the other to sit at home alone for dinner? For it is not to be expected that somebody else will on the very same night always ask the other of us. As likely as not, if there is another invitation for the same night, it will be for both of us, for I do not suppose that we shall all follow Mrs Ames' example, and model our hospitalities on hers.'

Mrs Altham paused a moment to eat her asparagus, which was getting cold.

'As a matter of fact, my dear, we do usually follow Mrs Ames' example,' he said. 'She may be said to be the leader of our society here.'

'And if you gave me a hundred guesses why we do follow her example,' said Mrs Altham rather excitedly, picking up a head of asparagus that had fallen on her napkin, 'I am sure I could not give you one answer that you would think sensible. There are a dozen of our friends in Riseborough who are just as well born as she is, and as many more much better off; not that I say that money should have anything to do with position, though you know as well as I do that you could buy their house over their heads, Henry, and afford to keep it empty, while, all the time, I, for one, don't believe that they have got three hundred a year between them over and above his pay. And as for breeding, if Mrs Ames' manners seem to you so worthy of copy, I can't understand what it is you find to admire in them, except that she walks into a room as if it all belonged to her, and looks over everybody's head, which is very ridiculous, as she can't be more than two inches over five feet, and I doubt if she's as much. I never have been able to see, and I do not suppose I ever shall be able to see, why none of us can do anything in Riseborough without asking Mrs Ames' leave. Perhaps it is my stupidity, though I do not know that I am more stupid than most.'

Henry Altham felt himself to blame for this agitated harangue. It was careless of him to have alluded to Mrs Ames' leadership, for if there was a subject in this world that produced a species of frenzy and a complete absence of full stops in his wife, it was that. Desperately before now had she attempted to wrest the sceptre from Mrs Ames' podgy little hands, and to knock the crown off her noticeably small head. She had given parties that were positively Lucullan in their magnificence on her first coming to Riseborough; the regimental band (part of it, at least) had played under the elm tree in her garden on the occasion of a mere afternoon party, while at a dance she had given (a thing almost unknown in Riseborough) there had been a cotillion in which the presents cost up to five and sixpence each, to say nothing of the trouble. She had given a party for children at which there was not only a Christmas tree, but a conjuror, and when a distinguished actor once stayed with her, she had, instead of keeping him to herself, which was Mrs Ames' plan when persons of eminence were her guests, asked practically the whole of Riseborough to lunch, tea and dinner. To all of these great parties she had bidden Mrs Ames (with a view to her deposition), and on certainly one occasion - that of the cotillion - she had heard afterwards unimpeachable evidence to show that that lady had remarked that she saw no reason for such display. Therefore to this day she had occasional bursts of volcanic amazement at Mrs Ames' undoubted supremacy, and made occasional frantic attempts to deprive her of her throne. There was no method of attack which she had not employed; she had flattered and admired Mrs Ames openly to her face, with a view to be permitted to share the throne; she had abused and vilified her with a view to pulling her off it; she had refrained from asking her to her own house for six months at a time, and for six months at a time she had refused to accept any of Mrs Ames' invitations. But it was all no use; the vilifications, so she had known for a fact, had been repeated to Mrs Ames, who had not taken the slightest notice of them, nor abated one jot of her rather condescending cordiality, and in spite of Mrs Altham's refusing to come to her house, had continued to send her invitations at the usual rate of hospitality. Indeed, for the last year or two Mrs Altham had really given up all thought of ever deposing her, and her husband, though on this occasion he felt himself to blame for this convulsion, felt also that he might reasonably have supposed the volcano to be extinct. Yet such is the disconcerting habit of these subliminal forces; they break forth with renewed energy exactly when persons of exactly average caution think that there is no longer any life in them.

He hastened to repair his error, and to calm the tempest, by fulsome agreement.

'Well, my dear,' he said, 'certainly there is a great deal in what you say, for we have no reason to suppose that everybody will ask husband and wife singly, or that two of this new set of invitations will always come for the same night. Then, too, there is the question of carriage hire, which, though it does not much matter to us, will be an important item to others. For, every time that husband and wife dine out, there will be two carriages needed instead of one. I wonder if Mrs Ames had thought of that.'

'Not she,' said Mrs Altham, whose indignation still oozed and spurted. 'Why, as often as not, she comes on foot, with her great goloshes over her evening shoes. Ah, I have it!'

A brilliant idea struck her, which did much to restore her equanimity.

'You may depend upon it,' she said, 'that Mrs Ames means to ask just husband or wife, as the case may be, and make that count. That will save her half the cost of her dinners, and now I come to think of it, I am sure I should not be surprised to learn that they have lost money lately. Major Ames may have been speculating, for I saw the Financial News on the table last time I was there. I daresay that is it. That would account, too, for the very poor dinner we got. Salmon was in season, I remember, but we only had plaice or something common, and the ordinary winter desert, just oranges and apples. You noticed it, too, Henry. You told me that you had claret that couldn't have cost more than eighteenpence a bottle, and but one glass of port afterwards. And the dinner before that, though there was champagne, I got little but foam. Poor thing! I declare I am sorry for her if that is the reason, and I am convinced it is.'

Mrs Altham felt considerably restored by this explanation, and got briskly up.

'I think I will just run round to Mrs Taverner's,' she said, 'to tell her there is no need for her to call on Mrs Ames, since you have heard the same story at the club, so that we can rest assured that it is true. That will do famously; it will account for everything. And there is Pritchard's cart at the gate. That will be the tongue. I wonder if he has told his man to take away the pale one. If not, as you say, it will serve for savouries.'

Summer had certainly come in earnest, and Mr Altham, when he went out on to the shaded verandah to the east of the house, in order to smoke his cigar before going up to the golf links, found that the thermometer registered eighty degrees in the shade. Consequently, before enjoying that interval of quiescence which succeeded his meals, and to which he felt he largely owed the serenity of his health, he went upstairs to change his cloth coat for the light alpaca jacket which he always wore when the weather was really hot. Last year, he remembered, he had not put it on at all until the end of July, except that on one occasion he wore it over his ordinary coat (for it was loosely made) taking a drive along an extremely dusty road. But the heat today certainly called for the alpaca jacket, and he settled himself in his chair (after tapping the barometer and observing with satisfaction that the concussion produced an upward tremor of the needle, which was at 'Set Fair' already) feeling much more cool and comfortable.

Life in general was a very cool and comfortable affair to this contented gentleman. Even in youth he had not been of very exuberant vitality, and he had passed through his early years without giving a moment's anxiety to himself or his parents. Like a good child who eats and digests what is given him, so Mr Altham, even in his early manhood, had accepted life exactly as he found it, and had seldom wondered what it was all about, or what it was made of. His emotions had been stirred when he met his wife, and he had once tried to write a poem to her - soon desisting, owing to the obvious scarcity of rhymes in the English language, and since then his emotional record had been practically blank. If happiness implies the power to want and to aspire, that quality must be denied him, but his content was so profound that he need not be pitied for the lack of the more effervescent emotions. All that he cared about was abundantly his: there was the Times to be read after breakfast, news to be gleaned at the club before lunch, golf to be played in the afternoon, and a little well-earned repose to be enjoyed before dinner, while at odd moments he looked at the thermometer and tapped the aneroid. He was distinctly kindly by nature, and would no doubt have cheerfully put himself to small inconveniences in order to lighten the troubles of others, but he hardly ever found it necessary to practise discomfort, since those with whom he associated were sunk in precisely the same lethargy of content as himself. Being almost completely devoid of imagination, no qualms or questionings as to the meaning of the dramas of life presented themselves to him, and his annual subscriptions to the local hospital and certain parish funds connoted no more to him than did the money he paid at the station for his railway ticket. He was, in fact, completely characteristic of the society of Riseborough, which largely consisted of men who had retired from their professions and spent their days, with unimportant variations, in precisely the same manner as he did. Necessarily they were not aware of the amazing emptiness of their lives, for if they had been, they would probably have found life very dull, and have tried to fill it with some sort of interest. As it was, golf, gardening, and gossip made the days pass so smoothly and quickly that it would really have been hazardous to attempt to infuse any life into them, for it might have produced upset and fermentation. But these chronicles would convey a very false impression if they made it seem as if life at Riseborough appeared dull or empty. The affairs of other people were so perennial a source of interest that it would only be a detached or sluggish mind that was not perpetually stimulated. And this stimulus was not of alcoholic character, nor was it succeeded by reaction and headache after undue indulgence. Mr Altham woke each morning with a clean palate, so to speak, and an appetite and digestion quite unimpaired. As yet, he had not to seek to fill the hours of the day with gardening, like Major Ames, or with continuous rubbers of bridge in the card room at the club; his days were full enough without those additional distractions, which he secretly rather despised as signs of senility, and wondered that Major Ames, who was still, he supposed, not much more than forty-five, should so soon have taken to a hobby that was better fitted for ladies and septuagenarians. It was not that he did not like flowers; he thought them pretty enough things in their place, and was pleased when he looked out of the bathroom window in the morning, and saw the neat row of red geraniums which ran along the border by the wall, between calceolarias and lobelias. Very likely when he was older, and other interests had faded, he might take to gardening, too; at present he preferred that the hired man should spend two days a week in superintending the operations of James. Certainly there would be some sense in looking after a vegetable garden, for there was an intelligible end in view there - namely, the production of early peas and giant asparagus for the table, but since the garden at Cambridge House was not of larger capacity than was occupied with a croquet lawn and a couple of flower borders, it was impossible to grow vegetables, and the production of a new red sweet pea, about which Major Ames had really rendered himself tedious last summer, was quite devoid of interest to him, especially since there were plenty of other red flowers before.

His cigar was already half-smoked before he recalled himself from this pleasant vacancy of mind which had succeeded the summer resumal of his alpaca jacket, and for the ten minutes that still remained to him before the cab from the livery stables which was to take him up the long hill to the golf links would be announced, he roused himself to a greater activity of brain. It was natural that his game with Mr Turner this afternoon should first occupy his thoughts. He felt sure he could beat him if only he paid a very strict attention to the game, and did not let his mind wander. A few days ago, Mr Turner had won merely because he himself had been rather late in arriving at the clubhouse, and had started with the sense of hurry about him. But today he had ordered the cab at ten minutes to three, instead of at the hour. Thus he could both start from here and arrive there without this feeling of fuss. Their appointed hour was not till a quarter past three, and it took a bare fifteen minutes to drive up. Also he had on his alpaca jacket; he would not, as on the last occasion of their encounter, be uncomfortably hot. As usual, he would play his adversary for the sum of half a crown; that should pay both for cab and caddie.

His thoughts took a wider range. Certainly it was a strange thing that Mrs Ames should ask husbands without their wives, and wives without their husbands. Of course, to ask Mrs Evans without the doctor was less remarkable than to ask General Fortescue without his wife, for it sometimes happened that Dr Evans was sent for in the middle of dinner to attend on a patient, and once, when he was giving a party at his own house, he had received a note which led him to get up at once, and say to the lady on his right, 'I am afraid I must go; maternity case,' which naturally had caused a very painful feeling of embarrassment, succeeded by a buzz of feverish and haphazard conversation. But to ask General Fortescue without his wife was a very different affair; it was not possible that Mrs Fortescue should be sent for in the middle of dinner, and cause dislocation in the party. He felt that if any hostess except Mrs Ames had attempted so startling an innovation, she would, even with her three-weeks' notice, have received chilling refusals coupled with frankly incredible reasons for declining. Thus with growing radius of thought he found himself considering the case of Mrs Ames' undoubted supremacy in the Riseborough world.

Most of what his wife had said in her excited harangue had been perfectly well founded. Mrs Ames was not rich, and a marked parsimony often appeared to have presided over the ordering of her dinners; while, so far as birth was concerned, at least two other residents here were related to baronets just as much as she was; Mrs Evans, for instance, was first cousin of the present Sir James Westbourne, whereas Mrs Ames was more distant than that from the same fortunate gentleman by one remove. Her mother, that is to say, had been the eldest sister of the last baronet but one, and older than he, so that beyond any question whatever, if Mrs Ames' mother had been a boy, and she had been a boy also, she would now have been a baronet herself in place of the cheerful man who had been seen by Mrs Altham driving his motorcar down the High Street that morning. As for General Fortescue, he was the actual brother of a baronet, and there was the end of the matter. But though Riseborough in general had a very proper appreciation of the deference due to birth, Mr Altham felt that Mrs Ames' supremacy was not really based on so wholesale a rearrangement of parents and sexes. Nor, again, were her manners and breeding such as compelled homage; she seemed to take her position for granted, and very seldom thanked her hostess for 'a very pleasant evening' when she went away. Nor was she remarkable for her good looks; indeed, she was more nearly remarkable for the absence of them. Yet, somehow, Mr Altham could not, perhaps owing to his lack of imagination, see anybody else, not even his own wife, occupying Mrs Ames' position. There was some force about her that put her where she was. You felt her efficiency; you guessed that should situations arise Mrs Ames could deal with them. She had a larger measure of reality than the majority of Mr Altham's acquaintances. She did not seem to exert herself in any way, or call attention to what she did, and yet when Mrs Ames called on some slightly doubtful newcomer to Riseborough, it was certain that everybody else would call too. And one defect she had of the most glaring nature. She appeared to take the most tepid interest only in what everyone said about every body else. Once, not so long ago, Mrs Altham had shown herself more than ready to question, on the best authority, the birth and upbringing of Mrs Turner, the election of whose husband to the club had caused so many members to threaten resignation. But all Mrs Ames had said, when it was clear that the shadiest antecedents were filed, so to speak, for her perusal, was, 'I have always found her a very pleasant woman. She is dining with us on Tuesday.' Or again, when he himself was full of the praise of Mrs Taverner, to whom Mrs Ames was somewhat coldly disposed - (though that lady had called three times, and was perhaps calling again this afternoon, Mrs Ames had never once asked her to lunch or dine, and was believed to have left cards without even inquiring whether she was in) - Mrs Ames had only answered his panegyrics by saying, 'I am told she is a very good-natured sort of woman.'

Mr Altham, hearing the stopping of a cab at his front-door, got up. It was still thirteen minutes to three, but he was ready to start. Indeed, he felt that motion and distraction would be very welcome, for there had stolen into his brain a strangely upsetting idea. It was very likely quite baseless and ill-founded, but it did occur to him that this defect on the part of Mrs Ames as regards her incuriousness on the subject of the small affairs of other people was somehow connected with her ascendency. He had so often thought of it as a defect that it was quite a shock to find himself wondering whether it was a quality. In any case, it was a quality which he was glad to be without. The possession of it would have robbed him of quite nine points of the laws that governed his nature. He would have been obliged to cultivate a passion for gardening, like Major Ames.

Of course, if you married a woman quite ten years your senior, you had to take to something, and it was lucky Major Ames had not taken to drink.

He felt quite cynical, and lost the first four holes. Later, but too late, he pulled himself together. But it was poor consolation to win the bye only.

MRS AMES put up her black and white sunshade as she stepped into the hot street outside Dr Evans' house, about half past six on the evening of the twenty-eighth of June, and proceeded afoot past the half-dozen houses that lay between it and the High Street. In appearance she was like a small, good-looking toad in half-mourning; or, to state the comparison with greater precision, she was small for a woman, but good-looking for a toad. Her face had something of the sulky and satiated expression of that harmless reptile, and her mourning was for her brother, who had mercifully died of delirium tremens some six months before. This scarcely respectable mode of decease did not curtail his sister's observance of the fact, and she was proposing to wear mourning for another three months.

She had not seen him much of late years, and, as a matter of fact, she thought it was much better that his inglorious career, since he was a hopeless drunkard, had been brought to a conclusion, but her mourning, in spite of this, was a faithful symbol of her regret. He had had the good looks and the frailty of her family, while she was possessed of its complementary plainness and strength, but she remembered with remarkable poignancy, even in her fifty-fifth year, bird's-nesting expeditions with him, and the alluring of fish in unpopulous waters. They had shared their pocket money together, also, as children, and she had not been the gainer by it. Therefore she thought of him with peculiar tenderness.

It would be idle to deny that she was not interested in the Riseborough view of his blackness. It was quite well known that he was a drunkard, but she had stifled inquiry by stating that he had died of 'failure'. What organ it was that failed could not be inquired into: anyone with the slightest proper feeling - and she was well aware that Riseborough had almost an apoplexy of proper feeling - would assume that it was some organ not generally mentioned. She felt that there was no call on her to gratify any curiosity that might happen to be rampant. She also felt that the chief joy in the possession of a sense of humour lies in the fact that others do not suspect it. Riseborough would certainly have thought it very heartless of her to derive any amusement from things however remotely connected with her brother's death; Riseborough also would have been incapable of crediting her with any tenderness of memory, if it had known that he had actually died of delirium tremens.

In this stifling weather she almost envied those who, like Dr Evans, lived at the top of the town, where, in Castle Street, was situated the charming Georgian house in the garden of which he for a little while only, and his wife for three hours, had been entertaining their friends and detractors at the garden party. Though the house was in a 'Street', and not a 'Road', it had a garden which anybody would expect to belong to a 'Road', if not a 'Place'. Streets seemed to imply small backyards looking into the backs of other houses, whereas Dr Evans' house did not, at its back, look on other houses at all, but extended a full hundred yards, and then looked over the railway cutting of the South-Eastern line, on open fields. Should you feel unkindly disposed, it was easy to ask whether the noise of passing trains was not very disagreeable, and indeed, Mrs Taverner, in a moment of peevishness arising from the fact that what she thought was champagne cup was only hock cup, had asked that very question of Millicent Evans this afternoon in Mrs Ames' hearing. But Millicent, in her most confiding and childlike manner, had given what Mrs Ames considered to be a wholly admirable and suitable answer. 'Indeed we do,' she had said, 'and we often envy you your beautiful big lawn.' For everybody, of course, knew that Mrs Taverner's beautiful big lawn was a small piece of black earth diversified by plantains, and overlooked and made odorous by the new gasworks. Mrs Taverner had, as was not unnatural, coloured up on receipt of this silken speech, until she looked nearly as red as Mrs Altham. For herself, Mrs Ames would not, even under this provocation, have made so ill-natured a reply, though she was rather glad that Millicent had done so, and to account for her involuntary smile, she instantly asked Mrs Altham to lunch with her the next day. Indeed, walking now down the High Street, she smiled again at the thought, and Mr Pritchard, standing outside his grocery store, thought she smiled at him, and raised his hat. And Mrs Ames rather hoped he saw how different a sort of smile she kept on tap, so to speak, for grocers.

Mrs Ames knew very well the manner of speeches that Mrs Altham had been indulging in during the last three weeks, about the little dinner-party she was giving this evening, for she had been indiscreet enough to give specimens of them to Millicent Evans, who had promptly repeated them to her, and it is impossible adequately to convey how unimportant she thought was anything that Mrs Altham said. But the fact that she had said so much was indirectly connected with her asking Mrs Altham ('and your husband, of course,' as she had rather pointedly added) to lunch tomorrow, for she knew that Mrs Altham would be bursting with curiosity about the success of the new experiment, and she intended to let her burst. She disliked Mrs Altham, but that lady's hostility to herself only amused her. Of course, Mrs Altham could not refuse to accept her invitation, because it was a point of honour in Riseborough that anyone bidden to lunch the day after a dinner party must, even at moderate inconvenience, accept, for otherwise what was to happen to the remains of salmon and of jelly too debilitated to be served in its original shape, even though untouched, but still excellent if eaten out of jelly glasses? So much malice, then, must be attributed to Mrs Ames, that she wished to observe the febrile symptoms of Mrs Altham's curiosity, and not to calm them, but rather excite them further.

Mrs Ames would not naturally have gone for social purposes to the house of her doctor, had he not married Millicent, whose father was her own first cousin, and would have been baronet himself had he been the eldest instead of the youngest child. As it was, Dr Evans was on a wholly different footing from that of an ordinary physician, for by marriage he, as she by birth, was connected with 'County', which naturally was the crown and cream of Riseborough society. Mrs Ames was well aware that the profession of a doctor was a noble and self-sacrificing one, but lines had to be drawn somewhere, and it was impossible to contemplate visiting Dr Holmes. A dentist's profession was self-sacrificing, too, but you did not dine at your dentist's, though his manipulations enabled you to dine with comfort and confident smiles elsewhere. Such lines as these she drew with precision, but automatic firmness, and the apparently strange case of Mr Turner, whom she had induced her husband to propose for election at the club, whom, with his wife, she herself asked to dinner, was really no exception. For it was not Mr Turner who had ever been a stationer in Riseborough, but his father, and he himself had been to a public school and a university, and had since then purged all taint of stationery away by twenty years' impartiality as a police magistrate in London. True, he had not changed his name when he came back to live in Riseborough, which would have shown a greater delicacy of mind, and the present inscription above the stationer's shop, 'Burrows, late Turner', was obnoxious, but Mrs Ames was all against the misfortunes of the fathers being visited on the children, and Riseborough, with the exception of Mrs Altham, had quite accepted Mr and Mrs Turner, who gave remarkably good dinners, which were quite equal to the finest efforts of the (Scotch) chef at the club. Mrs Altham said that the Turners had eaten their way into the heart of Riseborough society, which sounded almost witty, until Mrs Ames pointed out that it was Riseborough, not the Turners, who had done the eating. On which the wit in Mrs Altham's mot went out like a candle in the wind. It may, perhaps, be open to question whether Mrs Altham's rooted hostility to the Turners did not predispose Mrs Ames to accept them before their quiet amiability disposed her to do so, for she was neither disposed nor predisposed to like Mrs Altham.

Mrs Ames' way led through Queensgate Street, and she had to hold her black skirt rather high as she crossed the road opposite the club, for the dust was thick. She felt it wiser also to screw her small face up into a tight knot in order to avoid inhaling the fetid blue smoke from an over-lubricated motorcar that very rudely dashed by just in front of her. She did not regard motors with any favour, since there were financial reasons, whose validity was unassailable, why she could not keep one; indeed, partly no doubt owing to her expressed disapproval of them, but chiefly owing to similar financial impediments, Riseborough generally considered that hired flies were a more gentlemanly and certainly more leisurely form of vehicular transport. Mrs Altham, as usual, raised a dissentient voice, and said that she and her husband could not make up their minds between a Daimler and a Rolls-Royce. This showed a very reasonable hesitancy, since at present they had no data whatever with regard to either.

Mrs Ames permitted herself one momentary glance at the bow window of the club, as she regained the pavement after this dusty passage, and then swiftly looked straight in front of her again, since it was not quite QUITE to look in at the window of a man's club. But she had seen several things: her husband was standing there with face contorted by the imminent approach of a sneeze, which showed that his hay fever was not yet over, as he hoped it might be. There was General Fortescue with a large cigar in his mouth, and a glass, probably of sherry, in his hand; there was also the top of a bald head peering over the geraniums in the window like a pink full moon. That no doubt was Mr Turner (for no one was quite so bald as he), enjoying the privilege which she had been instrumental in securing for him. Then Mrs Altham passed her driving, and Mrs Ames waved and kissed her black-gloved hand to her, thinking how very angular curiosity made people, while Mrs Altham waved back thinking that it was no use trying to look important if you were only five foot two, so that honours were about divided. Finally, just before she turned into her own gate, she saw coming along the road, walking very fast, as his custom was, the man she respected and even revered more than anyone in Riseborough. She would have liked to wave her hand to him too, only the Reverend Thomas Pettit would certainly have thought such a proceeding to be very odd conduct. He was county too - very much county, although a clergyman - being the son of that wealthy and distressing peer, Lord Evesham, who occasionally came into Riseborough on county business. On these occasions he lunched at the club, instead of going to his son's house, but did not eat the club lunch, preferring to devour in the smoking room, like an ogre with false teeth, sandwiches which seemed to be made of fish in their decline. Mrs Ames, who could not be called a religious woman, but was certainly very high church, was the most notable of Mr Pettit's admirers, and, indeed, had set quite a fashion in going to the services at St Barnabas', which were copiously embellished by banners, vestments and incense. Indeed, she went there in adoration of him as much as for any other reason, for he seemed to her to be a perfect apostle. He was rich, and gave far more than half his goods to feed the poor; he was eloquent, and (she would not have used so common a phrase) let them all 'have it' from his pulpit, and she was sure he was rapidly wearing himself out with work. And how thrilling it would be to address her rather frequent notes to him with the title 'The Reverend The Lord Evesham'! . . . She gave a heavy sigh, and decided to flutter her podgy hand in his direction for a greeting as she turned into her gate.

The little dinner which had so agitated Riseborough for the last three weeks gave Mrs Ames no qualms at all.

CHAPTER TWO

Whatever happened at her house was right, and she never had any reason to wonder, like minor dinner givers, if things would go off well, since she and no other was responsible for the feast; it was Mrs Ames' dinner party. It was summoned for a quarter to eight, and at half past ten somebody's carriage would be announced, and she would say, 'I hope nobody is thinking of going away yet,' in consequence of which everybody would go away at twenty minutes to eleven instead. If anybody expected to play cards or smoke in the drawing room, he would be disappointed, because these diversions did not form part of the curriculum. The gentlemen had one cigarette in the dining room after their wine and with their coffee: then they followed the ladies and indulged in the pleasures of conversation. Mrs Ames always sat in a chair by the window, and always as the clock struck ten she re-sorted her conversationalists. That was (without disrespect) a parlour trick of the most supreme and unfathomable kind. There was always some natural reason why she should get up, and quite as naturally two or three people got up too. Then a sort of involuntary general post took place. Mrs Ames annexed the seat of the risen woman whose partner she intended to talk to, and instantly said, 'Do tell me, because I am so much interested . . . ' upon which her new partner sat down again. The ejected female then wandered disconsolately forward till she found herself talking to some man who had also got up. Therefore they sat down again together. But no one in Riseborough could do the trick as Mrs Ames could do it. Mrs Altham had often tried, and her efforts always ended in everybody sitting down again exactly where they had been before, after standing for a moment, as if an inaudible grace was being said. But Mrs Ames, though not socially jealous (for, being the queen of Riseborough society, she had nobody to be jealous of), was a little prone to spoil this parlour trick when she was dining at other houses, by suddenly developing an earnest conversation with her already existing partner, when she saw that her hostess contemplated a copy of her famous manoeuvre. Yet, after all, she was within her rights, for the parlour trick was her own patent, and it was quite proper to thwart the attempted infringement of it.

Having waggled her hand in the direction of Mr Pettit, she went straight to the dining room, where the dinner table was being laid. There was to be a company of eight tonight, and accordingly she took three little cardboard slips from the top left-hand drawer of her writing table, on each of which was printed:

PLEASE TAKE IN

TO DINNER.

These were presented in the hall to the men before dinner (it was unnecessary to write one for her husband), each folded, with the name of the guest in question being written on the back, while the name of the woman he was to take in filled the second line. Thus there were no separate and hurried communications to be made in the drawing room, as everything was arranged already. This was not so original as the other parlour trick, but at present nobody else in Riseborough had attempted it. Then out of the same drawer she took - what she took requires a fresh paragraph.

Printed menu cards. There were a dozen packets of them, each packet advertising a different dinner: an astounding device, requiring enlargement of explanation. She discovered them by chance in the Military Stores in London, selected a dozen packets containing fifty copies each, and kept the secret to herself. The parlour maids had orders to tweak them away as soon as the last course was served, so that no menu collector, if there was such retrospective glutton in Riseborough, could appropriate them, and thus, perhaps, ultimately get a clue which might lead him to the solution. For by a portent of ill luck, it might then conceivably happen that a certain guest would find himself bidden for the third or fourth time to eat precisely the same dinner as his odious collection told him that he had eaten six months before. But the tweaking parlourmaids obviated that risk, and if the menu cards were still absolutely 'unsoiled', Mrs Ames used them again. There was one very sumptuous dinner among the twelve, there were nine dinners good enough for anybody, there were two dinners that might be described as 'poor'. It was one of these, probably, which Mrs Altham had in her mind when she was so ruthless in respect to Mrs Ames' food. But, poor or sumptuous, it appeared to the innocent Riseborough world that Mrs Ames had her menu cards printed as required; that, having constructed her dinner, she sent round a copy of it to the printer's to be set up in type. Probably she corrected the proofs also. She never called attention to these menus, and seemed to take them as a matter of course. Mrs Altham had once directly questioned her about them, asking if they were not a great expense. But Mrs Ames had only shifted a bracelet on her wrist and said, 'I am accustomed to use them.'

Mrs Ames took four copies of one of these dinners which were good enough for anybody, and propped them up, two on each of the long sides of the table. Naturally, she did not want one herself, and her husband, also naturally, sometimes said, 'What are you going to give us tonight, Amy?' In which case one of them was passed to him. But he had a good retentive memory with regard to food, and with a little effort he could remember what the rest of the dinner was going to be, when the nature of the soup had given him his cue. Occasionally he criticized, saying in his hearty voice (this would be in the autumn or winter), 'What, what? Partridge again? Perdrix repetita, isn't it, General, if you haven't forgotten your Latin.' And Amy from the other end of the table replied, 'Well, Lyndhurst, we must eat the game our friends are so kind as to send us.' And yet Mrs Altham declared that she had seen partridges from the poulterers delivered at Mrs Ames' house! 'But they are getting cheap now,' she added to her husband, 'particularly the old birds. I got a leg, Henry, and the bird must have roosted on it for years before Mrs Ames' friends were so kind as to send it her.'

So Mrs Ames propped up the printed menu cards, and spoke a humorous word to her first parlourmaid.

'I have often told you, Parker, to wear gloves when you are putting out the silver. I am not a detective: I am not wanting to trace you by your fingerprints.'

Parker giggled discreetly. Somehow, Mrs Ames' servants adored their rather exacting mistress, and stopped with her for years. They did not get very high wages, and a great deal was required of them, but Mrs Ames treated them like human beings and not like machines. It may have been only because they were so far removed from her socially; but it may have been that there was some essential and innate kindliness in her that shut up like a parasol when she had to deal with such foolish and trying folk as Mrs Altham. Mrs Altham, indeed, had tried to entice Parker away with a substantial rise in wages, and the prospect of less arduous service. But that admirable servingmaid had declined to be tempted. Also, she had reported the occurrence to her mistress. It only confirmed what Mrs Ames already thought of the temptress. She did not add any further black mark.

CHAPTER TWO

The table at present was devoid of any floral decoration, but that was no part of Mrs Ames' province. Her husband, that premature gardener, was responsible for flowers and wine when Mrs Ames gave a party, and always returned home half an hour earlier, to pick such of his treasures as looked as if they would begin to go off tomorrow, and make a subterranean excursion with a taper and the wine book to his cellar. In the domestic economy of the house he paid the rent, the rates and taxes, the upkeep of the garden, the wine bills, and the cost of their annual summer holiday, while Mrs Ames' budget was responsible for coal, electric light, servants' wages, and catering bills. Arising out of this arrangement there occasionally arose clouds (though no bigger than Mrs Ames' own hand) that flecked the brightness of their domestic serenity. Occasionally - not often - Mrs Ames would be pungent about the possibility of putting out the electric light on leaving a room, occasionally her husband had sent for his coat at lunch time, to supplement the heat given out on a too parsimonious hearth. But such clouds were never seen by other eyes than theirs: the presence of guests led Major Ames to speak of the excellence of his wife's cook and say, "'Pon my word, I never taste better cooking than what I get at home,' and suggested to his wife to say to Mrs Fortescue, 'My husband so much enjoys having the General to dinner, for he knows a glass of good wine.' She might with truth have said that he knew a good many glasses.

Finally, the two shared in equal proportions the upkeep of a rather weird youth who was the only offspring of their marriage, and was mistakenly called Harry, for the name was singularly ill-suited to him. He had lank hair, protuberant eyes, and a tendency to write poetry. Just now he was at home from Cambridge, and had rather agitated his mother that afternoon by approaching her dreamily at the garden party and saying, 'Mother, Mrs Evans is the most wonderful creature I ever saw!' That seemed to her so wild an exaggeration as to be quite senseless, and to portend poetry. Harry made his father uncomfortable, too, by walking about with some quite common rose in his hand, and pretending that the scent of it was meat and drink to him. Also he had queer notions about vegetarianism, and said that a hunch of brown bread, a plate of beans, and a lump of cheese, contained more nourishment than quantities of mutton chops. But though not much of a hand at victuals, he found inspiration in what he called 'yellow wine', and he and a few similarly minded friends belonged to a secret Omar Khayyam Club at Cambridge, the proceedings of which were carried on behind locked doors, not for fear of the Jews, but of the Philistines. A large glass salad bowl filled with yellow wine and sprinkled with rose leaves was the inspirer of these mild orgies, and each Omarite had to write and read a short poem during the course of the evening. It was a point of honour among members always to be madly in love with some usually unconscious lady, and paroxysms of passion were punctuated by Byronic cynicism. Just now it seemed likely that Mrs Evans would soon be the fount of aspiration and despair. That would create quite a sensation at the next meeting of the Omar Club: nobody before had been quite so daring as to fall in love with a married woman. But no doubt that phenomenon has occurred in the history of human passion, so why should it not occur to an Omarite?

The wine at Mrs Ames' parties was arranged by her husband on a scale that corresponded with the food. At either of the two 'poor' dinners, for instance, a glass of Marsala was accorded with the soup, a light (though wholesome) claret moistened the rest of the meal, and a single glass of port was offered at dessert. The course of the nine dinners good enough for anybody was enlivened by the substitution of sherry for Marsala, champagne for claret, and liqueurs presented with coffee, while on the much rarer occasions of the one sumptuous dinner (which always included an ice) liqueur made its first appearance with the ice, and a glass of hock partnered the fish. Tonight, therefore, sherry was on offer, and when, the dinner being fairly launched, Mrs Ames took her first disengaged look round, she observed with some little annoyance, justifiable, even laudable, in a hostess, that Harry was talking in the wrong direction. In fact, he was devoting his attention to Mrs Evans, who sat between him and his father, instead of entertaining Elsie, her daughter, whom he had taken in, and who now sat isolated and silent, since General Fortescue, who was on her other side, was naturally conversing with his hostess. Certainly it was rubbish to call Mrs Evans a most wonderful creature; there was nothing wonderful about her. She was fair, with pretty yellow hair (an enthusiast might have called it golden), she had small regular features, and that look of distinction which Mrs Ames (drawing herself up a little as she thought of it) considered to be inseparable from any in whose veins ran the renowned Westbourne blood. She had also that slim, tall figure which, though characteristic of the same race, was unfortunately not quite inseparable from its members, for no amount of drawing herself up would have conferred it on Mrs Ames, and Harry took after her in this respect.

Dr Evans had not long been settled in Riseborough - indeed, it was only last winter that he had bought his practice here, and taken the delightful house in which his wife had given so populous a garden party that afternoon. Their coming, as advertised by Mrs Ames, had been looked forward to with a high degree of expectancy, since a fresh tenant for the Red House, especially when he was known to be a man of wealth (though only a doctor), was naturally supposed to connote a new and exclusive entertainer, while his wife's relationship to Sir James Westbourne made a fresh link between the 'town' and the 'county'. Hitherto, Mrs Ames had been the chief link, and though without doubt she was a genuine one (her mother being a Westbourne), she had been a little disappointing in this regard, as she barely knew the present head of the family, and was apt to talk about old days rather than glorify the present ones by exhibitions of the family to which she belonged. But it was hoped that with the advent of Mrs Evans a more living intimacy would be established.

Mrs Evans was the fortunate possessor of that type of looks which wears well, and it was difficult to believe that Elsie, with her eighteen years and elderly manner, was her daughter. She was possessed also of that unemotional temperament which causes the years to leave only the faintest traces of their passage, and they had graven on her face but little record of joys and sorrows. Her mouth still possessed the softness of a girl's, and her eyes, large and blue, had something of the shy, unconscious wonder of childhood in their azure. To judge by appearances (which we shall all continue to do until the end of time, though we have made proverbs to warn us against the fallibility of such conclusions), she must have had the tender and innocent nature of a child, and though Mrs Ames saw nothing wonderful about her, it was really remarkable that a woman could look so much and mean so little. She did not talk herself with either depth or volume, but she had, so to speak, a deep and voluminous way of listening which was immensely attractive. She made the man who was talking to her feel himself to be interesting (a thing always pleasant to the vainer sex), and in consequence he generally became interested. To fire the word 'flirt' at her, point-blank, would have been a brutality that would have astounded her - nor, indeed, was she accustomed to use the somewhat obvious arts which we associate with those practitioners, but it is true that without effort she often established relations of intimacy with other people without any giving of herself in return. Both men and women were accustomed to take her into their confidence; it was so easy to tell her of private affairs, and her eyes, so wide and eager and sympathetic, gave an extraordinary tenderness to her commonplace replies, which accurately, by themselves, reflected her dull and unemotional mind. She possessed, in fact, as unemotional but comely people do, the potentiality of making a great deal of mischief without exactly meaning it, and it would be safe to predict that, the mischief being made, she would quite certainly acquit herself of any intention of having made it. It would be rash, of course, to assert that no breeze would ever stir the pearly sleeping sea of her temperament: all that can be said is that it had not been stirred yet.

Mrs Ames could not permit Elsie's isolation to continue, and she said firmly to Harry, 'Tell Miss Evans all about Cambridge,' which straightened conversation out again, and allowed Mrs Evans to direct all her glances and little sentences to Major Ames. As was usual with men who had the privilege of talking to her, he soon felt himself a vivid conversationalist.

'Yes, gardening was always a hobby of mine,' he was saying, 'and in the regiment they used to call me Adam. The grand old gardener, you know, as Tennyson says. Not that there was ever anything grand about me.'

Mrs Evans' mouth quivered into a little smile.

'Nor old, either, Major Ames,' she said.

Major Ames put down the glass of champagne he had just sipped, in order to give his loud, hearty laugh.

'Well, well,' he said, 'I'm pretty vigorous yet, and can pull the heavy garden roller as well as a couple of gardeners could. I never have a gardener more than a couple of days a week. I do all the work myself. Capital exercise, rolling the lawn, and then I take a rest with a bit of weeding, or picking a bunch of flowers for Amy's table. Weeding, too -

'An hour's weeding a day
Keeps the doctor away.'

I defy you to get lumbago if you do a bit of weeding every morning.'

Again a little shy smile quivered on Millie Evans' mouth.

'I shall tell my husband,' she said. 'I shall say you told me you spend an hour a day in weeding, so that you shouldn't ever set eyes on him. And then you make poetry about it afterwards.'

Again he laughed.

'Well, now, I call that downright wicked of you,' he said, 'twisting my words about in that way. General, I want your opinion about that glass of champagne. It's a '96 wine, and wants drinking.'

The General applied his fishlike mouth to his glass.

'Wants drinking, does it?' he said. 'Well, it'll get it from me. Delicious! Goo' dry wine.'

Major Ames turned to Millie Evans again.

'Beg your pardon, Mrs Evans,' he said, 'but General Fortescue likes to know what's before him. Yes, downright wicked of you! I'm sure I wish Amy had asked Dr Evans tonight, but there - you know what Amy is. She's got a notion that it will make a pleasanter dinner table not to ask husband and wife always together. She says it's done a great deal in London now. But they can't put on to their tables in London such sweet peas as I grow here in my bit of a garden. Look at those in front of you. Black Michaels, they are. Look at the size of them. Did you ever see such sweet peas? I wonder what Amy is going to give us for dinner tonight. Bit of lamb next, is it? And a quail to follow. Hope you'll go Nap, Mrs Evans; I must say Amy has a famous cook. And what do you think of us all down at Riseborough, now you've had time to settle down and look about you? I daresay you and your husband say some sharp things about us, hey? Find us very stick-in-the-mud after London?'

She gave him one of those shy little deprecating glances that made him involuntarily feel that he was a most agreeable companion.

'Ah, you are being wicked now!' she said. 'Everyone is delightful. So kind, so hospitable. Now, Major Ames, do tell me more about your flowers. Black Michaels, you said those were. I must go in for gardening, and will you begin to teach me a little? Why is it that your flowers are so much more beautiful than anybody's? At least, I needn't ask: it must be because you understand them better than anybody.'

Major Ames felt that this was an uncommonly agreeable woman, and for half a second contrasted her pleasant eagerness to hear about his garden with his wife's complete indifference to it. She liked flowers on the table, but she scarcely knew a hollyhock from a geranium.

'Well, well,' he said, 'I don't say that my flowers, which you are so polite as to praise, don't owe something to my care. Rain or fine, I don't suppose I spend less than an average of four hours a day among them, year in, year out.

And that's better, isn't it, than sitting at the club, listening to all the gossip and tittle-tattle of the place?'

'Ah, you are like me,' she said. 'I hate gossip. It is so dull. Gardening is so much more interesting.'

He laughed again.

'Well, as I tell Amy,' he said, 'if our friends come here expecting to hear all the tittle-tattle of the place, they will be in for a disappointment. Amy and I like to give our friends a hearty welcome and a good dinner, and pleasant conversation about really interesting things. I know little about the gossip of the town; you would find me strangely ignorant if you wanted to talk about it. But politics now - one of those beastly Radical members of Parliament lunched with us only the week before last, and I assure you that Amy asked him some questions he found it hard to answer. In fact, he didn't answer them: he begged the question, begged the question. There was one, I remember, which just bowled him out. She said, 'What is to happen to the parks of the landed gentry, if you take them away from the owners?' Well, that bowled him out, as they say in cricket. Look at Sir James's place, for instance, your cousin's place, Amy's cousin's place. Will they plant a row of villas along the garden terrace? And who is to live in them if they do? Grant that Lloyd George - she said that - grant that Lloyd George wants a villa there, that will be one villa. But the terrace there will hold a dozen villas. Who will take the rest of them? She asked him that. They take away all our property, and then expect us to build houses on other people's! Don't talk to me!'

The concluding sentence was not intended to put a stop on this pleasant conversation; it was only the natural ejaculation of one connected with landed proprietors. Mrs Evans understood it in that sense.

CHAPTER TWO

'Do tell me all about it,' she said. 'Of course, I am only a woman, and we are supposed to have no brains, are we not? And to be able to understand nothing about politics. But will they really take my cousin James's place away from him? I think Radicals must be wicked.'

'More fools than knaves, I always say,' said Major Ames magnanimously. 'They are deluded, like the poor Suffragettes. Suffragettes now! A woman's sphere of influence lies in her home. Women are the queens of the earth; I've often said that, and what do queens want with votes? Would Amy have any more influence in Riseborough if she had a vote? Not a bit of it. Well, then, why go about smacking the faces of policemen and chaining yourself to a railing? If I had my way - '

Major Ames became of lower voice and greater confidence.

'Amy doesn't wholly agree with me,' he said, 'and it's a pleasure to thrash the matter out with somebody like yourself, who has sensible views on the subject. What use are women in politics? None at all, as you just said. It's for women to rock the cradle, and rule the world. I say, and I have always said, that to give them a vote would be to wreck their influence, God bless them. But Amy doesn't agree with me. I say that I will vote - she's a Conservative, of course, and so am I - I will vote as she wishes me to. But she says it's the principle of the thing, not the practice. But what she calls principle, I call want of principle. Home: that's the woman's sphere.'

Mrs Evans gave a little sigh.

'I never heard it so beautifully expressed,' she said. 'Major Ames, why don't you go in for politics?'

Major Ames felt himself flattered; he felt also that he deserved the flattery. Hence, to him now, it ceased to be flattery, and became a tribute. He became more confidential, and vastly more vapid.

'My dear lady,' he said, 'politics is a dirty business nowadays. We can serve our cause best by living a quiet and dignified life, without ostentation, as you see, but by being gentlemen. It is the silent protest against these socialistic ideas that will tell in the long run. What should I do at Westminster? Upon my soul, if I found myself sitting opposite those Radical louts, it would take me all my time to keep my temper. No, no, let me attend to my garden, and give my friends good dinners - bless my soul, Amy is letting us have an ice tonight - strawberry ice, I expect; that was why she asked me whether there were plenty of strawberries. Glace de fraises; she likes her menu cards printed in French, though I am sure "strawberry ice" would tell us all we wanted to know. What's in a name after all?'

Conversation had already shifted, and Major Ames turned swiftly to a dry-skinned Mrs Brooks who sat on his left. She was a sad high-church widow who embroidered a great deal. Her dress was outlined with her own embroideries, so, too, were many altar cloths at the church of St Barnabas. She and Mrs Ames had a sort of religious rivalry over its decoration; the one arranged the copious white lilies that crowned the cloth made by the other. Their rivalry was not without silent jealousy, and it was already quite well known that Mrs Brooks had said that lilies of the valley were quite as suitable as Madonna lilies, which shed a nasty yellow pollen on the altar cloth. But Madonna lilies were larger; a decoration required fewer 'blooms'. In other moods also she was slightly acid.

Mrs Evans turned slowly to her right, where Harry was sitting. She might almost be supposed to know that she had a lovely neck, at least it was hard to think that she had lived with it for thirty-seven years in complete unconsciousness of it. If she moved her head very quickly, there was just a suspicion of loose skin about it. But she did not move her head very quickly.

'And now let us go on talking,' she said. 'Have you told my little girl all about Cambridge? Tell me all about Cambridge too. What fun you must have! A lot of young men together, with no stupid women and girls to bother them. Do you play a great deal of lawn tennis?'

Harry reconsidered for a moment his verdict concerning the wonderfulness of her. It was hardly happy to talk to a member of the Omar Club about games and the advantages of having no girls about.

'No; I don't play games much,' he said. 'The set I am in don't care for them.'

She tilted her head a little back, as if asking pardon for her ignorance.

'I didn't know,' she said. 'I thought perhaps you liked games - football, racquets, all that kind of thing. I am sure you could play them beautifully if you chose. Or perhaps you like gardening? I had such a nice talk to your father about flowers. What a lot he knows about them!'

Flowers were better than games, anyhow; Harry put down his spoon without finishing his ice.

'Have you ever noticed what a wonderful colour La France roses turn at twilight?' he asked. 'All the shadows between the petals become blue, quite blue.'

'Do they really? You must show me sometime. Are there some in your garden here?'

'Yes, but father doesn't care about them so much because they are common. I think that is so strange of him. Sunsets are common, too, aren't they? There is a sunset every day. But the fact that a thing is common doesn't make it less beautiful.'

She gave a little sigh.

'But what a nice idea,' she said. 'I am sure you thought of it. Do you talk about these things much at Cambridge?'

Mrs Ames began to collect ladies' eyes at this moment, and the conversation had to be suspended. Millie Evans, though she was rather taller than Harry, managed, as she passed him on the way to the door, to convey the impression of looking at him.

'You must tell me all about it,' she said. 'And show me those delicious roses turning blue at twilight.'

Dinner had been at a quarter to eight, and when the men joined the women again in the drawing room, light still lingered in the midsummer sky. Then Harry, greatly daring, since such a procedure was utterly contrary to all established precedents, persuaded Mrs Evans to come out into the garden, and observe for herself the chameleonic properties of the roses. Then he had ventured on another violation of rule, since all rights of flower-picking were vested in his father, and had plucked her half a dozen of them. But on their return with the booty, and the establishment of the blue theory, his father, so far from resenting this invasion of his privileges, had merely said:

'The rascal might have found you something choicer than that, Mrs Evans. But we'll see what we can find you tomorrow.'

She had again seemed to look up at Harry.

'Nothing can be lovelier than my beautiful roses,' she said. 'But it is sweet of you to think of sending me some more. Cousin Amy, look at the roses Mr Harry has given me.'

Carriages arrived as usual that night at half past ten, at which hour, too, a gaunt, grenadier-like maid of certain age, rapped loudly on the front door, and demanded Mrs Brooks, whom she was to protect on her way home, and as usual carriages and the grenadier waited till twenty minutes to eleven. But even at a quarter to, no conveyance, by some mischance, had come for Mrs Evans, and despite her protests, Major Ames insisted on escorting her and Elsie back to her house. Occasionally, when such mistakes occurred, it had been Harry's duty to see home the uncarriaged, but tonight, when it would have been his pleasure, the privilege was denied him. So, instead, after saying goodnight to his mother, he went swiftly to his room, there to write a mysterious letter to a member of the Omar Club, and compose a short poem, which should, however unworthily, commemorate this amorous evening.

There is nothing in the world more rightly sacred than the first dawnings of love in a young man, but, on the other hand, there is nothing more ludicrous if his emotions are inspired, or even tinged, by self-consciousness and the sense of how fine a young spark he is. And our unfortunate Harry was charged with this absurdity; all through the evening it had been present to his mind, how dashing and Byronic a tale this would prove at the next meeting of the Omar Khayyam Club; with what fine frenzy he would throw off, in his hour of inspiration after the yellow wine, the little heart wail which he was now about to compose, as soon as his letter to Gerald Everett was written. And lest it should seem unwarrantable to intrude in the spirit of ridicule on a young man's rapture and despair, an extract from his letter should give solid justification.

'Of course, I can't give names,' he said, 'because you know how such things get about; but, my God, Gerald, how wonderful she is. I saw her this afternoon for the first time, and she dined with us tonight. She understands everything - whatever I said, I saw reflected in her eyes, as the sky is reflected in still water. After dinner I took her out into the garden, and showed her how the shadows of the La France roses turn blue at dusk. I quoted to her these two lines -

"O, thou art fairer than the evening air, Clad in the beauty of a thousand stars."

'And I THINK she saw that I quoted AT her. Of course, she turned it off, and said, "What pretty lines!" but I think she saw. And she carried my roses home. Lucky roses!

'Gerald, I am miserable! I haven't told you yet. For she is married. She has a great stupid husband, years and years older than herself. She has, too, a great stupid daughter. There's another marvel for you! Honestly and soberly she does not look more than twenty-five. I will write again, and tell you how all goes. But I think she likes me; there is clearly something in common between us. There is no doubt she enjoyed our little walk in the dusk, when the roses turned blue . . . Have you had any successes lately?'

He finished his letter, and before beginning his poem, lit the candle on his dressing table, and examined his small, commonplace visage in the glass. It was difficult to arrange his hair satisfactorily. If he brushed it back it revealed an excess of high, vacant-looking forehead; if he let it drop over his forehead, though his resemblance to Keats was distinctly strengthened, its resemblance to seaweed was increased also. The absence of positive eyebrow was regrettable, but was there not fire in his rather pale and far-apart eyes? He rather thought there was. His nose certainly turned up a little, but what, if not that, did tip-tilted imply? A rather long upper lip was at present only lightly fledged with an adolescent moustache, but there was decided strength in his chin. It stuck out. And having practised a frown which he rather fancied, he went back to the table in the window again, read a few stanzas of Dolores, in order to get into tune with passion and bitterness (for this poem was not going to begin or end happily) and wooed the lyric muse.

Major Ames, meantime, had seen Mrs Evans to her door, and retraced his steps as far as the club, where he was in half a mind to go in, and get a game of billiards, which he enjoyed. He played in a loud, hectoring and unskilful manner, and it was noticeable that all the luck (unless, as occasionally happened, he won) was invariably on the side of his opponent. But after an irresolute pause, he went on again, and let himself into his own house. Amy was still sitting in the drawing room, though usually she went to bed as soon as her guests had gone.

'Very pleasant evening, my dear,' he said, 'and your plan was a great success. Uncommonly agreeable woman Mrs Evans is. Pretty woman, too; you would never guess she was the mother of that great girl.'

'She was not considered pretty as a girl,' said his wife.

'No? Then she must have improved in looks afterwards. Lonely life rather, to be a doctor's wife, with your husband liable to be called away at any hour of the day or night.'

'I have no doubt Millie occupies herself very well,' said Mrs Ames. 'Goodnight, Lyndhurst. Are you coming up to bed?'

'Not just yet. I shall sit up a bit, and smoke another cigar.'

He sat in the window, and every now and then found himself saying half aloud, 'Uncommonly agreeable woman.' Just overhead Harry was tearing passion to shreds in the style (more or less) of Swinburne.

DR EVANS was looking out of the window of his dining room as he waited the next morning for breakfast to be brought in, jingling a pleasant mixture of money and keys in his trouser pockets and whistling a tune that sounded vague and De Bussy-like until you perceived that it was really an air familiar to streets and barrel organs, and owed its elusive quality merely to the fact that the present performer was a little uncertain as to the comparative value of tones and semitones. But this slightly discouraging detail was more than compensated for by the evident cheerfulness of the executant; his plump, high-coloured face, his merry eye, the singular content of his whole aspect betokened a personality that was on excellent terms with life.

His surroundings were as well furnished and securely comfortable as himself. The table was invitingly laid; a Sheffield-plate urn (Dr Evans was an amateur in Georgian decoration and furniture) hissed and steamed with little upliftings of the lid under the pressure within, and a number of hot dishes suggested an English interpretation of breakfast. Fine mezzotints after the great English portrait-painters hung on the walls, and a Chippendale sideboard was spread with fruit dishes and dessert plates. The morning was very hot, but the high, spacious room, with its thick walls, was cool and fresh, while its potentialities for warmth and cosiness in the winter were sponsored for by the large open fireplace and the stack of hot-water pipes which stood beneath the sideboard. Outside, the windows at which Dr Evans stood looked out on to the large and secluded lawn, which had been the scene of the garden party the day before. Red brick walls ran along the two sides of it at right angles to the house; opposite, a row of espaliered fruit trees screened off the homeliness of the kitchen garden beyond, and the railway cutting which formed the boundary of this pleasant place.

Wilfred Evans had whistled the first dozen bars of the 'Merry Widow Waltz' some six or seven times through, before, with the retarded consciousness that it was Sunday, he went on to 'The Church's One Foundation,' and though, with his usual admirable appetite, he felt the allure of the hot dishes, he waited, still whistling, for some other member of his household, wife or daughter, to appear. He was one of the most gregarious and clubbable of men, and no hecatomb of stalled oxen would have given him content, if he had had to eat his beef alone. A firm attachment to his domestic circle, combined with the not very exacting calls of his practice, but truly fervent investigations in the laboratory at the end of the garden, of the habits and economy of phagocytes, comfortably filled up, to the furthest horizon, the scenery of his mental territories.

He had not to wait long for his wife to appear, and he hailed her with his wonted cordiality.

'Morning, little woman,' he said. 'Slept well, I hope?'

Mrs Evans did not practise at home all those arts of pleasing with which she was so lavish in other people's houses. Also, this morning she felt rather cross, a thing which, to do her justice, was rare with her.

'Not very,' she said. 'I kept waking. It was stiflingly hot.'

'I'm sorry, my dear,' said he.

Mrs Evans busied herself with tea-making; her long, slender hands moved with extraordinary deftness and silence among clattering things, and her husband whistled the 'Merry Widow Waltz' once or twice more.

'Oh, Wilfred, do stop that odious tune,' she said, without the slightest hint of impatience in her voice. 'It is bad enough on your pianola, which, after all, is in tune!'

'Which is more than can be said for my penny whistle?' asked he, good-humouredly. 'Right you are, I'm dumb. Tell me about your party last night.'

'My dear, haven't you been to enough Riseborough parties to know that there is nothing to tell about any party?' she asked. 'I sat between Major Ames and the son. I talked gardening on one side with the father, and something which I suppose was enlightened Cambridge conversation on the other. Harry Ames is rather a dreadful sort of youth. He took me into the garden afterwards to show me something about roses. And the carriage didn't come. Major Ames saw me home. When did you get in?'

'Not till nearly three. Very difficult maternity case. But we'll pull them both through.'

Millie Evans gave a little shudder, which was not quite entirely instinctive. She emphasized it for her husband's benefit. Unfortunately, he did not notice it.

'Will you have your tea now?' she asked.

CHAPTER THREE

He looked at her with an air mainly conjugal but tinged with professionalism.

'Bit upset with the heat, little woman?' he asked. 'You look a trifle off colour. We can't have you sleeping badly, either. Show me the man who sleeps his seven hours every night, and I'll show you who will live to be ninety.'

This prospect did not for the moment allure his wife.

'I think I would sooner sleep less and die earlier,' she said in her even voice, 'though I'm sure Elsie will live to a hundred at that rate. You encourage her to be lazy in the morning, Wilfred. I'm sure anyone can manage to be in time for breakfast at a quarter past nine.'

He shook his head.

'No, no, little woman,' he said. 'Let a growing girl sleep just as much as she feels inclined. I would sooner stint a girl's food than her sleep. Give the red corpuscles a chance, eh?'

Millie got up from the table, and went to the sideboard to get some fruit. Then suddenly it struck her that all this was hardly worthwhile. It seemed a stupid business to come down every morning and eat breakfast, to manage the household, to go for a walk, perhaps, or sit in the garden, and after completing the round of these daily futilities, to go to bed again and sleep, just for the recuperation that sleep gave, to enable her to do it all over again. But the strawberries looked cool and moist, and standing by the sideboard she ate a few of them. Just above it hung the oblong Sheraton mirror, which her husband had bought so cheaply at a local sale and had brought home so triumphantly. That, too, seemed to tell her a stale story, and the reflection of her young face, crowned with the shimmer of yellow hair, against the dark oak background of the panelling seemed without purpose or significance. She was doing nothing with her beauty that stayed so long with her. But it would not stay many years longer: this morning even there seemed to be a shadow over it, making it dim . . . Soon nobody would care if she had ever been pretty or not; indeed, even now Elsie seemed by her height and the maturity of her manner to be reminding everybody of the fact that she herself must be approaching the bar which every woman has to cross when she is forty or thereabouts . . . And, strange enough it may appear, these doubts and questionings which looked at Millie darkly from the Sheraton glass above the sideboard, selfish and elementary as they were, resembled 'thought' far more closely than did the generality of those surface impressions that as a rule mirrored her mind. They were, too, rather actively disagreeable, and generally speaking, nothing disagreeable occurred to her. The experiences of every day might be mildly exhilarating, or mildly tedious. But, whatever they were, she was not accustomed to think closely about them. Now, for the moment, it seemed to her that some shadow, some vague presence confronted her, and menacingly demanded her attention.

Riseborough is notable for the number of its churches, and before long the air was mellow with bells. As a rule, Millie Evans went to church on Sunday morning with the same regularity as she ate hot roast beef for lunch when it was over, but this morning she easily let herself be persuaded to refrain from any act of public worship. It seemed quite within the bounds of possibility that she might feel faint during the psalms and, on her husband's advice, she settled to stop at home, leaving him and Elsie, who was quite unaware what faintness felt like, to attend. But it was not the fear of faintness that prompted her absence: she wanted, almost for the first time in her life, to be alone and to think. Even on the occasion of her marriage, she had not found it necessary to employ herself with original thought: her mother had done the thinking for her, and had advised her, as she felt quite sure, sensibly and well. Nor had she needed to think when she was expecting her only child, for on that occasion she had been perfectly content to do exactly as her husband told her. But now, at the age of thirty-seven, the sight of her own face in the glass had suggested to her certain possibilities, certain limitations.

Ill-health had, on infrequent Sundays, prevented her attendance at church, and now, following merely the dictates of habit, she took out with her to a basket chair below the big mulberry tree in the garden, a Bible and prayer book, out of which she supposed that she would read the psalms and lessons for the day. But the Bible remained long untouched, and when she opened it eventually at random, she read but one verse. It was at the end of Ecclesiastes that the leaves parted, and she read, 'When desire shall fail, because man goeth to his long home.'

That was enough, for it was that, here succinctly expressed, which had been troubling her this morning, though so vaguely, that until she saw her symptoms written down shortly and legibly, she had scarcely known what they were. But certainly this line and a half described them. No doubt it was all very elementary; by degrees one ceased to care, and then one died. But her case was rather different from that, for she felt that with her desire had not failed, simply because she never had had desire. She had waked and slept, she had eaten and walked, she had had a child; but all these things had been of about the same value. Once she had had a tooth out, without gas; that was a slightly more vivid experience. But it was very soon over: she had not really cared.

But though she had not cared for any of those things, she had not been bored with the repetition of them. It had seemed natural that one thing should follow another, that the days should become weeks, and the weeks should become months, insensibly. When the months added themselves into years, she took notice of that fact by having a birthday, and Wilfred, as he gave her some little present in a morocco case, told her that she looked as young as when they first met, which was very nearly true. She had a quantity of these morocco cases now: he never omitted the punctual presentation of each. And the mental vision of all these morocco cases, some round, some square, some oblong, and the thought of their contents - a little pearl brooch, a sapphire brooch, a pair of emerald earrings, a jewelled hatpin - suddenly came upon her with their cumulative effect. A lot of time had gone by; it chiefly lived in her now through the memory of the morocco cases.

By virtue of her unemotional temperament and serene bodily health she looked very young still, and certainly did not feel old. But as the bells for church ceased to jangle and clash in the hot still air, leaving only for the ear the hum of multitudinous bees in the long flowerbed, it dawned on her that whatever she felt, and however she looked, she would soon be on the other side of that barrier which for woman marks the end of their essential and characteristic life. There were a few years left her yet out of the years of which she made so little use, and with a spasm, the keenest perhaps she had ever known, even including the extraction of the tooth without gas, the horror of middle age fell upon her, making her shiver. All her life she had felt nothing: soon she would be incapable of feeling, except in so far as regret, that pale echo of what might once have been emotion, can be considered an affair of the heart. To feel, she readily perceived, implied the existence of something or somebody to feel about. But she did not know where to look for her participant. Long ago her husband had become as much part of that dead level of life as had her breakfast or her dressing for dinner. Never had he stirred her from her placid passivity, she had never yearned for him, in the sense in which a thirsty man desires water. She had no love of nature: 'the primrose by the river's brim' might have been a violet for anything that she cared; charity, in its technical sense, was distasteful to her, because the curious smell in the houses of the poor made her only long to get away. It was hard to know where to turn to find an outlet for that drowsily awakening recognition of life that today, so late and as yet so feebly, stirred within her. Yet, though it stirred but feebly, there was movement there: it wanted to be alive for a little, before it was indubitably dead.

Her thoughts went back to the topic concerning which she had told her husband that there was nothing to be told - namely, the dinnerparty at the Ames' last night. Certainly there was nothing remarkable about it: she had conducted herself as usual, with the usual result. She was accustomed to deal out her little smiles and deferential glances and flattering speeches to those who sat next her at dinner, because in herself a mild amiability prompted her to make herself pleasant, and because, with so little trouble to herself, she could make a man behave as agreeably as he was capable of behaving. She attracted men very easily, cursorily one might say, without attaching any importance to the interest she aroused, and without looking further than the dinner table for the fruits of the attraction she exercised. But this morning, this tardy and drowsy recognition of life, beside which, so to speak, lay the shadow of middle age, gave her pause. Was there some fruition and development of herself, before the withered and barren years came to her, to be found there? It would be quite beyond the mark to say that, sitting here, she definitely proposed to herself to try to make herself emotionally interested in somebody else, in case that might add a zest to life, but she considered the effect which she so easily produced in others, and wondered what it meant to feel like that. Certainly Major Ames had enjoyed escorting her home; certainly Harry had felt a touch of gauche romance when he showed her the effect of twilight on the complexion of some rose or other. He had given her a whole bunch of roses, with an attempt at a pretty speech. Yes, that was it - the shadows in them looked paleblue, and he had said that they were just the colour of her eyes. But the roses were pretty: she hoped that somebody had put them in water.

She was already more than a little interested in her reflections: there was something original and exciting to her in them, and it was annoying to have them broken in upon by the parlourmaid who came towards her from the house. Personally, she thought it absurd not to keep menservants, but Wilfred always maintained that a couple of good parlourmaids produced greater comfort with less disturbance, and yielding to him, as she always yielded to anybody who expressed a definite opinion, she had acquiesced in female service. But she always called the head parlourmaid Watkins, whereas her husband called her Mary.

'Major Ames wants to know if you will see him, ma'am,' said Watkins.

The interest returned.

'Yes, ask him to come out,' she said.

Watkins went back to the house and returned with Major Ames in tow, who carried a huge bouquet of sweet peas. There then followed the difficulty of meeting and greeting gracefully and naturally which is usual when the visitor is visible a long way off. The Major put on a smile far too soon, and had to take it off again, since Mrs Evans had not yet decided that it was time to see him. Then she began to smile, while he (without his smile) was looking abstractedly at the top of the mulberry tree, as if he expected to find her there. He looked there a moment too long, for one of the lower branches suddenly knocked his straw hat off his head, and he said, 'God bless my soul,' and dropped the sweet peas. However, this was not an unmixed misfortune, for the recognition came quite naturally after that. She hoped he was not hurt, was he SURE that silly branch had not hit his face? It must be taken off! WHAT lovely flowers! And were they for her? They were.

Major Ames replaced his hat rather hastily, after a swift manoeuvre with regard to his hair which Mrs Evans did not accurately follow. The fact was (though he believed the fact not to be generally known) that the top of Major Ames' head was entirely destitute of hair, and that the smooth crop which covered it was the produce of the side of his head - just above the ear - grown long, and brushed across the cranium so as to adorn it with seemingly local wealth and sleekness. The rough and unexpected removal of his hat by the bough of the mulberry tree had caused a considerable portion of it to fall back nearly to the shoulder of the side on which it actually grew, and his hasty manoeuvre with his gathered tresses was designed to replace them. Necessarily he put back his hat again quickly, in the manner of a boy capturing a butterfly.

His mind, and the condition of it, on this Sunday morning, would repay a brief analysis. Briefly, then, a sort of aurora borealis of youth had visited him: his heaven was streaked with inexplicable lights. He had told himself that a man of forty-seven was young still, and that when a most attractive woman had manifested an obvious interest in him, it was only reasonable to follow it up. He was not a coxcomb, he was not a loose liver; he was only a very ordinary man, well and healthy, married to a woman considerably older than himself, and living in a town which, in spite of his adored garden, presented but moderate excitements. But indeed, this morning call, paid with this solid tribute of sweet peas, was something of an adventure, and had not been mentioned by him to his wife. He had seen her start for St Barnabas, and then had hastily gathered his bouquet and set out, leaving Harry wandering dreamily about the cinder paths in the kitchen garden, in the full glory of the discovery that the colour of the scarlet runners was like a clarion. Major Ames had plucked almost his rarest varieties, for to pluck the rarest, since he wished to save their first bloom for seed, would have been on the further side of quixotism and have verged on imbecility, but he had brought the best of his second best. Last night, too, he had hinted at his own remissness in the matter of church attendance on Sunday morning, and on his way up here had permitted himself to wonder whether Millie would prove (in consequence, perhaps, of that) to have abstained from worship also, expecting, or at least considering possible, a morning call from him. As a matter of fact she had not indulged in any such hopes, since it had been a matter of pure indifference to her whether he went to church on Sunday or not. But when he found on inquiry at the door that she was at home, it was scarcely unreasonable, on the part of a rather vain and gallantly minded man, to connect the fact with the information he had given.

So he hastily readjusted his hat.

'My own stupidity entirely,' he said; 'do not blame the tree. Yes, I have brought you just a few flowers, and though they are not worthy of your acceptance, they are not the worst bunch of sweet peas I have ever seen, not the worst.

These, Catherine the Great, for instance, are not - well - they do not grow quite in every garden.'

Mrs Evans opened her blue eyes a little wider.

'And are they really for me, Major Ames?' she asked again. 'It is good of you. My precious flowers! They must be put in water at once. Watkins, bring me one of the big flower bowls out here. I will arrange them myself.'

'Lucky flowers, lucky flowers,' chuckled Major Ames.

'It's I who am lucky,' said she, acknowledging this subtle compliment with a little smile. 'I stop away from church rather lazily, and am rewarded by a pleasant visit and a beautiful nosegay. And what a charming party we had last night! I could hardly believe it when I came back here and found it was nearly half past eleven. Such hours!'

Major Ames gave his great loud laugh.

'You are making fun of us, Mrs Evans,' he said; ''pon my word you are making fun of us and our quiet ways down at Riseborough. I'll be bound that when you were in London, half past eleven was more the sort of time when you began to go out to your dances.'

'I used to go out a good deal when I was quite young,' she said. 'Wilfred used quite to urge me to go out, and certainly people were very kind in asking me. I remember one night in the season, I was asked to two dinner parties and a ball and an evening party. After all, it is natural to take pleasure in innocent gaiety when one is young.'

Major Ames felt very hot after his walk, and, forgetting the adventure of his hair, nearly removed his straw hat. But providentially he remembered it again just in time.

'Upon my word,' Mrs Evans, he said jovially, 'you make me feel a hundred years old when you talk like that, as if your days of youth and success were over. Why, someone at your garden party yesterday afternoon told me for a fact that Miss Elsie was the daughter of your husband's first wife. Wouldn't believe me when I said she was your daughter. Poor Sanders - it was Mr Sanders who said it - had to pay ten shillings to me for his positiveness. He betted, you know, he insisted on betting. But really, anyone who didn't happen to know would be right to make such a bet ninety-nine times out of a hundred.'

She gave him a little smile with lowered eyelids.

'Dear Elsie!' she said. 'She is such a comfort to me. She quite manages the house for me, and spares me all the trouble. She always knows how much asparagus ought to cost, and what happens to strawberry ice after a party. I never was a good housekeeper. Wilfred always used to say to me, "Go out and enjoy yourself, my dear, and I'll pay the bills." Of course, it was all his kindness, I know, but sometimes I wonder if it would not have been truer kindness to have made me think and contrive more. Elsie does it all now, but when my little girl marries it will be my turn again. Tell me, Major Ames, is it you or cousin Amy who makes everything go so beautifully at your house? I think - shall I say it - I think it must be you. When a man manages a house there is always more precision somehow: you feel sure that everything has been foreseen and provided for. Printed menu cards, for instance - so chic, so perfectly comme-il faut.'

Watkins had brought out a large dish, rather like a sponging tin, for the sweet peas, and Mrs Evans had begun the really Herculean labour of putting them in water. A grille of wire network fitted over the rim of it: each pea was stuck in separately. She looked up from her task at him.

'Am I right?' she asked.

Major Ames was not really an untruthful man, but many men who are not really untruthful get through a wonderful lot of misrepresentation.

'Oh, you mustn't give me the credit for that,' he said (truthfully so far); 'it's a dodge we always used to have at mess, so why not at one's own house also? It's better than written cards, which take a lot of time to copy out again and again, and then, you see, my dear Amy is not very strong at French, and doesn't want always to be bothering me to tell her whether there's an accent in one word, or two "s's" in another. Saves time and trouble.'

Mrs Evans applauded softly with pink fingertips.

'Ah, I knew it was you!' she said.

Now, clearly (though almost without intention) Major Ames had gone too far to retreat: also retreat implied a flat contradiction of what Mrs Evans said she knew, which would have been a rudeness from which his habitual gallantry naturally revolted. Consequently, being unable to retreat, he had to make himself as safe as possible, to entrench himself.

'Perhaps it's a little extravagance,' he said. 'Indeed, Amy thinks it is, and I never mention the subject of menu cards to her. She's apt to turn the subject a bit abruptly on the word menu card. Dear Amy! After all, it would be a very dull affair, our pleasant life down here, if we all completely agreed with each other.'

She gave a little sigh, shaking her head, and smiling at her sweet peas.

'Ah, how often I think that too,' she said. 'At least, now you say it, I feel I have often thought it. It is so true. Dear Wilfred is such an angel to me, you see! Whatever I do, he is sure to think right. But sometimes you wonder whether the people who know you best, really understand you. It is like - it is like learning things by heart. If you learn a thing by heart, you so often cease to think what it means.'

Mrs Evans, it must be confessed, did not mean anything very precisely by this: her life, that is to say, was not at all circumstanced in the manner that her speech implied it to be, except in so far that she often wished that more amusing things happened to her, and that she would not so soon be forty years old. But she certainly intended Major Ames to attach to her words their natural implication: she wanted to seem vaguely unappreciated. At the same time, she desired him to see that she in no way blamed her dear unconscious Wilfred. If Major Ames thought that, it would spoil a most essential feature of the picture she wished to present of herself. Why she wished to present it was also quite easy of comprehension. She wanted to be interesting, and was by nature silly. The fact that she was close on thirty-eight largely conduced to her speech.

Major Ames made a perfectly satisfactory interpretation of it. He saw all the things he was meant to see, and nothing else. And it was deliciously delivered, so affectionately as regarded Wilfred, so shyly as regarded herself. He instantly made the astounding mental discovery that she was somehow not very happy, owing to a failure in domestic affinities. He felt also that it was intuitive of him to have guessed that, since she had not actually said it. And he was tremendously conscious of the seduction of her presence, as she sat there, cool and white on this hot morning, putting in the last of the sweet peas he had brought her. She looked enchantingly young and fresh, and evidently she found something in him which disposed her to confidences. In justice to him, it may be said that he did not inquire in his own mind as to what that was, but it was easy to see she trusted him.

'I think we all must feel that at times, my dear lady,' he said, anxious to haul the circumstance of his own home into the discussion. 'I suppose that all of us who are not quite old yet, not quite quite old yet, let us say, in order to include me, feel at times that life is not giving us all that it might give; that people do not really understand us. No doubt many people, and I daresay those, as you said, who know one best, do not understand one. And then we mustn't mind that, but march straight on, march straight on, according to orders.'

He sat up very straight in his chair as if about to march, as he made thrillingly noble remarks, and hit himself a couple of sounding blows with his clenched fist on his broad chest. Then a sudden suspicion seized him that he had displayed an almost too Spartan unflinchingness, as if soldiers had no hearts.

'And then perhaps we shall meet someone who does understand us,' he added.

The critical observer, the cynic, and that rarest of all products, the entirely sincere and straightforward person, would have found in this conversation nothing that would move anything beyond his raillery or disgust. Here sitting under the mulberry tree in this pleasant garden, on a Sunday morning, were two people, the man nearly fifty, the woman nearly forty, both trying, with God knows how many little insincerities by the way, to draw near to each other. Both had reached ages that were dangerous to such as had lived (even as they had) extremely respectable and well-conducted lives, without any paramount reason for their morality. About Major Ames' mode of life before he married, which, after all, was at the early age of twenty-five, nothing need be said, because there is really very little to say, and in any case the conduct of a young man not yet in his twenty-fifth year has almost nothing to do with the character of the same man when he is forty-seven. In that very long interval he had conducted himself always as a married man should, and those years, married as he was to a woman much his senior, had not been at all discreditably passed. This chronicle does not in the least intend to impute to him any high principled character, for he had nothing of Galahad in his composition. But he was not a satyr. Consequently, for this is part of the ironical composition of a man - just in the years with which we are dealing, at a time of life when a man might have been condoned for having sown wild oats and seen the huskiness of them, he was in that far more precarious position of not having sown them (except, so to speak, in the smallest of flowerpots), nor of having experienced the jejune quality of such a crop. But it is not implied that he now regretted the respectability of those twenty-two years. He did not do so: he had had a happy and contented life, but he would soon be old. Nor did he now at all contemplate adventure. Merely an Odysseus who had never voyaged wondered what voyaging was like. He was not in love with this seductive long-lashed face that bent over the sweet peas he had brought her. But if he had the picking of those sweet peas over again, he would probably have picked the very best, regardless of the fact that he wanted the seeds for next year's sowing. So as regards him the cynic's sneers would have been out of place; he contemplated nothing that the cynic would have called 'a conquest'. The sincere, straightforward gentleman would have been equally excessive in his disgust. There was nothing, except the slight absurdity of Major Ames' nature, to justify either laughter or tears. He was a moderate man of middle age, about as well intentioned as most of us.

Mrs Evans, perhaps, was less laudable, and more deserved laughter and tears. She had consciously tried to produce a false impression without saying false things - a lamentable posture. She had wanted, as was her nature, to attract without being correspondingly attracted. She was prepared for him to go a little further, which is characteristic of the flirt. She succeeded, as the flirt usually does.

His last sentence was received in silence, and he thought well to repeat it with slight variation. The theme was clear.

'We may meet someone who understands us,' he said. 'Who looks into us, not at us, eh? Who sees not what we wish only, but what we want.'

She put the last sweet pea into the wire netting.

'Oh, yes, yes,' she said; 'how beautiful that distinction is.'

He was not aware of its being particularly beautiful, until she mentioned it, but then it struck him that it was rather fine. Also the respectability of all his long years tugged at him, as with a chain. He was quite conscious that he was encouraged, and so he was slightly terrified. He had not much power of imagination, but he could picture to himself a very uncomfortable home . . .

Providence came to his aid - probably Providence. Church time was spent, and two black Aberdeen terriers, followed by Elsie, followed by Dr Evans, came out of the drawing-room door on to the lawn. They were all in the genial exhilaration that accompanies the sense of duty done. The dogs had been let out from the house, where they were penned on Sunday morning to prevent their unexpected appearance in church; the other two had been let out from church.

Wilfred Evans had most clearly left church behind him: he had also left in the house not only his top hat but his coat, as befitted the heat of the morning, and appeared, stout, and strong, and brisk. Elsie was less vigorous: she sat down on the grass as soon as she reached the shade of the tree. She had the good sense to shake hands with Major Ames first: otherwise her mother would have made remarks to him about her manners. But she was markedly less elderly now than she had been at the formal dinner party of the night before.

Dr Evans arrived last at the mulberry tree.

'Jove! What jolly flowers,' he said. 'That's you, Major Ames, isn't it? How de'do? Well, little woman, how goes it? You did well not to come to church. Awfully hot it was.'

'And a very long sermon, Daddy,' said Elsie.

'Twenty-two minutes: I timed it. Very interesting, though. You'll stop to lunch, Major Ames, won't you? We lunch at one always on Sunday.'

Now Major Ames knew quite well that there was going to be at his house the lunch that followed parties, the resurrection lunch of what was dead last night. There would be little bits of salmon slightly greyer than on the evening before, peeping out from the fresh salad that covered them. There would be some sort of chaud-froid; there would be a pink and viscous fluid which was the debilitated descendant of the strawberry ice which Amy had given them. There would also be several people, including Mrs Altham, who had not been bidden to the feast last night, but who, since they came according to the authorized Riseborough version of festivities, to the lunch next day, would certainly be bidden to dinner on the next occasion. Also, he knew well, he would have to say to Mrs Altham, 'Amy has given us cold luncheon today. Well, I don't mind a cold luncheon on as hot a day as it is. Chaud-froid of chicken, Mrs Altham. I think you'll find that Amy's cook understands chaud-froid.'

And all the time he knew that chaud-froid meant a dinner-party on the night before. So did the viscous fluid in the jelly glasses, so did everything else. And of course

CHAPTER THREE

Mrs Altham knew: everybody knew all about the lunch that followed a dinner party. Even if the dinner party last night had been as secret as George the Fourth's marriage with Mrs Fitzherbert, the lunch today would have made it as public as any function at St Peter's, Eaton Square.

He thought over the unimaginable dislocation in all this routine that his absence would entail.

'I wonder if I ought to,' he said. 'I fancy Amy told me she had a few friends to lunch.'

Millie Evans looked up at him. Infinitesimal as was the point as to whether he should lunch here or at home, she knew that she definitely entered herself against his wife at this moment.

'Ah, do stop,' she said. 'If Cousin Amy has a few friends why shouldn't we have one?'

He got up: he nearly took off his hat again, but again remembered.

'I take it as a command,' he said. 'Am I ordered to stop?'

'Certainly. Telephone to Mrs Ames, Wilfred, and say that Major Ames is lunching with us.'

'À les ordres de votre Majesté,' said he brightly, forgetting for the moment that his wife came to him for help with the elusive language of our neighbours. But the Frenchness of his bearing and sentiment, perhaps, diverted attention from the curious character of his grammar.

IT was, of course, as inevitable as the return of day that Mrs Altham should start half an hour earlier than was necessary to go to church that morning, in order to return to Mrs Brooks, who had been dining last night at the Ames', a couple of books that had been lent her a month or two ago, and that Mrs Brooks should recount to her the unusual incident of Harry's taking Mrs Evans into the garden after dinner, and giving her a gradually growing bouquet of roses torn from his father's trees. Indeed, it was difficult to settle satisfactorily which part of Harry's conduct was the most astounding, with such completeness had he revolted against both beneficiaries of the fifth commandment.

'They can't have been out in the garden for less than twenty minutes,' said Mrs Brooks; 'and I shouldn't wonder if it was more. For we had scarcely settled ourselves after the gentlemen came in from the dining room, when they went out, and I'm sure we had hardly got talking again after they came back, before my maid was announced. To be sure the gentlemen sat a long time after dinner before joining us, which I notice is always the case when General Fortescue is at a party, but it can't have been less than half an hour that they were in the garden now one comes to add it up.'

Mrs Brooks surveyed for a moment in silence her piece of embroidery. Not for a moment must it be supposed that she would have done embroidery for her own dress on Sunday morning; this was a frontal for the lectern at St Barnabas, which would make it impossible for Mrs Ames to decorate the lectern any more with her flowers. There was a cross, and a crown, and some initials, and some rays of light, and a heart, and some passion flowers, and a dove worked on it, with a profusion of gold thread that was positively American in its opulence. Hitherto, the lectern had always been the field of one of Mrs Ames' most telling embellishments. When this embroidery was finished (which it soon would be) she would be driven from the lectern in disorder and discomfiture.

'A very rich effect,' said Mrs Altham sympathetically. 'Half an hour! Dear me! And then I think you said she came back with a dozen roses.'

Mrs Brooks closed her eyes, and made a short calculation.

'More than a dozen,' she said. 'I daresay there were twenty roses. It was very marked, very marked indeed. And if you ask me what I think of Mrs Ames' plan of asking husband without wife and wife without husband, I must say I do not like it at all. Depend upon it, if Dr Evans had come too, there would have been no walking about in the garden with our Master Harry. But far be it from me to say there was any harm in it, far! I hope I am not one who condemns other people's actions because I would not commit them myself. All I know is that the first time my late dear husband asked me to walk about the garden after dinner with him, he proposed to me; and the second time he asked me to walk in the garden with him he proposed again, and I accepted him. But then I was not engaged to anybody else at the time, far less married, like Mrs Evans. But it is none of my business, I am glad to say.'

'Indeed, no, it does not concern us,' said Mrs Altham, with avidity; 'and as you say, there may be no harm in it at all. But young men are very impressionable, even if most unattractive, and I call it distinct encouragement to a young man to walk about after dinner in the garden with him, and receive a present of roses. And I'm sure Mrs Evans is old enough to be his mother.'

Mrs Brooks tacked down a length of gold thread which was to form part of the longest ray of all, and made another little calculation. It was not completely satisfactory.

'Anyhow, she is old enough to know better,' she said; 'but I have noticed that being old enough to know better often makes people behave worse. Mind, I do not blame her: there is nothing I detest so much as this censorious attitude; and I only say that if I gave so much encouragement to any young man I should blame myself.'

'And the dinner?' asked Mrs Altham. 'At least, I need not ask that, since I am going to lunch there, and so I shall soon know as well as you what there was.'

Mrs Brooks smiled in a rather superior manner.

'I never know what I am eating,' she said. And she looked as if it disagreed with her, too, whatever it was.

This was not particularly thrilling, for though it was generally known that Harry had an emotional temperament and wrote amorous poems, he appeared to Mrs Altham an improbable Lothario. In any case, the slight interest that this aroused in her was nothing compared to that which awaited her and her husband when they arrived for lunch at Mrs Ames'.

There had been a long-standing feud between Mrs Altham and her hostess on the subject of punctuality. About two years ago Mrs Ames had arrived at Mrs Altham's at least ten minutes late for dinner, and Mrs Altham had very properly retorted by arriving a quarter of an hour late when next she was bidden to dinner with Mrs Ames, though that involved sitting in a dark cab for ten minutes at the corner of the next turning. So, next time that Mrs Altham 'hoped to have the pleasure of seeing you and Major Ames at dinner on Thursday at a quarter to eight,' she asked the rest of her guests at eight. With the effect that Mrs Ames and her husband arrived a few minutes before anybody else, and Riseborough generally considered that Mrs Altham had scored. Since then there had been but a sort of desultory pea-shooting kept up, such as would harm nobody, and today Mrs Altham and her husband arrived certainly within ten minutes of the hour named. Mr Pettit, who generally lunched with Mrs Ames or Mrs Brooks on Sunday, was already there with his sister. Harry was morosely fidgeting in a corner, and Mrs Ames was the only other person present in the small sitting room where she received her guests, instead of troubling them to go up to the drawing room and instantly to go down again. She gave Mrs Altham her fat little hand, and then made this remarkable statement.

'We are not waiting for anybody else, I think.'

Upon which they went into lunch, and Harry sat at the head of the table, instead of his father.

Mrs Ames was in her most conversational mood, and it was not until the chaud-froid, consisting mainly of the legs of chickens pasted over with a yellow sauce that concealed the long blue hair roots with which Nature has adorned their lower extremities, was being handed round, that Mrs Altham had opportunity to ask the question that had been effervescing like an antiseptic lozenge on the tip of her tongue ever since she remarked the Major's absence.

'And where is Major Ames?' she asked. 'I hope he is not ill? I thought he looked far from well at Mrs Evans' garden-party yesterday.'

Mrs Ames set her mind at rest with regard to the second point, and inflamed it on the first.

'Oh, no!' she said. 'Did you think he looked ill? How good of you to ask after him. But Lyndhurst is quite well. Mr Pettit, a little more chicken? After your sermon.'

Mr Pettit had a shrewd, ugly, delightful face, very lean, very capable. Humanly speaking, he probably abhorred Mrs Ames. Humanely speaking, he knew there was a great deal of good in her, and a quantity of debatable stuff. He smiled, showing thick white teeth.

'Before and after my sermon,' he said. 'Also before a children's service and a Bible class. I cannot help thinking that God forgot his poor clergymen when he defined the seventh day as one of rest.'

Mrs Ames hid a small portion of her little face with her little hand. She always said that Mr Pettit was not like a clergyman at all.

'How naughty of you,' she said. 'But I must correct you. The seventh day has become the first day now.'

Harry gave vent to a designedly audible sigh. The Omar Club were chiefly atheists, and he felt bound to uphold their principles.

'That is the sort of thing that confuses me,' he said. 'Mr Pettit says Sunday was called a day of rest, and my mother says that God meant what we call Monday, or Saturday. I have been behaving as if it was Tuesday or Wednesday.'

Mr Pettit gave him a kindly glance.

'Quite right, my dear boy,' he said. 'Spend your Tuesday or Wednesday properly and God won't mind whether it is Thursday or Friday.'

CHAPTER FOUR

Harry pushed back his lank hair, and became Omar-ish. 'Do you fast on Friday, may I ask?' he said.

Mrs Ames looked pained, and tried to think of something to say. She failed. But Mrs Altham thought without difficulty.

'I suppose Major Ames is away, Mr Harry?' she said.

Even then, though her intentions might easily be supposed to be amiable, she was not allowed the privilege of being replied to, for Mr Pettit cheerfully answered Harry's question, without a shadow of embarrassment, just as if he did not mind what the Omar Khayyam Club thought.

'Of course I do, my dear fellow,' he said, 'because our Lord and dearest friend died that day. He allows us to watch and pray with Him an hour or two.'

Harry appeared indulgent.

'Curious,' he said.

Mr Pettit looked at him for just the space of time anyone looks at the speaker, with cheerful cordiality of face, and then turned to his mother again.

'I want you at church next Sunday,' he said, 'with a fat purse, to be made thin. I am going to have an offertory to finance a children's treat. I want to send every child in the parish to the seaside for a day.'

Harry interrupted in the critical manner.

'Why the seaside?' he asked.

Mr Pettit turned to him with unabated cordiality.

'How right to ask!' he said. 'Because the sea is His, and He made it! Also, they will build sandcastles, and pick up shells. You must come too, my dear Harry, and help us to give them a nice day.'

Harry felt that this was a Philistine here, who needed to be put in his place. He was not really a very rude youth, but one who felt it incumbent on him to oppose Christianity, which he regarded as superstition. A bright idea came into his head.

'But His hands prepared the dry land,' he said, 'on the same supposition.'

'Certainly; and as the dear mites have always seen the dry land,' said Mr Pettit, with the utmost good humour, 'we want to show them that God thought of something they never thought of. And then there are the sand-castles.'

Harry was tired, and did not proceed to crush Mr Pettit with the atheistical arguments that were but commonplace to the Omar Khayyam Club. He was not worth argument: you could only really argue with the enlightened people who fundamentally agreed with you, and he was sure that Mr Pettit did not fulfil that requirement. So, indulgently, he turned to Mrs Altham.

'I saw you at Mrs Evans' garden party yesterday,' he said. 'I think she is the most wonderful person I ever met. She was dining here last night, and I took her into the garden - '

'And showed her the roses,' said Mrs Altham, unable to restrain herself.

Harry became a parody of himself, though that might seem to be a feat of insuperable difficulty.

'I supposed it would get about,' he said. 'That is the worst of a little place like this. Whatever you do is instantly known.'

The slightly viscous remains of the strawberry ice were being handed, and Mr Pettit was talking to Mrs Ames and his sister from a pitiably Christian standpoint.

'What did you hear?' asked Harry, in a low voice.

'Merely that she and you went out into the garden after dinner, and that you picked roses for her - '

Harry pushed back his lank hair with his bony hand.

CHAPTER FOUR

'You have heard all,' he said. 'There was nothing more than that. I did not see her home. Her carriage did not come: there was some mistake about it, I suppose. But it was my father who saw her home, not I.'

He laid down the spoon with which he had been consuming the viscous fluid.

'If you hear that I saw her home, Mrs Altham,' he said, 'tell them it is not true. From what you have already told me, I gather there is talk going on. There is no reason for such talk.'

He paused a moment, and then a line or two of the intensely Swinburnian effusion which he had written last night fermented in his head, making him infinitely more preposterous.

'I assure you that at present there is no reason for such talk,' he said earnestly.

Now Mrs Altham, with her wide interest in all that concerned anybody else, might be expected to feel the intensest curiosity on such a topic, but somehow she felt very little, since she knew that behind the talk there was really very little topic, and the gallant misgivings of poor, ugly Harry seemed to her destitute of any real thrill. On the other hand, she wanted very much to know where Major Ames was, and being endowed with the persistence of the household cat, which you may turn out of a particular armchair a hundred times, without producing the slightest discouragement in its mind, she reverted to her own subject again.

'I am sure there is no reason for such talk, Mr Harry,' she said, with strangely unwelcome conviction, 'and I will be sure to contradict it if ever I hear it. I am so glad to hear Major Ames is not ill. I was afraid that his absence from lunch today might mean that he was.'

Now Harry, as a matter of fact, had no idea where his father was, since the telephone message had been received by Mrs Ames.

'Father is quite well,' he said. 'He was picking sweet peas half the morning. He picked a great bunch.'

Mrs Altham looked round: the table was decorated with the roses of the dinner party of the evening before.

'Then where are the sweet peas?' she asked.

But Harry was not in the least interested in the question.

'I don't know,' he said. 'Perhaps they are in the next room. I showed Mrs Evans last night how the La France roses looked blue when dusk fell. She had never noticed it, though they turn as blue as her eyes.'

'How curious!' said Mrs Altham. 'But I didn't see the sweet peas in the next room. Surely if there had been a quantity of them I should have noticed them. Or perhaps they are in the drawing room.'

At this moment, Mrs Ames' voice was heard from the other end of the table.

'Then shall we have our coffee outside?' she said. 'Harry, if you will ring the bell - '

There was the pushing back of chairs, and Mrs Altham passed along the table to the French windows that opened on to the verandah.

'I hear Major Ames has been picking the loveliest sweet peas all the morning,' she said to her hostess. 'It would be such a pleasure to see them. I always admire Major Ames' sweet peas.'

Now this was unfortunate, for Mrs Altham desired information herself, but by her speech she had only succeeded in giving information to Mrs Ames, who guessed without the slightest difficulty where the sweet peas had gone, which she had not yet known had been picked. She was already considerably annoyed with her husband for his unceremonious desertion of her luncheon party, and was aware that Mrs Altham would cause the fact to be as well known in Riseborough as if it had been inserted in the column of local intelligence in the county paper. But she felt she would sooner put it there herself than let Mrs Altham know where he and his sweet peas were. She had no greater objection (or if she had, she studiously concealed it from herself even) to his going to lunch in this improvising manner with Mrs Evans than if he had gone to lunch with anybody else; what she minded was his non-appearance at an institution so firmly established and so faithfully observed as the lunch that followed the dinner party. But at the moment her entire mind was set on thwarting Mrs Altham. She looked interested.

'Indeed, has he been picking sweet peas?' she said. 'I must scold him if it was only that which kept him away from church. I don't know what he has done with them. Very likely they are in his dressing room: he often likes to have flowers there. But as you admire his sweet peas so much, pray walk down the garden, and look at them. You will find them in their full beauty.'

This, of course, was not in the least what Mrs Altham wanted, since she did not care two straws for the rest of the sweet peas. But life was scarcely worth living unless she knew where those particular sweet peas were. As for their being in his dressing room, she felt that Mrs Ames must have a very poor opinion of her intellectual capacities, if she thought that an old wives' tale like that would satisfy it. In this she was partly right: Mrs Ames had indeed no opinion at all of her mind; on the other hand, she did not for a moment suppose that this suggestion about the dressing room would content that feeble organ. It was not designed to: the object was to stir it to a wilder and still unsatisfied curiosity. It perfectly succeeded, and from by-ways Mrs Altham emerged full speed, like a motorcar, into the high road of direct question.

'I am sure they are lovely,' she said. 'And where is Major Ames lunching?'

Mrs Ames raised the pieces of her face where there might have been eyebrows in other days. She told one of the truths that Bismarck loved.

'He did not tell me before he went out,' she said. 'Perhaps Harry knows. Harry, where is your father lunching?'

Now this was ludicrous. As if it was possible that any wife in Riseborough did not know where her husband was lunching! Harry apparently did not know either, and Mrs Ames, tasting the joys of the bull-baiter, goaded Mrs Altham further by pointedly asking Parker, when she brought the coffee, if she knew where the Major was lunching. Of course Parker did not, and so Parker was told to cut Mrs Altham a nice bunch of sweet peas to carry away with her.

This pleasant duty of thwarting undue curiosity being performed, Mrs Ames turned to Mr Pettit, though she had not quite done with Mrs Altham yet. For she had heard on the best authority that Mrs Altham occasionally indulged in the disgusting and unfeminine habit of cigarette smoking. Mrs Brooks had several times seen her walking about her garden with a cigarette, and she had told Mrs Taverner, who had told Mrs Ames. The evidence was overwhelming.

'Mr Pettit, I don't think any of us mind the smell of tobacco,' she said, 'when it is out of doors, so pray have a cigarette. Harry will give you one. Ah! I forgot! Perhaps Mrs Altham does not like it.'

Mrs Altham hastened to correct that impression. At the same time she had a subtle and not quite comfortable sense that Mrs Ames knew all about her and her cigarettes, which was exactly the impression which that lady sought to convey.

These tactics were all sound enough in their way, but a profounder knowledge of human nature would have led Mrs Ames not to press home her victory with so merciless a hand. In her determination to thwart Mrs Altham's odious curiosity, she had let it be seen that she was thwarting it: she should not, for instance, have asked Parker if she knew of the Major's whereabouts, for it only served to emphasize the undoubted fact that Mrs Ames knew (that might be taken for granted) and that she knew that Parker did not, for otherwise she would surely not have asked her.

Consequently Mrs Altham (erroneously, as far as that went) came to the conclusion that the Major was lunching alone where his wife did not wish him to lunch alone. And in the next quarter of an hour, while they all sat on the verandah, she devoted the mind which her hostess so despised, to a rapid review of all houses of this description. Instantly almost, the wrong scent which she was following led her to the right quarry. She argued, erroneously, the existence of a pretty woman, and there was a pretty woman in Riseborough. It is hardly necessary to state that she made up her mind to call on that pretty woman without delay. She would be very much surprised if she did not find there an immense bunch of sweet peas and perhaps their donor.

Mrs Ames' guests soon went their ways, Mr Pettit and his sister to the children's service at three, the Althams on their detective mission, and she was left to herself, except in so far as Harry, asleep in a basket chair in the garden, can be considered companionship. She was not gifted with any very great acuteness of imagination, but this afternoon she found herself capable of conjuring up (indeed, she was incapable of not doing so) a certain amount of vague disquiet. Indeed, she tried to put it away, and refresh her mind with the remembrance of her thwarting Mrs Altham, but though her disquiet was but vague, and was concerned with things that had at present no real existence at all, whereas her victory over that inquisitive lady was fresh and recent, the disquiet somehow was of more pungent quality, and at last she faced it, instead of attempting any longer to poke it away out of sight.

Millie Evans was undeniably a good-looking woman, undeniably the Major had been considerably attracted last night by her. Undeniably also he had done a very strange thing in stopping to have his lunch there, when he knew perfectly well that there were people lunching with them at home for that important rite of eating up the remains of last night's dinner. Beyond doubt he had taken her this present of sweet peas, of which Mrs Altham had so obligingly informed her; beyond doubt, finally, she was herself ten years her husband's senior.

It has been said that Mrs Ames was not imaginative, but indeed, there seemed to be sufficient here, when it was all brought together, to occupy a very prosaic and literal mind. It was not as if these facts were all new to her: that disparity of age between herself and her husband had long lain dark and ominous, like a distant thundercloud on the horizon of her mind. Hitherto, it had been stationary there, not apparently coming any closer, and not giving any hint of the potential tempest which might lurk within it. But now it seemed to have moved a little up the sky, and (though this might be mere fancy on her part), there came from it some drowsy and distant echo of thunder.

It must not be supposed that her disquiet expressed itself in Mrs Ames' mind in terms of metaphor like this, for she was practically incapable of metaphor. She said to herself merely that she was ten years older than her husband. That she had known ever since they married (indeed, she had known it before), but till now the fact had never seemed likely to be of any significance to her. And yet her grounds for supposing that it might be about to become significant were of the most unsubstantial sort. Certainly if Lyndhurst had not gone out to lunch today, she would never have dreamed of finding disquiet in the happenings of the evening before; indeed, apart from Harry's absurd expedition into the garden, the party had been a markedly successful one, and she had determined to give more of those undomestic entertainments. But the principle of them assumed a strangely different aspect when her husband accepted an invitation of the kind instead of lunching at home, and that aspect presented itself in vivid colours when she reflected that he was ten years her junior.

Mrs Ames was a practical woman, and though her imagination had run unreasonably riot, so she told herself, over these late events, so that she already contemplated a contingency that she had no real reason to anticipate, she considered what should be her practical conduct if this remote state of affairs should cease to be remote. She had altogether passed from being in love with her husband, so much so, indeed, that she could not recall, with any sense of reality, what that unquiet sensation was like. But she had been in love with him years ago, and that still gave her a sense of possession over him. She had not been in the habit of guarding her possession, since there had never been any reason to suppose that anybody wanted to take it away, but she remembered with sufficient distinctness the sense that Lyndhurst's garden was becoming to him the paramount interest in his life. At the time that sense had been composed of mixed feelings: neglect and relief were its constituents. He had ceased to expect from her that indefinable sensitiveness which is one of the prime conditions of love, and the growing atrophy of his demands certainly corresponded with her own inclinations. At the same time, though this cessation on his part of the imperative need of her, was a relief, she resented it. She would have wished him to continue being in love with her on credit, so to speak, without the settlement of the bill being applied for. Years had passed since then, but today that secondary discontent assumed a primary importance again. It was more acute now than it had ever been, for her possession was not being quietly absorbed into the culture of impersonal flowers, but, so it seemed possible, was directly threatened.

There was the situation which her imagination presented her with, practically put, and she proceeded to consider it from a practical standpoint. What was she to do?

She had the justice to acknowledge that the first clear signals of coolness in their mutual relations, now fifteen years ago, had been chiefly flown by her: she had essentially welcomed his transference of affection to his garden, though she had secretly resented it. At the least, the cooling had been condoned by her. Probably that had been a mistake on her part, and she determined now to rectify it. She, pathetically enough, felt herself young still, and to confirm herself in her view, she took the trouble to go indoors, and look at herself in the glass that hung in the hall. It was inevitable that she should see there not what she really saw, but what, in the main, she desired to see. Her hair, always slightly faded in tone, was not really grey, and even if there were signs of greyness in it there was nothing easier, if you could trust the daily advertisements in the papers, than to restore the colour, not by dyes, but by 'purely natural means.' There had been an advertisement of one such desirable lotion, she remembered, in the paper today, which she had noticed was supplied by any chemist. Certainly there was a little grey in her hair: that would be easy to remedy. That act of mental frankness led on to another. There were certain premonitory symptoms of stringiness about her throat and of loose skin round her mouth and eyes. But who could keep abreast of the times at all, and not know that there were skin foods which were magical in their effect? There was one which had impressed itself on her not long before: an actress had written in its praise, affirming that her wrinkles had vanished with three nights' treatment. Then there was a little, just a little, sallowness of complexion, but after all, she had always been rather sallow. It was a fortunate circumstance: when she got hot she never got crimson in the face like poor Mrs Taverner . . . She was going to town next week for a night, in order to see her dentist, a yearly precaution, unproductive of pain, for her teeth were really excellent, regular in shape, white, undecayed. Lyndhurst, in his early days, had told her they were like pearls, and she had told him he talked nonsense. They were just as much like pearls still, only he did not tell her so. He, poor fellow, had had great trouble in this regard, but it might be supposed his trouble was over now, since artifice had done its utmost for him. She was much younger than him there, though his last set fitted beautifully. But probably Millie had seen they were not real. And then he was distinctly gouty, which she was not. Often had she heard his optimistic assertion that an hour's employment with the garden roller rendered all things of rheumatic tendency an impossibility. But she, though publicly she let these random statements pass, and even endorsed them, knew the array of bottles that beleaguered the washing stand in his dressing room, where the sweet peas were not.

The silent colloquy with the mirror in the hall occupied her some ten minutes, but the ten minutes sufficed for the arrival of one conclusion - namely, that she did not intend to be an old woman yet. Subtle art, the art of the hair restorer (which was not a dye), the art of the skin feeder must be invoked. She no longer felt at all old, now that there was a possibility of her husband's feeling young. And lip-salve: perhaps lipsalve, yet that seemed hardly necessary: a few little bitings and mumblings of her lips between her excellent teeth seemed to restore to them a very vivid colour.

She went back to the verandah, where her little luncheon party had had their coffee, and pondered the practical manoeuvres of her campaign of invasion into the territory of youth which had once been hers. The lotion for the hair, as she verified by a consultation with the Sunday paper, took but a fortnight's application to complete its work. The wrinkle treatment was easily comprised in that, for it took, according to the eminent actress, no more than three days. It might therefore be wiser not to let the work of rejuvenation take place under Lyndhurst's eye, for there might be critical passages in it. But she could go away for a fortnight (a fortnight was the utmost time necessary for the wonderful lotion to restore faded colour) and return again after correspondence that indicated that she felt much better and younger. Several times before she had gone to stay alone with a friend of hers on the coast of Norfolk: there would be nothing in the least remarkable in her doing it again.

An objection loomed in sight. If there was any reality in the supposition that prompted her desire to seem young again - namely, a possible attraction of her husband towards Millie Evans, she would but be giving facility and encouragement to that by her absence. But then, immediately the wisdom of the course, stronger than the objection to it, presented itself. Infinitely the wiser plan for her was to act as if unconscious of any such danger, to disarm him by her obvious rejection of any armour of her own. She must either watch him minutely or not at all. Mr Pettit had alluded in his sermon that morning to the finer of the two attitudes when he reminded them that love thought no evil. It seemed to poor Mrs Ames that if by her conduct she appeared to think no evil, it came to the same thing.

Her behaviour towards Lyndhurst, when he should come back from Millie's house, followed as a corollary. She would be completely genial: she would hope he had had a pleasant lunch, and, if he made any apology for his absence, assure him that it was quite unnecessary. Her charity would carry her even further than that: she would say that his absence had been deplored by her guests, but that she had been so glad that he had done as he felt inclined. She would hope that Millie was not tired with her party, and that she and her husband would come to dine with them again soon. It must be while Harry was at home, for he was immensely attracted by Millie. So good for a boy to think about a nice woman like that.

Mrs Ames carried out her programme with pathetic fidelity. Her husband did not get home till nearly teatime, and she welcomed him with a cordiality that would have been unusual even if he had not gone out to lunch at all. And to do him justice, it must be confessed that his wife's scheme, as already recounted, was framed to meet a situation which at present had no real existence, except in the mind of a wife wedded to a younger husband. There were data for the situation, so to speak, rather than there was danger of it. He, on his side, was well aware of the irregularity of his conduct, and was prepared to accept, without retaliation, a modicum of blame for it. But no blame at all awaited him; instead of that a cordiality so genuine that, in spite of the fact that a particularly good dinner was provided him, the possible parallel of the prodigal son did not so much as suggest itself to his mind.

Harry had retired to his bedroom soon after dinner with a certain wildness of eye which portended poetry rather than repose, and after he had gone his father commented in the humorous spirit about this.

'Poor old Harry!' he said. 'Case of lovely woman, eh, Amy? I was just the same at his age, until I met you, my dear.'

This topic of Harry's admiration for Mrs Evans, which his mother had intended to allude to, had not yet been touched on, and she responded cordially.

'You think Harry is very much attracted by Millie, do you mean?' she said.

He chuckled.

'Well, that's not very difficult to see,' he said. 'Why, the rascal tore off a dozen of my best roses for her last night, though I hadn't the heart to scold him for it. Not a bad thing for a young fellow to burn a bit of incense before a charming woman like that. Keeps him out of mischief, makes him see what a nice woman is like. As I said, I used to do just the same myself.'

'Tell me about it,' said she.

'Well, there was the Colonel's wife. God bless me, how I adored her. I must have been just about Harry's age, for I had only lately joined, and she was a woman getting on for forty. Good thing, too, for me, as I say, for it kept me out of mischief. They used to say she encouraged me, but I don't believe it. Every woman likes to know that she's admired, eh? She doesn't snub a boy who takes her out in the garden, and picks his father's roses for her. But we mustn't have Harry boring her with his attentions. That'll never do.'

CHAPTER FOUR

It seemed to Mrs Ames of singularly little consequence whether Harry bored Millie Evans or not. She would much have preferred to be assured that her husband did. But the subsequent conversation did not reassure her as to that.

'Nice little woman, she is,' he said. 'Thoroughly nice little woman, and naturally enough, my dear, since she is your cousin, she likes being treated in neighbourly fashion. We had a great talk after lunch today, and I'm sorry for her, sorry for her. I think we ought to do all we can to make life pleasant for her. Drop in to tea, or drop in to lunch, as I did today. A doctor's wife, you know. She told me that some days she scarcely set eyes on her husband, and when she did, he could think of nothing but microbes. And there's really nobody in Riseborough, except you and me, with whom she feels - dear me, what's that French word - yes, with whom she feels in her proper milieu. I should like us to be on such terms with her - you being her cousin - that we could always telephone to say we were dropping in, and that she would feel equally free to drop in. Dropping in, you know: that's the real thing; not to be obliged to wait till you are asked, or to accept weeks ahead, as one has got to do for some formal dinner party. I should like to feel that we mightn't be surprised to find her picking sweet peas in the garden, and that she wouldn't be surprised to find you or me sitting under her mulberry tree, waiting for her to come in. After all, intimacy only begins when formality ceases. Shall I give you some soda water?'

Mrs Ames did not want soda water: she wanted to think. Her husband had completely expressed the attitude she meant to adopt, but her own adoption of it had presupposed a certain contrition on his part with regard to his unusual behaviour. But he gave her no time for thought, and proceeded to propose just the same sort of thing as she (in her magnanimity) had thought of suggesting.

'Dinner, now,' he said. 'Up till last night we have always been a bit formal about dinner here in Riseborough. If you asked General Snookes, you asked Mrs Snookes; if you asked Admiral Jones, you asked Lady Jones. You led the way, my dear, about that, and what could have been pleasanter than our little party last night? Let us repeat it: let us be less formal. If you want to see Mr Altham, ask him to come. Mrs Altham, let us say, wants to ask me: let her ask me. Or if you meet Dr Evans in the street, and he says it is lunch time, go and have lunch with him, without bothering about me. I shall do very well at home. I'm told that in London it is quite a constant practice to invite like that. And it seems to me very sensible.'

All this had seemed very sensible to Mrs Ames, when she had thought of it herself. It seemed a little more hazardous now. She was well aware that this plan had caused a vast amount of talk in Riseborough, the knowledge of which she had much enjoyed, since it was of the nature of subjects commenting on the movements of their queen, without any danger to her of dethronement. But she was not so sure that she enjoyed her husband's cordial endorsement of her innovation. Also, in his endorsement there was some little insincerity. He had taken as instance the chance of his wishing to dine without his wife at Mrs Altham's, and they both knew how preposterous such a contingency would be. But did this only prepare the way for a further solitary excursion to Mrs Evans'? Had Mrs Evans asked him to dine there? She was immediately enlightened.

'Of course, we talked over your delightful dinner party of last night,' he said, 'and agreed in the agreeableness of it.

And she asked me to dine there, en garçon, on Tuesday next. Of course, I said I must consult you first; you might have asked other people here, or we might be dining out together. I should not dream of upsetting any existing arrangement. I told her so: she quite understood. But if there was nothing going on, I promised to dine there en garçon.'

That phrase had evidently taken Major Ames' fancy; there was a ring of youth about it, and he repeated it with gusto. His wife, too, perfectly understood the secret smack of the lips with which he said it: she knew precisely how he felt. But she was wise enough to keep the consciousness of it completely out of her reply.

'By all means,' she said; 'we have no engagement for that night. And I am thinking of proposing myself for a little visit to Mrs Bertram next week, Lyndhurst. I know she is at Overstrand now, and I think ten days on the east coast would do me good.'

He assented with a cordiality that equalled hers.

'Very wise, I am sure, my dear,' he said. 'I have thought this last day or two that you looked a little run down.'

A sudden misgiving seized her at this, for she knew quite well she neither looked nor felt the least run down.

'I thought perhaps you and Harry would take some little trip together while I was away,' she said.

'Oh, never mind us, never mind us,' said he. 'We'll rub along, en garçon, you know. I daresay some of our friends will take pity on us, and ask us to drop in.'

This was not reassuring: nor would Mrs Ames have been reassured if she could have penetrated at that moment unseen into Mrs Altham's drawing room. She and her husband had gone straight from Mrs Ames' house that afternoon to call on Mrs Evans, and had been told she was not at home. But Mrs Altham of the eagle eye had seen through the opened front door an immense bowl of sweet peas on the hall table, and by it a straw hat with a riband of regimental colours round it. Circumstantial evidence could go no further, and now this indefatigable lady was looking out Major Ames in an old army list.

'Ames, Lyndhurst Percy,' she triumphantly read out. 'Born 1860, and I daresay he is older than that, because if ever there was a man who wanted to be thought younger than his years, that's the one. So in any case, Henry, he is over forty-seven. And there's the front-door bell. It will be Mrs Brooks. She said she would drop in for a chat after dinner.'

There was plenty to chat about that evening.

MRS AMES might or might not have been run down when she left Riseborough the following week, but nothing can be more certain than that she was considerably braced up seven days after that. The delicious freshness of winds off the North Sea, tempering the heat of brilliant summer suns, may have had something to do with it, and she certainly had more colour in her face than was usual with her, which was the legitimate effect of the felicitous weather. There was more colour in her hair also, and though that, no doubt, was a perfectly legitimate effect too, being produced by purely natural means, as the label on the bottle stated, the sun and wind were not accountable for this embellishment.

She had spent an afternoon in London - chiefly in Bond Street - on her way here, and had gone to a couple of addresses which she had secretly snipped out of the daily press. The expenditure of a couple of pounds, which was already yielding her immense dividends in encouragement and hope, had put her into possession of a bottle with a brush, a machine that, when you turned a handle, quivered violently like a motorcar that is prepared to start, and a small jar of opaque glass, which contained the miraculous skin food. With these was being wrought the desired marvels; with these, as with a magician's rod, she was conjuring, so she believed, the remote enchantments of youth back to her.

After quite a few days change became evident, and daily that change grew greater. As regards her hair, the cost, both of time and material, in this miracle working, was of the smallest possible account. Morning and evening, after brushing it, she rubbed in a mere teaspoonful of a thin yellow liquid, which, as the advertisement stated, was quite free from grease or obnoxious smell, and did not stain the pillow. This was so simple that it really required faith to embark upon the treatment, for from the time of Hebrew prophets, mankind have found it easier to do 'some great thing' than merely to wash in the Jordan. But Mrs Ames, luckily, had shown her faith, and by the end of a week the marvellous lotion had shown its works. Till now, though her hair could not be described as grey, there was a considerable quantity of grey in it: now she examined it with an eye that sought for instead of shutting itself to such blemish, and the reward of its search was of the most meagre sort. There was really no grey left in it: it might have been, as far as colour could be taken as a test of age, the hair of a young woman. It was not very abundant in quantity, but the lotion had held out no promises on that score; quality, not quantity, was the sum of its beckoning. The application of the skin food was more expensive: she had to use more and it took longer. Nightly she poured a can of very hot water into her basin, and with a towel over her head to concentrate the vapour, she steamed her face over it for some twenty minutes. Emerging red and hot and stifled, she wiped off the streams of moisture, and with fingertips dipped in this marvellous cream, tapped and dabbed at the less happy regions between her eyebrows, outside her eyes, across her forehead, at the corners of her mouth, and up and down her neck. Then came the use of the palpitating machine; it whirred and buzzed over her, tickling very much. For half an hour she would make a patient piano of her face, then gently remove such of the skin food as still stayed on the surface, and had not gone within to do its nurturing work. Certainly this was a somewhat laborious affair, but the results were highly prosperous. There was no doubt that to a perfectly candid and even sceptical eye, a week's treatment had produced a change. The wrinkles were beginning to be softly erased: there was a perceptible plumpness observable in the leaner places. Between the bouts of tapping and dabbing she sipped the glass of milk which she brought up to bed with her, as the deviser of the skin food recommended. She drank another such glass in the middle of the morning, and digested them both perfectly.

As these external signs appeared and grew there went on within her an accompanying and corresponding rejuvenation of spirit. She felt very well, owing, no doubt, to the brisk air, the milk, the many hours spent out of doors, and in consequence she began to feel much younger. An unwonted activity and lightness pervaded her limbs: she took daily a walk of a couple of hours without fatigue, and was the life and soul of the dinner table, whose other occupants were her hosts, Mrs Bertram, a cold, grim woman with a moustache, and her husband, milder, with whiskers. Their only passion was for gardening, and they seldom left their grounds; thus Mrs Ames took her walks unaccompanied.

Miles of firm sands, when the tide was low, subtended the cliffs on which Mr Bertram's house stood, and often Mrs Ames preferred to walk along the margin of the sea rather than pursue more inland routes, and today, after her large and wholesome lunch (the physical stimulus of the east coast, combined with this mental stimulus of her object in coming here, gave her an appetite of dimensions unknown at Riseborough) she took a maritime way. The tide was far out, and the lower sands, still shining and firm from the retained moisture of its retreat, made uncommonly pleasant walking. She had abandoned heeled footgear, and had bought at a shop in the village, where everything inexpensive, from wooden spades to stamps and sticking plaster, was sold, a pair of canvas coverings technically known as sandshoes. They laced up with a piece of white tape, and were juvenile, light, and easily removable. They, and the great sea, and the jetsam of stranded seaweed, and the general sense of youth and freshness, made most agreeable companions, and she felt, though neither Mr nor Mrs Bertram was with her, charmingly accompanied. Her small, toadlike face expressed a large degree of contentment, and piercing her pleasant surroundings as the smell of syringa pierces through the odour of all other flowers, was the sense of her brown hair and fast-fading wrinkles. That gave her an inward happiness which flushed with pleasure and interest all she saw. In the lines of pebbles left by the retreating tide was an orange-coloured cornelian, which she picked up, and put in her pocket. She could have bought the same, ready polished, for a shilling at the cheap and comprehensive shop, but to find it herself gave her a pleasure not to be estimated at all in terms of silver coinage. Further on there was an attractive-looking shell, which she also picked up, and was about to give as a companion to the cornelian, when a sudden scurry of claw-like legs about its aperture showed her that a hermit crab was domiciled within, and she dropped it with a little scream and a sense of danger escaped both by her and the hermit crab. There were attractive pieces of seaweed, which reminded her of years when she collected the finer sorts, and set them, with the aid of a pin, on cartridge paper, spreading out their delicate fronds and fern-like foliage. There were creamy ripples of the quiet sea, long-winged gulls that hovered fishing; above all there was the sense of her brown hair and smoothed face. She felt years younger, and she felt she looked years younger, which was scarcely less solid a satisfaction.

It pleased her, but not acutely or viciously, to think of Mrs Altham's feelings when she made her rejuvenated appearance in Riseborough. It was quite certain that Mrs Altham would suspect that she had been 'doing something to herself,' and that Mrs Altham would burst with envy and curiosity to know what it was she had done. Although she felt very kindly towards all the world, she did not deceive herself to such an extent as to imagine that she would tell Mrs Altham what she had done. Mrs Altham was ingenious and would like guessing. But that lady occupied her mind but little. The main point was that in a week from now she would go home again, and that Lyndhurst would find her young. She might or might not have been right in fearing that Lyndhurst was becoming sentimentally interested in Millie Evans, and she was quite willing to grant that her grounds for that fear were of the slenderest. But all that might be dismissed now. She herself, in a week from now, would have recaptured that more youthful aspect which had been hers while he was still of loverlike inclination towards her. What might be called regular good looks had always been denied her, but she had once had her share of youth. Today she felt youthful still, and once again, she believed, looked as if she belonged to the enchanted epoch. She had no intention of using this recapture promiscuously: she scarcely desired general admiration: she only desired that her husband should find her attractive.

For a little while, as she took her quick, short steps along these shining sands, she felt herself grow bitter towards Millie Evans. A sort of superior pity was mixed with the bitterness, for she told herself that poor Millie, if she had tried to flirt with Lyndhurst, would speedily find herself flirting all alone. Very likely Millie was guiltless in intention; she had only let her pretty face produce an unchecked effect. Men were attracted by a pretty face, but the owners of such faces ought to keep a curb on them, so to speak. Their faces were not their faults, but rather their misfortunes. A woman with a pretty face would be wise to make herself rather reserved, so that her manner would chill anybody who was inclined . . . But the whole subject now was obsolete. If there had been any danger, there would not be any more, and she did not blame Millie. She must ask Millie to dine with them en famille, which was much nicer than en garçon, as soon as she got back.

It might be gathered from this account of Mrs Ames' self-communings that deep down in her nature there lay a strain of almost farcical fatuousness. But she was not really fatuous, unless it is fatuous to have preserved far out into the plains of middle age some vision of the blue mountains of youth. It is true that for years she had been satisfied to dwell on these plains; now, her fear that her husband, so much younger than herself, was turning his eyes to blue mountains that did not belong to him, made her desire to get out of the plains and ascend her own blue mountains again and wave to him from there, and encourage his advance. She felt exceedingly well, and in consequence told herself that in mind, as well as physical constitution, she was young still, while the effect of the bottles which she used with such regularity made her believe that the outward signs of age were erasible. She seemed to have been granted a new lease of life in a tenement that it was easy to repair. Her whole nature felt itself to be quickened and vivified.

She had gone far along the sands, and the tide was beginning to flow again. All round her were great empty spaces, a shipless sea, a cloudless sky, a beach with no living being in sight. A sudden unpremeditated impulse seized her, and without delay she sat down on the shore, and took off her shoes and stockings. Then, pulling up her skirts, she hastily ran down to the edge of the water, across a little belt of pebbles that tickled and hurt her soft-soled feet, and waded out into the liquid rims of the sea. She was astonished and amazed at herself that the idea of paddling had ever come into her head, and more amazed that she had had the temerity to put it into execution. For the first minute or two the cold touch of the water on her unaccustomed ankles and calves made her gasp a little, but for all the strangeness of these sensations she felt that paddling, playing like a child in the shallow waters, expressed the tone of her mind, just as the melody of a song expresses the words to which it is set. If she had had a spade, she would certainly have built a sandcastle and dug moats about it, and a smile lit up her small face at the thought of purchasing one at the universal shop, and furtively conveying it to these unfrequented beaches. And the smile almost ended in a blush when she tried to imagine what Riseborough society would say if it became known that their queen not only paddled in the sea, but seriously contemplated buying a wooden spade in order to conduct building operations on lonely shores.

The paddling, though quite pleasant, was not so joyous as the impulse to paddle had been, and it was not long before she sat down again on the beach and tried to get the sand out of the small, tight places between her toes, and to dry her feet and plump little legs with a most exiguous handkerchief. But even in the midst of these troublesome operations, her mind still ran riot, and she planned to secrete about her person one of her smaller bedroom towels when she went for her walk next day. And she felt as if this act of paddling must have aided in the elimination of wrinkles. For who except the really young could want to paddle? To find that she had the impulse of the really young was even better than to cultivate, though with success, the appropriate appearance. All the way home this effervescence of spirit was hers, which, though it definitely sprang from the effects of the lotion, the skin food and the tonic air, produced in her an illusion that was complete. She was certainly ascending her remote blue mountains again, and through a clarified air she could look over the plains, and see how very flat they had been. That must all be changed: there must be more variety and gaiety introduced into her days. For years, as she saw now, her life had been spent in small, joyless hospitalities, in keeping her place as accredited leader of Riseborough's socialities, in paying her share towards the expenses of the house. They did not laugh much at home: there had seemed nothing particular to laugh about, and certainly they did not paddle. She was forming no plan for paddling there now, irrespective of the fact that a muddy canal, which was the only water in the neighbourhood, did not encourage the scheme, but there must be introduced into her life and Lyndhurst's more of the spirit that had today prompted her paddling. Exactly what form it should take she did not clearly foresee, but when she had recaptured the spirit as well as the appearance of youth, there was no fear that it would find any difficulty in expressing itself suitably. All aglow, especially as to her feet, which tingled pleasantly, she arrived at her host's house again. They were both at work in the garden: Mrs Bertram was killing slugs in the garden beds, Mr Bertram worms on the lawn.

Major Ames proved himself during the next week to be a good correspondent, if virtue in correspondents is to be measured by the frequency of their communications. His letters were not long, but they were cheerful, since the garden was coming on well in this delightful weather, which he hoped embraced Cromer also, and since he had on two separate occasions made a grand slam when playing Bridge at the club. He and Harry were jogging along quite pleasantly, but there had been no gaieties to take them out, except a tea party with ices at Mrs Brooks'. Unfortunately, some disaster had befallen the ices: personally, he thought it was salt instead of sugar, but Harry had been unwell afterwards, which suggested sour cream. But his indisposition had been but short, though violent. He himself had dropped in to dine en garçon with the Evans', and the doctor was very busy. Finally (this came at the end of every letter), as the place was doing her so much good, why not stop for another week? He was sure the Bertrams (poor things!) would be delighted if she would.

But that suggestion did not commend itself to Mrs Ames. She had come here for a definite purpose, and when on the morning before her departure she looked very critically at herself in the glass, she felt that her purpose had been accomplished. Her skin had not, so much she admitted, the unruffled smoothness of a young woman's, but she had not been a young woman when she married. But search where she might in her hair, there was no sign of greyness in it all, while the contents of the bottle were not yet half used. But she would take back the more than moiety with her, since an occasional application when the hair had resumed its usual colour was recommended. It appeared to her that it undoubtedly had resumed its original colour: the change, though slight (for the grey had never been conspicuous), was complete; she felt equipped for youth again. And psychologically she felt equipped: every day since the first secret paddling she had paddled again in secret, and from a crevice in a tumble of fallen rock she daily extracted a small wooden spade, by aid of which, with many glancings around for fear of possible observers, she dug in the sand, making moats and ramparts. The 'first fine careless rapture' of this, it must be admitted, had evaporated: after one architectural afternoon she had dug not because this elementary pursuit expressed what she felt, so much as because it expressed what she desired to feel. After all, she did not propose to rejuvenate herself to the extent of being nine or ten years old again . . .

The manner of her return to Riseborough demanded consideration: it was not sufficient merely to look up in a railway guide the swiftest mode of transit and adopt it, for this was not quite an ordinary entry, and it would never do to take the edge off it by making a travel-soiled and dusty first appearance. So she laid down a plan.

The bare facts about the trains were these. A train starting at a convenient hour would bring her to London a short half-hour before another convenient train from another and distant terminus started for Riseborough. It was impossible to make certain of catching this, so she wrote to her husband saying that she would in all probability get to Riseborough by a later train that arrived there at eight. She begged him not to meet her at the station, but to order dinner for half past eight. It would be nice to be at home again. Then came the plan. Clearly it would never do to burst on him like that, to sit down opposite him at the dinner table beneath the somewhat searching electric light there, handicapped by the fatigues of a hot journey only imperfectly repaired by a hasty toilet. She must arrive by the early train, though not expected till the later. Thus she would secure a quiet two hours for bathing, resting and dressing. If Lyndhurst did not expect her to arrive till eight it was a practical certainty that he would be at the club till that hour, and walk home in time to welcome her arrival. He would then learn that she had already come and was dressing. She would be careful to let him go downstairs first, and a minute later she would follow. He should see . . .

So in order to catch this earlier train from town she left Cromer while morning was yet dewy, and had the peculiar pleasure, on her arrival at Riseborough, of seeing her husband, from the windows of her cab, passing along the street to the club. She had a moment's qualm that he would see her initialled boxes on the top, but by grace of a punctual providence Mrs Brooks came out of her house at the moment, and the Major raised a gallant hat and spoke a cheerful word to her. Certainly he looked very handsome and distinguished, and Mrs Ames felt a little tremor of anticipation in thinking of the chapters of life that were to be re-read by them. She felt confident also; it never entered her head to have any misgivings as to what the last fortnight, which had contained so much for her, might have contained for him.

Harry had gone back to Cambridge for the July term the day before, and she found on her arrival that she had the house to herself. The afternoon had turned a little chilly, and she enjoyed the invigoration of a hot bath, and a subsequent hour's rest on her sofa. Then it was time to dress, and though the dinner was of the simplest conjugal character, she put on a dress she had worn but some half-dozen of times before, but which on this one occasion it was meet should descend from the pompous existence that was its destiny for a year or two to come. It was of daring rose colour, the most resplendent possible, and never failed to create an impression. Indeed, she had, on one of its infrequent appearances, heard Lyndhurst say to his neighbour in an undertone, 'Upon my soul, Amy looks very well tonight.' And Amy meant to look very well again.

All happened as she had planned. Shortly after eight Lyndhurst tapped at her door on his return from the club, but could not be admitted, and at half past, having heard him go downstairs, she followed him. He had not dressed, according to their custom when they were alone.

Major Ames was writing a note when she entered, and only turned round in his chair, not getting up.

'Glad to see you home, my dear,' he said. 'Excuse me one moment. I must just direct this.'

She kissed him and waited while he scrawled an address. Then he got up and rang the bell.

'Just in time to catch the post,' he said. 'By Jove! Amy, you've put on the famous pink gown. I would have dressed if I had known. You're tired with your journey, I expect. It was a very hot day here, until a couple of hours ago.'

He gave the note to the servant.

'And dinner's ready, I think,' he said.

They sat down opposite each other at ends of the rather long table. There were no flowers on it, for it had not occurred to him to get the garden to welcome her home-coming, and the whole of her resplendency was visible to him. He began eating his soup vigorously.

'Capital plan in summer to have dinner at half past eight,' he said. 'Gives one most of the daylight and not so long an evening afterwards. Excellent pea soup, this. Fresh peas from my garden. The Evans' dine at eight-thirty. And how have you been, Amy?'

CHAPTER FIVE

Some indefinable chill of misgiving, against which she struggled, had laid cold fingers on her. Things were not going any longer as she had planned them. He had noticed her gown, but he had noticed nothing else. But then he had scarcely looked up since they had come into the dining room. But now he finished his soup, and she challenged his attention.

'I have been very well indeed,' she said. 'Don't I look it?'

He looked her straight in the face, saw all that had seemed almost a miracle to her - the softened wrinkles, the recovered colour of her hair.

'Yes, I think you do,' he said. 'You've got a bit tanned too, haven't you, with the sun?'

The cold fingers closed a little more tightly on her.

'Have I?' she said. 'That is very likely. I was out of doors all day. I used to take quite long walks every afternoon.'

He glanced at the menu card.

'I hope you'll like the dinner I ordered you,' he said. 'Your cook and I had a great talk over it this morning. "She'll have been in the train all day," I said, "and will feel a little tired. Appetite will want a bit of tempting, eh?" So we settled on a grilled sole, and a chicken and a macédoine of fruit. Hope that suits you, Amy. So you used to take long walks, did you? Is the country pretty round about? Bathing, too. Is it a good coast for bathing?'

Again he looked at her as he spoke, and for the moment her heartbeat quickened, for it seemed that he could not but see the change in her. Then his sole required dissection, and he looked at his plate again.

'I believe it is a good coast,' she said. 'There were a quantity of bathing machines. I did not bathe.'

'No. Very wise, I am sure. One has to be careful about chills as one gets on. I should have been anxious about you, Amy, if I had thought you would be so rash as to bathe.'

Some instinct of protest prompted her.

'There would have been nothing to be anxious about,' she said. 'I seldom catch a chill. And I often paddled.'

He laid down his knife and fork and laughed.

'You paddled!' he asked. 'Nonsense, nonsense!'

She had not meant to tell him, for her reasonable mind had informed her all the time that this was a secret expression of the rejuvenation she was conscious of. But it had slipped out, a thoughtless assertion of the youthfulness she felt.

'I did indeed,' she said, 'and I found it very bracing and invigorating.'

Then for a moment a certain bitterness welled up within her, born from disappointment at his imperceptiveness.

'You see I never suffer from gout or rheumatism like you, Lyndhurst,' she said. 'I hope you have been quite free from them since I have been away.'

But his amusement, though it had produced this spirit of rancour in her, had not been in the least unkindly. It was legitimate to find entertainment in the thought of a middle-aged woman gravely paddling, so long as he had no idea that there was a most pathetic side to it. Of that he had no inkling: he was unaware that this paddling was expressive of her feeling of recaptured youth, just as he was unaware that she believed it to be expressed in her face and hair. But this remark was distinctly of the nature of an attack: she was retaliating for his laughter. He could not resist one further answer which might both soothe and smart (like a patent ointment) before he changed the subject.

'Well, my dear, I'm sure you are a wonderful woman for your years,' he said. 'By Jove! I shall be proud if I'm as active and healthy as you in ten years' time'.

Dinner was soon over after this, and she left him, as usual, to have his cigarette and glass of port, and went into the drawing room, and stood looking on the last fading splendour of the sunset in the west. The momentary bitterness in her mind had quite died down again: there was nothing left but a vague, dull ache of flatness and disappointment. He had noticed nothing of all that had caused her such tremulous and secret joy. He had looked on her smoothed and softened face, and seen no difference there, on her brown unfaded hair and found it unaltered. He had only seen that she had put her best gown on, and she almost wished that he had not noticed that, since then she might have had the consolation of thinking that he was ill. It was not, it must be premised, that she meant she would find pleasure in his indisposition, only that an indisposition would have explained his imperceptiveness, which she regretted more than she would have regretted a slight headache for him.

For a few minutes she was incapable of more than blank and empty contemplation of the utter failure of that from which she had expected so much. Then, like the stars that even now were beginning to be lit in the empty spaces of the sky, fresh points in the dreary situation claimed her attention. Was he preoccupied with other matters, that he was blind to her? His letters, it is true, had been uniformly cheerful and chatty, but a preoccupied man can easily write a letter without betraying the preoccupation that is only too evident in personal intercourse. If this was so, what was the nature of his preoccupation? That was not a cheerful star: there was a green light in it . . . Another star claimed her attention. Was it Lyndhurst who was blind, or herself who saw too much? She had no idea, till she came to look into the matter closely, how much grey hair was mingled with the brown. Perhaps he had no idea either: its restoration, therefore, would not be an affair of surprise and admiration. But the wrinkles . . .

She faced round from the window as he entered, and made another call on her courage and conviction. Though he saw so little, she, quickened perhaps by the light of the green star, saw how good-looking he was. For years she had scarcely noticed it. She put up her small face to him in a way that suggested, though it did not exactly invite a kiss.

'It is so nice to be home again,' she said.

The suggestion that she meant to convey occurred to him, but, very reasonably, he dismissed it as improbable. A promiscuous caress was a thing long obsolete between them. Morning and evening he brushed her cheek with the end of his moustaches.

'Well, then, we're all pleased,' he said good-humouredly. 'Shall I ring for coffee, Amy?'

She was not discouraged.

'Do,' she said, 'and when we have had coffee, will you fetch a shawl for me, and we will stroll in the garden. You shall show me what new flowers have come out.'

The intention of that was admirable, the actual proposal not so happy, since a glimmering starlight through that fallen dusk would not conduce to a perception of colour.

'We'll stroll in the garden by all means,' he said, 'if you think it will not be risky for you. But as to flowers, my dear, it will be easier to appreciate them when it is not dark.'

Again she put up her face towards him. This time he might, perhaps, have taken the suggestion, but at that moment Parker entered with the coffee.

'How foolish of me,' she said. 'I forgot it was dark. But let us go out anyhow, unless you were thinking of going round to the club.'

'Oh, time for that, time for that,' said he. 'I expect you will be going to bed early after your long journey. I may step round then, and see what's going on.'

CHAPTER FIVE

Without conscious encouragement or welcome on her part, a suspicion darted into her mind. She felt by some process, as inexplicable as that by which certain people are aware of the presence of a cat in the room, that he was going round to see Mrs Evans.

'I suppose you have often gone round to the club in the evening since I have been away,' she said.

'Yes, I have looked in now and again,' he said. 'On other evenings I have dropped in to see our friends. Lonely old bachelor, you know, and Harry was not always very lively company. It's a good thing that boy has gone back to Cambridge, Amy. He was always mooning round after Mrs Evans.'

That was a fact: it had often been a slightly inconvenient one. Several times the Major had 'dropped in' to see Millie, and found his son already there.

'But I thought you were rather pleased at that, Lyndhurst,' she said. 'You told me you considered it not a bad thing: that it would keep Harry out of mischief.'

He finished his coffee rather hastily.

'Yes, within reason, within reason,' he said. 'Well, if we are to stroll in the garden, we had better go out. You wanted a shawl, didn't you? Very wise: where shall I find one?'

That diverted her again to her own personal efforts.

'There are several in the second tray of my wardrobe,' she said. 'Choose a nice one, Lyndhurst, something that won't look hideous with my pink silk.'

The smile, as you might almost say, of coquetry, which accompanied this speech, faded completely as soon as he left the room, and her face assumed that businesslike aspect, which the softest and youngest faces wear, when the object is to attract, instead of letting a mutual attraction exercise its inevitable power. Even though Mrs Ames' object was the legitimate and laudable desire to attract her own husband, it was strange how common her respectable little countenance appeared. She had adorned herself to attract admiration: coquetry and anxiety were pitifully mingled, even as you may see them in haunts far less respectable than this detached villa, and on faces from which Mrs Ames would instantly have averted her own. She hoped he would bring a certain white silk shawl: two nights ago she had worn it on the verandah after dinner at Overstrand, and the reflected light from it, she had noticed, as she stood beneath a light opposite a mirror in the hall, had made her throat look especially soft and plump. She stood underneath the light now waiting for his return.

Fortune was favourable: it was that shawl that he brought, and she turned round for him to put it on her shoulders. Then she faced him again in the remembered position, underneath the light, smiling.

'Now, I am ready, Lyndhurst,' she said.

He opened the French window for her, and stood to let her pass out. Again she smiled at him, and waited for him to join her on the rather narrow gravel path. There was actually room for two abreast on it, for, on the evening of her dinner party, Harry had walked here side by side with Mrs Evans. But there was only just room.

'You go first, Amy,' he said, 'or shall I? We can scarcely walk abreast here.'

But she took his arm.

'Nonsense, my dear,' she said. 'There: is there not heaps of room?'

He felt vaguely uncomfortable. It was not only the necessity of putting his feet down one strictly in front of the other that made him so.

'Anything the matter, my dear?' he asked.

CHAPTER FIVE

The question was not cruel: it was scarcely even careless. He could hardly be expected to guess, for his perceptions were not fine. Also he was thinking about somebody else, and wondering how late it was. But even if he had had complete knowledge of the situation about which he was completely ignorant, he could not have dealt with it in a more peremptory way. The dreary flatness to which she had been so impassive a prey directly after dinner, the sense of complete failure enveloped her like impenetrable fog. Out of that fog, she hooted, so to speak, like an under-vitalized siren.

'I am only so glad to get back,' she said, pressing his arm a little. 'I hoped you were glad, too, that I was back. Tell me what you have been doing all the time I have been away.'

This, like banns, was for the third time of asking. He recalled for her the days one by one, leaving out certain parts of them. Even at the moment, he was astonished to find how vivid his recollection of them was. On Thursday, when he had played golf in the morning, he had lunched with the Evans' (this he stated, for Harry had lunched there too) and he had culled probably the last dish of asparagus in the afternoon. He had dined alone with Harry that night, and Harry had toothache. Next day, consequently, Harry went to the dentist in the morning, and he himself had played golf in the afternoon. That he remembered because he had gone to tea with Mrs Evans afterwards, but that he did not mention, for he had been alone with her, and they had talked about being misunderstood and about affinities. On Saturday Harry had gone back to Cambridge, but, having missed his train, he had made a second start after lunch. He had met Dr Evans in the street that day, going up to the golf links, and since he would otherwise be quite alone in the evening, he had dined with them, 'en garçon'.

This catalogue of trivial happenings took quite a long time in the recitation. But below the trivialities there was a lurking significance. He was not really in love with Millie Evans, and his assurance to himself on that point was perfectly honest. But (this he did not put so distinctly to himself) he thought that she was tremendously attracted by him. Here was an appeal to a sort of deplorable sense of gallantry - so terrible a word only can describe his terrible mind - and mentally he called her 'poor little lady.' She was pretty, too, and not very happy. It seemed to be incumbent on him to interest and amuse her. His 'droppings in' amused her: when he got ready to drop out again, she always asked when he would come to see her next. These 'droppings in' were clearly bright spots to her in a drab day. They were also bright spots to him, for he was more interested in them than in all his sweet peas. There was a 'situation' come into his life, something clandestine. It would never do, for instance, to let Amy or the estimable doctor get a hint of it. Probably they would misunderstand it, and imagine there was something to conceal. He had the secret joys of a bloodless intrigue. But, considering its absolute bloodlessness, he was amazingly wrapped up in it. It was no wonder that he did not notice the restored colour of Amy's hair.

He, or rather Mrs Evans, had made a conditional appointment for tonight. If possible, the possibility depending upon Amy's fatigue, he was going to drop in for a chat. Primarily the chat was to be concerned with the lighting of the garden by means of Chinese lanterns, for a nocturnal fête that Mrs Evans meant to give on her birthday. The whole garden was to be lit, and since the entertainment of an illuminated garden, with hot soup, quails and ices, under the mulberry tree was obviously new to Riseborough, it would be sufficiently amusing to the guests to walk about the garden till suppertime. But there would be supererogatory diversions beyond that, bridge tables in the verandah, a small band at the end of the garden to intervene its strains between the guests and the shrieks of South-Eastern expresses, and already there was an idea of fancy dress. Major Ames favoured the idea of fancy dress, for he had a red velvet garment, sartorially known as a Venetian cloak, locked away upstairs, which was a dazzling affair if white tights peeped out from below it. He knew he had a leg, and only lamented the scanty opportunities of convincing others of the fact. But the lighting of the garden had to be planned first: there was no use in having a leg in a garden, if the garden was not properly lit. But the whole affair was as yet a pledged secret: he could not, as a man of honour, tell Amy about it. Short notice for a fête of this sort was of no consequence, for it was to be a post-prandial entertainment, and the only post-prandial entertainment at present existent in Riseborough was going to bed. Thus everybody would be able to be happy to accept.

A rapid résumé of this made an undercurrent in his mind, as he went through, in speaking voice, the history of the last days. Up and down the narrow path they passed, she still with her hand in his arm, questioning, showing an inconceivable interest in the passage of the days from which he had left out all real points of interest. His patience came to an end before hers.

'Upon my word, my dear,' he said, 'it's getting a little chilly. Shall we go in, do you think? I'm sure you are tired with your journey.'

There was nothing more coming: she knew that. But even in the midst of her disappointment, she found consolation. Daylight would show the re-establishment of her youthfulness more clearly than electric light had done.

Everyone looked about the same by electric light. And though, in some secret manner, she distrusted his visit to the club, she knew how impolitic it would be to hint, however remotely, at such distrust. It was much better this evening to acquiesce in the imputation of fatigue. Nor was the imputation groundless; for failure fatigues anyone when under the same conditions success would only stimulate. And in the consciousness of that, her bitterness rose once more to her lips.

'You mustn't catch cold,' she said. 'Let us go in.'

It was still only half past ten: all this flatness and failure had lasted but a couple of hours, and Major Ames, as soon as his wife had gone upstairs, let himself out of the house. His way lay past the doors of the club, but he did not enter, merely observing through its lit windows that there were a good many men in the smoking room. On arrival at the Doctor's he found that Elsie and her father were playing chess in the drawing room, and that Mrs Evans was out in the garden. He chose to go straight into the garden, and found her sitting under the mulberry, dressed in white, and looking rather like the Milky Way. She did not get up, but held out her hand to him.

'That is nice of you,' she said. 'How is Cousin Amy?'

'Amy is very well,' said he. 'But she's gone to bed early, a little tired with the journey. And how is Cousin Amy's cousin?'

He sat down on the basket chair close beside her which creaked with his weight.

'I must have a special chair made for you,' she said. 'You are so big and strong. Have you seen Cousin Amy's cousin's husband?'

'No: I heard you were out here. So I came straight out.'

She got up.

'I think it will be better, then, if we go in, and tell him you are here,' she said. 'He might think it strange.'

Major Ames jumped up with alacrity: with his alacrity was mingled a pleasing sense of adventure.

'By all means,' he said. 'Then we can come out again.'

She smiled at him.

'Surely. He is playing chess with Elsie. I do not suppose he will interrupt his game.'

Apparently Dr Evans did not think anything in the least strange. On the whole, this was not to be wondered at, since he knew quite well that Major Ames was coming to talk over garden illumination with his wife.

'Good evening, Major,' he said; 'kind of you to come. You and my little woman are going to make a pauper of me, I'm told. There, Elsie, what do you say to my putting my knight there? Check.'

'Pig!' said Elsie.

'Then shall we go out, Major Ames?' said Millie. 'Are you coming out, Wilfred?'

'No, little woman. I'm going to defeat your daughter indoors. Come and have a glass of whisky and soda with me before you go, Major.'

They went out again accordingly into the cool starlight.

'Wilfred is so fond of chess,' she said. 'He plays every night with Elsie, when he is at home. Of course, he is often out.'

This produced exactly the effect that she meant. She did not comment or complain: she merely made a statement which arose naturally from what was going on in the drawing room.

But Major Ames drew the inference that he was expected to draw.

'Glad I could come round,' he said. 'Now for the lanterns. We must have them all down the garden wall, and not too far apart, either. Six feet apart, eh? Now I'll step the wall and we can calculate how many we shall want there. I think I step a full yard still. Not cramped in the joints yet.'

It took some half hour to settle the whole scheme of lighting, which, since Major Ames was not going to pay for it, he recommended being done in a somewhat lavish manner. With so large a number of lanterns, it would be easily possible to see his leg, and he was strong on the subject of fancy dress.

'There'll be some queer turn-outs, I shouldn't wonder,' he said; 'but I expect there will be some creditable costumes too. By Jove! it will be quite the event of the year. Amy and I, with our little dinners, will have to take a back seat, as they say.'

'I hope Cousin Amy won't think it forward of me,' said Millie.

Major Ames said that which is written 'Pshaw'. 'Forward?' he cried. 'Why, you are bringing a bit of life among us. Upon my word, we wanted rousing up a bit. Why, you are a public benefactor.'

They had sat down to rest again after their labour of stepping out the brick walls under the mulberry tree, where the grass was dry, and only a faint shimmer of starlight came through the leaves. At the bottom of the garden a train shrieked by, and the noise died away in decrescent thunder. She leaned forward a little towards him, putting up her face much as Amy had done.

'Ah, if only I thought I was making things a little pleasant,' she said.

Suddenly it struck Major Ames that he was expected to kiss her. He leaned forward, too.

'I think you know that,' he said. 'I wish I could thank you for it.'

CHAPTER FIVE

She did not move, but in the dusk he could see she was smiling at him. It looked as if she was waiting. He made an awkward forward movement and kissed her.

There was silence a moment: she neither responded to him nor repelled him.

'I suppose people would say I ought not to have let you,' she said. 'But there is no harm, is there? After all, you are a - a sort of cousin. And you have been so kind about the lanterns.'

Major Ames was thinking almost entirely about himself, hardly at all about her. An adventure, an intrigue had begun. He had kissed somebody else's wife and felt the devil of a fellow. But with the wine of this emotion was mingled a touch of alarm. It would be wise to call a halt, take his whisky and soda with her husband, and get home to Amy.

MRS ALTHAM waited with considerable impatience next day for the return of her husband from the club, where he went on most afternoons, to sit in an armchair from teatime to dinner and casually to learn what had happened while he had been playing golf. She had been to call on Mrs Ames in the afternoon, and in consequence had matter of considerable importance to communicate. She could have supported that retarded spate of information, though she wanted to burst as soon as possible, but she had also a question to ask Henry on which a tremendous deal depended. At length she heard the rattle of his deposited hat and stick in the hall, and she went out to meet him.

'How late you are, Henry,' she said; 'but you needn't dress. Mrs Brooks, if she does come in afterwards, will excuse you. Dinner is ready: let us come in at once. Now, you were at the club last night, after dinner. You told me who was there; but I want to be quite sure.'

Mr Altham closed his eyes for a moment as he sat down. It looked as if he was saying a silent grace, but appearances were deceptive. He was only thinking, for he knew his wife would not ask such a question unless something depended on it, and he desired to be accurate.

Then he opened them again, and helped the soup with a name to each spoonful.

'General Fortescue,' he said. 'Young Morton. Mr Taverner, Turner, Young Turner.'

That was five spoonfuls - three for his wife, two for himself. He was not very fond of soup.

'And you were there all the time between ten and eleven?' asked his wife.

'Till half past eleven.'

'And there was no one else?'

Mr Altham looked up brightly.

'The club waiter,' he said, 'and the page. The page has been dismissed for stealing sugar. The sugar bill was preposterous. That was how we found out. Did you mean to ask about that?'

'No, my dear. Nor do I want to know.'

At the moment the parlourmaid left the room, and she spoke in an eager undertone.

'Mrs Ames told me that Major Ames went up to the club last night, when she went to bed at half past ten,' she said. 'You told me at breakfast whom you found there, but I wanted to be sure. Call them Mr and Mrs Smith and then we can go on talking.'

The parlourmaid came back into the room.

'Yes, Mr Smith apparently went up to the club at half past ten,' she said. 'But he can't have gone to the club, for in that case you would have seen him. It has occurred to me that he didn't feel well, and went to the doctor's.'

'It seems possible,' said Mr Altham, not without enthusiasm, understanding that 'doctor' meant 'doctor', and which doctor.

'We have all noticed how many visits he has been paying to - to Dr Jones,' said Mrs Altham, 'during the time Mrs Smith was away. But to pay another one on the very evening of her return looks as if - as if something serious was the matter.'

'My dear, there's nothing whatever to show that Major Ames went to the doctor's last night,' he said.

Mrs Altham gave him an awful glance, for the parlour-maid was in the room, and this thoughtless remark rendered all the diplomatic substitution of another nomenclature entirely void and useless.

'Mrs Smith, I should say,' added Mr Altham in some confusion, proceeding to make it all quite clear to Jane, in case she had any doubts about it.

'Suggest to me any other reasonable theory as to where he was, then,' said Mrs Altham.

'I can't suggest where he was, my dear,' said Mr Altham, finding his legal training supported him, 'considering that there is no evidence of any kind that bears upon the matter. But to know that a man was not in one given place does not show with any positiveness that he was at any other given place.'

'No doubt, then, he went shopping at half past ten last night,' said Mrs Altham, with deep sarcasm. 'There are so many shops open then. The High Street is a perfect blaze of light.'

Mr Altham could be sarcastic, too, though he seldom exercised this gift.

'It quite dazzles one,' he observed.

Mrs Altham no doubt was vexed at her husband's sceptical attitude, and she punished him by refraining from discussing the point any further, and from giving him the rest of her news. But this severity punished herself also, for she was bursting to tell him. When Jane had finally withdrawn, the internal pressure became irresistible.

'Mrs Ames has done something to her hair, Henry,' she said; 'and she has done something to her face. I had a good mind to ask her what she had used. I assure you there was not a grey hair left anywhere, and a fortnight ago she was as grey as a coot!'

'Coots are bald, not grey,' remarked her husband.

'That is mere carping, Henry. She is brown now. Is this another fashion she is going to set us at Riseborough? What does it all mean? Shall we all have to plaster our faces with cold cream, and dye our hair blue?'

Mr Altham was in a painfully literal mood this evening and could not disentangle information from rhetoric.

'Has she dyed her hair blue?' he asked in a slightly awe-stricken voice.

'No, my dear: how can you be so stupid? And I told you just now she was brown. But at her age! As if anybody cared what colour her hair was. Her face, too! I don't deny that the wrinkles are less marked, but who cares whether she is wrinkled or not?'

These pleasant considerations were discontinued by the sound of the postman's tap on the front door, and since the postman took precedence of everybody and everything, Mr Altham hurried out to see what excitements he had piloted into port. Unfortunately, there was nothing for him, but there was a large, promising-looking envelope for his wife. It was stiff, too, and looked like the receptacle of an invitation card.

'One for you, my dear,' he said.

Mrs Altham tore it open, and gave a great gasp.

'You would not guess in a hundred tries,' she said.

'Then be so kind as to tell me,' remarked her husband.

Mrs Altham read it out all in one breath without stops.

'Mrs Evans at home Thursday July 20 10 p.m. Shakespeare Fancy Dress well I never!'

For a little while the silence of stupefaction reigned. Then Mr Altham gave a great sigh.

'I have never been to a fancy dress ball,' he said. 'I think I should feel very queer and uncomfortable. What are we meant to do when we get there, Julia? Just stand about and look at each other. It will seem very strange. What would you recommend me to be? I suppose we ought to be a pair.'

Mrs Altham, to do her justice, had not thought seriously about her personal appearance for years. But, as she got up from the table, and consciously faced the looking glass over the chimney piece, it is idle to deny that she considered it now. She was not within ten years of Mrs Ames' age, and it struck her, as she carefully regarded herself in a perfectly honest glass, that even taking into full consideration all that Mrs Ames had been doing to her hair and her face, she herself still kept the proper measure of their difference of years between them. But it was yet too early to consider the question of her impersonation. There were other things suggested by the contemplation of a fancy dress ball to be considered first. There was so much, in fact, that she hardly knew where to begin. So she whisked everything up together, in the manner of a sea pie, in which all that is possibly edible is put in the oven and baked.

'There will be time enough to talk over that, my dear,' she said, 'for if Mrs Evans thinks we are all going to lash out into no end of expense in getting dresses for her party, she is wrong as far as I, for one, am concerned. For that matter you can put on your oldest clothes, and I can borrow Jane's apron and cap, and we can go as Darby and Joan. Indeed, I do not know if I shall go at all - though, of course, one wouldn't like to hurt Mrs Evans' feelings by refusing. Do you know, Henry, I shouldn't in the least wonder if we have seen the last of Mrs Ames and all her airs of superiority and leadership. You may depend upon it that Mrs Evans did not consult her before she settled to give a fancy dress party. It is far more likely that she and Major Ames contrived it all between them, while Mrs Ames was away, and settled what they should go as, and I daresay it will be Romeo and Juliet. I should not be in the least surprised if Mrs Ames did not go to the party at all, but tried to get something up on her own account that very night. It would be like her, I am sure. But whether she goes or not, it seems to me that we have seen the last of her queening it over us all. If she does not go, I should think she would be the only absentee, and if she does, she goes as Mrs Evans' guest. All these years she has never thought of a fancy dress party - '

Mrs Altham broke off in the middle of her address, stung by the splendour of a sudden thought.

'Or does all this staying away on her part,' she said, 'and dyeing her hair, and painting her face, mean that she knew about it all along, and was going to be the show-figure of it all? I should not wonder if that was it. As likely as not, she and Major Ames will come as Hamlet and Ophelia, or something equally ridiculous, though I am sure as far as the 'too too solid flesh' goes, Major Ames would make an admirable Hamlet, for I never saw a man put on weight in the manner he does, in spite of all the garden rolling, which I expect the gardener does for him really. But whatever is the truth of it all, and I'm sure everyone is so secretive here in Riseborough nowadays, that you never know how many dined at such a place on such a night unless you actually go to the poulterer's and find out whether one chicken or two was sent, - what was I saying?'

She had been saying a good deal. Mr Altham correctly guessed the train of thought which she desired to recall.

'In spite of the secretiveness - ' he suggested.

That served the purpose.

'No, my dear Henry,' said his wife rapidly, 'I accuse no one of secretiveness: if I did, you misunderstood me. All I meant was that when we have settled what we are to go as, we will tell nobody. There is very little sense in a fancy dress entertainment if you know exactly what you may expect, and as soon as you see a Romeo can say for certain that it is Major Ames, for instance; and I'm sure if he is to go as Romeo, it would be vastly suitable if Mrs Ames went as Juliet's nurse.'

'I am not sure that I shall like so much finery,' said Mr Altham, who was thinking entirely about his own dress, and did not care two straws about Major or Mrs Ames. 'It will seem very strange.'

'Nonsense, my dear; we will dine in our fancy dresses for an evening or two before, and you will get quite used to it, whatever it is. Henry, do you remember my white satin gown, which I scarcely wore a dozen times, because it seemed too grand for Riseborough? It was too, I am sure: you were quite right. It has been in camphor ever since. I used to wear my Roman pearls with it. There are three rows, and the clasp is of real pearls. The very thing for Cleopatra.'

'I recollect perfectly,' said Mr Altham. His mind instantly darted off again to the undoubted fact that whereas Major Ames was stout, he himself was very thin. If he had been obliged to describe his figure at that moment, he would have said it was boyish. The expense of a wig seemed of no account.

'Well, my dear, white dress and pearls,' said his wife. 'You are not very encouraging. With that book of

Egyptian antiquities, I can easily remodel the dress. And I remember reading in a Roman history that Cleopatra was well over thirty when Julius Caesar was so devoted to her. And by the busts he must have been much balder than you!'

It is no use denying that this was a rather heavy blow. Ever since the mention of the word Cleopatra, he had seen himself complete, with a wig, in another character.

'But Julius Caesar was sixty,' he observed, with pardonable asperity. 'I do not see how I could make up as a man of sixty. And for that matter, my dear, though I am sure no one would think you were within five years of your actual age, I do not see how you could make up as a mere girl of thirty. Why should we not go as 'Antony and Cleopatra, ten years later'? It would be better than to go as Julius Caesar and Cleopatra ten years before!'

Mrs Altham considered this. It was true that she would find it difficult to look thirty, however many Roman pearls she wore.

'I do not know that it is such a bad idea of yours, Henry,' she said. 'Certainly there is no one in the world who cares about her age, or wants to conceal it, less than I. And there is something original about your suggestion - Antony and Cleopatra ten years later - Ah, there is the bell, that will be Mrs Brooks coming in. And there is the telephone also. Upon my word, we never have a moment to ourselves. I should not wonder if half of Riseborough came to see us tonight. Will you go to the telephone and tell it we are at home? And not a word to anybody, Henry, as to what we are thinking of going as. There will be our surprise, at any rate, however much other people go talking about their dresses. If you are being rung up to ask about your costume, say that you haven't given it a thought yet.'

For the next week Mrs Altham was thoroughly in her element. She had something to conceal, and was in a delicious state of tension with the superficial desire to disclose her own impersonation, and the deep-rooted satisfaction of not doing so. To complete her happiness, the famous white satin still fitted her, and she was nearly insane with curiosity to know what Major and Mrs Ames 'were going to be', and what the whole history of the projected festivity was. In various other respects her natural interest in the affairs of other people was satiated. Mrs Turner was to be Mistress Page, which was very suitable, as she was elderly and stout, and did not really in the least resemble Miss Ellen Terry. Mr Turner had selected Falstaff, and could be recognized anywhere. Young Morton, with unwonted modesty, had chosen the part of the Apothecary in Romeo and Juliet. Mrs Taverner was to be Queen Catherine, and - almost more joyous than all - she had persuaded Mrs Brooks not to attempt to impersonate Cleopatra. What Mrs Brooks' feelings would be when it dawned on her, as it not inconceivably might, that Mrs Altham had seen in her a striking likeness to her conception of Hermione, because she did not want there to be two Cleopatras, did not particularly concern her. She had asked Mrs Brooks to dinner the day after the entertainment, and her acceptance would bury the hatchet, if indeed there was such a thing as a hatchet about. Finally, she had called on Mrs Evans, who had vaguely talked about *A Midsummer Night's Dream.* Mrs Altham had taken that to be equivalent to the fact that she would appear as Titania, and Mrs Evans had distinctly intended that she should so take it. Indeed, the idea had occurred to her, but not very vividly. Her husband was going to be Timon of Athens. That, again, was quite satisfactory: nobody knew at all distinctly who Timon of Athens was, and nobody knew much about Dr Evans, except that he was usually sent for in the middle of something. Probably the same thing happened to Timon of Athens.

Indeed, within a couple of hours of the reception of Mrs Evans' invitations, which all arrived simultaneously by the local evening post, a spirit of demoniacal gaiety, not less fierce than that which inspired Mrs Altham, possessed the whole of those invited. Though it was gay, it was certainly demoniacal, for a quite prodigious amount of ill-feeling was mingled with it which from time to time threatened to wreck the proceedings altogether. For instance, only two days after all the invitations had been accepted, Mrs Evans had issued a further intimation that there was to be dancing, and that the evening would open at a quarter past ten precisely with a quadrille in which it was requested that everybody would take part. It is easy to picture the private consternation that presided over that evening; how in one house, Mrs Brooks having pushed her central drawing-room table to one side, all alone and humming to herself, stepped in perplexed and forgotten measures, and how next door Mrs and Mr Altham violently wrangled over the order of the figures, and hummed different tunes, to show each other, or pranced in different directions. For here was the bitter affair: these pains had to be suffered in loneliness, for it was clearly impossible to confess that the practice of quadrilles was so long past that the memory of them had vanished altogether. But luckily (though at the moment the suggestion caused a great deal of asperity in Mrs Altham's mind) Mrs Ames came to the rescue with the suggestion that as many of them, no doubt, had forgotten the precise manner of quadrilles, she proposed to hold a class at half past four tomorrow afternoon, when they would all run through a quadrille together.

'There! I thought as much!' said Mrs Altham. 'That means that neither Major nor Mrs Ames can remember how the quadrille goes, and we, forsooth, must go and teach them. And she puts it that she is going to teach us! I am sure she will never teach me: I shall not go near the house. I do not require to be taught quadrilles by anybody, still less by Mrs Ames. There is no answer,' she added to Jane.

Mr Altham fidgeted in his chair. Last night he had been quite sure he was right, in points where he and his wife differed, and that the particular 'setting partners' which they had shown each other so often did not come in the quadrille at all, but occurred in lancers, just before the ladies' chain. But she had insisted that both the setting to partners and ladies' chain came in quadrilles. This morning, however, he did not feel quite so certain about it.

'You might send a note to Mrs Ames,' he observed, 'and tell her you are not coming.'

'No answer was asked for,' said his wife excitedly. 'She just said there was to be a quadrille practice at half past four. Let there be. I am sure I have no objection, though I do think you might have thought of doing it first, Henry.'

'But she will like to know how many to expect,' said Henry. 'If it is to be at half past four, she must be prepared for tea. It is equivalent to a tea party, unless you suppose that the class will be over before five.'

During the night Mrs Altham had pondered her view about the ladies' chain. It would be an awful thing if Henry happened to be right, and if, on the evening of the dance itself, she presented her hand for the ladies' chain, and no chain of any sort followed. She decided on a magnanimous course.

'Upon my word, I am not sure that I shall not go,' she said, 'just to see what Mrs Ames' idea of a quadrille is.

I should not wonder if she mixed it up with something quite different, which would be laughable. And after all, we ought not to be so unkind, and if poor Mrs Ames feels she will get into difficulties over the quadrille, I am sure I shall be happy to help her out. No doubt she has summoned us like this, so that she need not show that she feels she wants to be helped. We will go, Henry, and I daresay I shall get out of her what she means to dress up as! But pray remember to say that we, at any rate, have not given a thought to our costumes yet. And on our way, we may as well call in at Mr Roland's, for if I am to wear my three rows of pearls, he must get me a few more, since I find there is a good deal of string showing. I daresay that ordinary pearl beads would answer the purpose perfectly. I have no intention of buying more of the real Roman pearls. They belonged to my mother, and I should not like to add to them. And if you will insist on having some red stone in your cap, to make a buckle for the feather, I am sure you could not do better than get a piece of what he called German ruby that is in his shop now. I do not suppose anybody in Riseborough could tell it from real, and after all this is over, I would wear it as a pendant for my pearls. If you wish, I will pay half of it, and it is but a couple of pounds altogether.'

It did not seem a really handsome offer, but Henry had the sense to accept it. He wanted a stone to buckle the feather in a rather coquettish cap that they had decided to be suitable for Mark Antony, and did not really care what happened to it after he had worn it on this occasion, since it was unlikely that another similar occasion would arise. Deep in his mind had been an idea of turning it into a solitaire, but he knew he would not have the practical courage of this daring conception. It would want another setting, also.

In other houses there were no fewer anticipatory triumphs and present perplexities. There was also, in some cases, wild and secret intrigue. For instance, a few evenings after, Mrs Brooks next door, sorting out garments in her wardrobe from which she might devise a costume that should remind the beholder of Hermione, looked from her bedroom window, where her quest was in progress, and saw a strange sight in the next garden. There was a lady in white satin with pearls; there was a gentleman in Roman toga with a feathered cap. The Roman gentleman was a dubious figure; the lady indubitable. If ever there was an elderly Cleopatra, this was she.

Mrs Brooks sat heavily down, after observing this sight. It certainly was Cleopatra in the next garden: as certainly it was a snake in the grass. In a moment her mind was made up. She saw why she had been discouraged from being Cleopatra; the false Mrs Altham had wanted to be Cleopatra herself, without rival. But she would be Cleopatra too. Riseborough should judge between the effectiveness of the two representations. Of course, everyone knew that Mrs Altham had three rows of Roman pearls, which were nothing but some sort of vitreous enamel. But Mrs Brooks, as Riseborough also knew, had five or six rows of real seed-pearls. It was impossible to denigrer seed pearls: they were pearls, though small, and did not pretend to be anything different to what they were. But the Roman prefix, to any fair-minded person, invalidated the word 'pearls'. Besides, even as Cleopatra without pearls, she would have been willing to back herself against Mrs Altham. Cleopatra ought to be tall, which she was. Also Cleopatra ought to be beautiful, which neither was. And Mrs Altham had urged her to go as Hermione! Of course, she had to revise her toilet, but luckily it had progressed no further than the sewing of white rosettes on to a pair of slightly worn satin shoes, which were equally suitable for any of Shakespeare's heroines.

The week which had passed for Mr and Mrs Altham in a succession of so pleasing excitements and anxieties, had not been without incident to Mrs Ames. When (by the same post that bore their invitations to the other guests) the announcement of the fancy dress ball reached her, and she read it out to her husband (even as Mrs Altham had done) towards the end of dinner, he expressed his feelings with a good deal of poohing and the opinion that he, at any rate, was past the years of dressing-up. This attitude (for it had been settled that the invitation was to come as a surprise to him) he somewhat overdid, and found to his dismay that his wife quite agreed with him, and was prepared as soon as dinner was over to write regrets. The reason was not far to seek.

'I hope I am not what - what the servants call "touchy",' she said (and indeed, it was difficult to see what else the servants could call it), 'but I must say that, considering the length of time we have been in Riseborough, and the number of entertainments we have provided for the people here, I think dear Millie might have consulted me - or you, of course, Lyndhurst, in my absence - as to any such novelty as a fancy dress ball. I have no wish to interfere in any way with any little party that dear Millie may choose to give, but I suppose since she can plan it without me, she can also enjoy it without me. I am aware I am by no means necessary to the success of any party. And since you think that you are a little beyond the age of dressing up, Lyndhurst - though I do not say I agree with you - I think we shall be happier at home that night. I will write quite kindly to dear Millie, and say we are engaged. No doubt the Althams would dine with us, as I do not imagine that she would care to get up in fancy dress.'

Major Ames was not a quick thinker, but he saw several things without a pause. One was that he, at any rate, must certainly go, but that he did not much care whether Amy went or not. A second was that, having expressed surprise at the announcement of the party, it was too late now to say that he knew about it from the first, and was going to impersonate Antony, while Mrs Evans was to be Cleopatra. A third was that something had to be done, a fourth that he did not know what.

'I will leave you to your cigarette, Lyndhurst,' said his wife, rising, 'and will write to dear Millie. Let us stroll in the garden again tonight.'

She passed out of the dining room, he closed the door behind her, and she went straight to her writing table in the drawing room. Above it hung a looking glass, and (still not in the frame of mind which servants call 'touchy') she sat down to write the kind note. A considerable degree of sunset still lingered in the western sky, and there would be no need to light a candle to write by. There was light enough also for her to see a rosy-tinted image of herself in the glass, and she paused. She saw there, what she was aware Mrs Altham had seen this afternoon - namely, the absence of grey in her hair, and the softened and liquated wrinkles of her face. True, not even yet had her husband observed, or at any rate commented on those refurbished signals of her youth, but Mrs Ames had by no means yet despaired, and daily (as directed) tapped in the emollient cream. This rosy light of sunset gave her face a flush of delicate colour, and she unconsciously claimed for her own the borrowed enchantment of the light . . . Then that which was not touchiness underwent a similar softening to that of her wrinkles. She knew she had been guilty of sarcastic intention when she said she was aware that her presence was not necessary to the success of any party. It would be unkind to dear Millie if she refused to go, for a dinner party at home was no excuse at all; she could perfectly well go on there when carriages came at twenty minutes to eleven. Also it was absurd for Lyndhurst to say that he was past the age when 'dressing up' is seemly. In spite of his hair, which he managed very well, he was still young enough in face to excuse the yielding to the temptation of embellishing himself, and a Venetian mantle would naturally conceal his tendency to corpulence. No doubt dear Millie had not meant to put herself forward in any way; no doubt she had not yet really grasped the fact that Mrs Ames was acknowledged autocrat in all that concerned festivity.

All this train of thought needed but a few seconds for passage, and, as she still regarded herself, the name of the heroines of enchantment sounded delicately in her brain. Juliet and Ophelia she passed over without a pang, for she was not so unfocussed of imagination as to see her reflection capable of recapturing the budding spring of those, or the slim youthfulness of Rosalind. She wanted no girlish role, nor did she read into herself the precocious dignity of Portia. But was there not one who came down the green Nile to the sound of flutes in a gilded barge - no girl, but a woman in the charm of her full maturity?

The idea detailed itself in plan and manoeuvre. She wanted to burst on Lyndhurst like that, to let him see in a flash of revelation how bravely she could support the rôle of that sorceress . . . At the moment the drawing-room door opened, and simultaneously they both began a sentence in identical words.

'Do you know, my dear, I've been thinking . . . '

They both stopped, and he gave his genial laugh.

'Upon my soul, my dear Amy,' he said, 'I believe we always have the same thoughts. I'll tell you what you were going to say. You were going to say, "I've been thinking it wouldn't be very kind to dear Millie" - that is what YOU would say, of course - not very kind to Mrs Evans if we declined. And I agree with you, my dear. No doubt she should have consulted you first, or if you were away she might even, as you suggested, have mentioned it to me. But you can afford to be indulgent, my dear - after all, she is your cousin - and you wouldn't like to spoil her party, poor thing, by refusing to go. And if you go, why, of course, I shall put on one side my natural feelings about an old fogey like myself making a guy of himself, and I shall dress up somehow. I think I have an old costume with a Venetian cloak laid aside somewhere, though I daresay it's moth-eaten and rusty now, and I'll dress myself up somehow and come with you. I suppose there are some old stagers in Shakespeare - I must have a look at the fellow's plays again - which even a retired old soldier can impersonate. Falstaff, for instance - some stout old man of that sort.'

Some of this speech, to say the least of it, was not, it is to be feared, quite absolutely ingenuous. But then, Major Ames was not naturally quite ingenuous. He had already satisfied himself that the old costume in question had been perfectly preserved by the naphthaline balls which he was careful to renew from time to time, and was not in the least moth-eaten or rusty. Again, since he had settled to go as Antony, it was not perfectly straightforward to make allusion to Falstaff. But after all, the speech expressed all he meant to say, and it is only our most fortunate utterances that can do as much. Indeed, perhaps it leaned over a little to the further side of expression, for it struck Mrs Ames at that moment (struck her as violently and inexplicably as a coconut falling on her head) that the question of the Venetian cloak had not come into her husband's mind for the first time that evening. She felt, without being able to explain her feeling, that the idea of the fancy dress ball was not new to him. But it was impossible to tax him with so profound a duplicity; indeed, when she gave a moment's consideration to the question, she dismissed her suspicion. But the suspicion had been there.

She met him quite halfway.

'You have guessed quite right, Lyndhurst,' she said; 'I think it would be unkind to dear Millie if you and I did not go. I daresay she will have difficulty enough as it is to make a gathering. I will write at once.'

This was soon done, and even as she wrote, poor Mrs Ames' vision of herself grew more roseate in her mind. But she must burst upon her husband, she must burst upon him. Supposing her preposterous suspicion of a moment before was true, there was all the more need for bursting upon him, for Cleopatraizing herself . . . He, meantime, was wondering how on earth to keep the secret of his costume and his hostess's, should Amy proceed to discuss costumes, or suggest the King and Queen of Denmark as suitable for themselves. It might cvcn be better to accept the situation as such, and tell Mrs Evans that his wife wanted to go as 'a pair' (so Mrs Altham expressed it) and that it was more prudent to abandon the idea of a stray Antony and a stray Cleopatra meeting on the evening itself unpremeditatedly. But her next words caused all these difficulties to disappear; they vanished as completely as a watch or a rabbit under the wave of the conjurer's wand.

Mrs Ames never licked envelopes; she applied water on a camel-hair brush, from a little receptacle like a tear bottle.

'What nonsense, my dear Lyndhurst,' she said. 'Fancy you going as Falstaff! You must think of something better than that! Dear me, it is a very bold idea of Millie's, but really it seems to me that we might have great fun. I do hope that all Riseborough will not talk their costumes over together, so that we shall know exactly what to expect. There is little point in a fancy dress ball unless there are some surprises. I must think over my costume too. I am not so fortunate as to have one ready.'

She got up from the table, still with the roseate image of herself in her mind.

'I think I shall not tell you who I am going to be,' she said, 'even when I have thought of something suitable. I shall keep myself as a surprise for you. And keep yourself as a surprise for me, Lyndhurst. Let us meet for the first time in our costumes when the carriage is at the door ready to take us to the party. Do you not think that would be fun? But you must promise me, my dear, that you will not make yourself up as Falstaff, or any old guy. Else I shall be quite ashamed of you.'

He rang the bell effusively (the heartiness of the action was typical of the welcome he gave to his wife's suggestion), and ordered the note to be sent.

'By Jove! Amy,' he said, 'what a one you always are for thinking of things. And if you wish it, I'll try to make a presentable figure of myself, though I'm sure I should be more in place at home waiting for your return to hear all about it. But I'll do my best, I'll do my best, and I daresay the Venetian cloak isn't so shabby after all. I have always been careful to keep a bit of naphthaline in the box with it.'

Flirtation may not be incorrectly defined as making the pretence of being in love, and yet it is almost too solid a word to apply to Major Ames' relations with Mrs Evans during the week or two before the ball, and it would be more accurate to say that he was making the pretence of having a flirtation. Even as when he kissed her on that daring evening already described, he was thinking entirely about himself and the dashingness of this proceeding, so in the days that succeeded, this same inept futility and self-satisfaction possessed him. He made many secret visits to the house, entering like a burglar, in the middle of the afternoon, by an unfrequented passage from the railway cutting, at hours when she had told him that her husband and daughter would certainly be out, and the secrecy of those meetings added spice to them. He felt - so deplorable a frame of mind almost defies description - he felt a pleasing sense of wickedness which was endorsed, so to speak, by the certificate which attested to his complete innocence. As far as he was concerned, it was a mere farce of a flirtation. But the farce filled him with a kind of childish glee; he persuaded himself that his share in it was real, and that by a tragic fate he and the woman who were made for each other were forbidden to find the fruition of their affinity. It was an adventure without danger, a mine without gunpowder. For even on two occasions when he was paying one of these clandestine visits, Dr Evans had unexpectedly returned and found them together. The poor blind man, it seemed, suspected nothing; indeed, his welcome had been extremely cordial.

'Good of you to come and help my wife over her party,' he said. 'What you'd do without Major Ames, little woman, I don't know. Won't you stop for dinner, Major?'

Then, after a suitable reply, and a digression to other matters, the Major's foolish eye would steal a look at Millie, and for a moment her eyes would meet his, and flutter and fall. And considering that there was not in all the world probably a worse judge of human nature than Major Ames, it is a strange thing that his mental comment was approximately true.

'Dear little woman,' he said to himself; 'she's deuced fond of me!'

JUPITER Pluvius, or Mr J. Pluvius, by which name Major Ames was facetiously wont to allude to the weather, seemed amiably inclined to co-operate with Mrs Evans' scheme, for the evening of her party promised to be ideal for the purpose. The few days previous had been very hot, and no particle of moisture lurked in the baked lawns, so that her guests would be able to wander at will without risk of contracting catarrh, or stains on such shoes as should prove to be white satin. Moreover, by a special kindness of Providence, therc was no moon, so that the illumination of fairy lights and Chinese lanterns would suffer no dispiriting comparison with a more potent brightness. Over a large portion of the lawn Mrs Evans, at Major Ames' suggestion (not having to pay for these paraphernalia he was singularly fruitful in suggestions), had caused a planked floor to be laid; here the opening procession and quadrille and the subsequent dances would take place, while conveniently adjacent was the mulberry tree under shade of which were spread the more material hospitalities. Tree and dancing floor were copiously outlined with lanterns, and straight rows of fairy lights led to them from the garden door of the house. Similarly outlined was the garden wall and the hedge by the railway cutting, while the band (piano, two strings and a cornet of amazingly piercing quality) was to be concealed in the small cul-de-sac which led to the potting shed and garden roller. The shrubbery was less vividly lit; here Hamlets and Rosalinds could stray in sequestered couples, unharassed by too searching an illumination. Major Ames had paid his last clandestine visit this afternoon, and had expressed himself as perfectly pleased with the arrangements. Both Elsie and the doctor had been there.

The party had been announced to begin at half past ten, and it was scarcely that hour when Mrs Ames came downstairs from her bedroom where she had so long been busy since the end of the early dinner. Her arms were bare from finger-tip to her little round shoulders, over which were clasped, with handsome cairngorm brooches, the straps of her long tunic. But there was no effect of an excessive display of human flesh, since her arms were very short, and in addition they were plentifully bedecked. On one arm a metallic snake writhed from wrist to elbow, on the other there was clasped above the elbow a plain circlet of some very bright and shining metal. A net of blue beads altogether too magnificent to be turquoises, was pinned over her unfaded hair, and from the front of it there depended on her forehead a large pear-shaped pearl, suggestive of the one which the extravagant queen subsequently dissolved in vinegar. Any pearl, so scientists tell us, which is capable of solution in vinegar must be a curious pearl; that which Mrs Ames wore in the middle of her forehead was curious also. Art had been specially invoked, over and above the normal skin food tonight, in the matter of Mrs Ames' face, and a formal Egyptian eyebrow, as indicated in the illustration to 'Rameses' in the encyclopaedia, decorated in charcoal the place where her own eyebrow once was. Below her eye a touch of the same charcoal added brilliancy to the eye itself; several touches of rouge contributed their appropriate splendour to her cheeks.

The long tunic which was held up over her shoulders by the cairngorm brooches, reached to her knee. It was a little tight, perhaps, but when you have only one Arab shawl, shot with copious gold thread, you have to make it go as far as it can, and after all, it went to her knees. A small fold of it was looped up, and fell over her yellow girdle, it was parted at the sides below the hips, and disclosed a skirt made of two Arab shawls shot with silver, which, stitched together, descended to her ankle. She did not mean to dance anything except the opening quadrille. Below this silver-streaked skirt appeared, as was natural, her pretty plump little feet. On them she wore sandals which exhibited their plumpness and prettiness and smallness to the fullest extent. A correct strap lay between the great toe and the next, and the straps were covered with silver paper. For years Riseborough had known how small were her shoes; tonight Riseborough should see that those shoes had been amply large enough for what they contained. Round her neck, finally, were four rows of magnificent pearl beads; no wonder Cleopatra thought nothing of dissolving one pearl, when its dissolution would leave intact so populous a company of similar treasures.

As she came downstairs she heard a sudden noise in the drawing room, as if a heavy man had suddenly stumbled. It required no more ingenuity than was normally hers to conjecture that Lyndhurst was already there, and had tripped himself up in some novel accoutrement. And at that, a sudden flush of excitement and anticipation invaded her, and she wondered what he would be like. As regards herself she felt the profoundest confidence in the success of her garniture. He could scarcely help being amazed, delighted. And an emotion never keenly felt by her, but as such long outworn, shook her and made her knees tremulous. She felt so young, so daring. She wished that at this moment he would come out, for as she descended the stairs he could not but see how small and soft were her feet . . .

Almost before her wish was formed, it was granted.

A well-smothered oath succeeded the stumbling noise, and Major Ames, in white Roman toga and tights came out into the hall. There was no vestige of Venetian cloak about him; he was altogether different from what she had expected. A profuse wig covered his head, the toga completely masked what the exercise with the garden roller had not completely removed, and below, his big calves rose majestic over his classical laced shoes. If ever there was a Mark Antony with a military moustache, he was not in Egypt nor in Rome, but here; by a divine chance, without consultation, he had chosen for himself the character complementary to hers. He looked up and saw her, she looked down and saw him.

'Bless my soul,' he said. 'Amy! Cleopatra!'

She gave him a happy little smile.

'Bless my soul,' she said. 'Lyndhurst! Mark Antony!'

There was a long and an awful pause. It was quite clear to her that something had occurred totally unexpected. She had wanted to be unexpected, but there was something wrong about the quality of his surprise. Then such manliness as there was in him came to his aid.

'Upon my word,' he said, 'you have got yourself up splendidly, Amy. Cleopatra now, pearls and all, and sandals! Why, you'll take the shine out of them all! Here we go, eh? Antony and Cleopatra! Who would have thought of it! The cab's round, dear. We had better be starting, if we're to take part in the procession. Not want a cloak or anything? Antony and Cleopatra; God bless my soul!'

That was sufficient to allay the immediate embarrassment. True, he had not been knocked over by this apparition of her in the way she had meant, and the astonished pause, she was afraid, was not one of surrendering admiration. And yet, perhaps, he was feeling shy, even as she was; standing here in all this splendour of shining pantomime he might well feel her to be as strange to him, as she felt him to be to her. Moreover, she had not only to look Cleopatra, but to be Cleopatra, to behave herself with the gaiety and youth which her appearance gave him the right to expect. In the meantime he also had earned her compliments, for no man who thinks it worthwhile to assume a fancy dress has a soul so unhuman as to be unappreciative of applause.

She fell back a step or two to regard him comprehensively.

'My dear,' she said, 'you are splendid; that toga suits you to admiration. And your arms look so well coming out of the folds of it. What great strong arms, Lyndhurst! You could pick up your little Cleopatra and carry her back - back to Egypt so easily.'

Something of their irresponsibility which, as by a special Providence, broods over the audacity of assuming strange guises, descended on her. She could no more have made such a speech to him in her ordinary morning clothes, nor yet in the famous rose-coloured silk, than she could have flown. But now her costume unloosed her tongue. And despite the dreadful embarrassment that he knew would await him when they got to the party, and a second Cleopatra welcomed them, this intoxication of costume (liable, unfortunately, to manifest itself not only in vin gai) mounted to his head also.

'Ma reine!' he said, feeling that French brought them somehow closer to the appropriate Oriental atmosphere.

She held up her skirt with one hand, and gave him the other.

'We must be off, my Antony,' she said.

They got into the cab; a somewhat jaded-looking horse was lashed into a slow and mournful trot, and they rattled away down the hard, dry road.

A queue of carriages was already waiting to disembark its cargoes when they drew near the house, and leaning furtively and feverishly from the window, Mrs Ames saw a Hamlet or two and some Titanias swiftly and shyly cross the pavement between two rows of the astonished proletariat. Beside her in the cab her husband grunted and fidgeted; she guessed that to him this entrance was of the nature of bathing on a cold day; however invigorating might be the subsequent swim, the plunge was chilly. But she little knew the true cause of his embarrassment and apprehension; had his military career ever entailed (which it had not) the facing of fire, it was probable, though his courage was of no conspicuous a kind, that he would have met the guns with greater blitheness than he awaited the moment that now inevitably faced him. Then came their turn; there was a pause, and then their carriage door was flung open, and they descended from the innocent vehicle that to him was as portentous as a tumbril. In a moment Cleopatra would meet Cleopatra, and he could form no idea how either Cleopatra would take it. The Cleopatra-hostess, as he knew, was going to wear sandals also; snakes were to writhe up her long white arms . . .

Mrs Ames adjusted the pear-shaped pearl on her forehead.

'I think if we say half past one it will be late enough, Lyndhurst,' she said. 'If we are not ready he can wait.'

CHAPTER SEVEN

It seemed to Lyndhurst that half past one would probably be quite late enough.

The assemblage of guests took place in the drawing room which opened into the garden; a waiter from the 'Crown' inn, with a chin beard and dressed in a sort of white surplice and carrying a lantern in his hand, who might with equal reasonableness be supposed to be the Man in the Moon out of *A Midsummer Night's Dream*, or a gravedigger out of *Hamlet*, said, 'Character names, please, ma'am,' and preceded them to the door of this chamber. He bawled out 'Cleopatra and Mark Antony.'

Another Cleopatra, a 'different conception of this part', as the Kent Chronicle said in its next issue, a Cleopatra dim and white and willowy, advanced to them. She looked vexed, but as she ran her eyes up and down Mrs Ames' figure, like a practised pianist playing a chromatic scale, her vexation seemed completely to clear.

'Dear Cousin Amy,' she said, 'how perfectly lovely! I never saw - Wilfred, make your bow to Cleopatra. And Antony! Oh, Major Ames!'

Again she made the chromatic scale, starting at the top, so to speak (his face), with a long note, and dwelling there again when she returned to it.

Other arrivals followed, and this particular Antony and Cleopatra mingled with such guests as were already assembled. The greater part had gathered, and Mrs Ames' habitual manner and bearing suited excellently with her regal role. The Turner family, at any rate, who were standing a little apart from the others, not being quite completely 'in' Riseborough society, and, feeling rather hot and feverish in the thick brocaded stuffs suitable to Falstaff, Mistress Page and King Theseus, felt neither more nor less uncomfortable when she made a few complimentary remarks to them than they did when, with her fat prayer book in her hand, she spoke to them after church on Sunday. Elsewhere young Morton, with a white face and a red nose, was the traditional Apothecary, and Mrs Taverner was so copiously apparalled as Queen Catherine that she was looking forward very much indeed to the moment when the procession should go forth into the greater coolness of the night air. Then a stentorian announcement from the waiter at the Crown made everyone turn again to the door.

'Antony and Cleopatra ten years later,' he shouted.

There was a slight pause. Then entered Mr and Mrs Altham with high-held hands clasped at fingertips. They both stepped rather high, she holding her skirt away from her feet, and both pointing their toes as if performing a pavanne. This entry had been much rehearsed, and it was arresting to the point of producing a sort of stupefaction.

Mrs Evans ran her eye up and down the pair, and was apparently satisfied.

'Dear Mrs Altham,' she said, 'how perfectly lovely! AND Mr Altham. But ten years later! You must not ask us to believe that.'

She turned to her husband and spoke quickly, with a look on her face less amiable than she usually wore in public.

'Wilfred,' she said, 'tell the band to begin the opening march at once for the procession, in case there are any more - '

But he interrupted -

'Here's another, Millie,' he said cheerfully. 'Yes, we'd better begin.'

His speech was drowned by the voice of the brazen-lunged waiter.

'Cleopatra!' he shouted.

Mrs Brooks entered with all the rows of seed pearls.

CHAPTER SEVEN

Riseborough, if the census papers were consulted, might perhaps not prove to have an abnormally large percentage of inhabitants who had reached middle age, but certainly in the festivities of its upper circles, maturity held an overwhelming majority over youth. It was so tonight, and of the half-hundred folk who thus masqueraded, there were few who were not, numerically speaking, of thoroughly discreet years. The diffused knowledge of this undoubtedly gave confidence to their gaiety, for there was no unconscious standard of sterling youth by which their slightly mature exhilaration could be judged and found deficient in genuine and natural effervescence. Thus, despite the somewhat untoward conjunction of four matronly Cleopatras, a spirit of extraordinary gaiety soon possessed the entire party. Odious comparisons might conceivably spring up mushroom-like tomorrow, and (unmushroom-like) continue to wax and flourish through many days and dinners, but tonight so large an environment of elderly people gave to every one of those elderly people a pleasant sense of not suffering but rather shining in comparison with the others. Even the Cleopatras themselves were content; Mrs Ames, for instance, saw how sensible it was that Mrs Altham should announce herself as a Cleopatra of ten years later, while Mrs Altham, observing Mrs Ames, saw how supererogatory her titular modesty had been, and wondered that Mrs Ames cared to show her feet like that, while Mrs Brooks knew that everybody was mentally contrasting her queenliness of height with Mrs Ames' paucity of inches, and her abundance of beautiful hair with Mrs Altham's obvious wig. While, all the time, Mrs Evans, whom the appearance of a fourth Cleopatra had considerably upset for the moment, felt that at this rate she could easily continue being Cleopatra for more years than 'the ten after', so properly assumed by

Mrs Altham. In the same way Major Ames, with his six feet of solid English bone and muscle, and his fifth decade of years still but half-consumed, felt that Mr Altham had but provided a scale of comparison uncommonly flattering to himself. Simultaneously, Mr Altham, with a laurel wreath round his head, reflected how uncomfortable he would have felt if his laurel wreath was anchored on no sounder a foundation than a wig, and wondered if gardening (on the principle that all flesh is grass) invariably resulted in so great a growth of tissue. But all these pleasant self-communings were, indeed, but a minor tributary to the real river of enjoyment that danced and chattered through the starlit hours of this July night. Somehow the whole assembly seemed to have shifted off themselves the natural and inevitable burden of their years; they danced and mildly flirted, they sat out in the dim shrubbery, and played on the seashore of life again, finding the sandcastles had become real once more. Mrs Ames, for instance, had intended to dance nothing but the opening quadrille, but before the second dance, which was a waltz, had come to a close, she had accepted Mr Altham's offer, and was slowly capering round with him. A little care was necessary in order not to put too unjust a strain on the sandal straps, but she exercised this precaution, and was sorry, though hot, when the dance came to an end. Then Major Ames, who had been piloting Mrs Altham, joined them at the moselle-cup table.

''Pon my word, Altham,' he said, 'I don't know what to say to you. You've taken my Cleopatra, but then I've taken yours. Exchange no robbery, hey?'

His wife tapped him on the arm with her palmette fan.

'Lyndhurst, go along with you!' she said, employing an expression, the mental equivalent of which she did not know ever existed in her mind.

'I'll go along,' he said. 'But which is my Cleopatra?'

At the moment, Mrs Evans approached.

'My two Cleopatras must excuse me,' said this amazing man. 'I am engaged for this next dance to the Cleopatra of us all. Ha! Ha!'

He offered his arm to Mrs Evans, and they went out of the cave of the mulberry tree again.

The band had not yet struck up for the next dance, the majority of the guests were flocking under the mulberry tree at the conclusion of the last, and for the moment they had the cool starlit dusk to themselves. And then, all at once, the Major's sense of boisterous enjoyment deserted him; he felt embarrassed with a secret knowledge that he was expected to say something in tune with this privacy. How that expectation was conveyed he hardly knew; the slight pressure on his arm seemed to announce it unmistakably. It reminded him that he was a man, and yet with all that gaiety and gallantry that were so conspicuous a feature in his behaviour to women in public, he felt awkward and ill at ease. He embarked on a course of desperate and fulsome eulogy, longing in his private soul for the band to begin.

''Pon my soul, you are an enchantress, Millie!' he said. 'You come to our staid, respectable old Riseborough, and before you have been here six months you take us all into fairyland. Positively fairyland. And - and I've never seen you looking so lovely as tonight.'

'Let us stroll all round the garden,' she said. 'I want you to see it all now it is lit up. And the shrubbery is pretty, too, with - with the filter of starlight coming through the trees. Do tell me truthfully, like a friend, is it going all right? Are they enjoying themselves?'

'Kicking up their heels like two-year-olds,' said Major Ames.

'How wicked of you to say that! But really I had one bad moment, when - when the last Cleopatra came in.'

She paused a moment. Then in her clear, silky voice -

'Dear old things!' she said.

Now Mrs Evans was not in any way a clever woman, but had she had the brains and the wit of Cleopatra herself, she could not have spoken three more consummately chosen words. All the cool, instinctive confidence of a younger woman, and a pretty woman speaking of the more elderly and plain was there; there, too, was the deliberate challenge of the coquette. And Major Ames was quite helpless against the simplicity of such art. Mere manners, the ordinary code of politeness, demanded that he should agree with his hostess. Besides, though he was not in any way in love with her, he could not resist the assumption that her words implied, and, after all, she was a pretty woman, whom he had kissed, and he was alone in the star-hung dusk with her.

'Poor dear Amy!' he said.

Millie Evans gave a soft little sigh, as of a contented child. He had expressed with the most ruthless accuracy exactly what she wished him to feel. Then, in the manner of a woman whose nature is warped throughout by a slight but ingrained falsity, she spoke as if it was not she who had prompted the three words which she had almost made him say.

'She is enjoying herself so,' she said. 'I have never seen Cousin Amy look so thoroughly pleased and contented. I thought she looked so charming, too, and what dear, plump little feet she has. But, my dear, it was rather a surprise when you and she were announced. It looked as if this poor Cleopatra was going to be Antony-less! Dear me, what a word.'

Here was a more direct appeal, and again Major Ames was powerless in her soft clutch. Hers was not exactly an iron hand in a velvet glove, but a hand made of fly-catching paper. She had taken her glove off now. And he was beginning to stick to her.

'Pshaw!' he said.

That, again, had a perfectly satisfactory sound to her ears. The very abruptness and bluffness of it pleased her more than any protestation could have done. He was so direct, so shy, so manly.

She laughed softly.

'Hush, you mustn't say those things,' she said. 'Ah, there is the band beginning, and it is our dance. But let us just walk through the shrubbery before we go back. The dusk and quiet are such a relief after the glare. Lyndhurst - ah, dear me. Cousin Lyndhurst I ought to say - you really must not go home till my little dance is quite finished. You make things go so well. Dear Wilfred is quite useless to me. Does he not look an old darling as Timon of Athens? A sort of mixture between George the Fourth in tights and a lion tamer.'

Mrs Evans was feeling more actively alive tonight than she had felt for years. Her tongue, which was generally a rather halting adjutant to her glances and little sinuous movements, was almost vivified to wit. Certainly her description of her husband had acuteness and a sense of the ludicrous to inspire it. Through the boughs of laburnums in the shrubbery they could see him now, escorting the tallest and oldest Cleopatra, who was Mrs Brooks, to the end of the garden. Dimly, through the curtain of intervening gloom, they saw the populous wooden floor that had been laid down on the grass; Mrs Ames - the dance was a polka - was frankly pirouetting in the arms of a redoubtable Falstaff. Mrs Altham was wrestling with the Apothecary, and Elsie Evans, one of the few young people present, was vainly trying to galvanize

General Fortescue, thinly disguised as Henry VII, into some semblance of activity.

Mrs Evans gave another sigh, a sigh of curious calibre.

'It all seems so distant,' she said. 'All the lights and dancing are less real than the shadows and the stillness.'

That was not quite extemporaneous; she had thought over something of the sort. It had the effect of making Major Ames feel suddenly hot with an anxious kind of heat. He was beginning to perceive the truth of that which he had foppishly imagined in his own self-communings, namely, that this 'poor little lady' was very, very much attached to him. He had often dwelt on the thought before with odious self-centred satisfaction; now the thought was less satisfactory; it was disquieting and mildly alarming. Like the fly on the flypaper, with one leg already englued, he put down a second to get leverage with which to free the first, and found that it was adhering also.

Mrs Evans spoke again.

'I took such pleasure in all the preparations.' she said. 'You were so much interested in it all. Tell me, Cousin Lyndhurst, that you are not disappointed.'

It was hardly possible for him to do less than what he did. What he did was little enough. He pressed the arm that lay in his rather close to his white toga, and an unwonted romanticism of speech rose to his lips.

'You have enchanted me,' he said. 'Me, us, all of us.'

She gave a little laugh; in the dusk it sounded no louder than a breeze stirring.

'You needn't have added that,' she said.

Where she stood a diaper of light and shadow played over her. A little spray of laburnum between her face and the lights on the lawn outside, swaying gently in a breeze that had gone astray in this calm night, cast wavering shadows over her. Now her arms shone white under freckles of shadow, now it was her face that was a moon to him. Or again, both would be in shade and a diamond star on her bright yellow hair concentrated all the light into itself. All the elusive mysterious charm of her womanhood was there, made more real by the fantastic setting. He was kindled to a greater warmth than he had yet known, but, all the time, some dreadful creature in his semi-puritanical semi-immoral brain, told him that this was all 'devilish naughty'. He was as unused to such scruples as he was unused to such temptations, and in some curious fashion he felt as ashamed of the one as he felt afraid of the other. At length he summed up the whole of these despicable conclusions.

'Will you give me just one kiss, Millie!' he said; 'just one cousin kiss, before we go and dance?'

Such early worms next morning in Major Ames' garden as had escaped the early bird, must certainly have all been caught and laid out flat by the garden roller, so swift and incessant were its journeyings. For though the dawn had overspread the sky with the hueless tints of approaching day when Antony and Cleopatra were charioteered home again by a somnolent cabman; though Major Ames' repose had been of the most fragmentary kind, and though breakfast, in anticipation of late hours, had been ordered the night before at an unusual half past nine, he found his bed an intolerable abode by seven o'clock, and had hoped to expatriate somewhat disquieting thoughts from his mind by the application of his limbs to severe bodily exertion.

He and his wife had been the last guests to leave; indeed, after the others had gone they lingered a little, smoking a final cigarette. Even Mrs Ames had been persuaded to light one, but a convulsive paroxysm of coughing, which made the pear-shaped pearl to quiver and shake like an aspen leaf, led her to throw it away, saying she enjoyed it very much. He had danced with Mrs Evans three or four times; three or four times they had sat in the cool darkness of the shrubbery, and he had said to her several things which at the moment it seemed imperative to say, but which he did not really mean. But as the evening went on he had meant them more; she had a helpless, childlike charm about her that began to stir his senses. And yet below that childlike confiding manner he was dimly aware that there was an eager woman's soul that sought him. Her charm was a weapon; a very efficient will wielded it. All the same, he reflected as the honest dews of toil poured from his forehead this morning in the hot early sunlight, he had not said very much . . . he had said that Riseborough was a different place since she - or had he said 'they'? had come there; that her eyes looked black in the starlight, that - honestly, he could not remember anything more intimate than this. But that which had made his bed intolerable was the sense that the situation had not terminated last night, that his boat, so to speak, had not been drawn up safely ashore, but was still in the midst of accelerating waters. And yet it was in his own power to draw the boat ashore at any moment; he had but to take a decisive stroke to land, to step out and beach it, to return - surely it was not difficult - to his normal thoughts and activities. For years his garden, his club, his domestic concerns, his daily paper, had provided him with a sufficiency of pursuits; he had but to step back into their safe if monotonous circle, and look upon these disturbances as episodic. But already he had ceased to think of Mrs Evans as 'dear little woman' or 'poor little woman'; somehow it seemed as if she had got her finger - to use a prosaic metaphor - into his works. She was prodding about among the internal wheels and springs of his mechanism. Yet that was stating his case too strongly; it was that of contingency that he was afraid. But with the curious irresponsibility of a rather selfish and unimaginative man, the fact that he had allowed himself to prod about in her internal mechanism represented itself to him as an unimportant and negligible detail. It was only when she began prodding about in him, producing, as it were, extraordinary little whirrings and racings of wheels that had long gone slow and steady, that he began to think that anything significant was occurring. But, after all, there was nothing like a pull at the garden roller for giving a fellow an appetite for breakfast and for squashing worms and unprofitable reflections.

Though half past nine had seemed 'late enough for anybody', as Mrs Ames had said the evening before, it was not till nearly ten that she put an extra spoonful of tea into her silver teapot, for she felt that she needed a more than usually fortifying beverage, to nullify her disinclination for the day's routine. The sight of her Cleopatra costume also, laid upon the sofa in her bedroom, and shone upon by a cheerful and uncompromising summer sun, had awakened in her mind a certain discontent, a certain sense of disappointment, of age, of grievance. The gilt paper had moulted off one of the sandal straps, a spilt dropping of strawberry ice made a disfiguring spot on the tunic of Arab shawl, and she herself felt vaguely ungilded and disfigured.

The cigarette, too - she had so often said in the most liberal manner that she did not think it wicked of women to smoke, but only horrid. Certainly she did not feel wicked this morning, but as certainly she felt disposed to consider anybody else horrid, and - and possibly wicked. Decidedly a cup of strong tea was indicated.

Major Ames had gone upstairs again to have his bath, and to dress after his exercise in the garden, and came down a few minutes later, smelling of soap, with a jovial boisterousness of demeanour that smelt of unreality.

'Good morning, my dear Amy,' he said. 'And how do you feel after the party? I've been up a couple of hours; nothing like a spell of exercise to buck one up after late hours.'

'Will you have your tea now, Lyndhurst?' she asked.

'Have it now, or wait till I get it, eh? I'll have it now. Delicious! I always say that nobody makes tea like you.'

Now boisterous spirits at breakfast were not usual with Major Ames, and, as has been said, his wife easily detected a false air about them. Her vague sense of disappointment and grievance began to take more solid outlines.

'It is delightful to see you in such good spirits, Lyndhurst,' she observed, with a faint undertone of acidity. 'Sitting up late does not usually agree with you.'

There was enough here to provoke repartee. Also his superficial boisterousness was rapidly disappearing before his wife's acidity, like stains at the touch of ammonia.

'It does not, in this instance, seem to have agreed with you, my dear,' he said. 'I hope you have not got a headache. It was unwise of you to stop so late. However, no doubt we shall feel better after breakfast. Shall I give you some bacon? Or will you try something that appears to be fish?'

'A little kedjeree, please,' said Mrs Ames, pointedly ignoring this innuendo on her cook.

'Kedjeree, is it? Well, well, live and learn.'

'If you have any complaint to make about Jephson,' said she, 'pray do so.'

'No, not at all. One does not expect, a cordon bleu. But I dare say Mrs Evans pays no more for her cook than we do, and look at the supper last night.'

CHAPTER SEVEN

'I thought the quails were peculiarly tasteless,' said Mrs Ames; 'and if you are to be grand and have péches à la Melba, I should prefer to offer my guests real peaches and proper ice cream, instead of tinned peaches and custard. I say nothing about the champagne, because I scarcely tasted it.'

'Well then, my dear, I'm sure you are quite right not to criticize it. All I can say is that I never want to eat a better supper.'

Suddenly Mrs Ames became aware that another piece of solid outline had appeared round her vague discontent and reaction.

'No doubt you think that all Millie's arrangements are perfect in every way,' she observed.

'I don't know what you mean by that,' said he, rather hotly; 'but I do know that when a woman has been putting herself to all that trouble and expense to entertain her friends, her friends would show a nicer spirit if they refrained from carping and depreciating her.'

'No amount of appreciation would make tinned peaches fresh, or turn custard into ice cream,' said Mrs Ames, laying down the fork with which she had dallied with the kedjeree, which indeed was but a sordid sort of creation. 'It is foolish to pretend that a thing is perfect when it is not. Nor do I consider her manners as a hostess by any means perfect. She looked as cross as two sticks when poor Mrs Brooks appeared. I suppose she thought that nobody had a right to be Cleopatra besides herself. To be sure poor Mrs Brooks looked very silly, but if everybody who looked silly last night should have stayed away, there would not have been much dancing done.'

She took several more sips of the strong tea, while he unfolded and appeared engrossed in the morning paper, and under their stimulating influence saw suddenly and distinctly how ill-advised was her attack. She had yielded to temporary ill temper, which is always a mistake. It was true that in her mind she was feeling that Lyndhurst last night had spent far too much time with his hostess; in a word, she felt jealous. It was, therefore, abominably stupid, from a merely worldly point of view, to criticize and belittle Millie to him. If there was absolutely no ground for her jealousy - which at present was but a humble little green bud - such an attack was uncalled for; if there was ground it was most foolish, at this stage, at any rate, to give him the least cause for suspecting that it existed. But she was wise enough now, not to hasten to repair her mistake, but to repair it slowly and deliberately, as if no repair was going on at all.

'But I must say the garden looked charming,' she said after a pause. 'Did she tell you, Lyndhurst, whether it was she or her husband who saw to the lighting? The scheme was so comprehensive; it took in the whole of the lawn; there was nothing patchy about it. I suspect Dr Evans planned it; it looked somehow more like a man's work.'

A look of furtive guilt passed over the Major's face; luckily it was concealed by the Daily Mail.

'No; Evans told me himself that he had nothing to do with it,' he said. 'It was pretty, I thought; very pretty.'

'If the nights continue hot,' said she, 'it would be nice to have the garden illuminated one night, if dear Millie did not think we were appropriating her ideas. I do not think she would; she is above that sort of thing. Well, dear, I must go and order dinner. Have you any wishes?'

Clearly it was wiser, from the Major's point of view, to accept this bouquet of olive branches. After all, Amy was far too sensible to imagine that there could be anything to rouse the conjugal watchdog. Nor was there; hastily he told himself that. A cousinly kiss, which at the moment he would willingly have foregone.

Certainly last night he had been a little super-stimulated. There was the irresponsibility of fancy dress, there was the knowledge that Millie was not insensitive to him; there was the sense of his own big, shapely legs in tights, there was dancing and lanterns, and all had been potent intoxicants to Riseborough, which for so long had practised teetotalism with regard to such excitements. Amy herself had been so far carried away by this effervescence of gaiety as to smoke a cigarette, and Heaven knew how far removed from her ordinary code of conduct was such an adventure. Generously, he had forborne to brandish that cigarette as a weapon against her during this acrimonious episode at breakfast, and he had no conscious intention of hanging it, like Damocles' sword over her head, in case she pursued her critical and carping course against Millie. But whatever he had said last night, she had done that. Without meaning to make use of his knowledge, he knew it was in his power to do so. What would not Mrs Altham, for instance, give to be informed by an eyewitness that Mrs Ames had blown - it was no more than that - on the abhorred weed? So, conscious of a position that he could make offensive at will, he accepted the olive branch, and suggested a cold curry for lunch.

Breakfast at Mrs Altham's reflected less complicated conditions of mind. Both she and her husband were extremely pleased with themselves, and in a state of passion with regard to everybody else. Since their attitude was typical of the view that Riseborough generally took of last night's festivity, it may be given compendiously in a rhetorical flight of Mrs Altham's, with which her husband was in complete accord.

In palliation, it may be mentioned that they had both partaken of large quantities of food at an unusual hour. It is through the body that the entry is made by the subtle gateways of the soul, and vitriolic comments in the morning are often the precise equivalent of unusual indulgence the night before.

'Well, I'm sure if I had known,' said Mrs Altham, 'I should not have taken the trouble I did. Of course, everybody said 'How lovely your dress is,' simply to make one say the same to them. And I never want to hear the word Cleopatra again, Henry, so pray don't repeat it. Fancy Mrs Ames appearing as Cleopatra, and us taking the trouble to say we were Antony and Cleopatra ten years later! Twenty years before would have been more the date if we had known. Perhaps I am wrong, but when a woman arrives at Mrs Ames' time of life, whether she dyes her hair or not, she is wiser to keep her feet concealed, not to mention what she must have looked like in the face of half the tradesmen of Riseborough who were lining the pavements when she stepped out of her cab. I thought I heard a great roar of laughter as we were driving up the High Street; I should not wonder if it was the noise of them all laughing as she got out of her carriage. Of course, it was all very prettily done, as far as poor Mrs Evans was concerned, but I wonder that Dr Evans likes her to spend money like that, for, however unsuitable the supper was, I feel sure it was very expensive, for it was all truffles and aspic. There must have been a sirloin of beef in the cup of soup I took between two of the dances, and strong soup like that at dead of night fills one up dreadfully. And Mrs Brooks appearing as another Cleopatra, after all I had said about Hermione! Well, I'm sure if she chooses to make a silly of herself like that, it is nobody's concern but hers. She looked like nothing so much as a great white mare with the staggers. If you are going up to the club, Henry, I should not wonder if I came out with you. It seems to me a very stuffy morning, and a little fresh air would do me good. As for the big German ruby in your cap, I don't believe a soul noticed it. They were all looking at Mrs Evans' long white arms. Poor thing, she is probably very anaemic; I never saw such pallor. I saw little of her the whole evening. She seemed to be popping in and out of the shrubbery like a rabbit all the time with Major Ames. I should not wonder if Mrs Ames was giving him a good talking-to at this moment.'

Then, like all the rest of Riseborough, and unlike the scorpion, there was a blessing instead of a sting in her tail.

'But certainly it was all very pretty,' she said; 'though it all seemed very strange at the time. I can hardly believe this morning that we were all dressed up like that, hopping about out of doors. Fancy dress balls are very interesting; you see so much of human nature, and though I looked the procession up and down, Henry, I saw nobody so well dressed as you. But I suppose there is a lot of jealousy everywhere. And anyhow, Mrs Evans has quite ousted Mrs Ames now. Nobody will talk about anything but last night for the next fortnight, and I'm sure that when Mrs Ames had the conjurer who turned the omelette into the watch, we had all forgotten about it three days afterwards. And after all, Mrs Evans is a very pleasant and hospitable woman, and I wouldn't have missed that party for anything. If you hear anything at the club about her wanting to sell her Chinese lanterns and fairy lights second-hand, Henry, or if you find any reason to believe that she had hired them out for the night from the Mercantile Stores, you might ask the price, and if it is reasonable get a couple of dozen. If the weather continues as hot as this we might illuminate the garden when we give our August dinner party. At least, I suppose Mrs Evans does not consider that she has a monopoly of lighting up gardens!'

Henry found himself quite in accord with the spirit of this address.

'I will remember, my dear,' he said; 'if I hear anything said at the club. I shall go up there soon, for I should not be surprised if most of the members spent their morning there. I think I will have another cup of tea.'

'You have had two already,' said his wife.

He was feeling a little irritable.

'Then this will make three,' he observed.

Mrs Evans, finally, had breakfast in her room. When she came downstairs, she found that her husband had already left the house on his visits, which was a relief. She felt that if she had seen his cheerful smiling face this morning, she would almost have hated it.

She ordered dinner, and then went out into the garden. Workmen were already there, removing the dancing floor, and her gardener was collecting the fairy lights in trays, and carrying them indoors. Here and there were charred, burnt places on the grass, and below the mulberry tree the debris of supper had not yet been removed. But the shrubbery, as last night, was sequestered and cool, and she sat for an hour there on the garden bench overlooking the lawn. Little flakes of golden sunlight filtered down through the foliage, and a laburnum, delicate-sprayed, oscillated in the light breeze. She scarcely knew whether she was happy or not, and she gave no thought to that. But she felt more consciously alive than ever before.

DISCUSSION about the fancy dress ball, as Mrs Altham had said, was paramount over all other topics for at least a fortnight after the event, and the great question which annually became of such absorbing interest during July - namely, as to where to spend August, was dwarfed and never attained to its ordinary proportions till quite late on in the month. These discussions did not, as a rule, bear fruit of any kind, since, almost without exception, everybody spent August exactly where August had been spent by him for the last dozen years or so, but it was clearly wise to consider the problem afresh every year, and be prepared, in case some fresh resort suggested itself, to change the habit of years, or at least to consider doing so. The lists of hotels at the end of Bradshaw, and little handbooks published by the South-Eastern Railway were, as a rule, almost the only form of literature indulged in during these evenings of July, and Mr Altham, whose imagination was always fired by pictures of ships, often studied the sailings of River Plate steamers, and considered that the fares were very reasonable, especially steerage. The fact that he was an appalling bad sailor in no way diminished the zest with which he studied their sailings and the prices thereof. Subsequently he and Mrs Altham always spent August at Littlestone-on-Sea, in a completely detached villa called Blenheim, where a capable Scotchwoman, who, to add colour to the illusion, maintained that her name really was Churchill, boarded and lodged them on solid food and feather beds. During July, it may be remarked, Mrs Altham usually contrived to quarrel with her cook, who gave notice. Thus there was one mouth less to feed while they were away, and yearly, on their return, they had the excitement of new and surprising confections from the kitchen.

Mrs Ames, it may be remembered, had already enjoyed a fortnight's holiday at Overstrand this year, and the last week of July saw her still disinclined to make holiday plans. They had taken a sort of bungalow near Deal for the last year or two, which, among other advantages, was built in such a manner that any remark made in any part of the house could be heard in any other part of the house. It was enough almost for her to say, as she finished dressing, 'We are ready for breakfast,' to hear Parker replying from the kitchen, 'The kettle's just on the boil, ma'am.' This year, however, she had been late in inquiring whether it was vacant for August, and she found, when her belated letter was answered, that it was already engaged.

This fact she broke to her husband and Harry, who had returned from Cambridge with hair unusually wild and lank, with tempered indignation.

'Considering how many years we have taken it,' she said, 'I must say that I think they should have told us before letting it over our heads like this. But I always thought that Mrs Mackenzie was a most grasping sort of person who would be likely to take the first offer that turned up, and

I'm sure the house was never very comfortable. I have no doubt we can easily find a better without much bother!'

'My bedroom ceiling always leaked,' said Harry; 'and there was nowhere to write at!'

Mrs Ames had finished her breakfast and got up. She felt faintly in her mind that after the fancy dress ball it was time for her to do something original. Yet the whole idea was so novel . . . Riseborough would be sure to say that they had not been able to afford a holiday. But, after all, that mattered very little.

'I really don't know why we always take the trouble to go away to an uncomfortable lodging during August,' she said, 'and leave our own comfortable house standing vacant.'

Major Ames, had he been a horse, would have pricked up his ears at this. But the human ear being unadapted to such movements, he contented himself with listening avidly. He had seen little of Millie this last fortnight, and was beginning to realize how much he missed her presence. Between them, it is true, they had come near to an intimacy which had its dangers, which he really feared more than he desired, but he felt, with that self-deception that comes so easily to those who know nothing about themselves, that he was on his guard now. Meantime, he missed her, and guessed quite truly that she missed him. And, poor prig, he told himself that he had no right to cut off that which gave her pleasure. He could be Spartan over his own affairs, if so minded, but he must not play Lycurgus to others. And an idea that had privately occurred to him, which at the time seemed incapable of realization, suddenly leaped into the possible horizons.

'And you always complain of the dampness of strange houses, Lyndhurst,' she added; 'and as Harry says, he has no place for writing and study. Why should we go away at all?

I am sure, after the excitement of the last month, it would be a complete rest to remain here when everybody else is gone. I have not had a moment to myself this last month, and I should not be at all sorry to stop quietly here.'

Major Ames knew with sufficient accuracy the influence he had over his wife. He realized, that is to say, as far as regarded the present instance, that slight opposition on his part usually produced a corresponding firmness on hers. Accentuated opposition produced various results; sometimes he won, sometimes she. But mild remonstrance always confirmed her views in opposition to his. He had a plan of his own on this occasion, and her determination to remain in Riseborough would prove to be in alliance with it. Therefore he mildly remonstrated.

'You would regret it before the month was out,' he said. 'For me, I'm an old campaigner, and I hope I can make myself comfortable anywhere. But you would get bored before the end of August, Amy, and when you get bored your digestion is invariably affected.'

'I should like to stop in Riseborough,' said Harry. 'I hate the sea.'

'You will go wherever your mother settles to go, my boy,' said Major Ames, still pursuing his plan. 'If she wishes to go to Sheffield for August, you and I will go too, and - and no doubt learn something useful about cutlery. But don't try stopping in Riseborough, my dear Amy. At least, if you take my advice, you won't.'

Major Ames was not very intelligent, but the highest intelligence could not have done better. He had learned the trick of slight opposition, just as a stupid dog with a Conservative master can learn to growl for Asquith by incessant repetition. When it has learned it, it does it right. The Major had done it right on this occasion.

CHAPTER EIGHT

'I do not see why Harry should not have a voice in the question of where we spend his vacation,' she said. 'Certainly your room at the bungalow, Lyndhurst, was comfortable enough, but that was the only decent room in the house. In any case we cannot get the bungalow for this August. Have you any other plans as to where we should go?'

There was room for a little more of his policy of opposition.

'Well, now, Brighton,' he said. 'Why not Brighton? There's a club there; I dare say I should get a little Bridge in the evening, and no doubt you would pick up some acquaintances, Amy. I think the Westbournes went there last year.'

This remarkable reason for going to Brighton made Mrs Ames almost epigrammatic.

'And then we could go on to Margate,' she remarked, 'and curry favour there.'

'By all means, my dear,' said he. 'I dare say the curry would be quite inexpensive.'

Mrs Ames opened the door on to the verandah.

'Pray let me know, Lyndhurst,' she said, 'if you have any serious proposition to make.'

It was Major Ames' custom to start work in the garden immediately after breakfast, but this morning he got out one of his large-sized cheroots instead (these conduced to meditation), and established himself in a chair on the verandah. His mental development was not, in most regards, of a very high or complex order, but he possessed that rather rare attainment of being able to sit down and think about one thing to the exclusion of others. With most of us to sit down and think about one thing soon resolves itself into a confused survey of most other things; Major Ames could do better than that, for he could, and on this occasion did exclude all other topics from his mind, and at the end return, so to speak, 'bringing his sheaves with him.' He had made a definite and reasonable plan.

Harry had communicated the interesting fact of his passion for Mrs Evans to the Omar Khayyam Club, and was, of course, bound to prosecute his nefarious intrigue. He had already written several galloping lyrics, a little loose in grammar and rhyme, to his enchantress, which he had copied into a small green morocco notebook, the title page of which he had inscribed as 'Dedicated to M. E.'. This looked a Narcissus-like proceeding to anyone who did not remember what Mrs Evans' initials were. This afternoon, feeling the poetic afflatus blowing a gale within him, but having nothing definite to say, he decided to call on the inspirer of his muse, in order to gather fresh fuel for his fire. Arrayed in a very low collar, which showed the full extent of his rather scraggy neck, and adorned with a red tie, for socialism was no less an orthodoxy in the club than atheistic principles and illicit love, he set secretly out, and had the good fortune to find the goddess alone, and was welcomed with that rather timid, childlike deference that he had found so adorable before.

'But how good of you to come and see me,' she said, 'when I'm sure you must have so many friends wanting you. I think it is so kind.'

Clearly she was timid; she did not know her power. Her eyes were bluer than ever; her hair was of palest gold, 'As I remembered her of old,' he thought to himself, referring to the evening at the end of June. Indeed, there was a poem dated June 28, rather a daring one.

'The kindness is entirely on your side,' he said, 'in letting me come, and' - he longed to say - 'worship,' but did not quite dare - 'and have tea with you.'

'Dear me, that is a selfish sort of kindness,' she said. 'Let us go into the garden. I think it was very unkind of you, Mr Harry, not to come to my dance last week. But of course you Cambridge men have more serious things to think about than little country parties.'

'I thought about nothing else but your dance for days,' said he; 'but my tutor simply refused to let me come down for it. A narrow, pedantic fellow, who I don't suppose ever danced. Tell me about your dress; I like to picture you in a fancy dress.'

She could not help appearing to wish to attract. It was as much the fault of the way her head was set on to her neck, of the colour of her eyes, as of her mind.

'Oh, quite a simple white frock,' she said; 'and a few pearls. They - they wanted me to go as Cleopatra. So silly - me with a grown-up daughter. But my husband insisted.'

The fancy dress ball had not been talked about at Mrs Ames' lately, and he had heard nothing about it in the two days he had been at home. Both his parents had reason for letting it pass into the region of things that are done with.

'Did mother and father go?' he asked. 'I suppose they felt too old to dress up?'

'Oh, no. They came as Antony and Cleopatra. Have they not told you? Cousin Amy looked so - so interesting. And your father was splendid as Mark Antony.'

'Then was Dr Evans Mark Antony too?' asked Harry.

'No; he was Timon of Athens.'

'Then who was your Mark Antony?' he asked.

Mrs Evans felt herself flushing, and her annoyance at herself made her awkward in the pouring out of tea.

She felt that Harry's narrow, gimlet-like eyes were fixed on her.

'See how stupid I am,' she said. 'I have spilled your tea in the saucer. Dear Mr Harry, we had heaps of Cleopatras: Mrs Altham was one, Mrs Brooks was another. We danced with Hamlets, and - and anybody.'

But this crude, ridiculous youth, she felt, had some idea in his head.

'And did father and mother dance together all the evening?' he asked.

She felt herself growing impatient.

'Of course not. Everybody danced with everybody. We had quadrilles; all sorts of things.'

Then, with the mistaken instinct that makes us cautious in the wrong place, she determined to say a little more.

'But your father was so kind to me,' she said. 'He helped me with all the arrangements. I could never have managed it except for him. We had tremendous days of talking and planning about it. Now tell me all about Cambridge.'

But Harry was scenting a sonnet of the most remarkable character. It might be called The Rivals, and would deal with a situation which the Omar Khayyam Club would certainly feel to be immensely 'parful'.

'I suppose mother helped you, too?' he said.

This was Byronic, lacerating. She had to suffer as well as he . . . there was a pungent line already complete. 'But who had suffered as much as me?' was the refrain. There were thrills in store for the Omar Khayyam Club. After a sufficiency of yellow wine.

'Cousin Amy was away,' said Mrs Evans. 'She was staying at Cromer till just before my little dance. That is not far from Cambridge, is it? I suppose she came over to see you.'

Harry spared her, and did not press these questions. But enough had been said to show that she had broken faith with him. 'Rivals' could suitably become quite incoherent towards the close. Incoherency was sometimes a great convenience, for exclamatory rhymes were not rare.

He smoothed the lank hair off his forehead, and tactfully changed the subject.

'And I suppose you are soon going away now,' he said. 'I am lucky to have seen you at all. We are going to stop here all August, I think. My mother does not want to go away. Nor do I; not that they either of them care about that.'

Mrs Evans' slight annoyance with him was suddenly merged in interest.

'How wise!' she said. 'It is so absurd to go to stay somewhere uncomfortably instead of remaining comfortably. I wish we were doing the same. But my husband always has to go to Harrogate for a few weeks. And he likes me to be with him. I shall think of you all and envy you stopping here in this charming Riseborough.'

'You like it?' asked Harry.

'How should I not with so many delightful people being friendly to me? Relations too; Cousin Amy, for instance, and Major Ames, and, let me see, if Mrs Ames is my cousin, surely you are cousin Harry?'

Harry became peculiarly fascinating, and craned his long neck forward.

'Oh, leave out the "cousin",' he said.

'How sweet of you - Harry,' she said.

That, so to speak, extracted the poison-fangs from the projected 'Rivals', and six mysterious postcards were placed by the author's hand in the pillar box that evening. Each consisted of one mystic sentence. 'She calls me by my Christian name.' By a most convenient circumstance, too apt to be considered accidental, there had here come to birth an octosyllabic line, of honeyed sweetness and simplicity. He was not slow to take advantage of it, and the moon setting not long before daybreak saw another completed gem of the M. E. series.

Mrs Evans that afternoon, like Major Ames that morning, 'sat and thought,' after Harry had left her. Independently of the fact that all admirers, even the weirdest, always found welcome in her pale blue eyes, she felt really grateful to Harry, for he had given her the information on which she based a plan which was quite as sound and simple as Major Ames', and was designed to secure the same object. Since the night of the fancy dress ball she had only seen him once or twice, and never privately, and the greater vitality which, by the wondrous processes of affinity, he had stirred in her, hungered for its sustenance. It cannot be said that she was even now really conscious in herself of disloyalty to her husband, or that she actually contemplated any breach of faith. She had not at present sufficient force of feeling to imagine a decisive situation; but she could at most lash her helm, so to speak, so that the action of the wind would take her boat in the direction in which she wished to go, and then sit idly on deck, saying that she was not responsible for the course she was pursuing. The wind, the tide, the currents were irresistibly impelling her; she had nothing to do with the rudder; having tied it, she did not touch it. Like the majority in this world of miserable sinners, she did not actively court the danger she desired, but she hung about expectant of it. At the same time she kept an anxious eye on the shore towards which she was driving. Was it really coming closer? If so, why did she seem to have made no way lately?

Today her plan betokened a more active hand in what she thought of as fate, but unfortunately, though it was as sound in itself as Major Ames', it was made independently and ignorantly of that which had prompted his slight opposition this morning, so that, while each plan was admirable enough in itself, the two, taken in conjunction, would, if successful, result in a fiasco almost sublime in its completeness. The manner of which was as follows.

Elsie, it so happened, was not at home that evening, and she and her husband dined alone, and strolled out in the garden afterwards.

'You will miss your chess this evening, dear,' she said. 'Or would it amuse you to give me a queen and a few bishops and knights, and see how long it takes you to defeat me? Or shall we spend a little cosy chatty evening together? I hope no horrid people will be taken ill, and send for you.'

'So do I, little woman,' he said (she was getting to detest the appellation). 'And as if I shouldn't enjoy a quiet evening of talk with you more than fifty games of chess! But, dear me, I shall be glad to get away to Harrogate this year! I need a month of it badly. I shall positively enjoy the foul old rotten-egg smell.'

She gave a little shudder.

'Oh, don't talk of it,' she said. 'It is bad enough without thinking of it beforehand.'

'Poor little woman! Almost a pity you are not gouty too. Then we should both look forward to it.'

She sat down on one of the shrubbery seats, and drew aside her skirts, making room for him to sit beside her.

'Yes, but as I am not gouty, Wilfred,' she said. 'It is no use wishing I was. And I do hate Harrogate so. I wonder -'

She gave a little sigh and put her arm within his.

'Well, what's the little woman wondering now?' he asked.

'I hardly like to tell you. You are always so kind to me that I don't know why I am afraid. Wilfred, would you think it dreadful of me, if I suggested not going with you this year? I'm sure it makes me ill to be there. You will have Elsie; you will play chess as usual with her all evening. You see all morning you are at your baths, and you usually are out bicycling all afternoon with her. I don't think you know how I hate it.'

She had begun in her shy, tentative manner. But her voice grew more cold and decided. She put forward her arguments like a woman who has thought it all carefully over, as indeed she had.

'But what will you do with yourself, my dear?' he said. 'It seems a funny plan. You can't stop here alone.'

She sat up, taking her hand from his arm.

'Indeed, I should not be as lonely here as I am at Harrogate,' she said. 'We don't know anybody there, and if you think of it, I am really alone most of the time. It is different for you, because it is doing you good, and, as I say, you are bicycling with Elsie all the afternoon, and you play chess together in the evening.'

A shade of trouble and perplexity came over the doctor's face; the indictment, for it was hardly less than that, was as well ordered and digested as if it had been prepared for a forensic argument. And the calm, passionless voice went on.

'Think of my day there,' she said, going into orderly detail. 'After breakfast you go off to your baths, and I have to sit in that dreadful sitting room while they clear the things away. Even a hotel would be more amusing than those furnished lodgings; one could look at the people going in and out. Or if I go for a stroll in the morning, I get tired, and must rest in the afternoon. You come in to lunch, and go off with Elsie afterwards. That is quite right; the exercise is good for you, but what is the use of my being there? There is nobody for me to go to see, nobody comes to see me. Then we have dinner, and I have the excitement of learning where you and Elsie have been bicycling. You two play chess after dinner, and I have the excitement of being told who has won. Here, at any rate, I can sit in a room that doesn't smell of dinner, or I can sit in the garden. I have my own books and things about me, and there are people I know whom I can see and talk to.'

He got up, and began walking up and down the path in front of the bench where they had been sitting, his kindly soul in some perplexity.

'Nothing wrong, little woman?' he asked.

'Certainly not. Why should you think that? I imagine there is reason enough in what I have told you. I do get so bored there, Wilfred. And I hate being bored. I am sure it is not good for me, either. Try to picture my life there, and see how utterly different it is from yours. Besides, as I say, it is doing you good all the time, and as you yourself said, you welcome the thought of that horrible smelling water.'

He still shuffled up and down in the dusk. That, too, got on her nerves.

'Pray sit down, Wilfred,' she said. 'Your walking about like that confuses me. And surely you can say "Yes" or "No" to me. If you insist on my going with you, I shall go. But I shall think it very unreasonable of you.'

'But I can't say "Yes" or "No" like that, little woman,' he said. 'I don't imagine you have thought how dull Riseborough will be during August. Everybody goes away, I believe.'

For a moment she thought of telling him that the Ames' were going to stop here: then, with entirely misplaced caution, she thought wiser to keep that to herself. She, guilty in the real reason for wishing to remain here, though coherent and logical enough in the account she had given him of her reason, thought, grossly wronging him, that some seed of suspicion might hereby enter her husband's mind.

'There is sure to be someone here,' she said. 'The Althams, for instance, do not go away till the middle of August.'

'You do not particularly care for them,' said he.

'No, but they are better than nobody. All day at Harrogate I have nobody. It is not companionship to sit in the room with you and Elsie playing chess. Besides, the Westbournes will be at home. I shall go over there a great deal, I dare say. Also I shall be in my own house, which is comfortable, and which I am fond of. Our lodgings at Harrogate disgust me. They are all oilcloth and plush; there is nowhere to sit when they are clearing away.'

His face was still clouded.

'But it is so odd for a married woman to stop alone like that,' he said.

'I think it is far odder for her husband to want her to spend a month of loneliness and boredom in lodgings,' she said. 'Because I have never complained, Wilfred, you think I haven't detested it. But on thinking it over it seems to me more sensible to tell you how I detest it, and ask you that I shouldn't go.'

He was silent a moment.

'Very well, little woman,' he said at length. 'You shall do as you please.'

Instantly the cold precision of her speech changed. She gave that little sigh of conscious content with which she often woke in the morning, and linked her arm into his again.

'Ah, that is dear of you,' she said. 'You are always such a darling to me.'

He was not a man to give grudging consents, or spoil a gift by offering it except with the utmost cordiality.

'I only hope you'll make a great success of it, little woman,' he said. 'And it must be dull for you at Harrogate. So that's settled, and we're all satisfied. Let us see if Elsie has come in yet.'

She laughed softly.

'You are a dear,' she said again.

Wilfred Evans was neither analytical regarding himself nor curious about analysis that might account for the action of others. Just as in his professional work he was rather old-fashioned, but eminently safe and sensible, so in the ordinary conduct of his life he did not seek for abstruse causes and subtle motives. It was quite enough for him that his wife felt that she would be excruciatingly bored at Harrogate, and less acutely desolate here. On the other hand, it implied violation of one of the simplest customs of life that a wife should be in one place and her husband in another. That was vaguely disquieting to him. Disquieting also was the cold, precise manner with which she had conducted her case. A dozen times only, perhaps, in all their married life had she assumed this frozen rigidity of demeanour; each time he had succumbed before it. In the ordinary way, if their inclinations were at variance, she would coax and wheedle him into yielding or, though quietly adhering to her own opinion, she would let him have his way. But with her calm rigidity, rarely assumed, he had never successfully combated; there was a steeliness about it that he knew to be stronger than any opposition he could bring to it. Nothing seemed to affect it, neither argument nor conjugal command. She would go on saying 'I do not agree with you,' in the manner of cool water dripping on a stone. Or with the same inexorable quietness she would repeat, 'I feel very strongly about it: I think it very unkind of you.' And a sufficiency of that always had rendered his opposition impotent: her will, when once really aroused, seemed to paralyse his. Once or twice her line had turned out conspicuously ill. That seemed to make no difference: the cold, precise manner was on a higher plane than the material failure which had resulted therefrom. She would merely repeat, 'But it was the best thing to do under the circumstances.'

In this instance he wondered a little that she had used this manner over a matter that seemed so little vital as the question of Harrogate, but by next morning he had ceased to concern himself further with it. She was completely her usual self again, and soon after breakfast set off to accomplish some little errands in the town, looking in on him in his laboratory to know if there were any commissions she could do for him. His eye at the moment was glued to his microscope: a culture of staphylococcus absorbed him, and without looking up, he said -

'Nothing, thanks, little woman.'

He heard her pause: then she came across the room to him, and laid her cool hand on his shoulder.

'Wilfred, you are such a dear to me,' she said. 'You're not vexed with me?'

He interrupted his observations, and put his arm round her.

'Vexed?' he said. 'I'll tell you when I'm vexed.'

She smiled at him, dewily, timidly.

'That's all right, then,' she said.

So her plan was accomplished.

The affair of the staphylococcus did not long detain the doctor, and presently after Major Ames was announced. He had come to consult Dr Evans with regard to certain gouty symptoms into which the doctor inquired and examined.

'There's nothing whatever to worry about,' he said, after a very short investigation. 'I should recommend you to cut off alcohol entirely, and not eat meat more than once a day.

A fortnight's dieting will probably cure you. And take plenty of exercise. I won't give you any medicine. There is no use in taking drugs when you can produce the same effect by not taking other things.'

Major Ames fidgeted and frowned a little.

'I was thinking,' he said at length, 'of taking myself more thoroughly in hand than that. I've never approved of half-measures, and I can't begin now. If a tooth aches have it out, and be done with it. No fiddling about for me. Now my wife does not want to go away this August, and it seemed to me that it would be a very good opportunity for me to go, as you do, I think, and take a course of waters. Get rid of the tendency, don't you know, eradicate it. What do you say to that? Harrogate now; I was thinking of Harrogate, if you approved. Harrogate does wonders for gout, does it not?'

The doctor laughed.

'I am certainly hoping that Harrogate will do wonders for me,' he said. 'I go there every year. And no doubt many of us who are getting on in years would be benefited by it. But your symptoms are very slight. I think you will soon get rid of them if you follow the course I suggest.'

But Major Ames showed a strange desire for Harrogate.

'Well, I like to do things thoroughly,' he said. 'I like getting rid of a thing root and branch, you know. You see I may not get another opportunity. Amy likes me to go with her on her holiday in August, but there is no reason why I should stop in Riseborough. I haven't spoken to her yet, but if I could say that you recommended Harrogate, I'm sure she would wish me to go. Indeed, she would insist on my going. She is often anxious about my gouty tendencies, more anxious, as I often tell her, than she has any need to be. But an aunt of hers had an attack which went to her heart quite unexpectedly, and killed her, poor thing.

I think, indeed, it would be a weight off Amy's mind if she knew I was going to take myself thoroughly in hand, not tinker and peddle about with diet only. So would you be able to recommend me to go to Harrogate?'

'A course of Harrogate wouldn't be bad for any of us who eat a good dinner every night,' said Dr Evans. 'But I think that if you tried -'

Major Ames got up, waving all further discussion aside.

'That's enough, doctor,' he said. 'If it would do me good, I know Amy would wish me to go; you know what wives are. Now I'm pressed for time this morning, and so I am sure are you. By the way, you needn't mention my plan till I've talked it over with Amy. But about lodgings, now. Do you recommend lodgings or an hotel?'

Dr Evans did not mention that his wife was not going to be with him this year, for, having obtained permission to say that Harrogate would do him good, Major Ames had developed a prodigious hurry, and a few moments after was going jauntily home, with the address of Dr Evans' lodgings in his pocket. He trusted to his own powers of exaggeration to remove all possible opposition on his wife's part, and felt himself the devil of a diplomatist.

So his plan was arranged.

The third factor in this network of misconceived plots occurred the same morning. Mrs Ames, visiting the High Street on account of an advanced melon, met Cousin Millie on some similar errand to the butcher's on account of advanced cutlets, for the weather was trying. It was natural that she announced her intention of remaining in Riseborough with her family during August: it was natural also that Cousin Millie signified the remission from Harrogate. Cousin Amy was cordial on the subject, and returned home. Probably she would have mentioned this fact to her husband, if he had given her time to do it. But he was bursting with a more immediate communication.

'I didn't like to tell you before, Amy,' he said, 'because I didn't want to make you unnecessarily anxious. And there's no need for anxiety now.'

Mrs Ames was not very imaginative, but it occurred to her that the newly planted magnolia had not been prospering.

'No real cause for anxiety,' he said. 'But the fact is that I went to see Dr Evans this morning - don't be frightened, my dear - and got thoroughly overhauled by him, thoroughly overhauled. He said there was no reason for anxiety, assured me of it. But I'm gouty, my dear, there's no doubt of it, and of course you remember about your poor Aunt Harriet. Well, there it is. And he says Harrogate. A bore, of course, but Harrogate. But no cause for anxiety: he told me so twice.'

Mrs Ames gave one moment to calm, clear, oysterlike reflection, unhurried, unalarmed. There was no shadow of reason why she should tell him what Mrs Evans' plans were. But it was odd that she should suddenly decide to stop in Riseborough, instead of going to Harrogate, having heard from Harry that the Ames' were to remain at home, and Lyndhurst as suddenly be impelled to go to Harrogate, instead of stopping in Riseborough. A curious coincidence. Everybody seemed to be making plans. At any rate she would not add to their number, but only acquiesce in those which were made.

'My dear Lyndhurst, what an upset!' she said. 'Of course, if you tell me there is no cause for anxiety, I will not be anxious. Does Dr Evans recommend you to go to Harrogate now? You must tell me all he said. They always go in August, do they not? That will be pleasant for you. But I am afraid you will find the waters far from palatable.'

Major Ames felt that he had not made a sufficiently important impression.

'Of course, I told Dr Evans I could decide nothing till I had consulted you,' he said. 'It seems a great break-up to leave you and Harry here and go away like this. It was that I was thinking of, not whether waters are palatable or not. I have more than half a mind not to go. I daresay I shall worry through all right without.'

Again Mrs Ames made a little pause.

'You must do as Dr Evans tells you to do,' she said. 'I am sure he is not faddy or fussy.'

Major Ames' experience of him this morning fully endorsed this. Certainly he had been neither, whatever the difference between the two might be.

'Well, my dear, if both you and Dr Evans are agreed,' he said, 'I mustn't set myself up against you.'

'Now did he tell you where to go?'

'He gave me the address of his own lodgings.'

'What a convenient arrangement! Now, my dear, I beg you to waste no time. Send off a telegram, and pay the reply, and we'll pack you off tomorrow. I am sure it is the right thing to do.'

A sudden conviction, painfully real, that he was behaving currishly, descended on Major Ames. The feeling was so entirely new to him that he would have liked to put it down to an obsession of gout in a new place - the conscience, for instance, for he could hardly believe that he should be self-accused of paltry conduct. He felt as if there must be some mistake about it. He almost wished that Amy had made difficulties; then there would have been the compensatory idea that she was behaving badly too. But she could not have conducted herself in a more guilelessly sympathetic manner; she seemed to find no inherent improbability in Dr Evans having counselled Harrogate, no question as to the advisability of following his advice. It was almost unpleasant to him to have things made so pleasant.

But then this salutary impression was effaced, for anything that savoured of self-reproach could not long find harbourage in his mind. Instead, he pictured himself at Harrogate station, welcoming the Evans'. She would probably be looking rather tired and fragile after the journey, but he would have a cab ready for her, and tea would be awaiting them when they reached the lodgings . . .

A WEEK later Mrs Ames was sitting at breakfast, with Harry opposite her, expecting the early post, and among the gifts of the early post a letter from her husband. He had written one very soon after his arrival at Harrogate, saying that he felt better already. The waters, as Amy had conjectured, could not be described as agreeable, since their composition chiefly consisted of those particular ingredients which gave to rotten eggs their characteristic savour, but what, so said the valiant, did a bad taste in the mouth matter, if you knew it was doing you good? An excellent band encouraged the swallowing of this disagreeable fluid, and by lunch time baths and drinking were over for the day. He was looking forward to the Evans' arrival; it would be pleasant to see somebody he knew. He would write again before many days.

The post arrived; there was a letter for her in the Major's large sprawling handwriting, and she opened it. But it was scarcely a letter: a blister of expletives covered the smoking pages . . . and the Evans' - two of them - had arrived.

Mrs Ames' little toadlike face seldom expressed much more than a ladylike composure, but had Harry been watching his mother he might have thought that a shade of amusement hovered there.

'A letter from your father,' she said. 'Rather a worried letter. The cure is lowering, I believe, and makes you feel out of sorts.'

Harry was looking rather yellow and dishevelled. He had sat up very late the night before, and the chase for rhymes had been peculiarly fatiguing and ineffectual.

'I don't feel at all well, either,' he said. 'And I don't think Cousin Millie is well.'

'Why?' asked Mrs Ames composedly.

'I went to see her yesterday and she didn't attend. She seemed frightfully surprised to hear that father had gone to Harrogate.'

'I suppose Dr Evans had not told her,' remarked Mrs Ames. 'Please telephone to her after breakfast, Harry, and ask her to dine with us this evening.'

'Yes. How curious women are! One day they seem so glad to see you, another you are no more to them than foam on a broken wave.'

This was one of the fragments of last night.

'On a broken what?' asked Mrs Ames. The rustling of the turning leaf of the Morning Post had caused her not to hear. There was no sarcastic intention in her inquiry.

'It does not matter,' said Harry.

His mother looked up at him.

'I should take a little dose, dear,' she said, 'if you feel like that. The heat upsets us all at times. Will you please telephone now, Harry? Then I shall know what to order for dinner.'

Mrs Ames' nature was undeniably a simple one; she had no misty profundities or curious dim-lit clefts on the round, smooth surface of her life, but on occasion simple natures are capable of curious complexities of feeling, the more elusive because they themselves are unable to register exactly what they do feel. Certainly she saw a connection between the non-arrival of dear Millie at Harrogate and the inflamed letter from her husband. She had suspected also a connection between dear Millie's decision to spend August at Riseborough and her belief that Major Ames was going to do so too. But the completeness of the fiasco sucked the sting out of the resentment she might otherwise have felt: it was impossible to be angry with such sorry conspirators. At the same time, with regard to her husband, she felt the liveliest internal satisfaction at his blistering communication, and read it through again. The thought of her own slighted or rather unperceived rejuvenescence added point to this; she felt that he had been 'served out'. Not for a moment did she suspect him of anything but the most innocent of flirtations, and she was disposed to credit dear Millie with having provoked such flirtation as there was. By this time also it must have been quite clear to both the thwarted parties that she was in full cognizance of their futile designs; clearly, therefore, her own beau rôle was to appear utterly unconscious of it all, and, unconsciously, to administer nasty little jabs to each of them with a smiling face. 'They have been making sillies of themselves,' expressed her indulgent verdict on the whole affair. Then in some strange feminine way she felt a sort of secret pride in her husband for having had the manhood to flirt, however mildly, with somebody else's wife; but immediately there followed the resentment that he had not shown any tendency to flirt with his own, when she had encouraged him. But, anyhow, he had chosen the prettiest woman in Riseborough, and he was the handsomest man.

But her mood changed; the thought at any rate of administering some nasty little jabs presented itself in a growingly attractive light. The two sillies had been wanting to dance to their own tune; they should dance to hers instead, and by way of striking up her own tune at once she wrote as follows, to her husband.

'MY DEAREST LYNDHURST,

'I can't tell you how glad I was to get your two letters, and to know how much good Harrogate is doing you. What an excellent thing that you went to Dr Evans (please remember me to him), and that he insisted so strongly on your taking yourself thoroughly in hand.'

She paused a moment, wondering exactly how strong this insistence had been. It was possible that it was not very strong. So much the more reason for letting the sentence stand. She now underlined the words 'so strongly'.

'Of course the waters are disgusting to take, and I declare I can almost smell them when I read your vivid description, but, as you said in your first letter, what is a bad taste in the mouth when you know it is doing you good? And your second letter convinces me how right you were to go, and when things like gout begin to come out, it naturally makes you feel a little low and worried. I want you to stop there the whole of August, and get thoroughly rid of it.

'Here we are getting along very happily, and I am so glad I did not go to the sea. Millie is here, as you will know, and we see a great deal of her. She is constantly dropping in, en fille, I suppose you would call it, and is in excellent spirits and looks so pretty. But I am not quite at ease about Harry (this is private). He is very much attracted by her, and she seems to me not very wise in the way she deals with him, for she seems to be encouraging him in his silliness. Perhaps I will speak to her about it, and yet I hardly like to.'

Again Mrs Ames paused: she had no idea she had such a brilliant touch in the administration of these jabs. What she said might not be strictly accurate, but it was full of point.

'I remember, too, what you said, that it was so good for a boy to be taken up with a thoroughly nice woman, and that it prevented his getting into mischief, I am sure Harry is writing all sorts of poems to her, because he sighs a great deal, and has a most inky forefinger, for which I give him pumice stone. But if she were not so nice a woman, and so far from anything like flirtatiousness, I should feel myself obliged to speak to Harry and warn him. She seems very happy and cheerful. I daresay she feels like me, and is rejoiced to think that Harrogate is doing her husband good.

'Write to me soon again, my dear, and give me another excellent account of yourself. Was it not queer that you settled to go to Harrogate just when Millie settled not to? If you were not such good friends, one would think you wanted to avoid each other! Well, I must stop. Millie is dining with us, and I must order dinner.'

She read through what she had written with considerable content. 'That will be nastier than the Harrogate waters,' she thought to herself, 'and quite as good for him.' And then, with a certain largeness which lurked behind all her littlenesses, she practically dismissed the whole silly business from her mind. But she continued the use of the purely natural means for restoring the colour of the hair, and tapped and dabbed the corners of her eyes with the miraculous skin food. That was a prophylactic measure; she did not want to appear 'a fright' when Lyndhurst came back from Harrogate.

Mrs Ames was well aware that the famous fancy dress ball had caused her a certain loss of prestige in her capacity of queen of society in Riseborough. It had followed close on the heels of her innovation of asking husbands and wives separately to dinner, and had somewhat taken the shine out of her achievement, and indeed this latter had not been as epoch-making as she had expected. For the last week or two she had felt that something new was required of her, but as is often the case, she found that the recognition of such a truth does not necessarily lead to the discovery of the novelty. Perhaps the paltriness of Lyndhurst's conduct, leading to reflections on her own superior wisdom, put her on the path, for about this time she began to take a renewed interest in the Suffragette movement which, from what she saw in the papers, was productive of such adventurous alarums in London. For herself, she was essentially law-abiding by nature, and though, in opposition to Lyndhurst, sympathetically inclined to women who wanted the vote, she had once said that to throw stones at Prime Ministers was unladylike in itself, and only drew on the perpetrators the attention of the police to themselves, rather than the attention of the public to the problem. But a recrudescence of similar acts during the last summer had caused her to wonder whether she had said quite the last word on the subject, or thought the last thought. Certainly the sensational interest in such violent acts had led her to marvel at the strength of feeling that prompted them. Ladies, apparently, whose breeding - always a word of potency with Mrs Ames - she could not question, were behaving like hooligans. The matter interested her in itself apart from its possible value as a novelty for the autumn. Also an election was probably to take place in November. Hitherto that section of Riseborough in which she lived had not suffered its tranquillity to be interrupted by political excitements, but like a man in his sleep, drowsily approved a Conservative member. But what if she took the lead in some political agitation, and what if she introduced a Suffragette element into the election? That was a solider affair than that a quantity of Cleopatras should skip about in a back garden.

She had always felt a certain interest in the movement, but it was the desire to make a novelty for the autumn, peppered, so to speak, by an impatience at the futile treachery of her husband's Harrogate plans, and an ambition to take a line of her own in opposition to him, that presented their crusade in a serious light to her. The militant crusaders she had hitherto regarded as affected by a strange lunacy, and her husband's masculine comment, 'They ought to be well smacked, by Jove!' had had the ring of common sense, especially since he added, for the benefit of such crusaders as were of higher social rank, 'They're probably mad, poor things.'

But during this tranquil month of August her more serious interest was aroused, and she bought, though furtively, such literature in the form of little tracts and addresses as was accessible on the subject. And slowly, though still the desire for an autumn novelty that would eclipse the memory of the congregations of Cleopatras was a moving force in her mind, something of the real ferment began to be yeasty within her, and she learned by private inquiry what the Suffragette colours were. Naturally the introduction of an abstract idea into her mind was a laborious process, since her life had for years consisted of an endless chain of small concrete events, and had been lived among people who had never seen an abstract idea wild, any more than they had seen an elephant in a real jungle. It was always tamed and eating buns, as in the zoo, just as other ideas reached them peptonized by the columns of daily papers. But a wild thing lurked behind the obedient trunk; a wild thing lurked behind the reports of ludicrous performances in the Palace Yard at Westminster.

CHAPTER NINE

August was still sultry, and Major Ames was still at Harrogate, when one evening she and Harry dined with Millie. Since nothing of any description happened in Riseborough during this deserted month, the introductory discussion of what events had occurred since they last met in the High Street that morning was not possible of great expansion. None of them had seen the aeroplane which was believed to have passed over the town in the afternoon, and nobody had heard from Mrs Altham. Then Mrs Ames fired the shot which was destined to involve Riseborough in smoke and brimstone.

'Lyndhurst and I,' she said, 'have never agreed about the Suffragettes, and now that I know something about them, I disagree more than ever.'

Millie looked slightly shocked: she thought of Suffragettes as she thought of the persons who figure in police news. Indeed, they often did. She knew they wanted to vote about something, but that was practically all she knew except that they expressed their desire to vote by hitting people.

'I know nothing about them,' she said. 'But are they not very unladylike?'

'They are a disgrace to their sex,' said Harry. 'We soon made them get out of Cambridge! They tried to hold a meeting in the backs, but I and a few others went down there, and - well, there wasn't much more heard of them. I don't call them women at all. I call them females.'

Mrs Ames had excellent reasons for suspecting romance in her son's account of his exploits.

'Tell me exactly what happened in the backs at Cambridge, Harry,' she said.

Harry slightly retracted.

'There is nothing much to tell,' he said. 'Our club felt bound to make a protest, and we went down there, as I said. It seemed to cow them a bit!'

'And then did the proctors come and cow you?' asked his inexorable mother.

'I believe a proctor did come; I did not wait for that. They made a perfect fiasco, anyhow. They told me it was all a dead failure, and we heard no more about it.'

'So that was all?' said Mrs Ames.

'And quite enough. I agree with father. They disgrace their sex!'

'My dear, you know as little about it as your father,' she said.

'But surely a man's judgement - ' said Millie, making weak eyes at Harry.

'Dear Millie, a man's judgement is not of any value, if he does not know anything about what he is judging. We have all read accounts in the papers, and heard that they are very violent and chain themselves up to inconvenient places like railings, and are taken away by policemen. Sometimes they slap the policemen, but surely there must be something behind that makes them like that. I am finding out what it is. It is all most interesting. They say that they have to pay their rates and taxes, but get no privileges. If a man pays rates and taxes he gets a vote, and why shouldn't a woman? It is all very well expressed. They seem to me to reason just as well as a man. I mean to find out much more about it all. Personally I don't pay rates and taxes, because that is Lyndhurst's affair, but if we had arranged differently and I paid for the house and the rates and taxes, why shouldn't I have a vote instead of him? And from what I can learn the gardener has a vote, just the same as Lyndhurst, although Lyndhurst does all the garden-rolling, and won't let Parkins touch the flowers.'

Mrs Evans sighed.

'It all seems very confused and upside down,' she said. 'Do smoke, Harry, if you feel inclined. Will you have a cigarette, Cousin Amy? I am afraid I have none. I never smoke.'

Harry was a little sore from his mother's handling, and was not unwilling to hit back.

'I never knew mother smoked,' he said. 'Do you smoke, mother? How delightful! How Eastern! I never knew you were Eastern. I always thought you said it was not wicked for women to smoke, but only horrid. Do be horrid. I am sure Suffragettes smoke.'

Mrs Ames turned a swift appealing eye on Millie, entreating confidence. Then she lied.

'Dear Millie, what are you thinking of?' she said. 'Of course I never smoke, Harry.'

But the appeal of the eyes had not taken effect.

'But on the night of my little dance, Cousin Amy,' she said, 'surely you had a cigarette. It made you cough, and you said how nice it was!'

Mrs Ames wished she had not been so ruthless about the Suffragettes at Cambridge.

'There is a great difference between doing a thing once,' she said, 'and making a habit of it. I think I did want to see what it was like, but I never said it was nice, and as for its being Eastern, I am sure I am glad to belong to the West. I always thought it unfeminine, and then I knew it. I did not feel myself again till I had brushed my teeth and rinsed my mouth. Now, dear Millie, I am really interested in the Suffragettes. Their demands are reasonable, and if we are unreasonable about granting them, they must be unreasonable too. For years they have been reasonable and nobody has paid any attention to them. What are they to do but be violent, and call attention to themselves? It is all so well expressed; you cannot fail to be interested.'

'Wilfred would never let me hit a policeman,' said Millie. 'And I don't think I could do it, even if he wanted me to.'

'But it is not the aim of the movement to hit policemen,' said Mrs Ames. 'They are very sorry to have to - '

'They are sorrier afterwards,' said Harry.

Mrs Ames turned a small, withering eye upon her offspring.

'If you had waited to hear what they had to say instead of running away before the proctor came,' she said, 'you might have learnt a little about them, dear. They are not at all sorry afterwards; they go to prison quite cheerfully, in the second division, too, which is terribly uncomfortable. And many of them have been brought up as luxuriously as any of us.'

'I could not go to prison,' said Mrs Evans faintly, but firmly. 'And even if I could, it would be very wrong of me, for I am sure it would injure Wilfred's practice. People would not like to go to a doctor whose wife had been in prison. She might have caught something. And Elsie would be so ashamed of me.'

Mrs Ames gave the suppressed kind of sigh which was habitual with her when Lyndhurst complained that the water for his bath was not hot, although aware that the kitchen boiler was being cleaned.

'But you need not go to prison in order to be a Suffragette, dear Millie,' she said. 'Prison life is not one of the objects of the movement.'

Mrs Evans looked timidly apologetic.

'I didn't know,' she said. 'It is so interesting to be told. I thought all the brave sort went to prison, and had breakfast together when they were let out. I am sure I have read about their having breakfast together.'

A faint smile quivered on her mouth. She was aware that Cousin Amy thought her very stupid, and there was a delicate pleasure in appearing quite idiotic like this. It made Cousin Amy dance with irritation inside, and explain more carefully yet.

'Yes, dear Millie,' she said, 'but their having breakfast together has not much to do with their objects - '

'I don't know about that,' said Harry; 'there is a club at Cambridge to which I belong, whose object is to dine together.'

'Then it is very greedy of you, dear,' said Mrs Ames, 'and the Suffragettes are not like that. They go to prison and do all sorts of unladylike things for the sake of their convictions. They want to be treated justly. For years they have asked for justice, and nobody has paid the least attention to them; now they are making people attend. I assure you that until I began reading about them, I had very little sympathy with them. But now I feel that all women ought to know about them. Certainly what I have read has opened my eyes very much, and there are a quantity of women of very good family indeed who belong to them.'

Harry pulled his handkerchief out of the sleeve of his dress coat; he habitually kept it there. Just now the Omar Khayyam Club was rather great on class distinctions.

'I do not see what that matters,' he said. 'Because a man's great-grandmother was created a duchess for being a king's mistress - '

Mrs Evans and Mrs Ames got up simultaneously; if anything Mrs Ames got up a shade first.

'I do not think we need go into that, Harry,' said Mrs Ames.

Millie tempered the wind.

'Will you join us soon, Harry?' she said. 'If you are too long I shall come and fetch you. We have been political tonight! Will it be too cold for you in the garden, Cousin Amy?'

Left to himself, Harry devoted several minutes' pitiful reflection to his mother's state of mind. In spite of her awakened interest in the Suffragette movement, she seemed to him deplorably old-fashioned. But with his second glass of port his thoughts assumed a rosier tone, and he determined to wait till Cousin Millie came to fetch him. Surely she meant him to do that: no doubt she wanted to have just one private word with him. She had often caught his eye during dinner, with a deprecating look, as if to say this tiresome rigmarole about Suffragettes was not her fault. He felt they understood each other . . .

There was a large Chippendale looking glass above the sideboard, and he got up from the table and observed the upper part of his person which was reflected in it. A wisp of hair fell over his forehead; it might more rightly be called a plume. He appeared to himself to have a most interesting face, uncommon, arresting. He was interestingly and characteristically dressed, too, with a collar Byronically low, a soft frilled shirt, and in place of a waistcoat a black cummerbund. Then hastily he mounted on a chair in order to see the whole of his lean figure that seemed so slender. It was annoying that at this moment of critical appreciation a parlourmaid should look in to see if she could clear away . . .

There is nothing that so confirms individualism in any character as periods of comparative solitude. In men such confirmation is liable to be checked by the boredom to which their sex is subject, but women, less frequently the prey of this paralysing emotion, when the demands made upon them by household duties and domestic companionship are removed, enter very swiftly into the kingdoms of themselves. This process was very strongly at work just now with Millie Evans; superficially, her composure and meaningless smoothness were unaltered, so that Mrs Ames, at any rate, almost wondered whether she had been right in crediting her with any hand in the Harrogate plans, so unruffled was her insipid and deferential cordiality, but down below she was exploring herself and discovering a capacity for feeling that astonished her by its intensity. All her life she had been content to arouse emotion without sharing it, liking to see men attentive to her, liking to see them attracted by her and disposed towards tenderness. They were more interesting like that, and she gently basked in the warmth of their glow, like a lizard on the wall. She had not wanted more than that; she was lizard, not vampire, and to sun herself on the wall, and then glide gently into a crevice again, seemed quite sufficient exercise for her emotions. Luckily or unluckily (those who hold that calm and complete respectability is the aim of existence would prefer the former adverb, those who think that development of individuality is worth the risk of a little scorching, the latter) she had married a man who required little or nothing more than she was disposed to give. He had not expected unquiet rapture, but a comfortable home with a 'little woman' always there, good-tempered, as Millie was, and cheerful and pliable as, with a dozen exceptions when the calm precision came into play, she had always been. Temperamentally, he was nearly as undeveloped as she, and the marriage had been what is called a very sensible one. But such sensible marriages ignore the fact that human beings, like the shores of the bay of Naples, are periodically volcanic, and the settlers there assume that their little property, because no sulphurous signs have appeared on the surface, is essentially quiescent, neglecting the fact that at one time or another emotional disturbances are to be expected. But because many quiet years have passed undisturbed, they get to believe that the human and natural fires have ceased to smoulder, and are no longer alive down below the roots of their pleasant vines and olive trees. All her life up till now, Millie Evans had been like one of these quiescent estates; now, when middle age was upon her, she began to feel the stir of vital forces. The surface of her life was still undisturbed, she went about the diminished business of the household with her usual care, and in the weeks of this solitary August knitted a couple of ties for her husband, and read a couple of novels from the circulating library, with an interest not more markedly tepid than usual. But subterranean stir was going on, though no fire-breathing clefts appeared on the surface. Subconsciously she wove images and dreams, scarcely yet knowing that it is out of such dreams that the events and deeds of life inevitably spring. She had scarcely admitted even to herself that her projects for August had gone crookedly: the conviction that Lyndhurst Ames had found himself gouty and in need of Harrogate punctually at the date when he knew that she might be expected there, sufficiently straightened them. The intention more than compensated the miscarriage of events.

Tonight, when her two guests had gone, the inevitable step happened: her unchecked impulses grew stronger and more definite, and out of the misty subconsciousness of her mind the disturbance flared upwards into the light of her everyday consciousness. With genuine flame it mounted; it was no solitary imagining of her own that had kindled it; he, she knew, was a conscious partner, and she had as sign the memory that he had kissed her. Somehow, deep in her awakening heart, that meant something stupendous to her. It had been unrealized at the time, but it had been like the touch of some corrosive, sweet and acid, burrowing down, eating her and yet feeding her. Up till now, it seemed to have signified little, now it invested itself with a tremendous significance. Probably to him it meant little; men did such things easily, but it was that which had burrowed within her, making so insignificant an entry, but penetrating so far. It was not a proof that he loved her, but it had become a token that she loved him. Otherwise, it could not have happened. There was something final in the beginning of it all. Then he had kissed her a second time on the night of the fancy dress ball. He had called that a cousinly kiss, and she smiled at the thought of that, for it showed that it required to be accounted for, excused. She felt a sort of tenderness for that fluttering, broken-winged subterfuge, so transparent, so undeceptive. If cousins kissed, they did not recollect their relationship afterwards, especially if there was no relationship. He had not kissed her because she was some sort of cousin to his wife.

Yet it was hardly stating the case correctly to say that he had kissed her. Doubtless, on that first occasion below the mulberry tree it was his head that had bent down to hers, while she but remained passive, waiting. But it was she who had made him do it, and she gloried in the soft compulsion she had put on him. Even as she thought of it this evening, her eye sparkled. 'He could not help it,' she said to herself. 'He could not help it.'

Out of the sequestered cloistral twilight of her soul there had stepped something that had slumbered there all her life, something pagan, something incapable of scruples or regrets, as void of morals as a nymph or Bacchanal on a Greek frieze. It did not trouble, so it seemed, to challenge or defy the traditions and principles in which she had lived all these years; it appeared to be ignorant of their existence, or, at the most, they were but shadows that lay in unsubstantial bars across a sunlit pavement. At present, it stood there trembling and quiescent, like a moth lately broken out from its sheathed chrysalis, but momently, now that it had come forth, it would grow stronger, and its crumpled wings expand into pinions feathered with silver and gold.

But she made no plans, she scarcely even turned her eyes towards the future, for the future would surely be as inevitable as the past had been. One by one the hot August days dropped off like the petals of peach blossom, which must fall before the fruit begins to swell. She neither wanted to delay or hurry their withering. There were but few days left, few petals left to fall, for within a week, so her husband had written, he would be back, vastly better for his cure, and Major Ames was coming with him. 'I shall be so glad to see my little woman again,' he had said. 'Elsie and I have missed her.'

Occasionally she tried to think about her husband, but she could not concentrate her mind on him. She was too much accustomed to him to be able to fix her thoughts on him emotionally. She was equally well accustomed to Elsie, or rather equally well accustomed to her complete ignorance about Elsie. She could no more have drawn a chart of the girl's mind than she could have drawn a picture of the branches of the mulberry tree under which she so often sat, beholding the interlacement of its boughs but never really seeing them. Never had she known the psychical bond of motherhood; even the physical had meant little to her. She was Elsie's mother by accident, so to speak; and she was but as a tree from which a gardener has made a cutting, planting it near, so that sapling and parent stem grow up in sight of each other, but quite independently, without sense of their original unity. Even when her baby had lain at her breast, helpless, and still deriving all from her, the sweet intimate mystery of the life that was common to them both had been but a whispered riddle to her; and that was long ago, its memory had become a faded photograph that might really have represented not herself and her baby, but any mother and child. It was very possible that before long Elsie would be transplanted by marriage, and she herself would have to learn a little more about chess in order to play with her husband in the evening.

Such, hitherto, had been her emotional life: this summary of it and its meagre total is all that can justly be put to her credit. She liked her husband, she knew he was kind to her, and so, in its inanimate manner, was the food which she ate kind to her, in that it nourished and supported her. But her gratitude to it was untinged with emotion; she was not sentimental over her breakfast, for it was the mission of food to give support, and the mission of her husband had not been to her much more than that. Neither wifehood nor motherhood had awakened her womanhood. Yet, in that she was a woman, she was that most dangerous of all created or manufactured things, an unexploded shell, liable to blow to bits both itself and any who handled her. The shell was alive still, its case uncorroded, and its contents still potentially violent. That violence at present lay dark and quiet within it; its sheath was smooth and faintly bright. It seemed but a plaything, a parlour ornament; it could stand on any table in any drawing room. But the heart of it had never been penetrated by the love that could transform its violence into strength: now its cap was screwed and its fuse fixed. Until the damp and decay of age robbed it of its power, it would always be liable to wreck itself and its surroundings.

These same days that for her were kindling dangerous stuff, passed for Mrs Ames in a crescendo of awakening interest. All her life she had been wrapped round like the kernel of a nut, in the hard, dry husk of conventionalities, her life had been encased in a succession of minute happenings, and, literally speaking, she had never breathed the outer air of ideas. As has been noticed, she gave regular patronage to St Barnabas' Church, and spent a solid hour or two every week in decorating it with the produce of her husband's garden, from earliest spring, when the faint, shy snowdrops were available, to late autumn, when October and November frosts finally blackened the salvias and chrysanthemums. But all that had been of the nature of routine: a certain admiration for the vicar, a passionless appreciation of his nobly ascetic life, his strong, lean face, and the fire of his utterances had made her attendance regular, and her contributions to his charities quite creditably profuse in proportion to her not very ample means. But she had never denied herself anything in order to increase them, while the time she spent over the flowers was amply compensated for when she saw the eclipse they made of Mrs Brooks' embroideries, or when the lilies dropped their orange-staining pollen on to the altar cloth. Stranger, perhaps, from the emotional point of view, had been her recently attempted rejuvenescence, but even that had been a calculated and materialistic effort. It had not been a manifestation of her love for her husband, or of a desire to awaken his love for her. It was merely a decorative effort to attract his attention, and prevent it wandering elsewhere.

But now, with her kindled sympathy for the Suffragette movement, there was springing up in her the consciousness of a kinship with her sex whom, hitherto, she had regarded as a set of people to whom, in the matter of dinner giving and entirely correct social behaviour, she must be an example and a law, while even her hospitalities had not been dictated by the spirit of hospitality but rather by a sort of pompous and genteel competition. Now she was beginning to see that behind the mere events of life, if they were to be worth anything, must lie an idea, and here behind this woman's crusade, with all its hooliganism, its hysteria, its apish fanaticism, lay an idea of justice and sisterhood. They seemed simple words, and she would have said offhand that she knew what they meant. But, as she began faintly to understand them, she knew that she had been as ignorant of them as of what Australia really was. To her, as it was a geographical expression only, so justice was an abstract expression. But the meaning of justice was known to those who gave up the comforts and amenities of life for its sake, and for its sake cheerfully suffered ridicule and prison life and misunderstanding. And the fumes of an idea, to one who had practically never tasted one, intoxicated her as new wine mounts to the head of a teetotaller.

Ideas are dangerous things, and should be kept behind a fireguard, for fear that the children, of whom this world largely consists, should burn their fingers, thinking that these bright, sparkling toys are to be played with. Mrs Ames, in spite of her unfamiliarity with them, did not fall into this error. She realized that if she was to warm herself, to get the glow of the fire in her cramped and frozen limbs, she must treat it with respect, and learn to handle it. That, at any rate, was her intention, and she had a certain capacity for thoroughness.

It was in the last week of August that Major Ames was expected back, after three weeks of treatment. At first, as reflected in his letters, his experiences had been horrifying;

the waters nauseated him, and the irritating miscarriage of the plan which was the real reason for his going to Harrogate, caused him fits of feeble rage which were the more maddening because they had to be borne secretly and silently. Also the lodgings he had procured seemed to him needlessly expensive, and all this efflux of bullion was being poured out on treatment which Dr Evans had told him was really quite unnecessary. Regular and sparkling letters from his wife, in praise of August spent at Riseborough, continued to arrive and filled him with impotent envy. He, too, might be spending August at Riseborough if he had not been quite so precipitate. As it was, his mornings were spent in absorbing horrible draughts and gently stewing in the fetid waters of the Starbeck spring: his meals were plain to the point of grotesqueness, his evenings were spent in playing inane games of patience, while Elsie and the doctor pored silently over their chessboard, saying 'Check' to each other at intervals. But through the days and their tedious uniformity there ran a certain unquietness and desire. It was clear that Millie, no less than he, had planned that they should be together in August, but his desire did not absorb him, rather it made him restless and anxious about the future. He did not even know if he was really in love with her; he did not even know if he wanted to be. The thought of her kindled his imagination, and he could picture himself in love with her: at the same time he was not certain whether, if the last two months could be lived over again, he would let himself drift into the position where he now found himself. There was neither ardour nor anything imperative in his heart; something, it is true, was heated, but it only smouldered and smoked. It was of the nature of such fire as bursts out in haystacks: it was born of stuffiness and packed confinement, and was as different as two things of the same nature can be, from the swift lambency and laudable flame of sun-kindled and breeze-fed flame. It disquieted and upset him; he could not soberly believe in the pictures his imagination drew of his being irresistibly in love with her: their colour quickly faded, their outlines were wavering and uncertain. And the background was even more difficult to fill in . . . how was the composition to be arranged? Where would Amy stand? What aspect would Riseborough wear? And then, after a long silence, Elsie said 'Check'.

Major Ames was due to arrive at Riseborough soon after four in the afternoon, and Mrs Ames was at pains to be at home by that hour to welcome him and give him tea, and had persuaded Harry to go up to the station to meet him. She had gathered a charming decoration of flowers to make the room bright, and had put a couple more vases of them in his dressing room. Before long a cab arrived from the station bearing his luggage, but neither he nor Harry occupied it. So it was natural to conclude that they were walking down, and she made tea, since they would not be many minutes behind the leisurely four-wheeler. She wanted very particularly to give him an auspicious and comfortable return: he must not think that, because this Suffragette movement occupied her thoughts so much, she was going to become remiss in care for him. But still the minutes went on, and she took a cup of tea herself, and found it already growing astringent. What could have detained him she could not guess, but certainly he should have another brew of tea made for him, for he hated what in moments of irritation he called tincture of tannin. Five o'clock struck, and the two quarters that duly followed it. Before that a conjecture had formed itself in her mind.

Then came the rattle of his deposited hat and stick in the hall, and the rattle of the door handle for his entry.

'Well, Amy,' he said, 'and here's your returned prodigal. Train late as usual, and I walked down. How are you?'

She got up and kissed him.

'Very well indeed, Lyndhurst,' she said; 'and there is no need to ask you how you are.'

She paused a moment.

'Your luggage arrived nearly an hour ago,' she said.

He had forgotten that detail.

'An hour ago? Surely not,' he said.

She gave him one more pause in which he could say more, but nothing came.

'You have had tea, I suppose,' she said.

'Yes; Evans insisted on my dropping in to his house, and taking a cup there. That rogue Harry has stopped on. Well, well: we were all young once! You remember the old story I told you about the Colonel's wife when I was a lad.'

She remembered it perfectly. She felt sure also that he had not meant to tell her where he had been since his arrival at the station.

THE day was of early October, and Dr Evans, who was driving his swift, steady cob, harnessed to the light dogcart, along the flat road towards Norton, had leisure to observe the beauty of the flaming season. He had but a couple of visits to make, and neither of the cases caused him any professional anxiety. But it was with conscious effort that he commanded his obedient mind to cease worrying, and drink in the beneficent influence of this genial morning that followed on a night that had given them the first frost of the year. The road, after leaving Riseborough, ran through a couple of level miles of delectable woodland; ditches filled and choked with the full-grown grass and herbage of the summer bordered it on each side. On the left, the sun had turned the frozen night-dews into a liquid heraldry, on the right where the roadside foliage was still in shadow, the faceted jewels of the frost that hinted of the coming winter still stiffened the herbage, and was white on the grey beards of the sprawling clematis in the hedges. But high above these low-growing tangles of vegetation, an ample glory flamed, and the great beech forest was all ablaze with orange and red flame tremulous in the breeze. Here and there a yew tree, tawny trunked and green velveted with undeciduous leaf, seemed like a black spot of unconsumed fuel in the fire of the autumn; here a company of sturdy oaks seemed like a group of square-shouldered young men amid the maidens of the woodland. It had its fairies too, the sylphlike birches, whose little leaves seemed shed about their white shapeliness like a shower of confetti. Then, in the more open glades, short and rabbit-cropped turf sparkled emerald-like amid the sober greys and browns of the withering heather and the russet antlers of the bracken. Now and then a rabbit with white scutt*, giving a dot-and-dash signal of danger to his family, would scamper into shelter at the rattle of the approaching dogcart. Now and then a pheasant, whose plumage seemed to reproduce in metal the tints of the golden autumn, strode with lowered head and tail away from the dangerous vicinity of man. Below the beeches the ground was uncarpeted by any vegetation, but already the 'fallen glories' of the leaf were beginning to lie there, and occasionally a squirrel ran rustling across them, and having gained the security of his lofty ways among the trees, scolded Puck-like at the interruption that had made him leave his breakfast of the burst beech nuts. To the right, below the high-swung level road, the ground declined sharply, and gave glimpses of the distant sun-burnished sea; above, small companies of feathery clouds, assembled together as if migrating for the winter, fluttered against the summer azure of the sky.

Dr Evans' alert and merry eye dwelt on those delectable things, and in obedience to his brain, noted and appreciated the manifold festivity of the morning, but it did so not as

* [Ed. note: An obsolete early Saxon word for a rabbit's white bob-tail.]

ordinarily, by instinct and eager impulses, but because he consciously bade it. It needed the spur; its alertness and its merriness were pressed on it, and by degrees the spur failed to stimulate it, and he fell to regarding the well-groomed quarters of his long-stepping cob, which usually afforded him so pleasant a contemplation of strong and harmonious muscularity. But this morning even they failed to delight him, and the rhythm of its firm trot made no music in his mind. There came a crease which deepened into a decided frown between his eyes, and he communed with the trouble in his mind.

There were various lesser worries, not of sufficient importance to disturb seriously the equanimity of a busy and well-balanced man, and though each was trivial enough in itself, and distinctly had a humorous side to a mind otherwise content, the cumulative effect of them was not amusing. In the first place, there was the affair of Harry Ames, who, in a manner sufficiently ludicrous and calfish, had been making love to his wife. As any other sensible man would have done, Wilfred Evans had seen almost immediately on his return to Riseborough that Harry was disposed to make himself ridiculous, and had given a word of kindly warning to his wife.

'Snub him a bit, little woman,' he had said. 'We're having a little too much of him. It's fairer on the boy, too. You're too kind to him. A woman like you so easily turns a boy's head. And you've often said he is rather a dreadful sort of youth.'

But for some reason she took the words in ill part, becoming rather precise.

'I don't know what you mean,' she said. 'Will you explain, please?'

'Easy enough, my dear. He's here too much; he's dangling after you. Laugh at him a little, or yawn a little.'

'You mean that he's in love with me?'

'Well, that's too big a word, little woman, though I'm sure you see what I mean.'

'I think I do. I think your suggestion is rather coarse, Wilfred, and quite ill-founded. Is everyone who is polite and attentive supposed to be in love with me? I only ask for information.'

'I think your own good sense will supply you with all necessary information,' he said.

But her good sense apparently had done nothing of the kind, and eventually Dr Evans had spoken to Harry's father on the subject. The visits had ceased with amazing abruptness after that, and Dr Evans had found himself treated to a stare of blank unrecognition when he passed Harry in the street, and a curl of the lip which he felt must have been practised in private. But the Omar Khayyam Club would be the gainers, for they owed to it those stricken and embittered stanzas called 'Parted'.

Here comedy verged on farce, but the farce did not amuse him. He knew that his own interpretation of Harry's assiduous presence was correct, so why should his wife have so precisely denied that those absurd attentions meant nothing? There was nothing to resent in the sensible warning that a man was greatly attracted by her. Nor was there warrant for Colonel Ames' horror and dismay at the suggestion, when the doctor spoke to him about it. 'Infamous young libertine' was surely a hyperbolical expression.

Dr Evans unconsciously flicked the cob rather sharply with his whiplash, to that excellent animal's surprise, for he was covering his miles in five minutes apiece, and the doctor conveyed his apologies for his unintentional hint with a soothing remark. Then his thoughts drifted back again. That was not all the trouble with the Ames' family, for his wife had had a quarrel with Mrs Ames. This kindly man hated to quarrel with anybody, and, for his part, successfully refused to do so, and that his wife should find herself in such a predicament was equally distressing to him. No doubt it was all a storm in a teacup, but if you happen to be living in the teacup too, a storm there is just as upsetting as a gale on the high seas. It is worse, indeed, for on the high seas a ship can run into fairer weather, but there is no escape from these teacup disturbances. The entire teacup was involved: all Riseborough, which a year ago had seemed to him so suitable a place in which to pursue an unexacting practice, to conduct mild original work, in the peace and quiet of a small society and domestic comfort, was become a tempest of conflicting winds. 'And all arising from such a pack of nonsense,' as the doctor thought impatiently to himself, only just checking the whiplash from falling again on the industrious cob.

The interest of Mrs Ames in the Suffragette movement had given rise to all this. She had announced a drawing-room meeting to be held in her house, now a fortnight ago, and the drawing-room meeting had exploded in mid-career, like a squib, scattering sparks and combustible material over all Riseborough. It appeared that Mrs Ames, finding that the comprehension of Suffragette aims extended to the middle-class circles in Riseborough, had asked the wives and daughters of tradesmen to take part in it. It wanted but little after that to make Mrs Altham remark quite audibly that she had not known that she was to have the privilege of meeting so many ladies with whom she was not previously acquainted, and the sarcastic intention of her words was not lost upon her new friends. Tea seemed but to increase the initial inflammation, and the interest Mrs Ames had intended to awake on the subject of votes for women was changed into an interest in ascertaining who could be most offensively polite, a very pretty game. It is not to be wondered at that, before twenty-four hours had passed, Mrs Altham had started an anti-Suffragette league, and Millie, still strong in the conviction that under no circumstances could she go to prison, had allowed herself to be drawn into it. Next night at dinner she softly made a terrible announcement.

'I passed Cousin Amy in the street just now,' she said; 'she did not seem to see me.'

'Perhaps she didn't see you, little woman,' said her husband.

'So I did not seem to see her,' added Millie, who had not finished her sentence. 'But if she cares to come to see me and explain, I shall behave quite as usual to her.'

'Come, come, little woman!' said Dr Evans in a conciliating spirit.

'And I do not see what is the good of saying "Come, come",' she said, with considerable precision.

All this was sufficient to cause very sensible disquiet to a man who attached so proper an importance to peaceful and harmonious conditions of life, yet it was but a small thing compared to a far deeper anxiety that brooded over him. Till now he had not let himself directly contemplate it, but today, as he returned from his two visits, he made himself face this last secret trouble. He felt it was necessary for him to ascertain, for the sake of others no less than himself, what part, if any, of his disquiet was grounded on certainty, what part, if any, might be the figment of an over-anxious imagination. But he knew he was not anxious by temperament, nor given to imagine troubles. If anything, he was more prone, in his desire for a pleasant and studious life, to shut his eyes to the apparent approach of storm, trusting that it would blow by. He was anxious about Millie, not without cause; a hundred symptoms justified his anxiety.

CHAPTER TEN

She who for so long had been of such imperturbable serenity of temper that a man who did not feel her charm might have called her jellyfish was the prey of fifty moods a day. She had strange little fits of tenderness to him, with squalls of peevishness quite as strange. She was restless and filled with an energy that flamed and flickered and vanished, leaving her indolent and inert. She would settle herself for a morning of letter writing, and after tearing up a couple of notes, put on her gardening gloves and get as far as the herbaceous bed. Then she would find an imperative reason for going into the town, and so sit down at her piano to practise. Her appetite, usually of the steady reliable order, failed her, and she passed broken and tossing nights. Had she been a girl, he would have said those symptoms all pointed one way; and it would probably not have been difficult to guess who was the young man in question. Yet he could scarcely face the conclusion applied to his wife. It was a hideous thing that a husband should harbour such a suspicion, more hideous that the husband should be himself. And perhaps more hideous of all, that he should guess - again without difficulty - who was the man in question.

He had no conception what to do, or whether to do nothing; it seemed that action and inaction might alike end in disaster. And, again, the whole of his explanation of Millie's symptoms might be erroneous. There might be other explanations - indeed, there were others possible. As to that, time would show; at present the best course, perhaps the only right course, was to be watchful, yet not suspicious, observant, not prying. Rather than pry or be suspicious he would go to Millie herself, and without reservation tell her all that had been in his mind. He was well aware what the heroic attitude, the attitude of the virile, impetuous Englishman, dear to melodrama, would have been. It was quite easy for him to 'tax' Major Ames with baseness, to grind his teeth at his wife, and then burst into manly tears, each sob of which seemed to rend him. But to his quiet, sensible nature, it seemed difficult to see what was supposed to happen next. In melodrama the curtain went down, and you started ten years later in Queensland with regenerated natures distributed broadcast. But in actual life it was impossible to start again ten years later, or ten minutes later. You had to go on all the time. Willingly would he, on this divine October morning, have started again, indefinitely later. The difficulty was how to go on now.

His cases had not long detained him, and it was still not long after noon when the cob, still pleased and alert with motion, but with smoking flanks, drew up at his door. The clear chill of the morning had altogether passed, and the air in the basin or teacup of a town was still and sultry. There was a familiar hat on the table in the hall, a bunch of long-stemmed tawny chrysanthemums lay by it. And at that sight some distant echo of barbaric and simple man, deplorable to the smoothness of civilization and altogether obsolete, was resonant in him. He pitched the chrysanthemums into the street, where they flew like a shooting star close by the head of General Fortescue, who was tottering down to the club, and slammed the door. It was melodramatic and foolish enough, but the desire that prompted it was quite sincere and irresistible, and if at the moment Major Ames had been in that cool oak-panelled hall, there is little doubt that Dr Evans would have done his best to pitch him out after his flowers.

The doctor gave himself a moment to recover from his superficial violence, and then went out into the garden. They were sitting together on the bench under the mulberry tree, and Major Ames got up with his usual briskness as he approached. Somehow Dr Evans felt as if he was being welcomed and made to feel at home.

CHAPTER TEN

'Good morning,' said Major Ames. 'Glorious day, isn't it? I just stepped over with a handful of flowers, and we've been having a bit of a chat, a bit of a chat.'

'Cousin Lyndhurst has very kindly come to talk over all these little disturbances,' said Millie.

She looked at him.

'Shall I explain?' she asked.

Dr Evans took the seat that Major Ames had vacated, leaving him free to sit down in a garden chair opposite, or to stand, just as he pleased.

'It is like this, Wilfred,' she said. 'Cousin Amy did not like my joining the anti-Suffragette league which Mrs Altham started, and I have told Lyndhurst that I did not care a straw one way or the other, except that I could not go to prison to please Cousin Amy or anyone else. But it looked like taking sides, she thought. So Lyndhurst thought it would make everything easy if I didn't join any league at all. I think it very clever and tactful of him to think of that, and I will certainly tell Mrs Altham I find I am too busy. Of course, there is no quarrel between Cousin Amy and me, and Lyndhurst wants to assure us that he isn't mixed up in it, though there isn't any - and, of course, if Cousin Amy didn't see me the other day when I thought she pretended not to, it makes a difference.'

Millie delivered herself of these lucid statements with her usual deferential air.

'I think it is very kind of Cousin Lyndhurst to take so much trouble,' she added. 'He is stopping to lunch.'

Major Ames made a noble little gesture that disclaimed any credit.

'It's nothing, a mere nothing,' he said, quite truly. 'But I'm sure you hate little domestic jars as much as I do. As Amy once said, my profession was to be a man of war, but my instinct was to be a man of peace. Ha! Ha! I'm only delighted my little olive branch has - has met with success,' he added rather feebly, being unable to think of any botanical metaphor.

The doctor got up. It is to be feared that, in his present state of mind, he felt not the smallest admiration or gratitude for the work of Lyndhurst the Peacemaker, but only saw in it a purely personal desire to secure an uninterrupted va et vient between the two houses.

'I'm sure I haven't the slightest intention of quarrelling with anybody,' he said. 'It seems to me the most deplorable waste of time and energy, besides being very uncomfortable. Let us go in to lunch, Millie; I have to go out again at two o'clock.'

Millie wrote an amiable and insincere little note to Mrs Altham, which Major Ames undertook to deliver on his way home, explaining how, since Elsie had gone to Dresden to perfect herself in the German language, she herself had become so busy that she did not know which way to turn, besides missing Elsie very much. She felt, therefore, that since she would not be able to give as much time as she wished to this very interesting anti-Suffragette movement, it would be better not to give to it any time at all. This she wrote directly after her husband had gone out again, and brought to Major Ames, who was waiting for it. He, too, had said he would have to be off at once. She gave him the note.

'There it is,' she said; 'and so many thanks for leaving it. But you are not hurrying away at once, are you?'

'Am I not keeping you in?' he asked.

She pulled down the lace blinds over the window that looked into the street; the October sun, it is true, beat rather hotly into the room, but the instinct that dictated her action was rather a desire for privacy.

CHAPTER TEN

'As if I would not sooner sit and talk to you,' she said, 'than go out. I have no one to go out with. I am rather lonely since Elsie has gone, and I daresay I shall not see Wilfred again till dinnertime. It is rather amusing that I have just written to Mrs Altham to say how busy I am.'

He came and sat a little closer to her.

'Upon my word,' he said, 'I am in the same boat as you. I haven't set eyes on Amy all morning, and this afternoon I know she has a couple of meetings. It's extraordinary how this idea of votes for women has taken hold of her. Not a bad thing, though, as long as she doesn't go making a fool of herself in public, and as long as she doesn't have any more quarrels with you.'

'What would you have done if she had really wished to quarrel with me over Mrs Altham's league?' she asked.

'Just what I told her. I said I would be no partner to it, and as long as you would receive me here en garçon I should always come.'

'That was dear of you,' she said softly.

She paused a moment.

'Sometimes I think we made a mistake in coming to settle here,' she said; 'but you know how obstinate Wilfred is, and how little influence I have with him. But then, again, I think of our friendship. I have not had many friends. I think, perhaps, I am too shy and timid with people. When I like them very much I find it difficult to express myself. It is rather sad not to be able to show what you feel quite frankly. It prevents your being understood by the people whom you most want to understand you.'

But beneath this profession of incompetence, it seemed to Major Ames that there lurked a very efficient strength. He felt himself being gradually overpowered by a superior force, a force that did not strike and disable and overbear, but cramped and paralysed the power of its adversary, enfolding him, clinging to him. There was still something in him, some part of his will which was hostile and opposed to her: it was just that which she assailed. And in alliance with that paralysing force was her attraction and charm - soft, yielding, feminine; the two advanced side by side, terrible twins.

He did not answer for a moment, and it flashed across his mind that this cool room, shaded from the street glare by the lace curtains, and suffused with the greenish glow of the sunlight reflected from the lawn outside, was like a trap . . . She gave a little laugh.

'See how badly I express myself,' she said. 'You are puzzling, frowning. Don't frown, you look best when you are laughing. I get so tired of frowning faces. Wilfred so often frowns all dinnertime when he is thinking over something connected with microbes. And he frowns over his chess, when he cannot make up his mind whether to exchange bishops. We play chess every evening.'

Instinctively she had drawn back a little, when she saw he did not advance to meet her, and spoke as if chess and the pathos of her dumbness to express friendship were things of equal moment. There was no calculation about it: it was the expression of one type, the eternal feminine attracted and wishing to attract. Her descent to these commonplaces restored his confidence; the room was a trap no longer, but the pleasant drawing room he knew so well, with its charming mistress seated by him. It was almost inevitable that he should contrast the hot plushes and saddle-bag cushions of his own, its angular chairs and Axminster carpets with the cool chintzes here, the lace-shrouded windows, the Persian rugs. More marked was the contrast between the mistresses of the two houses. Amy had been writing at her davenport a good deal lately, and her short, stiff back had been the current picture of her. Here was a woman, dim in the half light, wanting to talk to him, to make timid confidences, to make him realize how much his friendship meant to her. His confidence returned with disarming completeness.

'Well, I'm sure I should find it dismal enough at home,' he said, 'if I hadn't somewhere to go to, knowing I should find a welcome. Mind you, I don't blame Amy. For years now, when we've been alone in the evening, she has done her work, and I have read the paper, and I daresay we haven't said a dozen words till Parker brought in the bedroom candles, or sometimes we play picquet - for love. But now evenings spent like that seem to me very prosy and dismal. Perhaps it's Harrogate that has made me a bit more supple and youthful, though I'm sure it's ridiculous enough that a tough old campaigner like me should feel such things - '

Mrs Evans put forward her chin, raising her face towards him.

'But why ridiculous?' she asked. 'You must be so much younger than dear Cousin Amy. I wonder - I wonder if she feels that too?'

There was there a very devilish suggestion, the more so because, in proportion to the suggestion, so very little was stated. It succeeded admirably.

'Poor dear Amy!' said he.

He had said that once before, when Cleopatra-Amy was contrasted with Cleopatra-Millie. But there was a significance in the repetition of it. Once the assumed identity of character had suggested the comment, now there was no assumed character. It concerned Millie and Amy themselves.

Mrs Evans put back her chin.

'I am sure Cousin Amy ought to be very happy,' she said softly. 'You are so devoted to her, and all. I almost think you spoil her, Lyndhurst. It is all so romantic. Fancy being a woman, and as old as Cousin Amy, and yet having a young man so devoted. Harry, too!'

Again a billow of confidence tinged with self-appreciation surged over Major Ames. After all, his wife was much older than him, for he was still a young man, and his youth was being expanded on sweet peas and the garden roller. And he was stirred into a high flight of philosophical conjecture.

'My God, what a puzzle life is!' he observed.

She rose to this high-water mark.

'And it might be so simple,' she said. 'It should be so easy to be happy.'

Then Major Ames knew where he was. In one sense he was worthy of the occasion, in another he did not feel up to all that it implied. He rose hastily.

'I had better go,' he said rather hoarsely.

But he had smoked five cigarettes since lunch. The hoarseness might easily have been the result of this indulgence.

She did not attempt to keep him, nor did she make it incumbent on him to give her a kiss, however cousinly. She did not even rise, but only looked up at him from her low chair as she gave him her hand, smiling a little secretly, as Mona Lisa smiles. But she felt quite satisfied with their talk; he would think over it, and find fresh signals and private beckonings in it.

'Come and see me again,' she said. There was a touch of imperativeness in her tone.

She looked through the lace curtain and saw him go out into the street. There was something in the gutter of the roadway which he inquired into with the end of his stick. It looked like a withered bunch of dusty chrysanthemums.

Mrs Ames, meantime, had lunched at home, and gone off immediately afterwards, as her husband had conjectured, to a meeting. In the last month the membership of her league had largely increased, and it was no longer possible to convene its meetings in her own drawing room, for it numbered some fifty persons, including a dozen men of enlightened principles. Even at first, as has been seen, she had welcomed (thereby incurring Mrs Altham's disapproval) several ladies with whom she did not usually associate, and now the gathering was entirely independent of all class distinctions. The wife of the station master, for instance, was one of the most active members and walked up and down the platform with a large rosette of Suffragette colours selling current copies of the Clarion. And no less remarkable than this growth of the league was the growth of Mrs Ames. She was neither pompous nor condescending to those persons whom, a couple of months ago, she would have looked upon as being barely existent, except if they were all in church, when she would very probably have shared a hymn book with any of them, the 'Idea' for which they had assembled galvanizing them, though strictly temporarily, into the class of existent people. Now, the idea which brought them together in the commodious warehouse, kindly lent and sufficiently furnished by Mr Turner, had given them a permanent existence, and they were not automatically blotted out of her book of life the moment these meetings were over, as they would have been so short a time ago in church, when the last 'Amen' was said. The bonds of her barren and barbaric conventionality were bursting; indeed, it was not so much that others, not even those of 'her class', were becoming women to her, as that she was becoming a woman herself. She had scarcely been one hitherto; she had been a piece of perfect propriety. And how far she had travelled from her original conception of the Suffragette movement as suitable to supply a novelty for the autumn that would eclipse the memory of the Shakespearean ball, may be gathered from the fact that she no longer took the chair at these meetings, but was an ordinary member. Mr Turner had far more experience in the duties of a chairman: she had herself proposed him and would have seconded him as well, had such a step been in order.

Today the meeting was assembled to discuss the part which the league should take in the forthcoming elections. The Tory Government was at present in power, and likely to remain in office, while Riseborough itself was a fairly safe seat for the Tory member, who was Sir James Westbourne. Before polemical or obstructive measures could be decided on, it had clearly been necessary to ascertain Sir James' views on the subject of votes for women, and today his answer had been received and was read to the meeting. It was as unsatisfactory as it was brief, and their 'obedient servant' had no sympathy with, and so declined to promise any support to, their cause. Mr Turner read this out, and laid it down on his desk.

'Will ladies or gentlemen give us their views on the course we are to adopt?' he said.

A dozen simultaneously rose, and simultaneously sat down again. The chairman asked Mrs Brooks to address the meeting. Another and another succeeded her, and there was complete unanimity of purpose in their suggestions. Sir James' meetings and his speeches to his constituents must not be allowed to proceed without interruption. If he had no sympathy with the cause, the cause would show a marked lack of sympathy with him. Thereafter the league resolved itself into a committee of ways and means. The President of the Board of Trade was coming to support Sir James' candidature at a meeting the date of which was already fixed for a fortnight hence, and it was decided to make a demonstration in force. And as the discussion went on, and real practical plans were made, that strange fascination and excitement at the thought of shouting and interrupting at a public meeting, of becoming for the first time of some consequence, began to seethe and ferment. Most of the members were women, whose lives had been passed in continuous self-repression, who had been frozen over by the narcotic ice of a completely conventional and humdrum existence. Many of them were unmarried and already of middle age; their natural human instincts had never known the blossoming and honey which the fulfilment of their natures would have brought. To the eagerness and sincerity with which they welcomed a work that demanded justice for their sex, there was added this excitement of doing something at last. There was an opportunity of expansion, of stepping out, under the stimulus of an idea, into an experience that was real. In kind, this was akin to martyrs, who rejoiced and sang when the prospects of persecution came near; as martyrs for the sake of their faith thought almost with glee of the rack and the burning, so, minutely, the very prospect of discomfort and rough handling seemed attractive, if, by such means, the cause was infinitesimally advanced. To this, a sincere and wholly laudable desire, was added the more personal stimulus. They would be doing something, instead of suffering the tedium of passivity, acting instead of being acted on. For it is only through centuries of custom that the woman, physically weak and liable to be knocked down, has become the servant of the other sex. She is fiercer at heart, more courageous, more scornful of consequences than he; it is only muscular inferiority of strength that has subdued her into the place that she occupies, that, and the periods when, for the continuance of the race, she must submit to months of tender and strong inaction. There she finds fruition of her nature, and there awakes in her a sweet indulgence for the strange, childish lust of being master, of parading, in making of laws and conventions, his adventitious power, of the semblance of sovereignty that has been claimed by man. At heart she knows that he has but put a tinsel crown on his head, and robed himself in spangles that but parody real gold. She lays a woman's hand on his child-head, and to please him says, 'How wise you are, how strong, how clever.' And the child is pleased, and loves her for it. And there is her weakness, for the most dominant thing in her nature is the need of being loved. From the beginning it must have been so. When Adam's rib was taken from him in sleep, he lost more than was left him, and woke to find all his finer self gone from him. He was left a blundering bumblebee: to the rib that was taken from him clung the courage of the lioness, the wisdom of the serpent, the gentleness of the dove, the cunning of the spider, and the mysterious charm of the firefly that dances in the dusk. But to that rib also clung the desire to be loved. Otherwise, in the human race, the male would be slain yearly like the drone of the hive. But the strange thing that grew from the rib, like flowers from buried carrion, desired love. There was its strength and its weakness.

It desired love, and in its desire it suffered all degradation to obtain it. And no leanness of soul entered into the gratification of its desire. Only when its desire was pinched and rationed, or when, by the operation of civilized law, all fruit of desire was denied it, so that the blossom of sex was made into one unfruitful bud, did revolt come. Long generations produced the germ, long generations made it active. At length it swam up to sight, from subaqueous dimnesses, feeble and violent, conscious of the justice of its cause and demanding justice. But what helped to make the desire for justice so attractive was the violence, the escape from self-repression that the demand gave opportunity for, to many who, all their lives, had been corked or wired down in comfort, which no woman cares about, or sealed up in spinsterhood and decorous emptiness of days. There was justice in the demand, and hysterical excitement in demanding.

To others, and in this little league of Riseborough there were many such, the prospect of making those demands was primarily appalling, and to none more than to poor Mrs Ames, when the plan of campaign was discussed, decided on, and entrusted to the members of the league. It required almost more courage than the idea was capable of inspiring to face, even in anticipation, the thought of shouting 'Votes for Women' when good-humoured Cousin James rose and said 'Ladies and gentlemen!' Very possibly, as had often happened in Cousin James' previous candidatures, Lyndhurst would wish his wife to ask him and the President of the Board of Trade to dinner before the meeting, an occasion which would warrant the materialization of the most sumptuous of all the dinners tabulated on the printed menu cards, while sherry would be given with soup, hock with fish, and a constant flow of champagne be kept up afterwards, until port time. In that case Cousin James would certainly ask them to sit on the platform, and they would roll richly to the town hall in his motor, all blazing with Conservative colours, while she, in a small bag, would be surreptitiously conveying there her great Suffragette rosette, and a small steel chain with a padlock. She would be sitting probably next to the Mayor, who would introduce the speakers, and no doubt refer to 'the presence of the fair sex' who graced the platform. During this she would have to pin her colours on her dress, chain herself up like Andromeda, snap the patent spring lock of the padlock, and when Sir James rose . . . her imagination could not grapple with the picture: it turned sickly away, refusing to contemplate. And this to a cousin and a guest, who had just eaten the best salt, so to speak, of her table, from one who all her life had been so perfect a piece of propriety! She felt far too old a bottle for such new wine. Sitting surrounded by fellow-crusaders, and infected by the proximity of their undiluted enthusiasm, it would be difficult enough, but that she should chain herself, perhaps, to the very leg of the table which Cousin James would soon thump in the fervour of his oratory, as he announced all those Tory platitudes in which she so firmly believed, and which she must so shrilly interrupt, while sitting solitary in the desert of his sleek and staid supporters, was not only an impossible but an unthinkable achievement. Whatever horrors fate, that gruesome weaver of nightmares, might have in store for her, she felt that here was something that transcended imagination. She could not sit on the platform with Lyndhurst and Cousin James and the Mayor and Lady Westbourne, and do what was required of her, for the sake of any crusade. Curfew, so to speak, would have to ring that night.

She and Lyndhurst were dining alone the evening after this meeting of 'ways and means', he in that state of mind which she not inaptly described as 'worried' when she felt kind, and 'cross' when she felt otherwise. He had come home hot from his walk, and, having sat in his room where there was no fire, when evening fell chilly, had had a smart touch of lumbago. Thus there were clearly two causes for complaint against Amy, and a third disturbing topic, for there was no shadow of doubt that it was his bouquet of chrysanthemums that he had found in the road outside Dr Evans' house, and even before the lumbago had produced its characteristic pessimism, he had been unable to find any encouraging explanation of this floral castaway.

'I'm sure I don't know what was the good of my spending all August,' he said, 'in that filthy hole of a Harrogate, at no end of expense, too, if I'm to be crippled all winter. But you urged me to so strongly: should never have thought of going there otherwise.'

'My dear, you have only been crippled for half an hour at present,' she observed. 'It is a great bore, but if only you will take a good hot bath tonight, and have a very light dinner, I expect you will be much better in the morning. Parker, tell them to see that there is plenty of hot water in the kitchen boiler.'

'It'll be the only warm thing in the house, if there is,' said he. 'My room was like an ice house when I came in. Positively like an ice house. Enough to give a man pneumonia, let alone lumbago. Soup cold, too.'

'My dear, you should take more care of yourself,' said Mrs Ames placidly. 'Why did you not light the fire instead of being cold? I'm sure it was laid.'

'And have it just burning up at dinnertime,' said he, 'when I no longer wanted it.'

It was still early in the course of dinner.

'Light the fire in the drawing room, Parker,' said Mrs Ames. 'Let there be a good fire when we come out of dinner.'

'Get roasted alive,' said Major Ames, half to himself, but intending to be heard.

But Mrs Ames' mind had been feasting for weeks past on things which had a solider existence than her husband's unreasonable strictures. Since this new diet had been hers, his snaps and growls had produced no effect: they often annoyed her into repartee, and as likely as not, a few months ago, she would have said that his claret seemed a very poor kind of beverage. But tonight she felt not the smallest desire to retort. She was very sorry for his lumbago, but felt no inclination to carry the war into his territories, or to tell him that if people, perspiring freely, and of gouty habit, choose to sit down without changing, and get chilly, they must expect reprisal for their imprudence.

'Then we will open the window, dear,' she said, 'if we find we are frizzling. But I don't think it will be too hot. Evenings are chilly in October. Did you have a pleasant lunch, Lyndhurst? Indeed, I don't know where you lunched. I ordered curry for you. I sat down at a quarter to two as you did not come in.'

It was all so infinitesimal . . . yet it was the mental diet which had supported her for years. Perhaps after dinner they would play picquet. The garden, the kitchen, for years, except for gossip infinitely less real, these had been the topics. There had been no joy for him in the beauty of the garden, only a pleased sense of proprietorship, if a rare plant flowered, or if there were more roses than usual. For her, she had been vaguely pleased if Lyndhurst had taken two helpings of a dish, and both of them had been vaguely disquieted if Harry quoted Swinburne.

'I lunched with the Evanses,' he said. 'By the way, I met your cousin James Westbourne this afternoon, when I was on my walk. Extraordinarily cordial he gets when there's business ahead that brings him into Riseborough, and he wants to cadge a dinner or two. It's little notice he takes of us the rest of the year, and I'm sure it's a couple of years since he so much as sent you a brace of pheasants, and more than that since he asked me to shoot there. But as I say, when he wants to pick up a dinner or two in Riseborough, he's all heartiness, and saying he doesn't see half enough of us.

He doesn't seem to strain himself in trying to see more, and there's seldom a weekend when he and that great guy of a wife of his don't have the house packed with people. I suppose we're not smart enough for them, except when it's convenient to dine in Riseborough. Then he's not above drinking a bottle of my champagne.'

Mrs Ames was eager in support of her husband.

'I'm sure there's no call for you to open any more bottles for him, my dear,' she said. 'If Cousin James wants to see us, he can take his turn in asking us. And Harriet is a great guy, as you say, with her big fiddle-head.'

Major Ames shrugged his shoulders rather magnificently.

'I'm sure I don't grudge him his dinner,' he said, 'and, in point of fact, I told him he could come and dine with us before his first meeting. He's got some Cabinet Minister with him, and I said he could bring him too. You might get up a little party, that's to say if I'm not in bed with this infernal lumbago. And Cousin James will return our hospitality by giving us seats on the platform to hear him stamp and stammer and rant. An infernal bad speaker. Never heard a worse. Wretched delivery, nothing to say, and says it all fifty times over. Enough to make a man turn Radical. However, he'll have made himself at home with my Mumm, and perhaps he'll go to sleep himself before he sends us off.'

This, of course, represented the lumbago view. Major Ames had been fulsomely cordial to Cousin James, and had himself urged the dinner that he represented now as being forced on him.

'Have you actually asked him, Lyndhurst?' said Mrs Ames rather faintly. 'Did he say he would come?'

'Did you ever know your Cousin James refuse a decent dinner?' asked Lyndhurst. 'And he was kind enough to say he would like it at a quarter past seven. Cool, upon my word! I wish I had asked him if he'd have thick soup or clear, and if he preferred a wing to a leg. That's the sort of thing one never thinks of till afterwards.'

Mrs Ames was not attending closely: there was that below the surface which claimed all her mind. Consequently she missed the pungency of this irony, hearing only the words.

'Cousin James never takes soup at all,' she said. 'He told me it always disagreed.'

Major Ames sighed; his lumbago felt less acute, his ill temper had found relief in words, and he had long ago discovered that women had no sense of humour. On the whole, it was gratifying to find the truth of this so amply endorsed. For the moment it put him into quite a good temper.

'I'm afraid I've been grumbling all dinner,' he said. 'Shall we go into the other room? There's little sense in my looking at the decanters, if I mayn't take my glass of port. Eh! That was a twinge!'

'IT is no use, Henry,' said Mrs Altham on that same evening, 'telling me it is all stuff and nonsense, when I've seen with my own eyes the parcel of Suffragette riband being actually directed to Mrs Brooks; for pen and ink is pen and ink, when all is said and done. Tapworth measured off six yards of it on the counter- measure that gives two feet, for he gave nine lengths of it and put it in paper and directed it. Of course, if nine lengths of two feet doesn't make eighteen feet, which is six yards, I am wrong and you are right, and twice two no longer makes four. And there were two other parcels already done up of exactly the same shape. You will see if I am not right. Or do you suppose that Mrs Brooks is ordering it just to trim her nightgown with it?'

'I never said anything about Mrs Brooks' nightgown,' said Henry, who, to do him justice, had been goaded into slightly Rabelaisian mood: 'I never thought about Mrs Brooks' nightgown. I didn't know she wore one - I mean - '

Mrs Altham made what children would call 'a face'. Her eyes grew suddenly fixed and boiled, and her mouth assumed an acidulated expression as if with a plethora of lemon juice.

The 'face' was due to the entry of the parlourmaid with the pudding. It was jelly, and was served in silence. Mrs Altham waited till the door was quietly closed again.

'It is not a question of Mrs Brooks' nightgown,' she said, 'since we both agree that she would not order six yards of Suffragette riband to trim it. I spoke sarcastically, Henry, and you interpreted me literally, as you often do. It was the same at Littlestone in August, when the bacon was so salty one day that I said to Mrs Churchill that a little bacon in the bath would be equivalent to sea bathing. Upon which you must needs tell her next morning to send your bacon to the bathroom, which she did, and there was a plate of bacon on the sponge tray, so extraordinary. But all that is beside the point, though what she can have thought of you I can't imagine. After all, your gift of being literal may help you now. Why does Mrs Brooks want six yards of Suffragette riband, and why are there two similar parcels on Tapworth's counter? If I had had a moment alone I would certainly have looked at the other addresses, and seen where they were being sent. But young Tapworth was there all the time - that one with the pince-nez, and the ridiculous chin - and he put them into the errand-boy's basket, and told him to be sharp about it. So I had no chance of seeing.'

'You might have strolled along behind the boy to see where he went,' suggested Mr Altham.

'He went on a bicycle,' said Mrs Altham, 'and it is impossible to stroll behind a boy on a bicycle and hope to get there in time. But he went up the High Street. I should not in the least wonder if Mrs Evans had turned Suffragette, after that note to me about her not having time to attend the anti-Suffragette meetings.'

'Especially since there was only one,' said Henry, in the literal mood that had been forced on him, 'and nobody came to that. It would not have sacrificed very much of her time. Not that I ever heard it was valuable.'

'What she can do with her day I can't imagine,' said Mrs Altham, her mind completely diverted by this new topic. 'Her cook told Griffiths that as often as not she doesn't go down to the kitchen at all in the morning, and she's hardly ever to be seen shopping in the High Street before lunch, and what with Elsie gone to Dresden, and her husband away on his rounds all day, she must be glad when it's bedtime. And she's a small sleeper, too, for she told me herself that she considers six hours a good night, though I expect she sleeps more than she knows, and I daresay has a nap after lunch as well. Dear me, what were we talking about? Ah, yes, I was saying I should not wonder if she had turned Suffragette, though I can't recall what made me think so.'

'Because Tapworth's boy went up the High Street on a bicycle,' said Mr Altham, who had a great gift of picking out single threads from the tangle of his wife's conversation; 'though, after all, the High Street leads to other houses besides Mrs Evans'. The station, for instance.'

'You seem to want to find fault with everything I say, tonight, Henry. I don't know what makes you so contrary. But there it is: I saw eighteen yards of Suffragette riband being sent out when I happened to be in Tapworth's this morning, and I daresay that's but a tithe of what has been ordered, though I can't say as to that, unless you expect me to stand in the High Street all day and watch. And as to what it all means, I'll let you conjecture for yourself, since if I told you what I thought, you would probably contradict me again.'

It was no wonder that Mrs Altham was annoyed. She had been thrilled to the marrow by the parcels of Suffragette riband, and when she communicated her discovery, Henry, who usually was so sympathetic, had seen nothing to be thrilled about. But he had not meant to be unsympathetic, and repaired his error.

'I'm sure, my dear, that you will have formed a very good guess as to what it means,' he said. 'Tell me what you think.'

'Well, if you care to know,' said she, 'I think it all points to there being some demonstration planned, and I for one should not be surprised if I looked out of the window some morning, and saw Mrs Ames and Mrs Brooks and the rest of them marching down the High Street with ribands and banners. They've been keeping very quiet about it all, at least not a word of what they've been doing has come to my ears, and I consider that's a proof that something is going on and that they want to keep it secret.'

Mr Altham's legal mind cried out to him to put in the plea that a complete absence of news does not necessarily constitute a proof that exciting events are occurring, but he rightly considered that such logic might be taken to be a sign of continued 'contrariness'. So he gave an illogical assent to his wife's theory.

'Certainly it is odd that nothing more has been heard of it all,' he said. 'I wonder what they are planning. The election coming on so soon, too! Can they be planning anything in connection with that?'

Mrs Altham got up, letting her napkin fall on the floor.

'Henry, I believe you have hit it,' she said. 'Now what can it be? Let us go into the drawing room, and thresh it out.'

But the best threshing machines in the world cannot successfully fulfil their function unless there is some material to work upon; they can but show by their whirling wheels and rattling gear that they are capable of threshing should anything be provided for them. The poor Althams were somewhat in this position, for their rations of gossip were sadly reduced, their two chief sources being cut off from them. For ever since the mendacious Mrs Brooks had appeared as Cleopatra, when she had as good as promised to be Hermione, chill politeness had taken the place of intimacy between the two houses, since there was no telling what trick she might not play next, while the very decided line which Mrs Altham had taken when she found she was expected to meet people like tradesmen's wives had caused a complete rupture in relations with the Ames'. That Suffragette meetings were going on was certain, else what sane mind could account for the fact that only today a perfect stream of people, some of them not even known by sight to Mrs Altham, and therefore probably of the very lowest origin, with Mrs Ames and the wife of the station master among them, had been seen coming out of Mr Turner's warehouse. It was ridiculous 'to tell me' that they had been all making purchases (nobody had told her), and such a supposition was thoroughly negated by the subsequent discovery that the warehouse in question contained only a quantity of chairs. All this, however, had been threshed out at teatime, and the flywheels buzzed emp-tily. Against the probability of an election demonstration was the fact that the Unionist member, to whom these attentions would naturally be directed, was Mrs Ames' cousin, though 'cousin' was a vague word, and Mrs Altham would not wonder if he was a very distant sort of cousin indeed. Still, it would be worthwhile to get tickets anyhow for the first of Sir James' meetings, when the President of the Board of Trade was going to speak, so as to be certain of a good place. HE was not Mrs Ames' cousin, so far as

Mrs Altham knew, though she did not pretend to follow the ramifications of Mrs Ames' family.

The flywheels were allowed to run on in silence for some little while after this meagre material had been thoroughly sifted, in case anything further offered itself; then Mr Altham proposed another topic.

'You were saying that you wondered how Mrs Evans got through her time,' he began.

But there was no need for him to say another word, nor any opportunity.

Mrs Altham stooped like a hawk on the quarry.

'You mean Major Ames,' she said. 'I'm sure I never pass the house but what he's either going in or coming out, and he does a good deal more of the going in than of the other, in my opinion.'

Henry penetrated into the meaning of what sounded a rather curious achievement and corroborated.

'He was there this morning,' he said, 'on the doorstep at eleven o'clock, or it might have been a quarter past, with a bouquet of chrysanthemums big enough to do all Mrs Ames' decorations at St Barnabas. What is the matter, my dear?'

For Mrs Altham had literally bounced out of her chair, and was pointing at him a forefinger that trembled with a nameless emotion.

'At a quarter past one, or a few minutes later,' she said, 'that bouquet was lying in the middle of the road. Let us say twenty minutes past one, because I came straight home, took off my hat, and was ready for lunch. It was more like a haystack than a bouquet: I'm sure if I hadn't stepped over it, I should have tripped and fallen. And to think that I never mentioned it to you, Henry! How things piece themselves together, if you give them a chance! Now did you actually see Major Ames carry it into the house?'

CHAPTER ELEVEN

'The door was opened to him, just as I came opposite,' said Henry firmly, 'and in he went, bouquet and all.'

'Then somebody MUST have thrown it out again,' said Mrs Altham.

She held up one hand, and ticked off names on its fingers.

'Who was then in the house?' she said. 'Mrs Evans, Dr Evans, Major Ames. Otherwise the servants - how they can find work for six servants in that house I can't understand - and servants would never have thrown chrysanthemums into the street. So we needn't count the servants. Now can you imagine Mrs Evans throwing away a bouquet that Major Ames had brought her? If so, I envy you your power of imagination. Or - '

She paused a moment.

'Or can there have been a quarrel, and did she tell him she had too much of him and his bouquets? Or - '

'Dr Evans,' said Henry.

She nodded portentously.

'Turned out of the house, he and his bouquet,' she said. 'Dr Evans is a powerful man, and Major Ames, for all his size, is mostly fat. I should not wonder if Dr Evans knocked him down. Henry, I have a good mind to treat Mrs Ames as if she had not been so insulting to me that day (and after all that is only Christian conduct) and to take round to her after lunch tomorrow the book she said she wanted to see last July. I am sure I have forgotten what it was, but any book will do, since she only wants it to be thought that she reads. After all, I should be sorry to let Mrs Ames suppose that anything she can do should have the power of putting me out, and I should like to see if she still dyes her hair. After the chrysanthemums in the road I should not be the least surprised to be told that Major Ames is ill. Then we shall know all. Dear me, it is eleven o'clock already, and I never felt less inclined to sleep.'

Henry stepped downstairs to drink a mild whisky and soda after all this conversation and excitement, but while it was still half drunk, he felt compelled to run upstairs and tap at his wife's door.

'I am not coming in, dear,' he said, in answer to her impassioned negative. 'But if you find Major Ames is not ill?'

'No one will be more rejoiced than myself, Henry,' said she, in a disappointed voice.

Henry went gently downstairs again.

Mrs Ames was at home when the forgiving Mrs Altham arrived on the following afternoon, bearing a copy of a book of which there were already two examples in the house. But she clearly remembered having wanted to see some book of which they had spoken together, last July, and it was very kind of Mrs Altham to have attempted to supply her with it. Beyond doubt she had ceased to dye her hair, for the usual grey streaks were apparent in it, a proof (if Mrs Altham wanted a proof, which she did not) that artificial means had been resorted to. And even as Mrs Altham, with her powerful observation, noticed the difference in Mrs Ames' hair, so also she noticed a difference in Mrs Ames. She no longer seemed pompous: there was a kindliness about her which was utterly unlike her usual condescension, though it manifested itself only in the trivial happenings of an afternoon call, such as putting a cushion on her chair, and asking if she found the room, with its prospering fire, too hot. This also led to interesting information.

'It is scarcely cold enough for a fire today,' she said, 'but my husband is laid up with a little attack of lumbago.'

'I am so sorry to hear that,' said Mrs Altham feverishly. 'When did he catch it?'

'He felt it first last night before dinner. It is disappointing, for he expected Harrogate to cure him of such tendencies. But it is not very severe: I have no doubt he will be in here presently for tea.'

Mrs Altham felt quite convinced he would not, and hastened to glean further enlightenment.

'You must be very busy thinking of the election,' she said. 'I suppose Sir James is safe to get in. I got tickets for the first of his meetings this morning.'

'That will be the one at which the President of the Board of Trade speaks,' said Mrs Ames. 'My cousin and he dine with us first.'

Mrs Altham determined on more direct questions.

'Really, it must require courage to be a politician nowadays,' she said, 'especially if you are in the Cabinet. Mr Chilcot has been hardly able to open his mouth lately without being interrupted by some Suffragette. Dear me, I hope I have not said the wrong thing! I quite forgot your sympathies.'

'It is certainly a subject that interests me,' said Mrs Ames, 'though as for saying the wrong thing, dear Mrs Altham, why, the world would be a very dull place if we all agreed with each other. But I think it requires just as much courage for a woman to get up at a meeting and interrupt. I cannot imagine myself being bold enough. I feel I should be unable to get on my feet, or utter a word. They must be very much in earnest, and have a great deal of conviction to nerve them.'

This was not very satisfactory; if anything was to be learned from it, it was that Mrs Ames was but a tepid supporter of the cause. But what followed was still more vexing, for the parlourmaid announced Mrs Evans.

'So sorry to hear about Major Ames, dear cousin Amy,' she said. 'Wilfred told me he had been to see him.'

Mrs Ames made a kissing pad, so to speak, of her small toad's face, and Millie dabbed her cheek on it.

'Dear Millie, how nice of you to call! Parker, tell the Major that tea is ready, and that Mrs Evans and Mrs Altham are here.'

But by the time Major Ames arrived Mrs Altham was there no longer. She was thoroughly disgusted with the transformation into chaff of all the beautiful grain that they had taken the trouble to thresh out the night before. She summed it up succinctly to her husband when he came back from his golf.

'I don't believe the Suffragettes are going to do anything at all, Henry,' she said, 'and I shouldn't wonder if these chrysanthemums had nothing to do with anybody. The only thing is that her hair is dyed, because it was all speckled with grey again as thickly as yours, and I declare I left The Safety of the Race behind me, instead of bringing it back again, as I meant to do.'

Henry, who had won his match at golf, was naturally optimistic.

'Then you didn't actually see Major Ames?' he asked.

'No, but there was no longer any doubt about it all,' she said. 'I do not think I am unduly credulous, but it was clear there was nothing the matter with him except a touch of lumbago. And all this Suffragette business means nothing at all, in spite of the yards of riband. You may take my word for it.'

'Then there will be no point in going to Sir James' meeting,' said Henry, 'though the President of the Board of Trade is going to speak.'

'Not unless you want to hear the biggest windbag in the country buttering up the greatest prig in the county. I should be sorry to waste my time over it; and he is dining with the Ameses, and so I suppose all there will be to look at will be the row of them on the platform, all swollen with one of Mrs Ames' biggest dinners. We might have gone to bed at our usual time last night, for all the use that there has been in our talk. And it was you saw the chrysanthemums, from which you expected so much and thought it worthwhile to tell me about them.'

And Henry felt too much depressed at the utter flatness of all that had made so fair a promise, to enter any protest against the palpable injustice of these conclusions.

Major Ames' lumbago was of the Laodicean sort, neither hot nor cold. It hung about, occasionally stabbing him shrewdly, at times retreating in the Parthian mode, so that he was encouraged to drink a glass of port, upon which it shot at him again, and he had to get back to his stew of sloppy diet and depressing reflections. Most of all, the relations into which he had allowed himself to drift with regard to Millie filled him with a timorous yet exultant agitation, but he almost, if not quite, exaggerated his indisposition, in order to escape from the responsibility of deciding what should come of it. Damp and boisterous weather made it prudent for him to keep to the house, and she came to see him daily. Behind her demure quietness he divined a mind that was expectant and sure: there was no doubt as to her view of the situation that had arisen between them. She had played with the emotions of others once too often, and was caught in the agitation which she had so often excited without sharing in it. Mrs Ames was generally present at these visits, but when it was quite certain that she was not looking, Millie often raised her eyes to his, and this disconcerting conviction lurked behind them. Her speech was equally disconcerting, for she would say, 'It will be nice when you are well again,' in a manner that quite belied the commonplace words. And this force that lay behind strangely controlled him. Involuntarily, almost, he answered her signals, gave himself the lover-like privilege of seeming to understand all that was not said. All the time, too, he perfectly appreciated the bad taste of the affair - namely, that a woman who was in love with him, and to whom he had given indications of the most unmistakable kind that he was on her plane of emotion, should play these unacted scenes in his wife's house, coming there to make pass his invalid hours, and that he should take his part in them. It was common, and he could not but contrast that commonness with the unconsciousness of his wife. Occasionally he was inclined to think, 'Poor Amy, how little she sees,' but as often it occurred to him that she was too big to be aware of such smallnesses as he and Millie were guilty of. And, in reality, the truth lay between these extreme views. She was not too big to be aware of it; she was quite aware of it, but she was big enough to appear too big to be aware of it. She watched, and scorned herself for her watching. She fed herself with suspicions, but was robust enough to spew them forth again. Also, and this allowed the robuster attitude to flourish, she was concerned with a nightmare of her own which daily grew more vivid and unescapable.

A decade of streaming October days passed in this trying atmosphere of suspicion and uncertainty and apprehension. Of the three of them it was Major Ames who was most thoroughly ill at ease, for he had no inspiration which enabled him to bear this sordid martyrdom. He divined that Millie was evolving some situation in which he would be expected to play a very prominent part, and such ardour as was his he felt not to be of the adequate temperature, and he looked back over the peaceful days when his garden supplied him not only with flowers, but with the most poignant emotions known to his nature, almost with regret. It had all been so peaceful and pleasant in that land-locked harbour, and now she, like a steam tug, was slowly towing him out past the pier-head into a waste of breakers. Strictly speaking, it was possible for him at any moment to cast the towing rope off and return to his quiet anchorage, but he was afraid he lacked the moral power to do so. He had let her throw the rope aboard him, he had helped to attach it to the bollard, thinking, so to speak, that he was the tug and she the frail little craft. But that frail little craft had developed into an engined apparatus, and it was his turn to be towed, helpless and at least unwilling, and wholly uninspired. The others, at any rate, had inspiration to warm their discomfort: Mrs Ames the sense of justice and sisterhood which was leavening her dumpy existence, Mrs Evans the fire which, however strange and illicit are its burnings, however common and trivial the material from which it springs, must still be called love.

It was the evening of Sir James' first meeting, and Mrs Ames at six o'clock was satisfying herself that nothing had been omitted in the preparations for dinner. The printed menu cards were in place, announcing all that was most sumptuous; the requisite relays of knives, spoons and forks were on the sideboard; the plates of opalescent glass for ice were to hand, and there was no longer anything connected with this terrible feast, that to her had the horror of a murderer's breakfast on the last morning of his life, which could serve to distract her mind any more. Millie was to dine with them and with them come to the meeting, but just now it did not seem to matter in the slightest what Millie did. All day Mrs Ames had been catching at problematic straws that might save her: it was possible that Mr Chilcot would be seized with sudden indisposition, and the meeting be postponed. But she herself had seen him drive by in Cousin

James' motor, looking particularly hearty. Or Cousin James might catch influenza: Lady Westbourne already had it, and it was pleasantly infectious. Or Lyndhurst might get an attack of really acute lumbago, but instead he felt absolutely well again today, and had even done a little garden-rolling. One by one these bright possibilities had been extinguished - now no reasonable anchor remained except that dinner would acutely disagree with her (and that was hardly likely, since she felt incapable of eating anything) or that the motor which was to take them to the town hall would break down.

At half past six she went upstairs to dress; she would thus secure a quarter of an hour before the actual operation of decking herself began, in which to be alone and really face what was going to happen. It was no use trying to face it in one piece: taken all together the coming evening had the horror and unreality of nightmare brooding over it. She had to take it moment by moment from the time when she would welcome her guests, whom, so it seemed to her, she was then going to betray, till the time when, perhaps four hours from now, she would be back again here in her room, and everything that had happened had woven itself into the woolly texture of the past, in place of being in the steely, imminent future. There was dinner to be gone through; that was only tolerable to think of because of what was to follow: in itself it would please her to entertain her cousin and so notable a man as a cabinet minister. Clearly, then, she must separate dinner from the rest, and enjoy it independently. But when she went down to dinner she must have left here in readiness the little black velvet bag . . . that was not so pleasant to think of. Yet the little black velvet bag had nothing to do yet. Then there would follow the drive to the town hall: that would not be unpleasant: in itself she would rather enjoy the stir and pomp of their arrival. Sir James would doubtless say to the scrutinizing doorkeeper, 'These ladies are with me,' and they would pass on amid demonstrations of deference. Probably there would be a little procession on to the platform . . . the Mayor would very likely lead the way with her, her and her little black velvet bag . . .

And then poor Mrs Ames suddenly felt that if she thought about it any more she would have a nervous collapse. And at that thought her inspiration, so to speak, reached out a cool, firm hand to her. At any cost she was going through with this nightmare for the sake of that which inspired it. It was no use saying it was pleasant, nor was it pleasant to have a tooth out. But any woman with the slightest self-respect, when once convinced that it was better to have the tooth out, went to the dentist at the appointed hour, declined gas (Mrs Ames had very decided opinions about those who made a fuss over a little pain), opened her mouth, and held the arms of the chair very firmly. One wanted something to hold on to at these moments. She wondered what she would find to hold on to this evening. Perhaps the holding on would be done by somebody else - a policeman, for instance.

There was one more detail to attend to before dressing, and she opened the little black velvet bag. In it were two chains - light, but of steel: they had been sold her with the gratifying recommendation that either of them alone would hold a mastiff, which was more than was required. One was of such length as to go tightly round her waist: a spring lock with hasp passing through the last link of it, closing with an internal snap, obviated the necessity of a key. This she proposed to put on below the light cloak she wore before they started. The second chain was rather longer but otherwise similar. It was to be passed through the one already in place on her waist, and round the object to which she desired to attach herself. Another snap lock made the necessary connection.

She saw that all was in order and, putting the big Suffragette rosette on top of the other apparatus, closed the bag: it was useless to try to accustom herself to it by looking; she might as well inspect the dentist's forceps, hoping thus to mollify their grip. Cloak and little velvet bag she would leave here and come up for them after dinner. And already the quarter of an hour was over, and it was time to dress.

The daring rose-coloured silk was to be worn on this occasion, and she hoped that it would not experience any rough treatment. Yet it hardly mattered: after tonight she would very likely never care to set eyes on it again, and emphatically Lyndhurst would find it full of disagreeable associations. And then she felt suddenly and acutely sorry for him and for the amazement and chagrin that he was about to feel. He could not fail to be burningly ashamed of her, to choke with rage and mortification. Perhaps it would bring on another attack of lumbago, which she would intensely regret. But she did not anticipate feeling in the least degree ashamed of herself. But she intensely wished it had not got to be.

And now she was ready: the rose-coloured silk glowed softly in the electric light, the pink satin shoes which 'went with it' were on her plump, pretty little feet, the row of garnets was clasped round her neck. There was a good deal of colour in her face, and she was pleased to see she looked so well. The last time she had worn all these fine feathers was on the evening she returned home with brown hair and softened wrinkles from Overstrand. That was not a successful evening: it seemed that the rose-coloured silk was destined to shine on inauspicious scenes. But now she was ready: this was her last moment alone. And she plumped down on her knees by the bedside, in a sudden despair at what lay before her, and found her lips involuntarily repeating the words that were used in the hugest and most holy agony that man's spirit has ever known, when for one moment He felt that even He could not face the sacrifice of Himself or to drink of the cup. But next moment she sprang from her knees again, her face all aflame with shame at her paltriness. 'You wretched little coward!' she said to herself. 'How dare you?'

Dinner, that long expensive dinner, brought with it trouble unanticipated by Mrs Ames. Mr Chilcot, it appeared, was a teetotaller at all times, and never ate anything but a couple of poached eggs before he made a speech. He was also, owing to recent experiences, a little nervous about Suffragettes, and required reiterated assurances that unaccountable females had not been seen about.

'It's true that a week or two ago I received a letter asking me my views,' said Sir James, 'but I wrote a fairly curt reply, and have heard nothing more about it. My agent's pretty wide awake. He would have known if there was likely to be any disturbance. No thanks, Major, one glass of champagne is all I allow myself before making a speech. Capital wine, I know; I always say you give one the best glass of wine to be had in Kent. How's time, by the way? Ah, we've got plenty of time yet.'

'I like to have five minutes' quiet before going on to the platform,' said Mr Chilcot.

'Yes, that will be all right. Perhaps we might have the motor five minutes earlier, Cousin Amy. No, no sweetbread thanks. Dear me, what a great dinner you are giving us.'

An awful and dismal atmosphere descended. Mr Chilcot, thinking of his speech, frowned at his poached eggs, and, when they were finished, at the tablecloth. Cousin James refused dish after dish, Mrs Ames felt herself incapable of eating, and Major Ames and Mrs Evans, who was practically a vegetarian, were left to do the carousing. Wines went round untouched, silences grew longer, and an interminable succession of dishes failed to tempt anybody except Major Ames. At this rate, not one, but a whole series of luncheon parties would be necessary to finish up the untouched dainties of this ill-starred dinner. Outside, a brisk tattoo of rain beat on the windows, and the wind having got up, the fire began to smoke, and Mr Chilcot to cough. A readjustment of door and window mended this matter, but sluiced Cousin James in a chilly draught. Mr Chilcot brightened up a little as coffee came round, but the coffee was the only weak spot in an admirable repast, being but moderately warm. He put it down. Mrs Ames tried to repair this error.

'I'm afraid it is not hot enough,' she said. 'Parker, tell them to heat it up at once.'

Cousin James looked at his watch.

'Really, I think we ought to be off,' he said. 'I'm sure they can get a cup of coffee for Mr Chilcot from the hotel. We might all go together unless you have ordered something, Cousin Amy. The motor holds five easily.'

A smart, chill October rain was falling, and they drove through blurred and disconsolate streets. A few figures under umbrellas went swiftly along the cheerless pavements, a crowd of the very smallest dimensions, scarce two deep across the pavement opposite the town hall, watched the arrival of those who were attending the meeting. There was an insignificant queue of half a dozen carriages awaiting their disembarkments, but as the hands of the town hall clock indicated that the meeting was not timed to begin for twenty minutes yet, even Mr Chilcot could not get agitated about the possibility of a cup of coffee before his effort.

CHAPTER ELEVEN

Through the rain-streaked windows Mrs Ames could see how meagre, owing no doubt to the inclement night, was the assembly of the ticket holders. It was possible, of course, that crowds might soon begin to arrive, but Riseborough generally made a point of being in its place in plenty of time, and she anticipated a sparsely attended room. Mrs Brooks hurried by in mackintosh and goloshes, the cheerful Turner family, who were just behind them in a cab, dived into the wet night, and emerged again under the awning. Mrs Currie (wife of the station master), with her Suffragette rosette in a paper parcel, had a friendly word with a policeman at the door, and at these sights, since they indicated a forcible assemblage of the league, she felt a little encouraged. Then the car moved on and stopped again opposite the awning, and their party dismounted.

A bustling official demanded their tickets, and was summarily thrust aside by another, just as bustling but more enlightened, who had recognized Sir James, and conducted them all to the Mayor's parlour, where that dignitary received them. There was coffee already provided, and all anxiety on that score was removed. Mr Chilcot effaced himself in a corner with his cup and his notes, while the others, notably Sir James, behaved with that mixture of social condescension and official deference which appears to be the right attitude in dealing with mayors. Then the Mayoress said, 'George, dear, it has gone the half hour; will you escort Mrs Ames?'

George asked Mrs Ames if he might have the honour, and observed -

'We shall have but a thin meeting, I am afraid. Most inclement for October.'

Mrs Ames pulled her cloak a little closer round her, in order to hide a chain that was more significant than the

Mayor's, and felt the little black velvet bag beating time to her steps against her knee.

They walked through the stark bare passages, with stone floors that exuded cold moisture in sympathy with the wetness of the evening, and came out into a sudden blaze of light.

A faint applause from nearly empty benches heralded their appearance, and they disposed themselves on a row of plush armchairs behind a long oak table. The Mayor sat in the centre, to right and left of him Sir James and Mr Chilcot. Just opposite Mrs Ames was a large table leg, which had for her the significance of the execution shed.

She put her bag conveniently on her knees, and quietly unloosed the latch that fastened it. There were no more preparations to be made just yet, since the chain was quite ready, and in a curious irresponsible calm she took further note of her surroundings. Scarcely a hundred people were there, all told, and face after face, as she passed her eyes down the seats, was friendly and familiar. Mrs Currie bowed, and the Turner family, in a state of the pleasantest excitement, beamed; Mrs Brooks gave her an excited hand-wave. They were all sitting in encouraging vicinity to each other, but she was alone, as on the inexorable seas, while they were on the pier . . . Then the Mayor cleared his throat.

It had been arranged that the Mayor was to be given an uninterrupted hearing, for he was the local grocer, and it had, perhaps, been tacitly felt that he might adopt retaliatory measures in the inferior quality of the subsequent supplies of sugar. He involved himself in sentences that had no end, and would probably have gone on for ever, had he not, with commendable valour, chopped off their tails when their coils threatened to strangle him, and begun again. The point of it all was that they had the honour to welcome the President of the Board of Trade and Sir James Westbourne. Luckily, the posters, with which the town had been placarded for the last fortnight, corroborated the information, and no reasonable person could any longer doubt it.

He was rejoiced to see so crowded an assembly met together - this was not very happy, but the sentence had been carefully thought out, and it was a pity not to reproduce it - and was convinced that they would all spend a most interesting and enjoyable evening, which would certainly prove to be epoch-making. Politics were taken seriously in Riseborough, and it was pleasant to see the gathering graced by so many members of the fair sex. He felt he had detained them all quite long enough (no) and he would detain them no longer (yes), but call on the Right Honourable Mr Chilcot (cheers).

As Mr Chilcot rose, Mr Turner rose also, and said in a clear, cheerful voice, 'Votes for Women.' He had a rosette, pinned a little crookedly, depending from his shoulder. Immediately his wife and daughter rose too, and in a sort of Gregorian chant said, 'Women's rights', and a rattle of chains made a pleasant light accompaniment. From beneath her seat Mrs Currie produced a banner trimmed with the appropriate colours, on which was embroidered 'Votes for Women.' But the folds clung dispiritingly together: there was never a more dejected banner. Two stalwart porters whom she had brought with her also got up, wiped their mouths with the backs of their hands, and said in low, hoarse tones, 'Votes for Women.'

This lasted but a few seconds, and there was silence again. It was impossible to imagine a less impressive demonstration: it seemed the incarnation of ineffectiveness. Mr Chilcot had instantly sat down when it began, and, though he had cause to be shy of Suffragettes, seemed quite undisturbed; he was smiling good-naturedly, and for a moment consulted his notes again. And then, suddenly, Mrs Ames realized that she had taken no share in it; it had begun so quickly, and so quickly ended, that for the time she had merely watched. But then her blood and her courage came back to her: it should not be her fault, in any case, if the proceedings lacked fire. The Idea, all that had meant so much to her during these last months, seemed to stand by her, asking her aid. She opened the little black velvet bag, pinned on her rosette, passed the second chain (strong enough to hold a mastiff) through the first, and round the leg of the table in front of her, heard the spring lock click, and rose to her feet, waving her hand.

'Votes for Women!' she cried. 'Votes for Women. Hurrah!'

Instantly everyone on the platform turned to her: she saw Lyndhurst's inflamed and astonished face, with mouth fallen open in incredulous surprise, like a fish in an aquarium: she saw Cousin James' frown of distinguished horror. Mrs Evans looked as if about to laugh, and the Mayoress said, 'Lor'!' Mr Chilcot turned round in his seat, and his good-humoured smile faded, leaving an angry fighting face. But all this hostility and amazement, so far from cowing or silencing her, seemed like a draught of wine. 'Votes for Women!' she cried again.

At that the cry was taken up in earnest: by a desperate effort Mrs Currie unfurled her banner, so that it floated free, her porters roared out their message with the conviction they put into their announcements to a stopping train that this was Riseborough, the Turner family gleefully shouted together: Mrs Brooks, unable to adjust her rosette, madly waved it, and a solid group of enthusiasts just below the platform emitted loud and militant cries. All that had been flat and lifeless a moment before was inspired and vital. And Mrs Ames had done it. For a moment she had nothing but glory in her heart.

Mr Chilcot leaned over the table to her.

'I had no idea,' he said, 'when I had the honour of dining with you that you proposed immediately afterwards to treat me with such gross discourtesy.'

'Votes for Women!' shouted Mrs Ames again.

This time the cry was less vehemently taken up, for there was nothing to interrupt. Mr Chilcot conferred a moment quietly with Sir James, and Mrs Ames saw that Lyndhurst and Mrs Evans were talking together: the former was spluttering with rage, and Mrs Evans had laid her slim, white-gloved hand on his knee, in the attempt, it appeared, to soothe him. At present the endeavour did not seem to be meeting with any notable measure of success. Even in the midst of her excitement, Mrs Ames thought how ludicrous Lyndhurst's face was; she also felt sorry for him. As well, she had the sense of this being tremendous fun: never in her life had she been so effective, never had she even for a moment paralysed the plans of other people. But she was doing that now; Mr Chilcot had come here to speak, and she was not permitting him to. And again she cried 'Votes for Women!'

An inspector of police had come on to the platform, and after a few words with Sir James, he vaulted down into the body of the hall. Next moment, some dozen policemen tramped in from outside, and immediately afterwards the Turner family, still beaming, were being trundled down the gangway, and firmly ejected. Sundry high notes and muffled shoutings came from outside, but after a few seconds they were dumb, as if a tap had been turned off. There was a little more trouble with Mrs Currie, but a few smart tugs brought away the somewhat flimsy wooden rail to which she had attached herself, and she was taken along in a sort of tripping step, like a cheerful dancing bear, with her chains jingling round her, after the Turners, and quietly put out into the night. Then Sir James came across to Mrs Ames.

'Cousin Amy,' he said, 'you must please give us your word to cause no more disturbance, or I shall tell a couple of men to take you away.'

'Votes for Women!' shouted Mrs Ames again. But the excitement which possessed her was rapidly dying, and from the hall there came no response except very audible laughter.

'I am very sorry,' said Cousin James.

And then, with a sudden overwhelming wave, the futility of the whole thing struck her. What had she done? She had merely been extremely rude to her two guests, had seriously annoyed her husband, and had aroused perfectly justifiable laughter. General Fortescue was sitting a few rows off: he was looking at her through his pince-nez, and his red, good-humoured face was all a-chink with smiles. Then two policemen, one of whom had his beat in St Barnabas Road, vaulted up on to the platform, and several people left their places to look on from a more advantageous position.

'Beg your pardon, ma'am,' said the St Barnabas policeman, touching his helmet with imperturbable politeness. 'She's chained up too, Bill.'

Bill was a slow, large, fatherly looking man, and examined Mrs Ames' fetters. Then a broad grin broke out over his amiable face.

'It's only just passed around the table leg,' he said. 'Hitch up the table leg, mate, and slip it off.'

CHAPTER ELEVEN

It was too true . . . patent lock and mastiff-holding chain were slipped down the table leg, and Mrs Ames, with the fatherly looking policeman politely carrying her chains and the little velvet bag, was gently and inevitably propelled through the door which, a quarter of an hour ago, she had entered escorted by the Mayor, and down the stone passage and out into the dripping street. The rain fell heavily on to the rose-coloured silk dress, and the fatherly policeman put her cloak, which had half fallen off, more shelteringly round her.

'Better have a cab, ma'am, and go home quietly,' he said. 'You'll catch cold if you stay here, and we can't let you in again, begging your pardon, ma'am.'

Mrs Ames looked round: Mrs Currie was just crossing the road, apparently on her way home, and a carriage drove off containing the Turner family. A sense of utter failure and futility possessed her: it was cold and wet, and a chilly wind flapped the awning, blowing a shower of dripping raindrops on to her. The excitement and courage that had possessed her just now had all oozed away: nothing had been effected, unless to make herself ridiculous could be counted as an achievement.

'Call a cab for the lady, Bill,' said her policeman soothingly.

This was soon summoned, and Bill touched his helmet as she got in, and before closing the door pulled up the window for her. The cabman also knew her, and there was no need to give him her address. The rain pattered on the windows and on the roof, and the horse splashed briskly along through the puddles in the roadway.

Parker opened the door to her, surprised at the speediness of her return.

'Why, ma'am!' she exclaimed, 'has anything happened?'

'No, nothing, Parker,' said she, feeling that a dreadful truth underlay her words. 'Tell the Major, when he comes in, that I have gone to bed.'

She looked for a moment into the dining room. So short a time had passed that the table was not yet cleared: the printed menu cards had been collected, but the coffee, which had not been hot enough, still stood untasted in the cups, and the slices of pineapple, cut, but not eaten, were ruinously piled together. The thought of all the luncheons that would be necessary to consume all this expensive food made her feel sick . . . These little things had assumed a ridiculous size to her mind; that which had seemed so big was pitifully dwindled. She felt desperately tired, and cold and lonely.

'AND what's to be done now?' said Major Ames, chipping his bacon high into the air above his plate. 'If you didn't hear me, I said, "What's to be done now?" I don't know how you can look Riseborough in the face again, and, upon my word, I don't see how I can. They'll point at me in the street, and say, "That's Major Ames, whose wife made a fool of herself." That's what you did, Amy. You made a fool of yourself. And what was the good of it all? Are you any nearer getting the vote than before, because you've screamed "Votes for Women" a dozen times? You've only given a proof the more of how utterly unfit you are to have anything at all of your own, let alone a vote. I passed a sleepless night with thinking of your folly, and I feel infernally unwell this morning.'

This clearly constituted a climax, and Mrs Ames took advantage of the rhetorical pause that followed.

'Nonsense, Lyndhurst,' she said; 'I heard you snoring.'

'It's enough to make a man snore,' he said. 'Snore, indeed! Why couldn't you even have told me that you were going to behave like a silly lunatic, and if I couldn't have persuaded you to behave sanely, I could have stopped away, instead of looking on at such an exhibition? Every one will suppose I must have known about it, and have countenanced you. I've a good mind to write to the Kent Chronicle and say that I was absolutely ignorant of what you were going to do. You've disgraced us; that's what you've done.'

He took a gulp of tea, imprudently, for it was much hotter than he anticipated.

'And now I've burned my mouth!' he said.

Mrs Ames put down her napkin, left her seat, and came and stood by him.

'I am sorry you are so much vexed,' she said, 'but I can't and I won't discuss anything with you if you talk like that. You are thinking about nothing but yourself, whether you are disgraced, and whether you have had a bad night.'

'Certainly you don't seem to have thought about me,' he said.

'As a matter of fact I did,' she said. 'I knew you would not like it, and I was sorry. But do you suppose I liked it? But I thought most about the reason for which I did it.'

'You did it for notoriety,' said Major Ames, with conviction. 'You wanted to see your name in the papers, as having interrupted a cabinet minister's speech. You won't even have that satisfaction, I am glad to say. Your cousin James, who is a decent sort of fellow after all, spoke to the reporters last night and asked them to leave out all account of the disturbance. They consented; they are decent fellows too; they didn't want to give publicity to your folly. They were sorry for you, Amy; and how do you like half a dozen reporters at a pound a week being sorry for you? Your cousin James was equally generous. He bore no malice to me, and shook hands with me, and said he saw you were unwell when he sat down to dinner. But when a man of the world, as your cousin James is, says he thinks that a woman is unwell, I know what he means. He thought you were intoxicated. Drunk, in fact. That's what he thought. He thought you were drunk. My wife drunk. And it was the kindest interpretation he could have put upon it. Mad or drunk. He chose drunk. And he hoped I should be able to come over some day next week and help him to thin out the pheasants. Very friendly, considering all that had happened.'

Mrs Ames moved slightly away from him.

'Do you mean to go?' she asked.

'Of course I mean to go. He shows a very generous spirit, and I think I can account for the highest of his rocketters. He wants to smooth things over and be generous, and all that - hold out the olive branch. He recognizes that I've got to live down your folly, and if it's known that I've been shooting with him, it will help us. Forgive and forget, hey? I shall just go over there, en garçon, and will patch matters up. I dare say he'll ask you over again sometime. He doesn't want to be hard on you. Nor do I, I am sure. But there are things no man can stand. A man's got to put his foot down sometimes, even if he puts it down on his wife. And if I was a bit rough with you just now, you must realize, Amy, you must realize that I felt strongly, strongly and rightly. We've got to live down what you have done. Well, I'm by you. We'll live it down together. I'll make your peace with your cousin. You can trust me.'

These magnificent assurances failed to dazzle Mrs Ames, and she made no acknowledgement of them. Instead, she went back rather abruptly and inconveniently to a previous topic.

'You tell me that Cousin James believed I was drunk,' she said. 'Now you knew I was not. But you seem to have let it pass.'

Major Ames felt that more magnanimous assurances might be in place.

'There are some things best passed over,' he said. 'Let sleeping dogs lie. I think the less we talk about last night the better. I hope I am generous enough not to want to rub it in, Amy, not to make you more uncomfortable than you are.'

Mrs Ames sat down in a chair by the fireplace. A huge fire burned there, altogether disproportionate to the day, and she screened her face from the blaze with the morning paper. Also she made a mental note to speak to Parker about it.

'You are making me very uncomfortable indeed, Lyndhurst,' she said; 'by not telling me what I ask you. Did you let it pass, when you saw James thought I was drunk?'

'Yes; he didn't say so in so many words. If he had said so, well, I dare say I should have - have made some sort of answer. And, mind you, it was no accusation he made against you; he made an excuse for you!'

Mrs Ames' small, insignificant face grew suddenly very firm and fixed.

'We do not need to go into that,' she said. 'You saw he thought I was drunk, and said nothing. And after that you mean to go over and shoot his pheasants. Is that so?'

'Certainly it is. You are making a mountain out of - '

'I am making no mountain out of anything. Personally, I don't believe Cousin James thought anything of the kind. What matters is that you let it pass. What matters is that I should have to tell you that you must apologize to me, instead of your seeing it for yourself.'

Major Ames got up, pushing his chair violently back.

'Well, here's a pretty state of things,' he cried; 'that you should be telling me to apologize for last night's degrading exhibition! I wonder what you'll be asking next? A vote of thanks from the Mayor, I shouldn't wonder, and an illuminated address. You teaching me what I ought to do! I should have thought a woman would have been only too glad to trust to her husband, if he was so kind, as I have been, as to want to get her out of the consequences of her folly. And now it's you who must sit there, opposite a fire fit to roast an ox, and tell me I must apologize. Apologies be damned! There! It's not my habit to swear, as you well know, but there are occasions - Apologies be damned!'

And a moment later the house shook with the thunder of the slammed front door.

Mrs Ames sat for a couple of minutes exactly where she was, still shielding her face from the fire. She felt all the chilling effects of the reaction that follows on excitement, whether the excitement is rapturous or as sickening as last night's had been, but not for a moment did she regret her share either in the events of the evening before or in the sequel of this morning. Last night had ended in utter fiasco, but she had done her best; this morning's talk had ended in a pretty sharp quarrel, but again she found it impossible to reconsider her share in it. Humanly she felt beaten and ridiculed and sick at heart, but not ashamed. She had passed a sleepless night, and was horribly tired, with that tiredness that seems to sap all pluck and power of resistance, and gradually her eyes grew dim, and the difficult meagre tears of middle age, which are so bitter, began to roll down her cheeks, and the hard inelastic sobs to rise in her throat . . . Yet it was no use sitting here crying, lunch and dinner had to be ordered whether she felt unhappy or not; she had to see how extensive was the damage done to her pink satin shoes by the wet pavements last night; she had to speak about this oxroasting fire. Also there was appointed a Suffragette meeting at Mr Turner's house for eleven o'clock, at which past achievements and future plans would be discussed. She had barely time to wash her face, for it was unthinkable that Parker or the cook should see she had been crying, and get through her household duties, before it was time to start.

She dried her eyes and went to the window, through which streamed the pale saffron-coloured October sunshine. All the stormy trouble of the night had passed, and the air sparkled with 'the clear shining after rain'. But the frost of a few nights before had blackened the autumn flowers, and the chill rain had beaten down the glory of her husband's chrysanthemums, so that the garden beds looked withered and dishevelled, like those whose interest in life is finished, and who no longer care what appearance they present. The interest of others in them seemed to be finished also; it was not the gardener's day here, for he only came twice in the week, and Major Ames, who should have been assiduous in binding up the broken-stemmed, encouraging the invalids, and clearing away the havoc wrought by the storm, had left the house. Perhaps he had gone to the club, perhaps even now he was trying to make light of it all. She could almost hear him say, 'Women get queer notions into their heads, and the notions run away with them, bless them. You'll take a glass of sherry with me, General, won't you? Are you by any chance going to Sir James' shoot next week? I'm shooting there one day.' Or was he talking it over somewhere else, perhaps not making light of it? She did not know; all she knew was that she was alone, and wanted somebody who understood, even if he disagreed. It did not seem to matter that Lyndhurst utterly disagreed with her, what mattered was that he had misunderstood her motives so entirely, that the monstrous implication that she had been intoxicated seemed to him an excuse. And he was not sorry. What could she do since he was not sorry? It was as difficult to answer that as it was easy to know what to do the moment he was sorry. Indeed, then it would be unnecessary to do anything; the reconciliation would be automatic, and would bring with it something she yearned after, an opportunity of making him see that she cared, that the woman in her reached out towards him, in some different fashion now from that in which she had tried to recapture the semblance of youth and his awakened admiration. Today, she looked back on that episode shamefacedly. She had taken so much trouble with so paltry a purpose. And yet that innocent and natural coquetry was not quite dead in her; no woman's heart need be so old that it no longer cares whether she is pleasing in her husband's eyes. Only today, it seemed to Mrs Ames that her pains had been as disproportionate to her purpose as they had been to its result; now she longed to take pains for a purpose that was somewhat deeper than that for which she softened her wrinkles and refreshed the colour of her hair.

She turned from the window and the empty garden, wishing that the rain would be renewed, so that there would be an excuse for her to go to Mr Turner's in a shut cab. As it was, there was no such excuse, and she felt that it would require an effort to walk past the club window, and to traverse the length of the High Street. Female Riseborough, on this warm sunny morning, she knew would be there in force, popping in and out of shops, and holding little conversations on the pavement. There would be but one topic today, and for many days yet; it would be long before the autumn novelty lost anything of its freshness. She wondered how her appearance in the town would be greeted; would people smile and turn aside as she approached, and whisper or giggle after she had gone by? What of the Mayor who, like an honest tradesman, was often to be seen at the door of his shop, or looking at the 'dressing' of his windows? A policeman always stood at the bottom of the street, controlling the cross-traffic from St Barnabas Road. Would he be that one who had helped to further her movements last night? . . . She almost felt she ought to thank him . . . And then quite suddenly her pluck returned again, or it was that she realized that she did not, comparatively speaking, care two straws for any individual comment or by-play that might take place in the High Street, or for its accumulated weight. There were other things to care about. For them she cared immensely.

The High Street proved to be paved with incident. Turning quickly round the corner, she nearly ran into Bill, the policeman, off duty at this hour, and obviously giving a humorous recital of some sort to a small amused circle outside the public house. It was abruptly discontinued when she appeared, and she felt that the interest that his audience developed in the sunny October sky, which they contemplated with faint grins, would be succeeded by stifled laughter after she had passed. A few paces further on, controlling the traffic of market day, was her other policeman Bill, who smiled in a pleasant and familiar manner to her, as if there was some capital joke private to them. Twenty yards further along the street was standing the Mayor, contemplating his shop window; he saw her, and urgent business appeared to demand his presence inside. After that there came General Fortescue tottering to the club; he crossed the street to meet her, and took off his hat and shook hands.

'By Jove! Mrs Ames,' he said, 'I never enjoyed a meeting so much, and my wife's wild that she didn't go. What a lark! Made me feel quite young again. I wanted to shout too, and tell them to give the ladies a vote. Monstrously amusing! Just going to the club to have a chat about it all.'

And he went on his way, with his fat old body shaking with laughter. Then, feeling rather ill from this encounter, she heard rapid steps in pursuit of her, and Mrs Altham joined her.

'Oh, Mrs Ames,' she said. 'I could die of vexation that I was not there. Is it really true that you threw a glass of water at Mr Chilcot and hit the policeman? Fancy, that it should have been such a terribly wet night, and Henry and I just sat at home, never thinking that five minutes in a cab would make such a difference. We sat and played patience; I should have been most impatient if I had known. And what is to happen next? It was so stupid of me not to join your league; I wonder if it is too late.'

This was quite dreadful; Mrs Ames had been prepared for her husband's anger, and for pride and aversion from people like Mrs Altham. What was totally unexpected and unwelcome was that she was supposed to have scored a sort of popular success, that Riseborough considered the dreadful fiasco of last night as an achievement, something not only to talk about, but a kind of new game, more exciting than croquet or criticism. She had begun by thinking of the Suffragette movement as an autumn novelty, but leanness came very near her soul when she found that it now appeared to others as she had first thought of it herself. She had travelled since then; she had seen the hinterland of it; the idea that rose up behind it, austere and beautiful and wise. All that these others saw was just the hysterical jungle that bounded the coast. To her this morning, after her experience of it, the hysterical jungle seemed - an hysterical jungle. If it was only by that route that the heights could be attained, then that route must be followed. She was willing to try it again. But was there not somewhere and somehow a better road?

It was not necessary to be particularly cordial to Mrs Altham, and she held out no certain prospect of an immediate repetition of last night's scenes, nor of a desire for additional recruits. But further trials awaited her in this short walk. Dr Evans, driving the high-stepping cob, wheeled round, and dismounted, throwing the reins to the groom.

'I must just congratulate you,' he said, 'for Millie told me about last night. I've been telling her that if she had half your pluck, she would be the better for it. I hope you didn't catch cold; beastly night, wasn't it? Do let me know when it will come on again. I hate your principles, you know, but I love your practice. I shall come and shout, too!'

This was perfectly awful. Nobody understood; they all sympathized with her, but cared not two straws for that which had prompted her to do these sensational things . . . They liked the sensational things . . . it was fun to them. But it was no fun to those who believed in the principles which prompted them. They thought of her as a clown at a pantomime; they wanted to see Dan Leno . . .

She was some minutes late when she reached Mr Turner's house, depressed and not encouraged by this uncomprehending applause that took as an excellent joke all the manifestations which had been directed by so serious a purpose. What to her was tragic and necessary, was to them a farce of entertaining quality. But now she would meet her coreligionists again, those who knew, those whose convictions, of the same quality as hers, were of such weight as to make her feel that even her quarrel with Lyndhurst was light in comparison.

The jovial Turner family, father, mother, daughter, were in the drawing room, and they hailed her as a heroine. If it had not been for her, there would have been no 'scene' at all.

Did the policemen hurt? Mr Turner had got a small bruise on his knee, but it was quite doubtful whether he got it when he was taken out. Mrs Turner had lost a small pearl ornament, but she was not sure whether she had put it on before going to the meeting. Miss Turner had a cold today, but it was certain that she had felt it coming on before they were all put out into the rain. None of them had seen the end; it was supposed that Mrs Ames had thrown a glass of water at a policeman, and had hit Mr Chilcot. They were all quite ready for Sir James' next meeting; or would he be a coward, and cause scrutiny to be held on those who desired admittance?

Mrs Brooks arrived; she had not been turned out last night, but she had caught cold, and did not think that much had been achieved. Mr Chilcot had made his speech, apparently a very clever one, about Tariff Reform, and Sir James had followed, without interruption, telling the half empty but sympathetic benches about the House of Lords. There had been no allusion made to the disturbance, or to the motives that prompted it. Also she had lost her Suffragette rosette. It must have been torn off her, though she did not feel it go.

Mrs Currie brought more life into the proceedings. She could get four porters to come to the next meeting, and could make another banner, as well as ensuring the proper unfurling of the first, which had stuck so unaccountably. It had waved quite properly when she had tried it an hour before, and it had waved quite properly (for it had been returned to her after she had been ejected) when she tried it again an hour later at home. Two banners expanding properly would be a vastly different affair from one that did not expand at all. Her husband had laughed fit to do himself a damage over her account of the proceedings.

A dozen more only of the league made an appearance, for clearly there was a reaction and a cooling after last night's conflagration, but all paid their meed of appreciation to Mrs Ames. Their little rockets had but fizzed and spluttered until she 'showed them the way', as Mrs Currie expressed it. But to them even it was the ritual, so to speak, the disturbance, the shouting, the sense of doing something, rather than the belief that lay behind the ritual, which stirred their imaginations. Could the cause be better served by the endurance of an hour's solitary toothache, than by waving banners in the town hall, and being humanely ejected by benevolent policemen, there would have been less eagerness to suffer. And Mrs Ames would so willingly have passed many hours of physical pain rather than suffer the heartache which troubled her this morning. And nobody seemed to understand; Mrs Currie with her four porters and two banners, Mrs Brooks with her cold in the head and odour of eucalyptus, the cheerful Turners who thought it would be such a good idea to throw squibs on to the platform, were all as far from the point as General Fortescue, chatting at the club, or even as Lyndhurst with the high-chipped bacon and the slammed front door. It was a game to them, as it had originally presented itself to her, an autumn novelty for, say, Thursday afternoon from five till seven. If only the opposite effects had been produced; if they all had taken it as poignantly as Lyndhurst, and he as cheerily as they!

He, meantime, after slamming the front door, had stormed up St Barnabas Road, in so sincere a passion that he had nearly reached the club before he remembered that he had hardly touched his breakfast or glanced at the paper. So, as there was no sense in starving himself (the starvation consisting in only having half his breakfast), he turned in at those hospitable doors, and ordered himself an omelette. Never in his life had he been so angry, never in the amazing chronicle of matrimony, so it seemed to him, had a man received such provocation from his wife. She had insulted the guests who had dined with her, she made a public and stupendous ass of herself, and when, next morning, he, after making such expostulations as he was morally bound to make, had been so nobly magnanimous as to assure her that he would patch it all up for her, and live it down with her, he had been told that it was for him to apologize! No wonder he had sworn; Moses would have sworn; it would have been absolutely wrong of him not to swear. There were situations in which it was cowardly for a man not to say what he thought. Even now, as he waited for his omelette, he emitted little squeaks and explosive exclamations, almost incredulous of his wrongs.

He ate his omelette, which seemed but to add fuel to his rage, and went into the smoking room, where, over a club cigar, for he had actually forgotten to bring his own case with him, he turned to the consideration of practical details. It was not clear how to re-enter his house again. He had gone out with a bang that made the windows rattle, but it was hardly possible to go on banging the door each time he went in and out, for no joinery would stand these reiterated shocks. And what was to be done, even if he could devise an effective re-entry? Unless Amy put herself into his hands, and unreservedly took back all that she had said, it was impossible for him to speak to her. Somehow he felt that there were few things less likely to happen than this. Certainly it would be no good to resume storming operations, for he had no guns greater than those he had already fired, and if they were not of sufficient calibre, he must just beleaguer her with silence - dignified, displeased silence.

He looked up and saw that Mr Altham was regarding him through the glass door; upon which Mr Altham rapidly withdrew. Not long afterwards young Morton occupied and retired from the same observatory. A moment's reflection enabled Major Ames to construe this singular behaviour. They had heard of his wife's conduct, and were gluttonously feeding on so unusual a spectacle as himself in the club at this hour, and reconstructing in their monkey minds his domestic disturbances. They would probably ascertain that he had breakfasted here. It was all exceedingly unpleasant; there was no sympathy in their covert glances, only curiosity.

No one who is not a brute, and Major Ames was not that, enjoys a quarrel with his wife, and no one who is not utterly self-centred, and he was not quite that either, fails to desire sympathy when such a quarrel has occurred. He wanted sympathy now; he wanted to pour out into friendly ears the tale of Amy's misdeeds, of his own magnanimity, to hear his own estimation of his conduct confirmed, fairly confirmed, by a woman who would see the woman's point of view as well as his. The smoking room with these peeping Toms was untenable, but he thought he knew where he could get sympathy.

Millie was in and would see him; from habit, as he crossed the hall he looked to the peg where Dr Evans hung his hat and coat, and, seeing they were not there, inferred that the doctor was out. That suited him; he wanted to confide and be sympathized with, and felt that Evans' breezy optimism and out-of-door habit of mind would not supply the kind of comfort he felt in need of. He wanted to be told he was a martyr and a very fine fellow, and that Amy was unworthy of him . . .

Millie was in the green, cool drawing room, where they had sat one day after lunch. She rose as he entered and came towards him with a tremulous smile on her lips, and both hands outstretched.

'Dear Lyndhurst,' she said. 'I am so glad you have come. Sit down. I think if you had not come I should have telephoned to ask if you would not see me. I should have suggested our taking a little walk, perhaps, for I do not think I could have risked seeing Cousin Amy. I know how you feel, oh, so well. It was abominable, disgraceful.'

Certainly he had come to the right place. Millie understood him: he had guessed she would. She sat down close beside him, and for a moment held her hand over her eyes.

'Ah, I have been so angry this morning,' she said; 'and it has given me a headache. Wilfred laughed about it all; he said also that what Amy did showed a tremendous lot of pluck. It was utterly heartless. I knew how you must be suffering, and I was so angry with him. He did not understand. Oh no, my headache is nothing; it will soon be gone – now.'

She faintly emphasized the last word, stroked it, so to speak, as if calling attention to it.

'I'm broken-hearted about it,' said Major Ames, which sounded better than to say, 'I'm in a purple rage about it.' 'I'm broken-hearted. She's disgraced herself and me – '

'No, not you.'

'Yes; a woman can't do that sort of thing without the world believing that her husband knew about it. And that's not all. Upon my word I'm not sure whether what she did this morning isn't worse than what you saw last night.'

Millie leaned forward.

'Tell me,' she said, 'if it doesn't hurt you too much.'

He decided it did not hurt him too much.

'Well, I came down this morning,' he said, 'willing and eager to make the best of a bad job. So were we all: James

Westbourne last night was just as generous, and asked the reporters to say nothing about it, and invited me to a day's shooting next week. Very decent of him. As I say, I came down this morning, willing to make it as easy as I could. Of course, I knew I had to give Amy a good talking to: I should utterly have failed in my duty to her as a husband if I did not do that. I gave her a blowing up, though not half of what she deserved, but a blowing up. Even then, when I had said my say I told her we would live it down together, which was sufficiently generous, I think. But, for her good, I told her that James Westbourne said he saw she was unwell, and that when a man says that he means that she is drunk. Perhaps Westbourne didn't mean that, but that's what it sounded like. And would you believe it, just because I hadn't knocked him down and stamped on his face, she tells me I ought to apologize to her for letting such a suggestion pass. Well, I flared up at that: what man of spirit wouldn't have flared up? I left the house at once, and went and finished my breakfast at the club. I should have choked - upon my word, I should have choked if I had stopped there, or got an apoplexy. As it is, I feel devilish unwell.'

Millie got up, and stood for a moment in silence, looking out of the window, white and willowy.

'I can never forgive Cousin Amy,' she said at length. 'Never!'

'Well, it is hard,' said Major Ames. 'And after all these years! It isn't exactly the return one might expect, perhaps.'

'It is infamous,' said Millie.

She came and sat down by him again.

'What are you going to do?' she asked.

'I don't know. If she apologizes, I shall forgive her, and I shall try to forget. But I didn't think it of her. And if she doesn't apologize - I don't know. I can't be expected to eat my words: that would be countenancing what she has done. I couldn't do it: it would not be sincere. I'm straight, I hope: if I say a thing it may be taken for granted that I mean it.'

She looked up at him with her chin raised.

'I think you are wonderful,' she said, 'to be able even to think of forgiving her. If I had behaved like that, I should not expect Wilfred to forgive me. But then you are so big, so big. She does not understand you: she can't understand one thing about you. She doesn't know - oh, how blind some women are!'

It was little wonder that by this time Major Ames was beginning to feel an extraordinarily fine fellow, nor was it more wonderful that he basked in the warm sense of being understood. But from the first Millie had understood him. He felt that particularly now, at this moment, when Amy had so hideously flouted and wronged him. All through this last summer, the situation of today had been foreshadowed; it had always been in this house rather than in his own that he had been welcomed and appreciated. He had been the architect and adviser in the Shakespeare ball, while at home Amy dealt out her absurd printed menu cards without consulting him. And the garden which he loved - who had so often said, 'These sweet flowers, are they really for me?' Who, on the other hand, had so often said, 'The sweet peas are not doing very well, are they?' And then he looked at Millie's soft, youthful face, her eyes, that sought his in timid, sensitive appeal, her dim golden hair, her mouth, childish and mysterious. For contrast there was the small, strong, toad's face, the rather beady eyes, the hair - grey or brown, which was it? Also, Millie understood; she saw him as he was - generous, perhaps, to a fault, but big, big, as she had so properly said. She always made him feel so comfortable, so contented with himself. That was the true substance of a woman's mission, to make her husband happy, to make him devoted to her, instead of raising hell in the town hall, and insisting on apologies afterwards.

'You've cheered me up, Millie,' he said; 'you've made me feel that I've got a friend, after all, a friend who feels with me. I'm grateful; I'm - I'm more than grateful. I'm a tough old fellow, but I've got a heart still, I believe. What's to happen to us all?'

It was emotion, real and genuine emotion, that made Millie clever at that moment. Her mind was of no high order; she might, if she thought about a thing, be trusted to exhibit nothing more subtle than a fair grasp of the obvious. But now she did not think: she was prompted by an instinct that utterly transcended any achievement of which her brain was capable.

'Go back to your house,' she said, 'and be ready for Cousin Amy to say she is sorry. Very likely she is waiting for you there now. Oh, Lyndhurst - '

He got up at once: those few words made him feel completely noble; they made her feel noble likewise. The atmosphere of nobility was almost suffocating . . .

'You are right,' he said; 'you are always all that is right and good and delicious? Ha!'

There was no question about the cousinly relations between them. So natural and spontaneous a caress needed no explanation.

The house was apparently empty when he got back, but he made sufficiently noisy an entry to advise the drawing room, in any case, that he was returned, and personally ready, since he did not enter 'full of wrath', like Hyperion, to accept apologies. Eventually he went in there, as if to look for a paper, in case of its being occupied, and, with the same pretext, strolled into his wife's sitting room. Then, still casually, he went into his dressing room, where he had slept last night, and satisfied himself that she was not in her bedroom. Her penitence, therefore, which would naturally be manifested by her waiting, dim-eyed, for his return, had not been of any peremptory quality.

He went out into the garden, and surveyed the damage of last night's rain. There was no need to punish the plants because Amy had been guilty of behaviour which her own cousin said was infamous: he also wanted something to employ himself with till lunchtime. As his hands worked mechanically, tying up some clumps of chrysanthemums which had a few days more of flame in their golden hearts, removing a debris of dead leaves and fallen twigs, his mind was busy also, working not mechanically but eagerly and excitedly. How different was the sympathy with which he was welcomed and comforted by Millie from the misunderstandings and quarrels which made him feel that he had wasted his years with one who was utterly unappreciative of him. Yet, if Amy was sorry, he was ready to do his best. But he wondered whether he wanted her to be sorry or not.

At half past one the bell for lunch sounded, and, going into the drawing room, he found that she had returned and was writing a note at her table. She did not look up, but said to him, just as if nothing had happened -

'Will you go in and begin, Lyndhurst? I want to finish my note.'

He did not answer, but passed into the dining room. In a little while she joined him.

'There seems to have been a good deal of rain in the night,' she said. 'I am afraid your flowers have suffered.'

Certainly this did not look like penitence, and he had no reply for her. In some strange way this seemed to him the dignified and proper course.

Then Mrs Ames spoke for the third time.

'I think, Lyndhurst, if we are not going to talk,' she said, 'I shall see what news there is. Parker, please fetch me the morning paper.'

At that moment he hated her.

THREE days later Major Ames was walking back home in the middle of the afternoon, returning from the house in which he had lately spent so considerable a portion of his time. But this was the last day on which he would go there, nor would he, except for this one time more, cross the threshold of his own house. The climax had come, and within an hour or two he and Millie were going to leave Riseborough together.

Now that their decision had been made, it seemed to him that it had been inevitable from the first. Ever since the summer, when, from some mixture of genuine liking and false gallantry, he had allowed himself to drift into relations with her, the force that drew and held him had steadily increased in strength, and today it had proved itself irresistible. The determining factor no doubt had been his quarrel with his wife; that gave the impulse that had been still lacking, the final push which upset the equilibrium of that which was tottering and ready to fall over.

The scene this afternoon had been both short and quiet, as such scenes are. Dr Evans had been called up to town on business yesterday morning, returning possibly this evening but more probably tomorrow, and they had lunched alone. Afterwards Major Ames had again spoken of his wife.

'The situation is intolerable,' he had said. 'I can't stand it. If it wasn't for you, Millie, I should go away.'

She had come close to him.

'I'm not very happy, either,' she said. 'If it wasn't for you, I don't think I could stand it.'

And then it was already inevitable.

'It's too strong for us,' she said. 'We can't help it. I will face anything with you. We will go right away, Lyndhurst, and live, instead of being starved like this.'

She took both his hands in hers, completely carried away for the first time in her life by something outside herself. Treacherous and mean as was that course on which she was determined, she was, perhaps, a finer woman at this moment of supreme disloyalty than in all the years of her blameless married life.

'I've never loved before, Lyndhurst,' she said quietly, 'nor have I ever known what it meant. Now I can't consider anything else; it doesn't matter what happens to Wilfred and Elsie. Nothing matters except you.'

This time it was not he who kissed her; it was she who pressed her mouth to his.

There was but little to settle, their plans were perfectly simple and ruthless. They would cross over to Boulogne that night, and, as soon as the law set them free, marry each other. A train to Folkestone left Riseborough in a little over an hour's time, running in connection with the boat. They could easily catch it. But it was wiser not to go to the station together: they would meet there.

As he walked home through the gleaming October afternoon, Major Ames was conscious neither of struggle nor regret. The power which Millie had had over him all these months, so that it was she always who really took the lead, and urged him one step forward and then another, gripped him and led him on here to the last step of all. He still obeyed and followed that slender, fragile woman who so soon would be his; it was as necessary to do her bidding here as it had been to kiss her, when first, under the mulberry tree, she had put up her face towards his. These last days seemed to have killed all sense of loyalty and manhood within him; he gave no thought at all to his wife, and thought of Harry only as Amy's son. Besides, he was not responsible: man though he was, he was completely in the hands of this woman. All his life he had had no real principles to direct him, he had lived a decent life only because no temptation to live otherwise had ever really come near him, and even now it was in no way the wickedness of what he purposed that at all dragged him back; it was mere timidity at taking an irrevocable step.

Amy, he knew, was out: at breakfast she had announced to him that she did not expect to be in till dinnertime, and he had told her that he would be out for dinner. Such sentences dealing with household arrangements had been the sum of their discourse for the last days, and they were spoken not so much to each other as to the air, heard by, rather than addressed to anyone in particular.

And yet the prospect of the life that should open for him, when once this irrevocable step had been taken, did not fill him with the resistless longing which, though it cannot excuse, at any rate accounts for the step itself. Millie, though throughout she had led him on until the climax was reached, had at least the authentic goad to drive her: life with him seemed to her to be real life: it was passionately that she desired it. But with him, apart from the force with which she dominated him, it was the escape from the very uncomfortable circumstances of home that chiefly attracted him. In a way, he loved her; he felt for her a warmth and a tenderness of stronger quality than he could remember having ever experienced before, and since it is not given to all men to love violently, it may be granted that he was feeling the utmost fire of which his nature was capable. But it was of sufficient ardour to burn up in his mind the rubbish of minor considerations and material exigencies.

Cabs were of infrequent occurrence at this far end of St Barnabas Road, and meeting one by hazard just outside his house, he told the driver to wait. Then, letting himself in, he went straight up to his dressing room. There was not time for him to pack his whole wardrobe, and a moderate portmanteau would be all he really needed. And here the trivialities began to wax huge and engrossing: though the afternoon was warm, it would no doubt be fresh, if not chilly on the boat, and it would certainly be advisable to take his thick overcoat, which at present had not left its summer quarters. Those were in a big cupboard in the passage outside, overlooking the garden, where it was packed away with prophylactic little balls of naphthaline. These had impregnated it somewhat powerfully, but it was better to be odorously than insufficiently clad. Passing the window he saw that the chrysanthemums had responded bravely to his comforting a few mornings ago: if there was no more frost they would be gay for another fortnight yet. Should he take a bouquet of them with him? He did not see why he should not have the enjoyment of them. Yet there was scarcely time to pick them: he must hurry on with the packing of his small portmanteau, which presented endless problems.

A panama hat should certainly be included; also a pair of white tennis shoes, in which he saw himself promenading on the parade: a white flannel suit, though it was October, seemed to complete the costume. He need not cumber himself with a dress coat: a dinner jacket was all that would be necessary. She had told him she had six hundred a year of her own: he had another three. It was annoying that his sponge was rather ragged; he had meant to buy a new one this morning. Perhaps Parker could draw it together with a bit of thread. An untidy sponge always vexed him: it was unsoldierly and slovenly. 'Show me a man's washhand-stand,' he had once said, 'and I'll tell you about the owner.' His own did not invite inspection, with its straggly sponge.

Then for a moment all these trivialities stood away from him, and for an interval he saw where he stood and what he was doing - the vileness, the sordidness, the vulgarity of it. High principles, nobility of life were not subjects with which hitherto he had much concerned himself, and it would be useless to expect that they should come to his rescue now, but for this moment his kindliness, such as it was, his affection for his wife, such as it was, but above all the continuous, unbroken smug respectability of his days read him a formidable indictment. What could he plead against such an accusation? No irresistible or imperative necessity of soul that claimed Millie as his by right of love. He knew that his desire for her was not of that fiery order, for he could see, undazzled and unburned, the qualities which attracted him. He admired her frail beauty, the youth that still encompassed her, he fed with the finest appetite on the devotion and admiration which she brought him. He loved being the god and the hero of this attractive woman, and it was this, far more than the devotion he brought her, that dominated him.

Respectability cried out against him and his foolishness. There would be no more strutting and swelling about the club among the mild and honourable men who frequented it, and looked up to him as an authority on India and gardening, nor any more of those pompous and satisfactory evenings when General Fortescue assured him that there was not such a good glass of port in Kent as that with which the Major supplied his guests. To be known as Major Ames, late of the Indian Army, had been to command respect; now, the less that he was known as Major Ames, late of Riseborough, the better would be the chance of being held in esteem. And to what sort of life would he condemn the woman, who for his sake was leaving a respectability no less solid than his own? To the companionship of such as herself, to the soiled doves of a French watering place. That, of course, would be but a temporary habitation, but after that, what? Where was the society which would receive them, by which there would be any satisfaction in being received? Neither of them had the faintest touch of Bohemianism in their natures: both were of the school that is accustomed to silver teapots and life in houses with a garden behind. For a moment he hesitated as he folded back the sleeves of his dinner jacket: then the tide of trivialities swept over him again, and he noticed that there was a spot of spilled wax on the cuff.

Among other engagements that Saturday afternoon, Mrs Ames was occupied with the decoration of St Barnabas' Church for the Sunday service next day, and she had gone there after lunch with an adornment of foliage tinted red by October, for she had not felt disposed to ask Lyndhurst if she might pick the remnant of his chrysanthemums. She, too, like him, felt the impossibility of the present situation, and, as she worked, she asked herself if it was in any way in her power to end this parody of domestic life. Every day she had made the attempt to begin the breaking of this ridiculous and most uncomfortable silence which lay between them, by the introduction of ordinary topics, hoping by degrees to build up again the breach that yawned between them, but at present she had got no sense of the slightest answering effort on his side. Psychically no less than conversationally he had nothing whatever to say to her. If in the common courtesies of daily life he had nothing for her, it seemed idle to hope to find further receptiveness if she opened discussion of their quarrel. Besides, a certain very natural pride blocked her way: he owed her an apology, and when she indicated that, he had sworn at her. It did not seem unreasonable (even when decorating a church) to expect the initiatory step to be taken by him. But what if he did not do so?

Mrs Ames gave a little sigh, and her mouth and throat worked uncomfortably. The quarrel was so childish, yet it was serious, for it was not a light thing, whatever her provocation might have been, to pass days like these. Half a dozen times she went over the circumstances, and half a dozen times she felt that it was only just that he should make the advance to her, or at any rate behave with ordinary courtesy in answer to her ordinary civilities. It was true that the original dissension was due to her, but she believed with her whole heart in the cause for which she provoked it. All these last months she had felt her nature expand under the influence of this idea: she knew herself to be a better and a bigger woman than she had been. She believed in the rights of her sex, but had they not their duties too? It was nearly twenty-five years since she had voluntarily undertaken a certain duty. What if that came first, before any rights or privileges? What if that which she had undertaken then as a duty was in itself a right?

Yet even then, what could she do? In itself, she was very far from being ashamed of the part she had taken, yet was it possible to weigh this independently, without considering the points at which it conflicted with duties which certainly concerned her no less? She could not hope to convince her husband of the justice of the cause, nor of the expediency of promoting it in ways like these. For herself, she knew the justice of it, and saw no other expedient for promoting it. Those who had worked for the cause for years said that all else had been tried, that there remained only this violent crusading. But was not she personally, considering what her husband felt about it, debarred from taking part in the crusade? She had deeply offended and vexed him. Could anything but the stringency of moral law justify that? Nothing that he had done, nothing that he could do, short of the violation of the essential principles of married life, could absolve her from the accomplishment of one tittle of her duty towards him.

For a moment, in spite of her perplexity and the difficulty of her decision, Mrs Ames smiled at herself for the mental use of all these great words like duty and privilege, over so small an incident. For what had happened? She had been a militant Suffragette on one occasion only, and at breakfast next morning he had, in matters arising therefrom, allowed himself to swear at her. Yet it seemed to her that, with all the pettiness and insignificance of it, great laws were concerned. For the law of kindness is broken by the most trumpery exhibition of inconsiderateness, the law of generosity by the most minute word of spite or backbiting. Indeed, it is chiefly in little things, since most of us are not concerned with great matters, that these violations occur, and in cups of cold water that they are fulfilled. And for once Mrs Ames did not finish her decoration with tidiness and precision, a fact clearly noted by Mrs Altham next day.

CHAPTER THIRTEEN

There was a Suffragette meeting at four, but she was prepared to be late for that, or, if necessary, to fail in attendance altogether. In any case, she would call in at home on her way there, on the chance that her husband might be in. She made no definite plan: it was impossible to forecast her share in the interview. But she had determined to try to suffer long, to be kind . . . to keep the promise of twenty-five years ago. There was a cab drawn up at the entrance, and it vaguely occurred to her that Millie might be here, for she had not seen her for some days, and it was possible she might have called. Yet it was hardly likely that she would have waited, since the servants would have told her that she herself was not expected home till dinnertime. Or was Lyndhurst giving her tea? And Mrs Ames grew suddenly alert again about matters to which she had scarcely given a thought during these last months.

She let herself in, and went to the drawing room: there was no one there, nor in the little room next it where they assembled before dinner on nights when they gave a party. But directly overhead she heard steps moving: that was in Lyndhurst's dressing room.

She went up there, knocked, and in answer to his assent went in. The portmanteau was nearly packed, he stood in shirtsleeves by it. In his hand was his sponge bag - he had anticipated the entry of Parker with the stitched sponge.

She looked from the portmanteau to him, and back and back again.

'You are going away, Lyndhurst?' she asked.

He made a ghastly attempt to devise a reasonable answer, and thought he succeeded.

'Yes, I'm going - going to your cousin's to shoot. I told you he had asked me. You objected to my going, but I'm going all the same. I should have left you a note. Back tomorrow night.'

Then she felt she knew all, as certainly as if he had told her.

'Since when has Cousin James been giving shooting parties on Sunday?' she asked. 'Please don't lie to me, Lyndhurst. It makes it much worse. You are not going to Cousin James, and - you are not going alone. Shall I tell you any more?'

She was not guessing: all the events of the last month, the Shakespeare ball, Harrogate, their own quarrel, and on the top this foolish lie about a shooting party made a series of data which proclaimed the conclusion. And the suddenness of the discovery, the magnitude of the issues involved, but served to steady her. There was an authentic valour in her nature; even as she had stood up to interrupt the political meeting, without so much as dreaming of shirking her part, so now her pause was not timorous, but rather the rallying of all her forces, that came eager and undismayed to her summons.

Apparently Lyndhurst did not want to be told any more: he did not, at any rate, ask for it. Just then Parker came in with the mended sponge. She gave it him, and he stood with sponge bag in one hand, sponge in the other.

'Shall I bring up tea, ma'am?' she said to Mrs Ames.

'Yes, take it to the drawing room now. And send the cab away. The Major won't want it.'

Lyndhurst crammed the sponge into its bag.

'I shall want the cab, Parker,' he said. 'Don't send it away.'

Mrs Ames whisked round on Parker with amazing rapidity.

'Do as I tell you, Parker,' she said, 'and be quick!'

It was a mere conflict of will that, for the next five seconds, silently raged between them, but as definite and as hard-hitting as any affair of the prize ring. And it was impossible that there should be any but the one end to it, for Mrs Ames devoted her whole strength and will to it, while from the first her husband's heart was not in the battle. But she was fighting for her all, and not only her all, but his, and not only his, but Millie's. Three existences were at stake, and the ruin of two homes was being hazarded. And when he spoke, she knew she was winning.

'I must go,' he said. 'She will be waiting at the station.'

'She will wait to no purpose,' said Mrs Ames.

'She will be' - no word seemed adequate - 'be furious,' he said. 'A man cannot treat a woman like that.'

Any blow would do: he had no defence: she could strike him as she pleased.

'Elsie comes home next week,' she said. 'A pleasant homecoming. And Harry will have to leave Cambridge!'

'But I love her!' he said.

'Nonsense, my dear,' she said. 'Men don't ruin the women they love. Men, I mean!'

That stung; she meant that it should.

'But men keep their word,' he said. 'Let me pass.'

'Keep your word to me,' said she, 'and try to help poor Millie to keep hers to her husband. It is not a fine thing to steal a man's wife, Lyndhurst. It is much finer to be respectable.'

'Respectable!' he said. 'And to what has respectability brought us? You and me, I mean?'

'Not to disgrace, anyhow,' she said.

'It's too late,' said he.

'Never quite too late, thank God,' she said.

Mrs Ames gave a little sigh. She knew she had won, and quite suddenly all her strength seemed to leave her. Her little trembling legs refused to uphold her, a curious buzzing was in her ears, and a crinkled mist swam before her eyes.

'Lyndhurst, I'm afraid I am going to make a goose of myself and faint,' she said. 'Just help me to my room, and get Parker - '

She swayed and tottered, and he only just caught her before she fell. He laid her down on the floor and opened the door and window wide. There was a flask of brandy in his portmanteau, laid on the top, designed to be easily accessible in case of an inclement crossing of the Channel. He mixed a tablespoonful of this with a little water, and as she moved, and opened her eyes again, he knelt down on the floor by her, supporting her.

'Take a sip of this, Amy,' he said.

She obeyed him.

'Thank you, my dear,' she said. 'I am better. So silly of me.'

'Another sip, then.'

'You want to make me drunk, Lyndhurst,' she said.

Then she smiled: it would be a pity to lose the opportunity for a humorous allusion to what at the time had been so far from humour.

'Really drunk, this time,' she said. 'And then you can tell Cousin James he was right.'

She let herself rest longer than was physically necessary in the encircling crook of his arm, and let herself keep her eyes closed, though, if she had been alone, she would most decidedly have opened them. But those first few minutes had somehow to be traversed, and she felt that silence bridged them over better than speech. It was appropriate, too, that his arm should be round her.

'There, I am better,' she said at length. 'Let me get up, Lyndhurst. Thank you for looking after me.'

CHAPTER THIRTEEN

She got on to her feet, but then sat down again in his easy chair.

'Not quite steady yet?' he said.

'Very nearly. I shall be quite ready to come downstairs and give you your tea by the time you have unpacked your little portmanteau.'

She did not even look at him, but sat turned away from him and the little portmanteau. But she heard the rustle of paper, the opening and shutting of drawers, the sound of metallic articles of toilet being deposited on dressing table and washing stand. After that came the click of a hasp. Then she got up.

'Now let us have tea,' she said.

'And if Millie comes?' he asked.

She had been determined that he should mention her name first. But when once he had mentioned it she was more than ready to discuss the questions that naturally arose.

'You mean she may come back here to see what has happened to you?' she asked. 'That is well thought of, dear. Let us see. But we will go downstairs.'

She thought intently as they descended the staircase, and busied herself with tea-making before she got to her conclusion.

'She will ask for you,' she said, 'if she comes, and it would not be very wise for you to see her. On the other hand, she must be told what has happened. I will see her, then. It would be best that way.'

Major Ames got up.

'No, I can't have that,' he said. 'I can't have that!'

'My dear, you have got to have it. You are in a dreadful mess. I, as your wife, am the only person who can get you out of it. I will do my best, anyhow.'

She rang the bell.

'I am going to tell Parker to tell Millie that you are at home if she asks for you, and to show her in here,' she said. 'There is no other way that I can see. I do not intend to have nothing more to do with her. At least I want to avoid that, if possible, for that is a weak way out of difficulties. I shall certainly have to see her some time, and there is no use in putting it off. I am afraid, Lyndhurst, that you had better finish your tea at once, or take it upstairs. Take another cup upstairs; you have had but one, and drink it in your dressing room, in the comfortable chair.'

There was an extraordinary wisdom in this minute attention to detail, and it was by this that she was able to rise to a big occasion. It was necessary that he should feel that her full intention was to forgive him, and make the best of the days that lay before them. She had no great words and noble sentiment with which to convey this impression, but, in a measure, she could show him her mind by minute arrangements for his comfort. But he lingered, irresolute.

'You have got to trust me,' she said. 'Do as I tell you, my dear.'

She had not long to wait after he had gone upstairs. She heard the ring at the bell, and next moment Millie came into the room. Her face was flushed, her breathing hurried, her eyes alight with trouble, suspense, and resentment.

'Lyndhurst,' she began. 'I waited - '

Then she saw Mrs Ames, and turned confusedly about, as if to leave the room again. But Amy got up quickly.

'Come and sit down at once, Millie,' she said. 'We have got to talk. So let us make it as easy as we can for each other.'

Millie was holding her muff up to her face, and peered at her from above it, wild-eyed, terrified.

'It isn't you I want,' she said. 'Where is Lyndhurst? I - I had an appointment with him. He was late - we - we were going for a drive together. What do you know, Cousin Amy?' she almost shrieked; 'and where is he?'

'Sit down, Millie, as I tell you,' said Mrs Ames very quietly. 'There is nothing to be frightened of. I know everything.'

'We were going for a drive,' began Millie again, still looking wildly about. 'He did not come, and I was frightened. I came to see where he was. I asked you if you knew - if you knew anything about him, did I not? Why do you say you know everything?'

Suddenly Mrs Ames saw that there was something here infinitely more worthy of pity than she had suspected. There was no question as to the agonized earnestness that underlay this futile, childish repetition of nonsense. And with that there came into her mind a greater measure of understanding with regard to her husband. It was not so wonderful that he had been unable to resist the face that had drawn him.

'Let us behave like sensible women, Millie,' she said. 'You have come down from the station. Lyndhurst was not there. Do you want me to tell you anything more?'

Millie wavered where she stood, then she stumbled into a chair.

'Has he given me up?' she said.

'Yes, if you care to put it like that. It would be truer to say that he has saved you and himself. But he is not coming with you.'

'You made him?' she asked.

'I helped to make him,' said Mrs Ames.

Millie got up again.

'I want to see him,' she said. 'You don't understand, Cousin Amy. He has got to come. I don't care whether it is wicked or not. I love him. You don't understand him either.

You don't know how splendid he is. He is unhappy at home; he has often told me so.'

Mrs Ames took hold of the wretched woman by both hands.

'You are raving, Millie,' she said. 'You must stop being hysterical. You hardly know whom you are talking to. If you do not pull yourself together, I shall send for your husband, and say you have been taken ill.'

Millie gave a sudden gasp of laughter.

'Oh, I am not so stupid as you think!' she said. 'Wilfred is away. Where is Lyndhurst?'

Mrs Ames did not let go of her.

'Millie,' she said, 'if you are not sensible at once, I will tell you what I shall do. I shall call Parker, and together we will put you into your cab, and you shall be driven straight home. I am perfectly serious. I hope you will not oblige me to do that. You will be much wiser to pull yourself together, and let us have a talk. But understand one thing quite clearly. You are not going to see Lyndhurst.'

The tension of those wide, childish eyes slowly relaxed, and her head sank forward, and there came the terrible and blessed tears, in wild cataract and streaming storm. And Mrs Ames, looking at her, felt all her righteousness relax; she had only pity for this poor destitute soul, who was blind to all else by force of that mysterious longing which, in itself, is so divine that, though it desires the disgraceful and the impossible, it cannot wholly make itself abominable, nor discrown itself of its royalty. Something of the truth of that, though no more than mere fragments and moulted feather, came to Mrs Ames now, as she sat waiting till the tempest of tears should have abated. The royal eagle had passed over her; as sign of his passage there was this feather that had fallen, and she understood its significance.

CHAPTER THIRTEEN

Slowly the tears ceased and the sobs were still, and Millie raised her dim, swollen eyes.

'I had better go home,' she said. 'I wonder if you would let me wash my face, Cousin Amy. I must be a perfect fright.'

'Yes, dear Millie,' said she; 'but there is no hurry. See, shall I send your cab back to your house? It has your luggage on it; yes? Then Parker shall go with it, and tell them to take it back to your room and unpack it, and put everything back in place. Afterwards, when we have talked a little, I will walk back with you.'

Again the comfort of having little things attended to reached Millie, that and the sense that she was not quite alone. She was like a child that has been naughty and has been punished, and she did not much care whether she had been naughty or not. What she wanted primarily was to be comforted, to be assured that everybody was not going to be angry with her for ever. Then, returning, Mrs Ames made her some fresh tea, and that comforted her too.

'But I don't see how I can ever be happy again,' she said.

There was something childlike about this, as well as childish.

'No, Millie,' said the other. 'None of us three see that exactly. We shall all have to be very patient. Very patient and ordinary.'

There was a long silence.

'I must tell you one thing,' said Millie, 'though I daresay that will make you hate me more. But it was my fault from the first. I led him on - I - I didn't let him kiss me, I made him kiss me. It was like that all through!'

She felt that Mrs Ames was waiting for something more, and she knew exactly what it was. But it required a greater effort to speak of that than she could at once command. At last she raised her eyes to those of Mrs Ames.

'No, never,' she said.

Mrs Ames nodded.

'I see,' she said baldly. 'Now, as I said, we have got to be patient and ordinary. We have got, you and I, to begin again. You have your husband, so have I. Men are so easily pleased and made happy. It would be a shame if we failed.'

Again the helpless, puzzled look came over Millie's face.

'But I don't see how to begin,' she said. 'Tomorrow, for instance, what am I to do all tomorrow? I shall only be thinking of what might have happened.'

Mrs Ames took up her soft, unresisting, unresponsive hand.

'Yes, by all means, think what might have happened,' she said. 'Utter ruin, utter misery, and - and all your fault. You led him on, as you said. He didn't care as you did. He wouldn't have thought of going away with you, if he hadn't been so furious with me. Think of all that.'

Some straggler from that host of sobs shook Millie for a moment.

'Perhaps Wilfred would take me away instead,' she said. 'I will ask him if he cannot. Do you think I should feel better if I went away for a fortnight, Cousin Amy?'

Mrs Ames' twisted little smile played about her mouth.

'Yes,' she said. 'I think that is an excellent plan. I am quite sure you will feel better in a fortnight, if you can look forward like that, and want to be better. And now would you like to wash your face? After that, I will walk home with you.'

IT was a brisk morning in November, and Mr and Mrs Altham, who breakfasted at half past eight in the summer, and nine in the winter, were seated at breakfast, and Mr Altham was thinking how excellent was the savour of grilled kidneys. But he was not sure if they were really wholesome, and he was playing an important match at golf this afternoon. Perhaps two kidneys approached the limits of wisdom. Besides, his wife was speaking of really absorbing things; he ought to be able to distract his mind from the kidneys he was proposing to deny himself, under the sting of so powerful a counter-interest.

'And to think that Mrs Ames isn't going to be a Suffragette any more!' she said. 'I met Mrs Turner when I took my walk just now, and she told me all about it.'

A word of explanation is necessary. The fact was that Swedish exercises, and a short walk on an empty stomach, were producing wonderful results in Riseborough at the moment, especially among its female inhabitants. They now, instead of meeting in the High Street before lunch, to stand about on the pavement and exchange news, met there before breakfast, when on these brisk autumn mornings it was wiser not to stand about. They therefore skimmed rapidly up and down the street together, in short skirts and walking boots. Rain and sunny weather, in this first glow of enthusiasm, were alike to them, and they had their baths afterwards. These exercises gave a considerable appetite for breakfast, and produced a very pleasant and comfortable feeling of fatigue. But this fatigue was a legitimate, indeed, a desirable effect, for their systems naturally demanded repose after exertion, and an hour's rest after breakfast was recommended. Thus this getting up earlier did not really result in any actual saving of time, though it made everybody feel very busy, and they all went to bed a little earlier.

Mr Altham found he got on very nicely without these gymnastics, but then he played golf after lunch. It was no use playing tricks with your health if it was already excellent: you might as well poke about in the works of a punctual watch. He had already had a pretty sharp lesson on this score, over the consumption of sour milk. It had made him exceedingly unwell, and he had sliced his drive for a fortnight afterwards. Just now he weaned his mind from the thoughts of kidneys, and gave it in equitable halves to marmalade and his wife's conversation. To enjoy either, required silence on his part.

'She went to a meeting yesterday,' said Mrs Altham, 'so Mrs Turner told me, and said that though she had the success of the cause so deeply at heart as ever, she would not be able to take any active part in it. That is a very common form of sympathy. I suppose, from what one knows of Mrs Ames, we might have expected something of the sort. Do you remember her foolish scheme of asking wives without husbands, and husbands without wives? I warned you at the time, Henry, not to take any notice of it, because

I was sure it would come to nothing, and I think I may say I am justified. I don't know what YOU think.'

Mr Altham, by a happy coincidence, had finished masticating his last piece of toast at this moment, and was at liberty to reply.

'I do not think anything about it at present,' said he. 'I daresay you are quite right, but why?'

Mrs Altham gave a little shrill laugh. The sprightliness at breakfast produced by this early walk and the exercises was very marked.

'I declare,' she said, 'that I had forgotten to tell you. Mrs Ames wrote to ask us both to dine on Saturday. I had quite forgotten! There is something in the air before breakfast that makes one forgetful of trifles. It says so in the pamphlet. Worries and household cares vanish, and it becomes a joy to be alive. I don't think we have any engagement. Pray do not have a third cup of tea, Henry. Tannin combines the effects of stimulants and narcotics. A cup of hot water, now - you will never regret it. Let me see! Yes, dinner at the Ameses on Saturday, and she isn't a Suffragette any longer. As I said, one might have guessed. I daresay her husband gave her a good talking-to, after the night when she threw the water at the policeman. I should not wonder if there was madness in the family. I think I heard that Sir James' mother was very queer before she died!'

'She lived till ninety,' remarked Mr Altham.

'That is often the case with deranged people,' said Mrs Altham. 'Lunatics are notoriously long-lived. There is no strain on the brain.'

'And she wasn't any relation of Mrs Ames,' continued Henry. 'Mrs Ames is related to the Westbournes. She has no more to do with Sir James' mother than I have to do with yours. I will take tea, my dear, not hot water.'

'You want to catch me up, Henry,' said she, 'and prove I am wrong somehow. I was only saying that very likely there is madness in Mrs Ames' family, and I was going to add that I hoped it would not come out in her. But you must allow that she has been very flighty. You would have thought that an elderly woman like that could make up her mind once and for all about things, before she made an exhibition of herself. She thinks she is like some royal person who goes and opens a bazaar, and then has nothing more to do with it, but hurries away to Leeds or somewhere to unveil a memorial. She thinks it is sufficient for her to help at the beginning, and get all the advertisement, and then drop it all like cold potatoes.'

'Hot,' said Henry.

'Hot or cold: that is just like her. She plays hot and cold. One day she is a Suffragette and the next day she isn't. As likely as not she will be a vegetarian on Saturday, and we shall be served with cabbages.'

'Major Ames went over to Sir James' to shoot, - she wasn't asked,' said Henry, reverting to a previous topic.

'There you are!' exclaimed Mrs Altham. 'That will account for her abandoning this husband and wife theory. I am sure she did not like that, she being Sir James' relative and not being asked. But I never could quite understand what the relationship is, though I daresay Mrs Ames can make it out. There are people who say they are cousins, because a grandmother's niece married the other grandmother's nephew. We can all be descendants of Queen Elizabeth or of Charles the Second at that rate.'

'It would be easier to be a descendant of Charles the Second than of Queen Elizabeth, my dear,' remarked Henry.

Mrs Altham pursed her lips up for a moment.

'I do not think we need enter into that,' she said. 'I was asking you if you wished to accept Mrs Ames' invitation for

Saturday. She says she expects Sir James and his wife, so perhaps we shall hear some more about this wonderful relationship, and Dr Evans and his wife and one or two others. To my mind that looks rather as if the husband and wife plan was not quite what she expected it would be. And giving up all active part in the Suffragette movement, too! But I daresay she feels her age, though goodness only knows what it is. However, it is clearly going to be a grand party on Saturday, and the waiter from the Crown will be there to help Parker, going round and pouring a little foam into everybody's glass. I do not know where Major Ames gets his champagne from, but I never get anything but foam. But I am sure I do not wish to be unkind, and certainly poor Major Ames does not look well. I daresay he has worries we do not know of, and, of course, there is no reason why he should speak of them to us. The Evanses, too! I never satisfied myself as to why they went away in October. They must have been away nearly three weeks, for it was only yesterday that I saw them driving down from the station, with so much luggage on the top of the cab I wonder it did not fall over.'

'It can't have been yesterday, my dear,' said Mr Altham, 'because you spoke of it to me two days ago.'

'You shall have it your own way, Henry,' said she. 'I am quite willing that you should think it was a twelvemonth ago, if you choose. But I suppose you will not dispute that they went away in October, which is a very odd time to take for a holiday. Of course, Mrs Evans stopped here all August, or so she says, and she might answer that she wanted a little change of air. But for my part, I think there must have been something more, though, as I say, I cannot guess what it is. Luckily, it is no concern of mine, and I need not worry my head about it. But I have always thought Mrs Evans looked far from strong, and it seems odd that a doctor's wife should not be more robust, when she has all his laboratory to choose from.'

Henry lit his cigarette, and strolled to the window. The lawn was still white with the unmelted hoar frost, and the gardener was busy in the beds, putting things tidy for the winter. This consisted in plucking up anything of vegetable origin and carrying it off in a wheelbarrow. Thus the beds were ready to receive the first bedded-out plants next May.

'I remember, my dear,' said Henry, 'that you once thought that there had been some - some understanding between Mrs Evans and Major Ames, and some misunderstanding between Major Ames and Dr Evans.'

Mrs Altham brought her eyebrows together and put her finger on her forehead.

'I seem to remember some ridiculous story of yours, Henry, about a bunch of chrysanthemums in the road outside Dr Evans' house, how you had seen Major Ames take them in, and there they were afterwards in the road. I seem to remember your being so much excited about it that I made a point of going round to Mrs Ames' next day with - with a book. I think that at the time - correct me if I am wrong - I convinced you that there was nothing whatever in it... Or have you seen or heard anything since that makes you think differently?' she added rather more briskly.

'No, my dear, nothing whatever,' said he.

Mrs Altham got up.

'I am glad, very glad,' she said. 'At any rate, we know in Riseborough that we are safe from that sort of thing. I declare when I went to London last week, I hardly slept with thinking of the dreadful things that might be going on round me. Dear me, it is nearly ten o'clock. I do not know whether the hours or the days go quickest! It is always half an hour later than I expect it to be, and here we are in November already. I shall rest for an hour, Henry, and I will write to Mrs Ames before lunch saying we shall be delighted to come on Saturday. November the twelfth, too! Nearly half November will be gone by then, and that leaves us but six weeks to Christmas, and it will be as much as we shall be able to manage to get through all that has to be done before that. But with these Swedish exercises, I declare I feel younger every day, and more able to cope with everything. You should take to them, Henry; by eleven o'clock they are finished and you have had your rest. With a little management you would find time for everything.'

Henry sat over the dining-room fire, considering this. As has been mentioned, he did not want to make any change in his excellent health, but, on the other hand, a little rest after breakfast would be pleasant, and when that was over it would be almost time to go to the club.

But it was impossible to settle a question like that offhand. After he had read the paper he would think about it.

Mrs Altham came hurrying back into the room.

'Henry, you would never guess what I have seen!' she said. 'I glanced out of the window in the hall on the way to my room, and there was Mrs Ames wobbling about the road on a bicycle. Major Ames was holding it upright with both hands, and it looked to be as much as he could manage. Yet she has no time for Suffragettes! I should be sorry if I thought I should ever make such a hollow excuse as that. And at her age, too! I had no time to call you, but I dare say she will be back soon if you care to watch. The window seat in the hall is quite comfortable.'

Henry took his paper there.

The Bloomsbury Group: a new library of books from the early twentieth-century chosen by readers, for readers

ALSO AVAILABLE IN THE SERIES

RACHEL FERGUSON

THE BRONTËS WENT TO WOOLWORTHS

As growing up in pre-war London looms large in the lives of the Carne sisters, Deirdre, Katrine and young Sheil still cannot resist making up stories as they have done since childhood; from their talking nursery toys to their fulsomely-imagined friendship with real high-court Judge Toddington. But when Deirdre meets the judge's real-life wife at a charity bazaar the sisters are forced to confront the subject of their imaginings. Will the sisters cast off the fantasies of childhood forever? Will Toddy and his wife, Lady Mildred, accept these charmingly eccentric girls? And when fancy and reality collide, who can tell whether Judge Toddington truly wears lavender silk pyjamas or whether the Brontës did indeed go to Woolworths?

*

'Marvellously successful'
A.S BYATT

'The family at its most eccentric and bohemian – a pure concoction of wonderful invention. What an extraordinary meeting I have just had with the Carnes'
DOVEGREYREADER.TYPEPAD.COM

*

ISBN: 978 1 4088 0293 9 · PAPERBACK · £7.99

WOLF MANKOWITZ

A KID FOR TWO FARTHINGS

Six year-old Joe knows a unicorn when he sees one. His neighbour Mr Kandinsky has told him all about them, and there isn't anything in the world that this wise tailor doesn't know. So when Joe sees a little white goat in a Whitechapel market he has to have him. He knows it's just a matter of time before the tiny bump on the unicorn's head becomes the magic horn to grant his every wish.

For in the embattled working-class community of 1950s East End London, there are plenty of people in need of good fortune. The only thing Mr Kandinsky wants is a steam press for his shop; his assistant Shmule, a wrestler, just needs to buy a ring for his girl; and all Joe and his mother wish for, more than anything, is to join his father in Africa. But maybe, just maybe, Joe's unicorn can sprinkle enough luck on all his friends for their humble dreams to come true.

*

'Wolf Mankowitz possessed the now largely vanished gift of being able to write about romance and sentiment without being ever sentimental'
DENNIS NORDEN

'A small miracle. He writes of the teeming streets round the Whitechapel Road with such glowing warmth and love that they come triumphantly alive. Wolf Mankowitz, you are not a star. You are a planet'
DAILY EXPRESS

*

ISBN: 978 1 4088 0294 6 · PAPERBACK · £7.99

BLOOMSBURY

ADA LEVERSON

LOVE'S SHADOW

Edith and Bruce Ottley live in a very new, very small, very white flat in Knightsbridge. On the surface they are like every other respectable couple in Edwardian London and that is precisely why Edith is beginning to feel a little bored. Excitement comes in the form of the dazzling and glamorous Hyacinth Verney, who doesn't understand why Edith is married to one of the greatest bores in society. But then, Hyacinth doesn't really understand any of the courtships, jealousies and love affairs of their coterie: why the dashing Cecil Reeve insists on being so elusive, why her loyal friend Anne is so stubbornly content with being a spinster, and why she just can't seem to take her mind off love...

A wry, sparklingly observed comedy of manners, *Love's Shadow* brims with the wit that so endeared Ada Leverson to Oscar Wilde, who called her the wittiest woman in the world.

*

'Saki meets Jane Austen in the delectable Edwardian comedies of Ada Leverson. A great discovery awaits her new readers'

BARRY HUMPHRIES

'A perceptive, witty and wise portrayal of an ill-assorted marriage and unrequited love'

RANDOMJOTTINGS.TYPEPAD.COM

*

ISBN: 978 1 4088 0382 0 · PAPERBACK · £7.99

BLOOMSBURY

FRANK BAKER

MISS HARGREAVES

When, on the spur of a moment, Norman Huntley and his friend Henry invent an eighty-three year-old woman called Miss Hargreaves, they are inspired to post a letter to their new fictional friend. It is only meant to be a silly, harmless game – until she arrives on their doorstep, complete with her cockatoo, her harp and – last but not least – her bath. She is, to Norman's utter disbelief, exactly as he had imagined her: eccentric and endlessly astounding. He hadn't imagined, however, how much havoc an imaginary octogenarian could wreak in his sleepy Buckinghamshire home town, Cornford.

Norman has some explaining to do, but how will he begin to explain to his friends, family and girlfriend where Miss Hargreaves came from when he hasn't the faintest clue himself?

*

'A fantasy of the most hilarious description – the kind of novel, I fancy, that is badly wanted at the moment, and its central idea is one which has rarely, if, indeed, ever, been used before'
SUNDAY TIMES

'Having met Miss Hargreaves, you won't want to be long out of her company – Frank Baker's novel is witty, joyful, and moving but above all an extraordinary work of the imagination'
STUCK-IN-A-BOOK.BLOGSPOT

*

ISBN: 978 1 4088 0282 3 · PAPERBACK · £7.99

BLOOMSBURY

D.E. STEVENSON

MRS TIM OF THE REGIMENT

Vivacious, young Hester Christie tries to run her home like clockwork, as would befit the wife of British Army officer, Tim Christie. Left alone for months at a time whilst her husband is with his regiment, Mrs Tim resolves to keep a diary of events large and small in her family life.

When a move to a new regiment in Scotland uproots the Christie family, Mrs Tim is hurled into a whole new drama of dilemmas; from settling in with a new set whilst her husband is away, to disentangling a dear friend from an unsuitable match. And who should stride into Mrs Tim's life one day but the dashing Major Morley, hell-bent on pursuit of our charming heroine. Hester soon finds herself facing unexpected crossroads...

*

'The writer's unflagging humour, her shrewd, worldly wisdom, and her extremely realistic pictures of garrison life make it all good reading'
TIMES LITERARY SUPPLEMENT

'Delightful domestic comedy'
FRISBEEWIND.BLOGSPOT.COM

*

ISBN: 978 1 4088 0346 2 · PAPERBACK · £7.99

BLOOMSBURY

JOYCE DENNYS

HENRIETTA'S WAR

NEWS FROM THE HOME FRONT 1939–1942

Spirited Henrietta wishes she was the kind of doctor's wife who knew exactly how to deal with the daily upheavals of war. But then, everyone in her close-knit Devonshire village seems to find different ways to cope: there's the indomitable Lady B, who writes to Hitler every night to tell him precisely what she thinks of him; flighty Faith who is utterly preoccupied with flashing her shapely legs; and then there's Charles, Henrietta's hard-working husband who manages to sleep through a bomb landing in the neighbour's garden.

With life turned upside down under the shadow of war, Henrietta chronicles the dramas, squabbles and loyal friendships of a sparkling community of determined troupers.

*

'Wonderfully evocative of English middle-class life at the time ... never fails to cheer me up'
SUSAN HILL, GOOD HOUSEKEEPING

'Warm and funny, but candid and telling too. A real delight!'
CORNFLOWER.TYPEPAD.COM

*

ISBN: 978 1 4088 0281 6 · PAPERBACK · £7.99

BLOOMSBURY

JOYCE DENNYS

HENRIETTA SEES IT THROUGH

MORE NEWS FROM THE HOME FRONT 1942-45

The war is now in its third year and although nothing can dent the unwavering patriotism of Henrietta and her friends, everyone in the Devonshire village has their anxious moments. Henrietta takes up weeding and plays the triangle in the local orchestra to take her mind off things; the indomitable Lady B, now in her late seventies, partakes in endless fund-raising events to distract herself from thoughts of life without elastic; and Faith, the village flirt, finds herself amongst the charming company of the American GIs. With the war nearing its end, hope seems to lie just around the corner and as this spirited community muddle through, Lady B vows to make their friendships outlast the hardship that brought them together.

*

'Anyone who wants to get the feel of the period must read [this]'
DAILY TELEGRAPH

'I haven't smirked, giggled and laughed out loud at a book so much in quite some time. A perfect and delightful book'
SAVIDGEREADS.WORDPRESS.COM

*

ISBN: 978 1 4088 0855 9 · PAPERBACK · £7.99

BLOOMSBURY

PAUL GALLICO

MRS HARRIS GOES TO PARIS & MRS HARRIS GOES TO NEW YORK

Mrs Harris is a salt-of-the-earth London charlady who cheerfully cleans the houses of the rich. One day, when tidying Lady Dant's wardrobe, she comes across the most beautiful thing she has ever seen – a Dior dress. She's never seen anything as magical and she's never wanted anything as much. Determined to make her dream come true, Mrs Harris scrimps, saves and slaves away until one day, she finally has enough money to go to Paris. Little does she know how her life is about to be transformed forever...

Part charlady, part fairy godmother, Mrs Harris's adventures take her from her humble Battersea roots to the heights of glamour in Paris and New York as she learns some of life's greatest lessons along the way.

*

'It is almost impossible not to succumb to Gallico's spell'
TIMES LITERARY SUPPLEMENT

'Mrs Harris is one of the great creations of fiction – so real that you feel you know her, yet truly magical as well. I can never have enough of her'
JUSTINE PICARDIE

*

ISBN: 978 1 4088 0856 6 · PAPERBACK · £7.99

B L O O M S B U R Y

ROHAN O'GRADY

LET'S KILL UNCLE

When recently-orphaned Barnaby Gaunt is sent to stay with his uncle on a remote Canadian island, he is all set to have the perfect summer holiday. Except for one small problem: his uncle is trying to kill him. Heir to a ten-million-dollar fortune, Barnaby tries to tell anyone who will listen that his uncle is after his inheritance, but no one will believe him. That is, until he tells the only other child on the island, Christie, who concludes that there is only one way to stop his demonic uncle: Barnaby will just have to kill him first. With the unexpected help of One-ear, the aged cougar who has tormented the island for years, Christie and Barnaby hatch a fool-proof plan... Playful, dark and witty, *Let's Kill Uncle* is a surprising tale of two ordinary children who conspire to execute an extraordinary murder – and get away with it.

*

'A dark, whimsical, startling book, far ahead of its time'
DONNA TARTT

'A thrilling, original book, exquisitely written, and unforgettable – a classic, rediscovered'
HANAN AL-SHAYKH

*

ISBN: 978 1 4088 0857 3 · PAPERBACK · £7.99

B L O O M S B U R Y

The History of Bloomsbury Publishing

Bloomsbury Publishing was founded in 1986 to publish books of excellence and originality. Its authors include Margaret Atwood, John Berger, William Boyd, David Guterson, Khaled Hosseini, John Irving, Anne Michaels, Michael Ondaatje, J.K. Rowling, Donna Tartt and Barbara Trapido. Its logo is Diana, the Roman Goddess of Hunting.

In 1994 Bloomsbury floated on the London Stock Exchange and added both a paperback and a children's list. Bloomsbury is based in Soho Square in London and expanded to New York in 1998 and Berlin in 2003. In 2000 Bloomsbury acquired A&C Black and now publishes *Who's Who, Whitaker's Almanack, Wisden Cricketers' Almanack* and the *Writers' & Artists' Yearbook.* Many books, bestsellers and literary awards later, Bloomsbury is one of the world's leading independent publishing houses.

Launched in 2009, The Bloomsbury Group continues the company's tradition of publishing books with perennial, word-of-mouth appeal. This series celebrates lost classics written by both men and women from the early twentieth century, books recommended by readers for readers. Literary bloggers, authors, friends and colleagues have shared their suggestions of cherished books worthy of revival. To send in your recommendation, please write to:

The Bloomsbury Group
Bloomsbury Publishing Plc
36 Soho Square
London
W1D 3QY
Or e-mail: thebloomsburygroup@bloomsbury.com

For more information on all titles in
The Bloomsbury Group series
and to submit your recommendations online please visit
www.bloomsbury.com/thebloomsburygroup

For more information on all Bloomsbury authors and for all the latest news please visit www.bloomsbury.com